FAT DOG

Krish Day

FAT DOG

A Canine Odyssey
Across the Human Landscape

Matador
9 Priory Business Park,
Wistow Road, Kibworth Beauchamp,
Leicestershire. LE8 0RX
Tel: (+44) 116 279 2299
Fax: (+44) 116 279 2277
Email: books@troubador.co.uk
Web: www.troubador.co.uk/matador

ISBN 978 1784621 643

British Library Cataloguing in Publication Data.
A catalogue record for this book is available from the British Library.

Printed and bound by CPI Group (UK) Ltd, Croydon, CR0 4YY
Typeset in 11pt Aldine401 BT Roman by Troubador Publishing Ltd, Leicester, UK

Matador is an imprint of Troubador Publishing Ltd

For
MADDALENA DAY-AMBONI
with Love and Gratitude

Digressions, incontestably, are the sunshine;
take them out of this book for instance;
they are the life, the soul of reading;
you might as well take the book along with them.
LAURENCE STERNE

my heart goes out to the wretch. It is beyond my imagining, to be orphaned and homeless, tramping alone through the days of an entire life under rain and snow, unloved, uncherished. The mere thought filling me with dread and despair, I hurry away to join the Professor.

2

We know what young Albert likes," says Martha with a kindly smile as her matronly figure towers above me. "And what will you have this evening, Professor?"

It's a rhetorical query, for the menu at Martha's is not an extensive one, the dish of the day and another choice or two. And always as prelude there are small offerings, hors d'oeuvres of pickled mushrooms, sauerkraut cakes, brawn in vinaigrette to waken the palate. Yet Martha's kitchen is famed in the town and the countryside around. Her skills come from a distant past, when women toiled long hours at the stove, tinned and bottled foodstuffs were a rarity or brought out in moments of urgency, meats simmered on the fire through half a day and the aroma of rich sauces filled the air with promise of goodness and fulfilment. Martha cooked, her son Ulrich served, and the diners' compliments went beyond mere words of praise. Only once in the long years had she failed in her mission, when the Head Mother of the Mothers of the Fatherland had become querulous at table and in the ensuing scuffle abandoned her dentures in a bowl of mustard.

With Gretchen gone, often in the evenings the Professor dines at Martha's and I sit by his feet at this corner table, awaiting my turn to be taken to the kitchen by Ulrich. Beside us, on the wide grate of the chimney a bright fire crackles, greedily consuming a stout log, sending out comforting waves of warmth through the luminous interior of what was once a timbered barn, now spaced with a score of tables set with white and green checked linen, heavy cutlery, glasses that catch the glow of the flames on their burnished surface.

The late winter chill shutting people indoors, it is a slow evening at the restaurant. At the far end, by the tall windows looking out on the night, school teacher Vogel stares past his wife impatiently, fixing the Professor through his thick lenses as though mesmerized. Unable to restrain himself, finally he walks over to greet the Professor.

"A devilish night to be out," he says. "Inge insisted on reminding me it was our wedding anniversary," he adds with unconcealed grievance. The tone is perfectly in keeping with Herr Vogel's credo, that the company of women is one of mere necessity, to be eluded at all times or whenever possible without jeopardizing life and limb.

"Anniversaries! A perverse invention of modern sentimentalism," the teacher announces glumly, glancing back unhappily at his wife, a gaunt figure with a lantern jaw and shrewish lineaments. "Wouldn't you say, Ernst?"

The Professor agrees whole-heartedly, fearing that the least sign of dissent might precipitate an instant debate, with Herr Vogel pulling up a chair and launching into a minute analysis of the salient points of his thesis.

The Professor is halfway through stripping the knuckle of his generous plate of Schweinshaxe when Ulrich comes to fetch me and I follow him into the kitchen, a brightly-lit spacious workplace with a long metal plate covered worktable in the middle, outsize stoves and heavy-handled ovens along one side, the walls hung with neat rows of fryers, baking dishes, griddle irons, the dimpled bronze of the saucepans glinting bright and burnished. The air redolent with the nose-tingling aroma of roasted meats, Ulrich sets a low stool by the door that opens on to the back yard and places on it a capacious white enamel bowl filled to the brim.

Good-hearted Uli has slipped the joint of meat of the shank clean off the bone, to save my ancient molars coming loose with an untoward encounter. Burrowing in the bowl, my tongue seeks out the conveniently-sized morsels that melt away in the mouth without effort, my senses replete with the plenitude and goodness of the fare. "You've got to finish it all, Albert!" Ulrich says brightly, one hand

4

slowly stroking my coat. His word is my command and it's not long before my tongue has licked dry the bowl of the juices that have trickled out of the meat.

A young man now, Uli has never quite managed to come to manhood, his mind caught forever in the realms of boyhood, his spirit hovering between the child and the man. Dim-witted he might be, as some say. For me Uli remains a paradigm of the human heart in all its unblemished innocence, goodness and warmth that ask for nothing in return. Ever spirited and playful, the bright blue eyes in the impish face topped with sparse strands of light hair, Uli radiates the light of an early sun, pristine and pure, new-born.

Martha comes in and stands for a moment beside him, gently smoothing his head, mother and son looking down kindly as I lift my head from the empty bowl. The chord never severed at birth, she still carries him within her, safe, secure from the censure and derision of the world. This gentle infant, seemingly still in her womb, is her only worldly possession, for whom she lives, has lived, toiled, known pain and despair. Tireless and unsparing with herself, severe in her own habits, Uli's precarious hold on the world has over the years mellowed her, imbued her with grace and a good-humoured tolerance of the frailties and failings of those less able to make their way through the intricacies and entanglements of life's demands.

"Ma, I think Albert's still hungry," Uli says with an ill-concealed wink at me. "Can he have some more?"

"No, Uli," Martha shakes her head, softly stroking his cheeks. "Dr. Hammes says Albert's not to be fed too much. Soon he'll not be able to get to his feet."

Uli smiles conspiratorially, his eyes directing my gaze to the large tin of salt biscuits on the shelf. Sometimes I think that had my Maker chosen to fashion me into a human, I would have wanted to be like him, guileless and endearing, with a child's unsullied, undenying heart. And I should have wanted Martha for a mother.

3

She seemed to have come from nowhere, arriving in town one day holding a small boy by hand, clutching in the other a dull green fibre-glass suitcase. Alighting from the train she stood on the empty platform for long minutes, hesitant and uncertain.

Not a soul about this warm summer afternoon, finally she caught sight of the station master at the gate. She set down the suitcase, extracted from the pocket of the worn, dun-coloured raincoat a slip of paper and held it out. It was the name and address of a distant relative, her mother's cousin whom she had never seen and who, apparently, was now more distant than ever. The station master shook his head regretfully. Yes, he said, he knew the person, but the old lady had passed away some months ago. Pneumonia, he thought.

Martha thanked him, picked up the case and clutching the child's hand walked out into the sunlight. A life signed with the milestones of defeat, she had become accustomed to the weariness of dejection, the tristful sinking of the heart's hopes, prayers voiced and prayers unanswered. But now it was different. She could no longer passively yield to the caprice of the gods, admit defeat and surrender. She looked down at the child, smoothing the sparse strands of his fair head. She had fled towards this new life, not for herself, for him, thinking to give him a morrow without fear and deception, to live a life of his own choosing, for well or ill.

She looked about her, at the few passers-by, noting how different were the clothes they wore, how out of place her drab raincoat on this close and sultry summer noon. Then, resolute in mind yet hesitant in spirit, clutching in her hands the sum of her worldly possessions she set off down the tree-lined street on a journey whose destination she could neither divine nor imagine.

4

Lodged at widow Ansel's old stone house by the river, she started out early the next morning. Little Ulrich by her side, she did the rounds of the shops and stores, Gersten's bakery, Farber's haberdashery, Gärtner's flower shop, Daecher's hardware store. All her life Martha had worked. Now she offered her able hands. She could serve at the counter, clean and sweep, keep accounts, she could even cook. But her willingness to toil at whatever came her way found no takers. Polite and courteous, the tradesmen listened patiently, Gersten offering the child a small freshly-baked roll, florist Gärtner a toffee.

True, the dark apocalyptic days were behind, peace it seemed had come to stay, times were better, the promise of prosperity in the air. But memories were still alive, fear still lurked in minds like a stubborn shadow that refused to lift and fade away. Henschel at the Gasthaus could recall the times when the occasional guest had to be shown to his room by candle-light. Farber still remembered his mother sending him out with a wad of notes to fetch a box of matches. Hovering between hope and a past too ruinous and recent to be erased out of sight, timorous and hesitant the small shop owners to a man thought it was still much too early in the day to be able to afford the luxury of a hired hand.

Bewildered, Martha stood with the child in the bright morning sun. Where she came from, work was a birthright, bread if not pastry was assured on the family table, the entire nation ate the same food, the very same dishes, but they ate. Some toiled more, some less or little, but hunger and destitution were no longer matters of circumstance. It now came to her that this land that had seemingly held out the promise of plenty, so long dreamt of, held alongside also the prospect of want and indigence.

She looked around her. Not merely a new town, it was a new world. Accustomed since youth to a life of dull monotone, the aridity of land-locked minds and landscapes of drab, grey artefacts, the mise-en-scène of forced pageantry and feigned laughter, Martha looked at the people in the street, their easy gait and unhurried pace, the casual encounter, the cheerful greeting for her from the odd passer-by. She was startled when a woman went past and a parrot's head popped up from the wicker basket in her hand to cackle a brisk, peremptory "Good morning!".

Quiet and uncomplaining, the child looked about him in wonder, eyes glued to the shop windows, colourful and bounteous, so miraculously abundant with both the necessary and the superfluous, clothing of a variety Martha had never seen, foodstuffs in quantities to sate the appetites of the greedy and the glutton. She stared wide-eyed at a display of ladies toiletries, amazed at the variety of lotions, creams, cosmetics and perfumes. She had never imagined that beauty necessitated such profusion and extravagance.

Weary then, slowly she walked across the park towards the monumental mass of the town library, little Ulrich tugging at her arm, animated by the sight of a pair of swans skimming with fluttering wings the waters of the small lake in the middle of the green. Drawing the reluctant child to her side, she mounted the wide steps rising up to the tall columns of the Roman temple façade of the library. It was an imposing structure, perhaps she could find something there, whatever, cleaning, dusting, reordering the books on the shelves. She had had schooling, could read and write.

A soothing light filtered down through the high, green-tinted glass roof. There were no visitors. A reposeful silence reigned over the row on row of tall book-laden shelves drawn up like a phalanx of battlements. Martha was taken aback, that there should be so grand a temple of knowledge in a small town such as this.

Uncertain, a little awed even, Martha approached the counter behind which sat an elderly grey-haired woman. Briefly she explained the purpose of her call. The librarian looked up with a kindly smile. Something about this woman's hesitant plea seemed to awaken a distant echo in her. She rose and beckoned Martha towards the small reading room on the side of the main hall, sat mother and son down at the long table, excused herself and went out, to return with a colourful animal alphabet book for the child.

The librarian was familiar with Martha's aged relative who had recently passed away. A kind woman, she said, who over the years had fallen on hard times, after both her husband and son had perished in the last days of the war. Towards the end she had been fed and cared for with municipal funds. There were no heirs, nor inheritance. Martha listened passively.

She had come here neither for charity nor in hopes of patrimony, she said. It was merely to seek a refuge in these early days, until she found her feet. She did not recount her story, merely the bare facts of her escape, the loss of a loved one during the flight. Now here she was, in the land of her fathers yet a world new and unknown, hoping to set out afresh.

Sat across the table, the librarian listened, occasionally lowering her gaze in pensive recollection. She who had herself once known pain and adversity saw the same shades of loss and hurt in Martha's eyes, heard the echoes of dusk in her quiet, remissive voice. Long ago, when the world had teetered on the brink of the abyss, she herself had fled from the scenes of madness and terror, finding a benign sanctuary in this forgotten town. It was all so far away, yet she had not forgotten. The purgatory of having to live several lives in the span of one lifetime was still with her. Dulled by time, the reminiscence of pain still lingered like a faded palimpsest between the leaves of her memory. So that her heart now went out to this woman in a silent embrace.

"It's a quiet town," she said writing down on a sheet of paper a name and an address. Proffering the note, she held Martha's hand for a brief moment. "It might seem difficult now, but you'll find your feet, I'm sure. There are good men here."

5

Kelb was a good man. Almost all who knew him thought so, his neighbours, fellow tradesmen, the customers who frequented his shop. There were no conditionals, no reservations, it was stated simply as a matter of fact, much as one might announce the hour of the day. The Burgomaster who had known Kelb since childhood once said that the most apt epitaph on Kelb's tomb would be "*A GOOD MAN*"; his wife lightly chiding him with "Could you at least wait for the poor man to die first!"

It was the older part of the town. The cobbled street wound around a small square lined with ancient houses, the bare stone façades darkened with age. There were a few shops, their weathered signs relics from another age. The elaborate hand-painted board above Schübler's Stationary had faded out of recognition, leaving only the faintest image of a quill in an inkpot. The wooden boot that had hung outside cobbler Freitag's little shop had flown away on a stormy night long ago, leaving only the chain which gave out a dull chime when the wind was up.

Most of the shop owners lived on the premises, the homes of forefathers passed down the generations. The street and the square had known better times. Now, with much of the trade moved elsewhere and many of the residents grown old, the area had an air of unhurried neglect. Sometimes, looking out through the glass front, Kelb felt he had never been beyond the confines of this tiny corner of the earth.

In truth, Kelb had once been out of town briefly. Called up in youth to stave off the ruinous fall of the fatherland, he had left with high hopes of seeing the world. But the expectations of his boyish heart were short-lived. He did not serve on the front, nor sailed the seas. Dim of sight in one eye since childhood, during the brief training before being despatched for combat he had managed to wound a fellow recruit in the foot and come close to blowing off the instructor sergeant's head. Relegated to the rank of kitchen hand, he had barely taken up duty when the nation met its destined end and went down in flames.

But the wanderlust remained with young Kelb. At school his keen interest in the Australian continent had earned him the appellation of "Captain Joachim Cook". By the time he reached manhood, his interest in geography had grown into a veritable passion. With the same avid curiosity that others brought to collecting stamps or coins, he gathered maps, atlases, facts and figures about the five continents, climate and topography, charts of sea lanes, land routes, railway networks.

His mother feigned weariness with the numerous old cardboard boxes strewn about his room, in which the assorted collection of his dreams was stored. But with silent pride she punctually dusted them, stacking them in good order in one corner, scrupulously respecting the categories young Joachim had assigned them with neat labels: continents, countries, climate, vegetation, fauna, transport. His teachers thought he might take up cartography. But family tradition assigned him a more mundane destiny.

The Kelbs had been in the meat trade since the time of the Guilds, owners of the town's abattoir on the edge of the wood, suppliers of prime cuts to the affluent, offal and trimmings to the poor. The shop itself dated back to the time of the first Kaiser. The family had prospered, managing to weather the troubled times after the Great War and, then, the dark days that followed the second, ruinous conflict. Joachim was the only child and it was beyond the family's imagining that he could do other than follow in the footsteps of his forbears. Mild-tempered, docile and unassuming, Joachim acquiesced. The dream of the world beyond lodged in the cardboard boxes nourished his imagination while he learned the family trade from his father.

6

At the time Martha came into his life, Kelb was in his mid-fifties, a tall burly figure with a thinning head of hair and a pair of heavy spectacles sat atop a barely aquiline nose. He had never been handsome, nor with the pale angular face and tepid blue eyes that peered uncertainly through the lenses did he resemble much the proverbial ruddy-faced butcher with meaty hands and jocular manners. Quietly pleasant and considerate, sober with measured words, he might have belonged to a profession that called for thought and reflection rather than wielding cleavers and boning knives, donning a blood-stained apron, hacking and chopping.

Inheriting the business after his father's death, he had shut down the abattoir, for a brand new slaughter-house had come up in town with facilities in pace with the times. He kept the shop. Its faithful clientèle provided a comfortable living. Besides, there was some money in the family. But Kelb's needs were few, even less after his mother passed away some years later. His one indulgence was the cartographic material he regularly ordered by mail, which postman Scholl dropped at the door as regularly, but not without the occasional fleeting cogitation that despite appearances the butcher could well be a secret agent of some enemy nation. Why else should a retiring figure in the meat trade need to be familiar with the names of obscure cities and distant lands, railway networks and ferry crossings.

Kelb had never married. Years ago the long courtship of the mill owner's daughter had abruptly come to an end when one afternoon, taking the short cut through the woods on the way to the abattoir, he had come across his bride-to-be in the arms of the municipal clerk. But there was neither ire nor rage, it was not in his nature. Soundlessly he traced his steps back through the trees, as though tiptoeing unheard and unseen across a stage from the scene of a drama. Afterwards he showed neither offence nor resentment. It was almost as if he did not mind. If there was pain, it was well concealed in the silent retreats of his heart.

There were other women who would have gladly come into his life. Times were hard and a great many widows about, whose husbands had perished in fields far and near, who saw in Kelb an escape from their famished lives, the promise of a future. Seemingly impervious to charm and beauty, the needs of the flesh and the siren call of domestic bliss, he met the offers and overtures with courteous passivity. It was only with Martha's appearance did he seem to become aware that a life could be shared.

Until then, his days were circumscribed within the confines of the shop on the ground floor of the large family house he had inherited and the rooms above where he lived, tending the patch of garden at the back in warm weather, hibernating in the long winter evenings nourishing the one passion of his life. The boyhood predilection for the physical details of the world at large had never left him. From a mere pastime it had become in manhood the universe of his inner life.

In flight from the mundane routine of the day, suppliers, customers, accounts, the innumerable details of running the shop single-handed, in the peace of the after-hours, sitting by the fire in the grate, his spirit took wing, soaring over continents, the vast spaces of creation, rivers, plains and deserts, as straining his dim sight he poured over the maps and charts, the cartographic material that had now grown to a formidable collection that filled the shelves of an entire room at the back of the house and would have certainly rivalled the archives of many a library.

People sometimes said in jest that Kelb was preparing himself for a journey that would put to shame the amateurish navigations of a Magellan or Columbus. One of the town wags had it that the Great Powers meant to send him off on a secret mission of reconnaissance to some distant planet, Mars or Saturn, perhaps even the Sun. Never contrary or vexed, Kelb accepted the teasing with a good-humoured smile.

Sometimes, too, now that times were better and people had begun to travel abroad, there were those who sought his council on improbable matters. Coming into the shop one afternoon and undecided between kidney and liver for dinner, Frau Lutze enquired with some concern if the following week it would rain in Spain, where her daughter was to honeymoon after the wedding. Miffed by Kelb's inability to provide a sure forecast and going for the liver, peevishly she said, "You could look up those papers of yours!"

Very likely Kelb could have told Frau Lutze of the seasonal rains over Malaga. He knew of the time of the year the westerly monsoon broke over the central Ghats of India, the average number of storms

13

in a year in the South China seas, the late summer hurricanes that roared in from the ocean and laid waste the eastern coastline of Mexico. But he never vaunted, rarely exhibited the pages of the encyclopaedic tomes he carried in his head. Once, meaning to put an end to a heated debate between two septuagenarian survivors of the war, he interjected that the railroad from Sebastopol did indeed run through Dnepropetrovsk; only to earn the piqued gaze of the loser.

There were some who thought it odd that a man so little travelled, whose steps had almost never carried him beyond the well-trodden paths of a small town, should be the depository of such detailed knowledge of the earth's latitudes and longitudes. Then there were the women, ageing widows whose attentions and ambitions he had gently, politely thwarted, who thought it not quite right that a good man, honest and upright, and of some means too, should spend his evenings and spare hours immersed in a sterile pursuit rather than fathering a family and keeping the loving company of a good woman.

7

Martha was in the prime of her life when she first met Kelb, a tall handsome woman, broad-shouldered and strong-legged, with rounded hips that would take on matronly girth in time to come. A good head of dark chestnut hair coiffed loosely in a bun gave the slightly heavy set face an air of severity of purpose. But in repose the lineaments softened, the light eyes at rest with a pensive tenderness, a mother contemplating her young, a lover in middle life.

She brought to Kelb's shop-keeping order, precision and punctuality. By mid-morning the various cuts of meat were in place, the mound of mince heaped neatly, the cross cuts evenly sliced, chops meticulously shorn of excess fat, ribs laid out in rows on the tray. Customers were surprised by the brisk service, staring wide-eyed at Kelb who hovered in the background. They were perplexed by the precision of Martha's weighing and counting, where Kelb had always been generous, throwing in an extra slice, an extra slab of liver. And at the till Martha demanded and received payment to the last penny, where Kelb had been in the habit of waiving off small change, saying "Oh, don't bother!" or "Next time you come in."

Passing in the street, some of the older women paused to look through the shop window and their imaginations toiled at suppositions and conjectures. Looking at Martha's tall figure moving about behind the counter, Frau Klagges who assiduously worked the town's rumour-mill thought she knew where the woman came from. "She's come over the Wall!" she pronounced with infallible conviction. "She could have tunnelled under the Wall," said Frau Schiedermair, offering an alternative with equal certainty. "Like a mole!" added Frau Klinger whose task it was to take a thought to its logical conclusion.

Widow Ansel was of a different mind. She had known the grief of loss and was apt to see her own misfortune reflected in those of others. "Poor dear," she said shaking her head. "And with that child, too."

The days of ordeal behind her, the memory of the loss of a loved one still with her but in slow recession, gradually Martha found her feet. Coming through the storm and finding anchorage in this quiet harbour, her spirit discovered a new-found serenity. Kelb's retiring presence and kind-humoured encouragement when she erred gave her a sense of security. She could not yet read into the future, the road ahead remained uncharted, but she found comfort and hope in the present.

Little Uli had taken to Kelb. Busy at work, filling the trays, arranging the display, serving customers, occasionally Martha glanced towards the corner in the rear of the shop, at the child nestling against Kelb as he peered at a map of the world's fauna spread on his knee, Uli's little finger picking out the tiny animal figures inhabiting the various continents. Familiar and at ease, it was as if the child and the man had always known each other, old friends with a shared interest. Martha's gaze softened at the sight, her heart warming with comfort, a wordless prayer rising to her lips.

Often now, leaving Kelb and Uli, she went upstairs to prepare a meal. She minded the shop while they sat a long idle hour at lunch, Kelb describing for the child quietly and in simple words the wonders of a world he had never set eyes on but imagined, vast planes on which wild herds grazed in the tall grass, man-high locomotives and carriages that wound around mountains, volcanoes on remote islands billowing smoke and tongues of flame. The boy, whose wandering mind made him slow of speech, listened rapt and unmoving, the wide blue eyes bright with wonder and trust gazing up at Kelb.

8

It was perhaps a year later that Martha and Uli left widow Ansel's cottage and moved to the rear of Kelb's house, occupying two of the empty rooms that gave onto a field beyond which stood the old mill beside the winding curve of the river. It was decided without Martha asking or Kelb's offering. It was done simply, wordless almost and tacit, without agreement or conditions, as an occurrence in the natural course of events. Kelb confining himself to the front of the upper floor, the rest of the house was mostly empty, shut and shuttered, furniture piled in the corners and draped against dust. Martha's presence, cleaning, ordering, tidying, the child's feet running on the boards and the bustle of the quotidian brought the rooms to life again, making of the house something of a home.

Tongues wagged. Some in the neighbourhood, others who came to the shop, saw it otherwise. "A man and a woman all alone!" Frau Klagges remarked with a censorious frown. "Alone together in a house!" Frau Schiedermair exclaimed swallowing her outrage. "And alone at night," Frau Klinger shook her head with indisputable certitude, putting her finger on the crux of the scandal.

Though with Martha's move she had lost the rent from the

lodging, widow Ansel failed to share the vociferous indignation. She was pleased, but fearing the censure of her companions she kept her council, merely saying in a meek tone that people needed each other.

The women envied Martha, the menfolk envied Kelb. "The Queen Bee's found her honey pot!" sneered one old spinster who once had been particularly keen on Kelb. "And a big pot at that!" added her cousin who herself had not been averse to trying to work her way into Kelb's favour.

"Old Joachim's fallen on his feet. Lucky man!" said the Burgomaster watching Martha's rounded figure coming down the street. "I suppose you wish you had," his wife remarked with a vaguely snide undertone.

But Schübler from the stationer's shop, who had known Kelb as a boy, put things right whenever some dubious inference was made within his earshot. "Joachim's a good man. A Gentleman," he said firmly. And there the truth resided.

Martha and Kelb lived under the same roof, within a distance of a few rooms. Martha kept house, cleaned, scrubbed, tidied, cooked. They ate at the same table, spent the day together in the shop. Yet they lived separate lives, apparently uncurious, almost never delving into the other's past, never peering into the twilight where thoughts and passion dwell. The inner sanctuary of each unrevealed, unviolated, their lives ran parallel, skimming the surface of the daily round of work and repose, the days busy, the nights separate.

Yet the jostle of living at arm's length, the silent discovery of the other's tastes and habits, the sight of each other morning and evening, reading the weariness in the lineaments at the close of a long day, gradually brought with it a sense of familiarity and, with it, the dawn of an unspoken sympathy and friendship. They were at ease with one another, nothing to vaunt, to put on display nor to conceal. It was as though they had known each other, lived at each other's door through a lifetime.

Martha did not know what to expect. Perhaps she had no expectations, content only that she had found a shelter in the unfamiliar landscape of this new world, gained a corner of the earth that appeared to assure survival and a future for the child, the only possession that marked the beat of her heart. Beyond that lay her infinite gratitude that the uncertain meanders of life could still offer the kindness and goodness of a man such as Kelb.

Timid and retiring, Kelb himself did not know what to think. Unfamiliar with the young, inadvertently he had grown fond of little Uli. Sat in the corner, his arms around the frail shoulders as the child's tiny hand worked a crayon imitating a giraffe's neck, he looked at the mother as Martha stood at the counter talking with a customer.

He felt admiration. The brisk energy she brought to her task, her skill in running the affairs of the shop, running the household, impressed him. He admired, too, the woman in Martha, the tall statuesque figure when she stood still, the tilt of the face when she smiled, the feigned severity of the rich head of burnished hair swept up from the nape. But a confused thread of uncertainty ran through his contemplation. He could not decide how he was meant to consider her, sister, wife, or lover.

Then one late summer evening, as the light outside slowly dimmed and the sky took on a darker shade of night blue, with the child upstairs, alone with Martha as silently she tidied up in the empty shop, unthinking and without volition, as though his voice had taken on a life of its own, he asked her.

"Martha! Do you think we ought to marry?"

"I do," she replied engrossed in her task, unmindful, much like the set response of an antiphony. After a long moment, the import of her answer dawning, surprised and confused she lowered her head, asking softly then "And you, Joachim?"

"Yes, I do."

9

The marriage could have lasted longer, into old age. He would have entered his dotage, feeble and tottering, she holding him by the arm, her hair gone white, body broadened to matronly girth but still vigorous, hands strong enough to shore up this man she might have loved through to his journey's end. Instead, the interlude was a short one, the space of mere years. For a long time afterwards Martha could not understand why providence should have asked of her a price so exorbitant for a heart's contentment so brief and ephemeral.

Though short-lived, the union was one of quietude and amity. A gentle encounter, considerate and affable, that demanded little and offered the intimacy of closeness and companionship. Martha had known men, once known the ardour of passion. But with the onset of mid-life and the travails of half a lifetime etched on the spirit, she could now no longer rekindle the fires of youth, the racing pulse of a lover's yearning. She gave Kelb care and affection, the warmth of a solicitous heart, surrendering in his hands without reserve her own life and that of the child.

Joachim on his part was grateful. For so long he had lived outside himself, an existence apart from the rote and routine of the quotidian. In his younger days he had dreamt of a different life. But circumstances, the times, had forced his hand. Living in the shadow of his forebears he had plied a trade not after his heart. There were no regrets, it was not in him to glance over his shoulder, mourn what might have been. "It's only a life to be got through," he once said to Rebekha Steiner, surprising the librarian with the rare moment of self-revelation.

Only a life, but to be lived as best as one could, Martha thought. She retrieved him from the uncertain and featureless world in whose narrow confines he had lived so long. Once again he knew the warmth of companionship, discovered the comfort of another beside him at night, discovering too the pleasures of the palate, for Martha was unusually and surprisingly skilled at the stove. She fed him, nourished his body with hers, filled the void of his days. He gave her the surety of a future free from the whims of life.

And then there was the child. Joachim could not be the father little Ulrich had hardly known and lost so early. But he did give of himself, unsparing and patient, ever gentle and companionable.

Melding the fancies of the infant mind with his own fertile imaginings, in spare hours and sitting by the fire on winter evenings he told of fabled lands and far-off worlds. Martha watched, glad and grateful, as the boy listened rapt and wide-eyed, occasionally his stuttering tongue turning to speech, small words long delayed. She could not have wished for a better man to father Uli's mind as he took the first faltering steps away from the flaw nature had chosen to endow him with at birth.

Frau Klugge and the circle of gossiping crones might have grudgingly approved that with wedlock the couple had abandoned their sinful ways. But women of dubious provenance coming to town to make away with their honest men folk, that was another matter. They never forgave Martha, ever after a scarlet woman in their eyes. "She'll pay for her sin one day," Frau Klugge asserted with absolute foreknowledge. Frau Schiedermair seconded her, adding that the price would not be a small one. "The wages of sin never are!" Frau Klinger pronounced with a righteous toss of her oblong head.

10

It was soon after Uli's seventh birthday. One afternoon, coming out of the cold storage, Joachim sat down in the corner complaining of a pain in the chest. Martha thought it was indigestion. He had been greedy with the veal in cream sauce, one of his favourites since she had started making it. Seeing then the pallor of the frozen expression on his face, she took his arm and helped him up the stairs.

His body suddenly awkward and unwieldy, she managed to lay him on the bed. Slipping off the shoes and unbuttoning his shirt, asking him to lie still, she made to go back downstairs. But his fingers closing around her wrist, the still eyes fixed on her face would not let her free. She said she would run down and close the shop. He understood, nodded his head imperceptibly. Martha bent over and put her lips to his forehead, before hurrying out of the room. When minutes later she returned, Joachim was gone, the palm of one outstretched arm open, as if it had awaited the healing touch of her hand.

Martha did not shed bitter tears. Only in the depths of the night, lying awake, sometimes her eyes would moisten. Wiping away the damp, staring at the faint glimmer of light on the ceiling, her hand reached out to where he would have been, where now her boy lay curled fast in sleep. She thought it odd that one so modest and unobtrusive should now more than ever fill so ample a space within her. There lingered in her the shadow of a regret that she had not needed him more, drawn him closer into herself. There were depths in him she would now never discover. And slipping into the folds of sleep she wondered why in death those we have loved still keep on growing inside us.

11

Some months after Kelb's death Martha sold the shop. The meat trade was not for her, it was a man's world and she knew little of its dealings. But she kept the house, and the abandoned abattoir, which was a large timbered barn now locked and fallen into disuse. There was also some farmland the Kelbs had owned. And there was some money.

Joachim had no siblings, nor close relatives. What he left was Martha's. She had arrived here without shelter or a discernible future, her few earthly possessions packed in a small suitcase. She now found herself a woman of some means. The modest affluence wisely employed would have sufficed for her to retire to a placid life with no other call than that of bringing up her boy. As Kelb's widow she had gained acceptance and a place in the town. "A good woman," said the Burgomaster. "But please don't anticipate what should be written on her headstone!" his wife mildly rebuked looking up from her knitting.

Handsome in her maturity, a small fortune on her hands, she

21

could have had other men, another man. She could have remarried, chosen a companion for herself and given little Uli the anchor of a male presence in the house. And indeed, drawn by the promise of her body and her bearing, perhaps also the endowment she had come into, there were those who solicited her attention, suitors who sidled into sight timidly courting the new widow, offering vague prospects.

Cobbler Freitag's wandering eye came to settle on her, as he repeatedly hinted that as a widower he was entirely at her disposal. Lawyer's clerk Wetzel was more insistent, coming into the shop every other day; but timid and tongue-tied, unable to give voice to the scheme in his head, on each occasion he left with cuts of meat much in excess of the needs of a bachelor who lived with an aged aunt.

But Martha had not run the gauntlet and fled to the haven of this other half of her native land merely to settle into humdrum domesticity with the first eager admirer who came her way. It had been different with Kelb. Now in the middle passage of her life, shorn of youthful notions of love and romance, she wanted no further entanglements of the heart. Now, too, she had found her feet. She had come with a purpose and circumstances, sorrowful yet fortuitous, had strengthened her will. She would stand alone, be her own woman, raise the child and lead the life she deemed best for Uli and herself. That, she thought, was the sense of being newborn and free.

She had the old slaughter house rebuilt and extended. The slate roof remained, wide windows were opened in the sturdy timbered walls, hardwood parquet laid on the stone flooring, a large fireplace installed on one side of the sizeable hall which at the far end led into an airy and spacious kitchen furnished with worktables, ample basins, wood and coal-fired stoves, ovens capacious enough to feed a wedding party. In an adjacent store room, alongside a cold box and an outsize refrigerator, shelves and cupboards rose to the ceiling. When months later the work was done, a kitchen hand taken on and a lad to serve at table, a wooden sign went up on the front bearing large green letters that read simply MARTHA.

People in the town were curious. Passers-by paused in the street to ponder over the sign and wonder. An eatery, a restaurant. They wondered how one who came from where Martha had come could offer a repast, dining and wining that could satisfy the palate. Hearsay had it that it was a dull grey world devoid of joy and the pleasures of living, fenced in and shut to the winds of change that had begun to usher in the new and the unexplored, novelty in mores and manners, in apparel and fashion, in fads as much as foods. Papers carried pictures of that other world across a blind Wall that showed a still landscape of mean habitations and dreary streets, weary and wary faces frozen by the camera's lens.

With half a lifetime spent in a land petrified and held in hostage, where the past had survived and lived on in the mind, in customs and habits, Martha's cooking had not kept pace with the times, offered nothing newfangled or supposedly modern. Learnt from her mother and her mother's mother, her culinary skills harked back to a now distant time, an age when dieting was the involuntary choice of the impoverished and Hippocrates had not yet come between a man and his table.

Martha was lavish with what the doctor peering over his spectacles had begun to forbid, butter and cream, suet, lard and liver. It made for old-fashioned cooking, sound food with strong aromas and rich on the palate. Emptying their plates of the belly pork and trotters, duck, geese and game drowned in sauces vinous, spicy and sour, older diners found themselves recalled to childhood and youth by the evocation of tastes and fragrances long forgotten, embedded and dormant in the folds of faded memory.

On the occasion of the opening of the restaurant, Martha invited a dozen well-wishers and acquaintances, a handful of friends she had made in the town, Rebekha Steiner the librarian, Schübler from the stationer's shop. The burgomaster and his wife were there, Herr Schreck the lawyer who had seen to the legal work after Kelb's death, the manager of the local bank who had helped with money matters with the inheritance of Kelb's estate.

Seated amidst the simple décor of tables dressed with checked linen, set with white polished Bavarian china and solid Solingen cutlery, the company looked around, expectant yet uncertain. Martha herself served the meal, as the young lad she had taken on brought in the courses from the kitchen.

Timid at first, conversing almost in hushed tones, the guests warmed as the food arrived, plates of liverwurst, pickled mushrooms, tureens of goose giblet soup. Animated and astounded, complimenting Martha with each mouthful, they reached for the dishes of devilled pigs' feet, drowned the brochettes of pork in the sour cream sauce. heaping their plates with generous helpings of the green kale with chestnut. "Kaiser Wilhelm is still on the throne and I'm back at my grandmother's!" old lawyer Schreck remarked with a fond smile of recollection.

Hearing the amiable table-talk, the tintinnabulation of glass and cutlery, watching the diners as they heartily downed the food with long sips of wine and beer, acknowledging the compliments with a modest smile, Martha felt a sense of the relief and repose at a journey's end. She looked about her, at the sleeping embers on the grate in the chimney, the brightly lit interior laid out with a score of tables, at the centre of each an imitation Meissen vase with a small posy of red and white carnations.

It had been a long road, beset with peril and fear, a faltering trek into the unknown. Half listening to the voices around her, looking out through the wide glazed glass windows as night closed in on the evanescent last light of the autumn evening, perhaps for the first time Martha felt she was home, anchored, with the certitude of permanence. And a fleeting shadow of melancholy rising from the heart, she wished Joachim could be here now with her.

When at length the food was gone, the diners sated and the dishes cleared, the Burgomaster raised a toast to Martha. "If only one could dine like this every day," he sighed, replete and heavy, as he gained his seat. "Then," said his wife with fond good-humour, "we'd have to find in a hurry the words to put on your gravestone!"

Dr. HAMMES

1

Dr. Thomas Hammes was our local vet. He was also one of the most likeable humans I had ever come across. Tall and suitably built to deal with some of his larger patients on the farms and in the stables, the imposing frame was topped off with a large head of dark curly hair shading to faint silver here and there. The lively eyes behind the round steel spectacles looked out on the world with an air of good-humoured tolerance, as though they had seen it all before and there could be no further surprises.

Dr. Hammes was at his kindest with members of the animal kingdom, both large and small. His patience stretched even to Montevideo, Frau Krause's incorrigible parrot, whose overtly exhilarating antics he put up with cheerful forbearance; for which, he said, he expected to be handsomely rewarded in the hereafter.

I myself was treated as a companion and confidant. Alone with me on the old wrought-iron bench outside, watching Fräulein Ulrike move about in the surgery, he would say in a ruminant tone, "Well, old friend Albert, what do you say? Should I marry the good woman? Or shall we go on as we are?" With a vigorous rub of my neck, he would then smile down at me to add, "I wish you would say something!"

With his fellow humans he was rather more dismissive, his wry humour disposing of them with a witty phrase, an ironic remark. No great love lost between them, Fraulein Breitfuss once said that Dr. Hammes was best approached on four legs. A less than generous remark, in keeping with the persona of the young lady, a late-comer in our midst and a harbinger of grief. The doctor, instead, had long been a close family friend, fond of Gretchen and an intimate of the Professor.

An inveterate bachelor despite his wistful musings about nurse Ulrike, the doctor lived with his mother in a rambling old house set on extensive grounds near the park. At a short distance, in the same untended and weed-choked compound, Dr. Hammes had his surgery in the oddest of constructions, a large glass house with a dome of green tinted glass. Lying on the surgical table, surrounded by bottles of tablets and capsules, jars of salve and ointment, rolls of bandage, looking up through the green dome at the emerald clouds moving idly by in the sky, I would drift into reveries of other times; until the doctor's quite voice brought me to. "Albert," he would say with an amused chuckle to nurse Ulrike, "is a born dreamer!"

The doctor's house and the conservatory had a curious history. I heard it said that a very long time ago one of our great Kaisers had met a young lady who had been rather pleasant to him for several years. Later, wishing to reward her pleasantness, he had gifted her the land and house; and had a conservatory built on the grounds, for she greatly loved orchids and had often offered one to her King, saying "Will your Majesty have my pink orchid?"

2

Once a month I was taken to Dr. Hammes for a routine check-up. I quite enjoyed the visits, which consisted of nothing more than my lying on my back while Dr. Hammes peered at my tongue, pulled my ears, scratched my stomach and pinched my scrotum a time or two.

In truth, the visits had more to do with my weight, which in later years caused Gretchen much concern. While I could keep pace with humans, long gone were the days when one could frantically rush through the woods at the sight of a squirrel or dash back with a twig between the teeth.

While Fräulein Ulrike laboriously set me down on the weighing scales, Gretchen would look on anxiously. "Lost anything?" she would ask.

"Lost?" The doctor's tone was one of mild surprise, as though she had enquired after an improbable phenomenon. "No, not really. I would say Albert's holding his own."

Seeing Gretchen crestfallen then, he would put a consoling arm around her and pronounce philosophically, "Weight, dear Gretchen, is character. Would I be the kind, caring and loving person that I am," he would add playfully as his eyes sought out Ulrike's, "without my mass? Nor would Albert be so gentle and companionable without some ballast"

Gretchen smiled at his good humour but was less than convinced. Her brow furrowed with concern as she sought his council: "Ought I to take him to Dr. Schneidhuber's clinic?"

The very sound of the name sent a series of shivers down my back, for the dread doctor's name was not entirely unfamiliar and one had on occasion heard talk of his terrifying weight-loss cures, which surpassed by far any atrocity that Hubert the Horrid could have thought up.

"If you must," Dr. Hammes sighed with a lofty air. Then grasping my right paw and giving it a firm shake, in sorrowful tones he said, "So the end is near. Adieu, good friend. Till we meet again on the far shore!"

Gretchen never again mentioned Schneidhuber's Pet-Weight Clinic; and I felt that I owed Dr. Hammes the debt of my life.

3

Today the Professor has accompanied me to the surgery. Now he sits reading on the bench in the grounds outside, while I lie on my back looking through the glass dome at sea-green tufts of cloud loitering in the sky. Bent over me, Dr. Hammes has prised my jaws open and is giving my teeth and tongue the one over.

"All's well Albert, you may chomp away as usual," he pronounces distantly, and then, "You were unkind to me last night, Ulrike."

"And you were cruel!" Nurse Ulrike says over her shoulder, her voice grieved but uncomplaining.

"You know I wouldn't hurt a fly! Would I, Albert?" he quips affably, with a light tickle under my chin

"You did hurt my feelings."

He turns and drawing her down to him plants a fleeting kiss on her cheek, saying "Feelings are meant to be hurt now and again. Otherwise what use would feelings be?"

Ulrike presses her cheek against his. "Oh Thomas! What is to happen to us?" she pleads with tender exasperation.

"Nothing much, I expect," he says evenly, putting an arm around her shapely hips. "We'll live a while, grow old, dribble into our soup, wear nappies again. And then we'll be gone!"

Over time, lying on my back in the surgery, in the suffused light filtering through the glass, I had been witness to many such exchanges, Ulrike's gentle ardour and the doctor's easy-going manner that nevertheless veiled, I felt, affection and attachment.

4

"Oh no! It's her again. And that bird!" Ulrike exclaimed peering out through the glass.

Dr. Hammes turned to look. I craned my neck to catch the sight. Sure enough, there striding hurriedly up the path through the weed-choked grounds was Frau Krause, the long greying hair trailing behind her in the wind like a tattered flag. The bird in question was Montevideo. But there was no sign of the fatuous fowl, Frau Krause holding in her arms merely a mass of green feathers. While wishing none of God's creatures any ill, the rising hope shared by all in the surgery was that finally the inane bird had done itself in. The sanguine expectation was dashed within moments, as the good woman burst into the surgery.

"Doctor! Doctor!"

Nurse Ulrike rushed to the entrance to block the intrusion. "The doctor's busy. I'm sorry, you'll have to wait."

Frau Krause evaded the barrier with a surprisingly energetic skip and hop and rushed towards Dr. Hammes. "Oh Doctor, Monty's lost his head!" she cried trying to catch her breath.

The doctor looked at the long, angular face with sunken grey eyes. "Not to worry," he assured her with jovial nonchalance, "we'll stick it back on!"

"But it can't be found!" Frau Krause lamented frantically. "He's hidden it somewhere."

"We'll ask him."

"You can't, Doctor. The poor thing can't talk without his head!" she moaned.

"We'll, most people do!" In a business-like manner the doctor then reached out to take the bunch of feathers.

Frau Kraus hopped back a step. "You won't hurt him, will you, doctor?"

Dr. Hammes turned to Nurse Ulrike and asked in a professional tone, "One wouldn't ever hurt a cock-or-two, would you Ulrike?" She returned a coy smile.

"Oh, please be gentle, doctor," the old lady pleaded. "After all, you've taken the hypocritical oath."

The doctor looked nonplussed for a moment. "Oh, have I?" With that his hands shot out and plucked clean the mass of feathers from her arm. From where I lay on the surgical table, it looked much like one of those ladies' wedding hats made of exotic green feathers. Dr. Hammes plunged his hand through the top and grasping it by the neck pulled forth Montevideo's little parrot head.

The bird looked not a little surprised. Sleepily it turned its small beady eyes around to take in the scene; bending it's head first to one side and then the other, as if to take a crick out of its neck. All of a sudden, as though a spring inside had begun to uncoil, it came alive.

Head thrown back, the bird fixed Dr. Hammes and peremptorily enquired: "I Montevideo Who you?" Not getting an immediate response, it varied the query "Me Montevideo You who?"

"Who you? Who you?" it insisted.

Dr. Hammes held it up at arms length to get the cackle out of his ears, when the bird caught sight of Nurse Ulrike.

"Who he?" it asked incredulous.

"Oh, Monty dear, she's a lady," Frau Krause informed him tenderly, stretching out her arms to take him.

Montevideo shook his head violently. "Who he she? Who he she?" Exasperated, refusing to part from the doctor, in a beseeching cackle that got louder it demanded again and again and again, "Heeshehoo, hoo, heesheehoo, hoo, hoo…"

The deranged bird must have got its tongue tied in knots, for the inane crescendo ceased abruptly. Opening its beak in a lazy yawn, it lowered its head and appeared to fall into a deep coma; only to open one drowsy eye, look down at me indifferently and ask with a small gurgle "Whohee?"

Dr. Hammes handed the quiescent fowl back to the owner. "Poor dear, he's tired," said Frau Krause laying her withered cheeks against the feathers. "Will you give him something, doctor?"

"Sleep, sleep is what he needs," Dr. Hammes said kindly, adding in a murmur, "Eternal sleep."

Nurse Ulrike was about to show the old lady out when the Professor appeared at the door. And all hell broke loose. Montevideo's head shot up with a such a convulsion that it could well have detached itself from the rest of him and flown off. Eyes petrified and fixed on the Professor, Monty gave out the most agonized screech, as if it's neck had been placed on the executioner's block: "Who heee? Who heee?" he pleaded, "Hoo hee! Hoohee! Ooee! Hoo hoo!" The ear-splitting scream rising in a cacophonous peal rent the air and would have certainty shattered the glass dome of the conservatory had not Dr. Hammes hurriedly taken Frau Krause by the arm and led her briskly to the exit.

The Professor, Dr. Hammes, Nurse Ulrike and I watched Frau Krause wend her way slowly through the grounds clutching her feathered treasure to her bosom. The orange-beaked head still bobbed up and down and the hooheeing urgent cry enquiring the Professor's identity slowly receded and ceased altogether as Frau Krause turned the corner towards the gate.

Ulrike followed the disappearing figure pensively. "I wonder if sailor Krause will ever come home again," she said staring out at the grey, murky day outside. A woman's hope in a woman's heart!

5

Perhaps some small ember of hope still lingered under the ashes of her life. But no one ever came to know, for she never spoke nor pronounced sailor Krause's name. Perhaps she had long ago secreted away the tiny spark in some hidden recess within her, to be kindled anew should he one day come to her again with that swinging gait and hearty laughter.

Until then Frau Krause remained a daily sight around town, always and ever accompanied by her inseparable Monty. She did her morning round of the baker, the butcher, the greengrocer, with Montevideo's head peeping out of the wicker basket.

Buried up to the neck in a jumble of beets and swedes, greens and meat, he watched the world around him, storing away in his puny brain the oft-repeated words and phrases, occasionally echoing his mistress with the odd "Hullo!" or "Morning!" as she greeted and was greeted in turn in the shops and stores. In time he had become the unacknowledged mascot of the town, with passers-by peering down at the bobbing head in the basket and asking "And how's Monty doing this morning?"; to which, depending on his humour, he croaked "Monty not doing" or "Monty well. Monty all too well." In truth, I much envied him his gift of speech; thinking though that with a bird-brain such as his, the blessing had been ill-bestowed.

So Montevideo tittered and conversed, so to speak, with one and all, as Frau Krause did her rounds, to trudge back then to her silent and solitary day in the small brown cottage a stone's throw from the station where it had all begun.

<h1 style="text-align:center">6</h1>

It was all so long ago that the people in our town could only recall it dimly, and the young not at all. It was before my time, when Gretchen was but a child with curls in her hair, the picture-box was black and white, and certainly a great many years before men went to the moon – it ever remained beyond the reach of my canine comprehension why any living being would want to go to the moon at all!

He had alighted from the train midway on his journey to the port to join his ship; for somewhere along the way he had lost his papers. It was a small station, the name of the locality unknown to him. Not that it mattered, as he meant to board the next train back to procure fresh documents.

The whistle blew once, and again, and enveloping the station in a fog of steam and a cloud of ash grey smoke, the engine jerked forward, laboriously gathering speed. The carriages slipped past, the air cleared, and there she stood in the pale sunlight of a late spring morning, a tall awkward girl in a bottle-green coat and a red scarf that framed a clean angular face set with large pearl-grey eyes.

She had waited since the chill of daybreak for a father who had failed to arrive, yet again. Now on the silent and empty platform she saw him, a short muscular young man turned out in trim sailor's rig, white and blue, with a ribbon-circled cap atop a close-cropped head. Afterwards she could not tell, nor he, how long they had stood there gazing at each other, only to look away and then look back till their eyes met again. At last he strolled up to her with a slow swinging gait and asked the name of the town.

Motherless, fathered by a man who had left for his country's glory when she was yet an infant in arms, now freed after years of captivity and much awaited by his only child but never to return, she worked at Henschel's Gasthaus to earn her keep. The sailor lodged there the first night, and then a second, and yet another, idling away the hours roaming the small town till her work was done.

They made an odd couple, she a head taller than him, slender, almost wiry, with a head full of fine dark hair that fell like a cascade of silk; he stocky, with large heavy hands, the dark eyes alive and luminescent. She was then perhaps merely eighteen, meek and retiring, the hesitant smile witness of wounded hope, uncertainly awaiting a better life to come. He was some years older, with never a care and brimming with life, filling the space with easy laughter, as though a gurgling, giggling infant had suddenly come to manhood and never known the least burden of sorrow or bereavement.

He missed his ship and stayed a week, then another, and yet another. And he swept her off her uncertain feet and carried her away on his carefree wings to other worlds, regaling her with tales of far off places and faces. She felt giddy and fell in his arms as he told her of the moon in the tropics, the balmy nights in the southern seas, the voracious man-eating fish in the Amazon, the unnatural and unspeakable antics of the donkey lady in Suez.

Then he left. The small station again and, the short shrill whistle of the engine piercing her heart, the train lurched forward and pulled out, and through the billowing clouds of steam she caught the round laughing face in the carriage window and the cheerful wave of a short stout arm. She raised a timid hand and stood motionless watching the empty track as the last carriage blurred in the distance. Orphaned once, and orphaned once again, she did not weep, but her days were petrified by the void of a cold stillness.

In the long months that followed, there was no news of him. She heard nothing, felt only the slow ebbing of a tenuous hope. Then one day, unexpectedly, a large parcel arrived, filled with a wondrous array from far away, things she had never seen before; a beige ivory comb, a silver bracelet set with luminous green stone lozenges, a translucent mother of pearl pendant, a coat in shimmering green shantung that buttoned right up to the neck.

He had said he would return, and he did. And when he came, she met him sheathed in the sea-green shantung which set off the pale guileless lineaments. The sheen of her long fine hair matched the shine of the silk as she ran to him and his strong arms folded around Ilse's tall spare body. In the quickness of her heart she felt then that he would always return. And he did.

Season after season he came, bringing her gifts from the corners of the earth, souvenirs, odds and ends, strange and exotic objects, some useful, others less so. The small cottage slowly filled with the chinoserie and bric-à-brac, taking on the semblance in miniature of a fair where the world at large had come together. And he sent her money during the long absences when he sailed the seas.

Now in her womanhood, Ilse gave up her menial job at Henschel's Gasthaus and became a housekeeper and home-maker. She cleaned and washed, dusted the hundred and one objects and placed each precious memento in its allotted place and niche; the black carved hardwood head from Africa on the mantelpiece, the Japanese parasol in the bedroom, the porcelain spoons and lacquered bowels in the glass case, the terracotta Chinese figurines on the table by the chimney. She hoed, raked and weeded the small patch behind the house and planted flowers, daisies, antirrhinum, and trained a nasturtium up the kitchen wall. It was as if each single day she expected her man on the morrow.

At times he wrote of his arrival, as often as not he would arrive unannounced and unexpected. He stayed weeks, a month, more, and once an entire summer. Then they would go out each evening, dressed in the colourful and exotic garments he brought back; his head often topped with a red fez with a swinging gold tassel or shadowed by a wide-brimmed sombrero; her tall figure trim and fetching in a tartan skirt and beret.

With time the town grew accustomed to their carnivalesque progression down the streets, sailor Krause's arms firmly wound around her waist, head thrown back in mirth as the gold tassel of the fez gyrated and swung. At first seen as an oddity, a curious even bizarre presence in the placid, uneventful pace of the town, in time people came to like him, the smiling courtesy, the ever jovial air, the infectious laughter, not least the raconteur's gift of weaving together tales both true and far-fetched. He told them of hermits who slept on beds of nails, needles driven through the tongue, men buried underground for long weeks and waking to serene life when unearthed, lengths of rope that snaked up climbing the air to the sound of music, white-gowned men who danced twirling on their toes for days; God's entire floral creation stamped on bodies tattooed from head to foot; and more.

And they discerned in him an unexpected vein of kindness and largesse, for he never failed to bring back a gift, large or small, for one or the other of his acquaintances: a Venetian gondola in glass, a tiny marble replica of the Taj Mahal, the Great Pyramid in plaster, a papier mâchè nodding clown. When years later Adolf opened his Adolf's Antiques near Herr Himmel's bookshop, many of the supposed antiques adorning the glass case were in truth nothing more than sailor Krause's mementoes.

Some said they were man and wife. The gossips said they lived in sin. It was true that once they had been away an entire week and came back with a glow of contentment. Some said they looked blessed on their return and saw in Ilse's radiance the aura of a bride. Frau Mittelfàrt, the head gossip, discovered a wedding-like ring on Ilse, but it was on the wrong finger; which was of immense relief to her, for it proved that the couple continued to lie on a sinful bed.

Herr Freitag the cobbler vowed that he had seen sailor Krause enter the cottage carrying Ilse in his arms. But then Herr Freitag saw several things that no one else ever did. He often saw bright saucer-like objects glide by in the night sky; glowing green men wandering the countryside in the dark; once he even saw a lady's bejewelled hand beckoning to him from the middle of the lake in the park: much to the disappointment of many he had failed to take up the invitation. Not surprisingly Freitag's sighting of sailor Krause's prowess in lifting women over the threshold was entirely discredited.

7

So it could have gone on; and it did for many long years. Then one season he did not return, nor the next. There was no news, nor did he keep the rendezvous with his accustomed autumn homecoming. The months passed, Ilse waited, thinking his ship had been docked in some distant port for major repairs. She thought of shipwrecks, bought papers, listened to the radio. The months turned to a whole year.

Cleaning, dusting, tidying, ever readying the house for his homecoming, in the quiet of the afternoon she sometimes walked over to the station and sat on the bench under the old wrought-iron lamp post. It was where a lifetime ago she had waited for her lost father on the morning of the first encounter with her sailor. Now, stranded in a timeless biding, she watched as trains rattled past, halted, passengers alighted, the whistle blew, hissing steam filled the air, and the carriages slipped past lazily, to disappear finally in the haze of the late summer sun. And she still waited for a sight of the sailors rig and the jaunty walk.

The first year of his absence ushered in a second. She turned to the authorities. They knew nothing of sailor Krause, even less about his whereabouts. Ilse would not be turned away. Modest and retiring all her life, she now became stubborn and demanding, patiently enduring interminable hours of waiting outside offices, badgering officials. Finally she was directed to the shipping company.

She wrote. For the very first time she committed herself to his name, signing the letter "Ilse Krause". It was several weeks before the reply arrived. She sat in the pallid autumn sun in her little patch at the back of the house, turning the unopened envelope in her hands. The season's blooms were fading, the annuals at the end of their short gaudy journey. The nasturtium on the kitchen wall was seeding and this summer she had not put the swollen little green pellets under brine.

The spare lines under an artist's heading in blue of an ocean-going liner ploughing through the swells informed Ilse that Sailor Krause's vessel had made a brief call at the port of Valparaiso, where the crew had been given leave to go ashore for a few hours. Sailor Krause had presumably jumped ship, for he had not returned with his mates. The vessel had left port without him. He had not contacted the shippers' agents since and at the present time his whereabouts were unknown.

Ilse neither wept nor mourned, but she kept her pain. She took his name, not so much in memory as in expectation. There had been other occasions, though not quite as long, when he had been away without word or a brief line. She was still young, time was with her. She would wait and one day, suddenly, on the wings of a bright and blessed morning he would appear at her doorstep.

But he never came to her again. Instead, some time later, she was brought a last wordless gift from him: a parrot. Born, bred and tutored half a world away, for a year or more it had wandered through the other half, held back by customs, quarantined, misaddressed. Finally landing on her doorstep in a battered cage, it presented itself: "*I Montevideo Who You?*"

Some in town said it was sailor Kraus impersonating a bird. The gossips and tattlers were satisfied that it was nothing more than the well-deserved wages of sin. Adolf the future antiquarian, who dabbled in things and thoughts Oriental, suggested that it might be the sailor reincarnated. Dr. Hammes thought the sailor might have chosen a somewhat more intelligent species than a foolish fowl for his reincarnation.

8

"I just wonder if one day he'll come back to her again," said Ulrike quietly, looking out at the grey, murky day.

"You go on wondering, dear girl!" the doctor said jovially. "We're off to lunch."

With that we left Ulrike wondering as she tidied up the surgery and I followed the Professor and Dr. Hammes to his house across the scruffy grounds with tussocks of tall grass burnt straw-brown by the long winter.

Frau Hammes had set the table for lunch in the sun lounge at the back. It was a warm airy space which offered a clear view of the conservatory-cum-surgery and the tympanum of the town library beyond the line of trees. There was a tall cactus with tiny scarlet flowers in one corner and, maintaining a sentimental if tenuous link with the past, an orchid hung from the sun-roof at the far end, the violet blooms strung out on a single long bough.

It was said that the Kaiser's orchid lady had in later years sat in this lounge to write her memoirs, a slender work titled "An Orchid for My Kaiser," of which she arranged to have printed only a single copy, which she subsequently addressed to her king. In the turmoil of war the book gathered dust in some country post office. When finally it was delivered, the Kaiser had gone and the House of Hohenzollern fallen. The original manuscript was still in the house and occasionally Dr. Hammes had read from it to Gretchen, when she came to lunch.

Today Frau Hammes served Wiener Rostbraten, a perennial favourite of the Professor's. Now as they sat at table, as always the talk inevitably turned to the old lady's favourite subject: what her son might have become and had not, how far he might have gone and how he had fallen short, and what the Surgeon-General might have thought of his son's modest progress through life. She interspersed her cahier de doleances with moments from the distant past, how the Surgeon-General had step by step scaled the heights, held positions of indubitable prestige, treated and cured the great and the mighty, and ended the latter days of his life fêted and honoured.

But there was neither bitterness nor recrimination in her tone, merely a fond regret, a harking back to the felicity of cloudless days and the love of a good man. Small and seemingly frail, she was yet vigorous in her bird-like movements and manners. She doted on her son, chiding him with nothing more, nor less, than the ever nourishing warmth of heart of a mother with a truant child. He met her with affectionate banter and the loving courtesy of courtship.

Gently beating about the bush, circling her prey, Frau Hammes asked, "Have you had many visits today from your friends in the animal kingdom, Thomas?"

Dr. Hammes was perfectly familiar with such parting shots and he led her on with a precise account of his morning's work. "Well, there's Konrad's foal, not keeping well, I'm afraid. Then, of course, Albert came in for his check-up. Frau Krause's Monty lost his head and I had to screw it back on." For good measure he added, "I was to visit Karla's canaries this morning, but she didn't turn up. They must have all died, poor tots"

True to form, his mother took the expected bait. Serving the Professor turnips, she stopped half way and said sadly "Putting back parrots' heads and visiting dead canaries! I ask you, Professor, is this the way for an able and intelligent person to spend his days?"

"I take it, Mother, that the kind compliment is for me. Thank you!" and the doctor took the dish of turnips from her.

Frau Hammes ignored the playful remark. "And to think," she said with a sorrowful mien, "that in medical school, Thomas always topped his class. And he even won a medal, didn't you dear, for anatomy or autopsy. Or was it appendicitis? Something of the sort. The Surgeon-General was the proudest man on earth that day." She always referred to her dead husband as the Surgeon-General.

"Mother, please don't give away family secrets," Dr. Hammes chided through a mouthful. "Topping a class of dunces was no mean task. Most of them couldn't tell a human liver from a slab of steak! As for the medal, they had to give it to someone."

"A medal's a medal," the Professor said solemnly pouring Frau Hammes more wine.

She thought she had found an ally. "That's what I say," she started off eagerly. "Did you know, Professor, he passed out with flying colours. They gave him quite a few medals,"

"With the boxful knocking about the house somewhere, I could set up stall in the market offering medical medals!" the doctor laughed.

Frau Hammes failed to share the humour. "Oh, we had great hopes, the Surgeon-General and I. Thomas could have gone into practice in the best of places, the Surgeon-General would have seen to it."

"It's called nepotism, Mother!"

Ignoring her son's high ideals, she spoke only with the Professor. "I remember the Surgeon-General always said that it was a man's born duty to cure his fellow men"

It was the cue for Dr. Hammes to trot out his routine proverb. That man was incurable; in any case largely futile, an entirely wasted effort.

But the old lady was not to be derailed by her son's philosophising. "Don't you think, Professor, that it's an honour to heal people, even those we may not particularly like? Did you know that the Suregeon-General was once even called to treat the great Herr Himmler?"

"Great, Mother?" Dr. Hammes quizzed with some severity, "Great?"

"Well, I mean," the old lady hesitated, adding uncertainly "he was great then."

The doctor laughed, rose to his feet, brushed her silver head with his lips and went to fetch another bottle of wine. The momentary absence allowed Frau Hammes to launch into her reminiscence unfettered by interruptions.

"You see, Professor, the Surgeon-General would never have gone on his own. It was Herr Himmler who insisted. And you can't say no to great men, can you?" She looked cautiously through the door as her son returned to the table. "The Surgeon-General and I were on our honeymoon in Breslau…"

"Now I ask you, Ernst," Dr. Hammes interrupted with mock indignation, uncorking the bottle, "why would anyone want to honeymoon in Breslau of all places."

"One day, Thomas, when you decide to take a wife, you'll find that one has to go on honeymoon somewhere," his mother said somewhat peevishly, before proceeding with her tale of the ailing

Herr Himmler. "Did you know Professor that the great…I mean the Herr Himmler suffered from terrible migraines. He had to stop work and neglect his great affairs of the state."

"Pity he didn't suffer a permanent migraine!"

Frau Hammes ignored the malicious innuendo. "He was in Breslau at the same time as the Surgeon General and I and this terrible migraine came over him. His personal physician, a Swedish doctor, Kessel the Quack they used to call him, well he was on leave. The Surgeon-General was summoned. Of course he was so young then, but already known in medical circles. And would you believe it, Professor, they sent two cars!" she added almost breathlessly.

"Have another drop, Mother," Dr. Hammes said pouring, "you'll feel better."

But the old lady was not to be distracted. "Well, he went, and in no time Herr Himmler was on his feet. He told the Surgeon-General that he felt born again."

"Why was he ever born at all!"

"Please don't interrupt, Thomas! That evening the… Herr Himmler sent me at the hotel where we were staying the largest bouquet of red roses I had ever seen. Goodness me! He must have ordered his people to cut every rose in Breslau. There was a note, too, with the flowers, written by Herr Himmler in his own hand. It was signed HH and said…What did it say, Thomas?"

"It said that HH had an elephant's memory and that he would not forget the Surgeon-General's kindness. It also proved that HH, who had been a chicken farmer in his earlier avatar, could actually read and write!" Dr. Hammes added flippantly.

"Oh! And imagine, Professor, when we got back from Breslau, we found that Herr Himmler had arranged for us to holiday in Switzerland. Two of his very nice men brought us the papers and money and told us all arrangements had been made to travel the week after. The Surgeon-General didn't want to go but I insisted. You couldn't possibly say no Herr Himmler, could you? It was so kind of him, he would have felt hurt had we not accepted the gift."

"I'm glad mother you didn't say no to HH. Otherwise I might not be here now!"

"He sent one of those big cars with flags to take us to the station. On the train we had a coupè all to ourselves. And he even arranged for us to be accompanied by a very nice young man. A captain, I think. I can't remember his name, Thomas."

"Captain Spy, Mother."

"He was so kind, escorting us everywhere, taking care of everything. But so well-mannered. He never dined with us, always at a separate table. And he had orders to buy us all kinds of gifts…"

"The cuckoo is dead, but we still have the clock somewhere!" the doctor said sitting back from the table and smiling at his mother with affectionate tolerance.

"And the Helvetians were so kind to us when we went to buy things in the shops."

"The Helvetians, as you put it, will do anything at the sight of money. I wouldn't be in the least surprised if it turned out that not Judas but the Swiss who pocketed the thirty shekels when Christ was handed over to the Romans!"

"Really, Thomas, how rude of you! And please try not to be blasphemous. You see, Professor, things were a little difficult then and there we were, having a second honeymoon. It was all so wonderful, such nice things to eat, and so much of it, too. We were ever so grateful to Herr Himmler."

"So grateful, mother, that the Surgeon-General had half a mind not to go back!"

"Well, it's such a beautiful country. All those lakes and mountains. One could stay on forever."

"Which you and the Surgeon-General nearly did."

"It wouldn't have been nice, would it, Professor? What would Herr Himmler have said."

Dr. Hammes laughed. "He would have simply torn out his hair and got another migraine!"

Frau Hammes gazed at her son thoughtfully; then with a wistful look said, "I do believe, Thomas, that it was during the second honeymoon that you…"

"Goodness, Mother! You are not telling me now that I was conceived in the land of twittering clocks and perforated cheese!"

Afterwards, quietly conversing between puffs of the doctor's cigar, the two men sat outside in the pallid sunshine. Frau Hammes had fed me generously on the Wiener Rostbraten and, replete and relaxed, I had stretched out beside the Professor's chair. Lying in the shadow of their company, half listening to their amiable voices, I wondered why the gift of friendship had not been granted to my tribe, why humans alone were blessed with the bonds of warm and comforting amity. In another life, if there was to be one, I would pray to be endowed with this most precious of sentiments.

GRETCHEN

1

After breakfast the Professor picks up the flowers Matilde has placed on the dining table and we set out on our fortnightly pilgrimage. Gretchen, the housekeeper thinks, might have tired of the hothouse-grown white roses that have accompanied our visits through the winter months. This morning she has got the florist to make up a large bouquet of lilies of the valley. "Frau Gärten says they are early this year," she adds.

The Professor holds the tiny white blooms to his nose. "Our Lady's Tears," he says with a faint smile of recollection.

"Oh!" Matilde looks at the pristine bell flowers with pursed lips. "I didn't know that," she apologizes awkwardly.

"Neither did I. Gretchen once told me. I'm sure they'll make a nice change," the Professor adds trying to put the housekeeper at ease.

Out through the back garden, we climb the steps to the road that skirts the woods. The warming morning sun lifts the chill of the early hour. There's a hint of spring in the air. The first birds have returned from their hibernal retreat and now flutter about among the still gaunt trees, the swollen tips of the boughs and branches waiting to unfurl their greenery.

The Professor's brisk step leaves me lagging behind. "Come along, Albert!" he calls glancing over his shoulder. Weighed down by the generous bulk of my aged frame, breath shortening I try to keep up with his trim pace. In the early months of our visit to Gretchen, our mournful stroll towards the cemetery was slow and ponderous. With time, the acceptance of her absence, the melancholy excursion has taken on the routine of our usual morning walks, apparently carefree and unburdened, the ache of loss seemingly enfolded in the habits of everyday life.

Below us, the town still dormant, idle wisps of smoke rising from chimney stacks here and there, the houses recede and fall out of sight as we turn the wide bend in the road. Above the cold green waters of the river winding between the shallow descent of the wooded valley, the cemetery laid out on a gentle slope comes into sight.

School teacher Vogel maintains that it is the site of an ancient burial ground, where horsemen once emerged from the dark forests to bid farewell to their dead on burning pyres whose leaping flames lit up the twilight of the surrounding countryside. Teaching history and something of an expert on legend and lore, Herr Vogel should know.

The fires extinguished, the chestnut-bearded horsemen long gone to join their dead kinsmen in the land of their forbears where warriors ride again, the hallowed ground now lies steeped in pastoral silence, the dead at peace on this verdant mantle that overlooks the seemingly endless greenery of the woods and forests that stretch unbroken towards the horizon. The older tombs jostle one another, weather-beaten and moss-coated, jagged like worn teeth protruding from the earth, nameless and consigned to the oblivion of memory. Close by the rust-ridden iron gate lie the Kelbs in a long irregular row, Joachim the last of the tribe, visited by Martha once in a while. Gretchen lies at the far end under a long slab of clear marble.

The Professor places the flowers on the tomb, gazes at the simple inscription with Gretchen's name before sitting down on the edge. I stretch out alongside, resting my chin on the cold marble. The Professor's hand reaches out, his fingers gently ploughing through my fur. We rest in silence a long while, his eyes contemplating the horizon where the timid morning light has grown to a pale brightness.

I cannot fathom the elusive depths of human sorrow, cannot pretend to read the thoughts that graze through his mind. For one of my kind this inheritance of pain merely crowds the head with memories. So that rising up from beneath the cold stone, she once again walks the earth, once again her light laughter rings in my ears, the grace of her lithe body filling my sight, ineffable tenderness in her voice as she calls my name, as though calling to herself the child of her heart. And leaping up to be enfolded in her arms, I abruptly awake to find my paw scratching at the marble. The professor quietly pats my head as I come to my self. "Shall we go, Albert?"

Our spirit dulled by the aching ebb and tide of memory, we saunter back through the woods, the Professor's pace no longer brisk, I laboriously weaving my way between the trees. An early squirrel darts across my path, stops at a short distance and looks back, hoping perhaps for a chase. But the time for such play and pursuit is long past, beyond the dignity and demeanour of age. Besides, it suffices that I can barely keep pace with the Professor's stride. But his eye catching the scene, "Off you go, Albert," he says with a smile of encouragement.

The Professor resumes his walk back to the house. Out of obedience, for Dr. Hammes thinks I am to exercise a little more if I am to shed some weight, I follow the squirrel. Like a feather duster the bushy tail, upright and teasing, swings to and fro as I laboriously follow in its wake. Cunning and patient, keeping its distance, the little creature waits for me with the courteous forbearance of an old companion. Grateful for the friendly charity, mourning my exhausted vigour, I cannot help but wonder at the cruel depredations of time and age.

Tiring then of the senile pace of my forced indolence, the little fellow suddenly makes off, leaping out of sight. Relieved of the unsolicited company, I slow my steps and ambling through the morning air make my way for a brief respite in my secret den.

Long years ago, warring men had put up on the wooded slope overlooking the town an odd structure, a round hat box the size of a small room, with cemented walls and two narrow, oblong slits that let in the daylight. Sunk in the ground and almost entirely hidden from sight by overgrowth, it now sat there with its blind eyes like the petrified head of some monstrous creature drowned in the earth.

Once, out walking with Gretchen, nosing about in the shrubs, I had come on this mysterious den, finding myself suddenly on the inside, the floor heaped high with dead leaves that had drifted in over the seasons, a dim light filtering in through the eyelets. And ever since, when on warm summer afternoons Gretchen strolled through the woods or sat reading nearby on the old trunk of the fallen larch, it had become my secret refuge. I would then wander away to retire in the twilight retreat, stretch out on the soft bed of dead foliage, doze and drowse for an hour or two in the entombed silence. Sometimes, the mind languid with the high summer heat, the fancy stole into my head that should I, like my ancestors, ever take to the wilderness, it was here, in this sculpted cavern, that I would choose to end my days. Fleeing from the lugubrious dream, I would wake with a start to hear Gretchen's voice calling me to herself.

2

A mournful day, when abruptly shorn of illusions, wings clipped, one falls back to earth. Robbed of birth and lineage, the fanciful flights of imagination, today I discover what it is to be merely one of the herd, indistinct, without identity, like any common mongrel of uncertain descent and dubious parentage.

Helping out Matilde with the household chores, sometimes at mid-morning Gretchen would retire with a coffee to the living room for a brief rest, putting up her feet on the old pouffe and turning on the picture box. Stretched out by her feet, I would keep her company. Often at that hour the picture box showed a program on the animal kingdom. Over time I saw and learned of the oddest of creatures inhabiting the earth, fauna large and small, birds and bees, mammals, reptiles, amphibians, carnivore and herbivore, tiny beings that lived in our company but unknown to us.

There were sights that raised a growl in my throat, others that made me whimper as cowering I watched lions with long manes and heads as large as gardener Bauer's outsize flower pots idling in the tall grass, immense herds of gnu racing at breakneck speed across vast plains, the jaundiced eyes of crocodiles floating disembodied in muddy waters, the heart-pounding sight of tigers stalking their prey in the forests of night. One morning, then, there were images that filled my being with pride, raised my spirit to heights of regard and esteem that set me apart from my fellow canines, mostly common, low-born specimens on whom I could look down with pity and sympathy.

In a pristine world whitened with snow stretching to the mountain-etched horizon, across a frozen waste echoing with the sibilant whisper of an icy wind sweeping down from the void of a colourless sky, raced a wolverine pack with bared fangs and eyes glinting with a breath-seizing ferocity, the smooth silver coat over lithe muscle-bound bodies speckled with glistening droplets. The lion and the tiger were tame, household creatures in comparison. "Labrador," Gretchen said looking down at me with a fond smile. "That's where your ancestors come from, Albert."

Could it be, I wondered afterwards, that one such as myself, gentle and docile, tamed by man's kindness and care, ever alive to the call of the human heart, could it at all be that I had descended from the same tree as these feral creatures with blood-lust dripping from their eyes. But so it was. Gretchen's words remained imprinted within me, endowing me with the certainty of lineage, an ancestral nobility of blood that raised me above others of my race, the button-eyed, sniffling little Pekinese in Frau Gärtner's flower shop, music teacher Forkel's Florenz, a daft creature with an orange-sized head and tall, stilt-like legs, something out of a pantomime. And for a long time afterwards, at night, cradled in sleep, I found myself racing across the arctic wilderness alongside the untamed companions of my breed, our fiery breath frosting the boreal air, the ululation of our primordial hunting call echoing across the snow-bound wastes.

And then today the sudden fall from grace, cruel and unexpected. Abruptly discarded and disowned, outcast from the realms of the noble and the high-born, I found myself adrift, unanchored and helpless.

Now with youth far behind her, Matilde's accustomed housekeeping, brisk and energetic, sometimes left her a little breathless. Cleaning, sweeping, dusting, putting out the rugs and carpets to air, washing the curtains, ironing the Professor's clothes, all the household chores on her hands now that Gretchen was no longer with us, Matilde's mornings were without respite, a flurry of ceaseless activity. So that tiring and out of breath, occasionally she too would pause, sitting down briefly in front of the picture box to watch whatever was on offer.

This morning, sat alongside her, it came as no little surprise to see a near image of myself, but years earlier, in the prime of my days, rampant and vigorous, the body bursting with youthful energy, the coat sleek and shiny. Bewildered I watched this former self in the company of a tweed-jacketed figure with a flat cap standing perfectly still among the tall reeds of a marshland, a long barrelled rifle raised skywards.

Suddenly, the tips of the vegetation parting, in a flutter of wings and with a harsh cry, a brace of ducks rose in the air. The dull echo of a shot seemed to arrest one of the birds in its upward lift. For a brief moment it appeared to float in the air, plummeting then headlong towards the ground like a deadweight. My youthful self at once leapt and raced into the reeds, disappearing for a long minute, to emerge finally with the dead fowl daintily held between the jaws, which then was gently deposited at the master's feet.

"That's what you should have been doing, young man," said Matilde kindly slapping my rump. "You'd have a little less of this!"

As she made to rise and return to her labours, I listened astonished to the voice from the picture box describing me as a "gun dog", whatever that meant, the only gun I had ever set eyes on being the Professor's ancient, family revolver when occasionally Matilde cleaned and oiled the weapon. Even more astounding was the news that I had been bred for the sole purpose of accompanying hunters, carrying and fetching the game they downed.

"Come along, Albert, you don't want to be looking at yourself all day long!" Matilde invited me out of the room turning off the box.

Confused and deflated I padded out to the garden. The late morning sun could do little to dispel the cold and emptiness that had taken hold of my spirit. Bred to fetch and carry! And what now of the imagined pedigree reaching back to ancient lineage, the vision of the ancestral rites of hunt and chase, running free, wild and untamed, under the endless expanse of frozen northern skies. All gone, like the last dreams of dawn, vaporous and evanescent, melting into thin air at the first light of day. With her doltish expression and preposterous mincing gait, music teacher's Florenz was a foolish creature, no doubt about it. But how should I meet her gaze when next our paths crossed?

How blessed were humans, I thought watching old gardener Bauer training the new tendrils of the passiflora along the wall. An only kind, created in a single image, free and unburdened like the little passarine now hopping about on the grass around me, apparently humankind made no distinction between one breed and another, indifferent to height, hue and girth, untroubled by the variety among the tribes of man. A gift worthy of envy.

3

Today we have an eminent guest to lunch. No stranger to the house, his preferences at table are familiar to Matilde. Dr. Süssmayr's tastes are eclectic, which is to say he eats anything placed before him, forgetting on the instant whatever might have passed his lips. Food he considers merely an item of nourishment, much as the air, inhaled and expelled. Only once was he seen to pause in contemplation as he briefly noticed the contents of his raised fork before swiftly demolishing the piece of turnip with an unaccustomed expression of satisfaction. The event had not gone unregistered, so that along with the other dishes Matilde today has placed on the table a generous bowl of buttered baby turnips.

The head of neurosurgery at the hospital, Dr. Meinrad Süssmayr is a solemn figure, mostly silent save for the subject of his particular interest. Tall and lean, heavy-browed and greying at the temples, an intense look of pain or preoccupation shadows his expression at all times. Pensive and academic, over the years he has authored several works of some weight, most notably a trilogy, the three consecutive volumes being titled "Death," "Dying" and "The Dead". While his thoughts have earned him a degree of notoriety elsewhere, in the town library none of the books have ever gone out on loan. Dr. Hammes had once made a half-hearted attempt at the first volume, persevered through several pages of the first chapter before definitively abandoning the learned work, admitting nevertheless that the writing was a cut above that of the local telephone directory, though the contents somewhat less comprehensible.

What assailed Dr. Süssmayr's thoughts through his waking hours, perhaps his nights as well, was the conundrum surrounding the hour of death. For decades he had studied, researched, contemplated and meditated in an attempt to arrive at a precise and unequivocal determination of the moment when death becomes definitive. When are the dead finally dead? Pastor Schaffgott's claim that death occurred when the soul flew out of the body the doctor rejected outright. It was not a clinical proposition, besides which the flying soul was mostly a rare sight.

Dr. Süssmayr had attended to Gretchen through her last illness. It had brought him close to the Professor, who had become an occasional confidante of the doctor's thoughts and doubts. Dissimilar in outlook, manner and habits, yet there was a likeness between the two men that might have been mistaken for a family trait. Both of a tall, stately bearing, both immersed in a cerebral solitude that found rare fellowship in the town; yet their lives had trodden very different paths, the doctor austere in mien, spartan in habits, a bachelor wedded to his mind and work; the Professor more amenable to comfort and companionship, susceptible to the graces and gifts life had to offer, friendship, affection, desire.

Now talking over lunch in a quiet but grave voice, touching briefly on the malady that had carried Gretchen away, Dr. Süssmayr admitted to an occasional sense of helplessness. "The truth, Ernst, is that we still know so little of what goes on up here," he said touching his temple briefly; adding, to Matilde's terrified look as she cleared the dishes, "The only way to shed some light is to slice the brain." He looked at the platter of meat. "As fine as those slices. Fortunately science has relieved us of the blood and butchery. Today machines do the job."

The doctor had reverted to the query uppermost in his mind as Matilde served the desert and hurried back to the kitchen rolling her eyes. "When are the dead really dead?" she asked aloud mimicking the doctor's solemn tone as she removed the baking dish from the oven.

"When they are dead!" said gardener Bauer startled as he sat with his mug of beer by the kitchen door.

"The doctor doesn't think so."

"Oh!" His head full of the seeds and seedlings for the summer annuals, the old man was not at ease with abstruse cogitations. "But," he stammered, "but if the dead are not dead, when are they dead?"

"That's what the doctor would like to know."

Bauer scratched his grizzled head. "People are dead when they are buried, aren't they?" he asked helplessly.

"Oh!" Matilde laughed, arrested by the novelty of the thought. "Why, would you bury them before they're dead?"

It may have been the dull glare of the sunlight outside, but for a mere instant I thought I saw Gretchen standing in the haze of the doorway looking down at Bauer with a kindly smile. She had always been fond of the old gardener.

FREUDE

1

The trees look ever so tall from where I lie in the back of the car, the early sun playing truant through the branches, painting the new leaves lucent green. We drive through the morning woods, the road arrow-straight along the shallow valley sloping down to the river's dark-emerald waters. Not a soul about, neither habitation nor trace of life, only flora and foliage, the wakening blue of the sky overhead, the world appears new-born, still and undiscovered.

As I drowse, lulled by the even purring hum of the motor, once again I feel her hand reach out to me, resting weightless on my head, smoothing my fur, infinitely gentle. And somewhere, in an unknown recess within my head, yet distant and beyond, once again I hear her voice, but disembodied and ethereal with the soundlessness of air.

A hare busy on his morning errands crosses our path and the car slows, coming almost to a halt. Jarred out of my reverie I open my eyes as the Professor turns to look at me, saying "All well there, Albert?" He turns back to the wheel and we resume our journey.

We resume our journey and I look at the empty seat beside the Professor, thinking then of the many mornings of my life we have travelled this country road on the way to the Baron's estate. She was then always there, the soft cadence of her voice barely rising above the sound of the car, and in that soothing lull she would turn her head to bestow on me a quiet smile, a word, her hand reaching back to touch my coat in a brief caress. Dear Gretchen! It makes me wonder why my Maker should have thought it fit that one of my kind be blessed with such solicitude, so much affection, only to be suddenly bereft of the sun that lit these mornings and the days of my life.

Now the valley narrowing, we leave behind the larch and birch of the woods as the pines multiply, grow dense, and the dark green closes in on us, shutting out the sunlight. Flanked by the forest of sentinel evergreens we drive a while longer. The road then broadening, the car slows down and in the midst of the virgin forestland the trees part to reveal an opening. We turn into an ancient gateway of lichen-covered black stone with an intricate and ponderous wrought-iron arch topped with a large, stained brass casting of an heraldic insignia. Figuring a fierce canine head with bared fangs and lolling tongue, an upright sword in one gauntleted hand, it is the coat of arms of the Monfleury-Pischendorpf family. Ferocity of the kind I had never seen in one of my tribe and it made me think of the peculiar habit of humans of attributing their own inclinations to lesser creatures.

We pass through the gate and drive briefly through a shadowed avenue of pines and dense undergrowth, light-less and secluded. Abruptly then the wilderness falls back and as if in a dream a magical world appears before us, a vast sunlit meadow alive with the offerings of early spring, daisy and cowslip, the riotous hues of crocus here and there woven into the undulating carpet of white and gold. As though guarding a hallowed space, a seemingly impenetrable forest of evergreens encircles the pasture.

We drive up the winding road towards the manor house. Set back from the green, almost in the shadows of the trees, it is a large awkward structure almost entirely covered with ancient ivy, looking as though sculpted by nature out of the surrounding green, a rambling habitation from the vegetable kingdom set with jewelled windows of shiny glass. In origin, the Baron once said, it was meant to be a sort of château. "But great grandfather Wilhelm was something of a gothic soul. And then his wife, who had several English cousins, was an admirer of the Georgian. Thank heavens it was before the time of the Bauhaus and the Chicago School! Quite a pastiche, as it is."

At the far end of the meadow stands an oak, a giant of a tree, regal and ancient, a veritable Methuselah. And half hidden behind it's towering spread lurks a dark, ominous shape, seemingly hewn from a mountain of night. Built by the founder of the House of Monfleury-Pischendorpf, long abandoned by the living, Hubert's castle sits silent and sinister, like a monstrous beast, an ogre, escaped from the twilight gloom of the surrounding forest.

As if to contrast the tenebrous past, at the other end of the vast green, nearer the mansion, is the garden, a singular creation covering a full acre, the immense plot laid out with rose bushes, shrubs of an endless variety, roses of every hue, size and shape. Neat gravel paths wind through the endless maze of beds. On early summer evenings when the fading light stands still, the riotous colours of the blooms tinge the air with lilac and red, pale liquescent gold, linen white. And the fragrant breath of unknown perfumes lingers in the closing twilight like wisps of imagined memory.

Baroness Gertrude once recounted to Gretchen of a summer long ago, a month's holiday at the Monfleury-Pischendorpf estate. She was young then. "Yes, dear, I too was young once," she said looking up at Gretchen, the irony of her faint smile lost in the parchment folds of her face. She was young, barely twenty, her head in the clouds, brimming with airy notions of romance, mysterious encounters, impossible loves. One evening towards the end of her stay, the air redolent with the fragrance of rose, the hush of dusk settling on the green of the meadow, the young scion of the family had asked for her hand. Looking out over the immense patchwork of deepening colours afloat in the fading light, feeling faint and weightless in the enchantment of a dream, she had assented, granted him his desire. They were wed a year later. "It was this garden that I married," she said looking pensively over the shrubs in bloom. "Armin's father left us long ago. But the roses, they are still here. I did well, wouldn't you say, dear?" she added, her voice impassive, without mirth.

Now as the car winds its way up to the mansion, we catch sight of butler Otfried idly manoeuvring the wrought-iron wheel chair along the labyrinthine paths of the rose garden, the old lady sitting upright, leisurely waving her cane with feigned severity over gardener Schwarzbauer as he crouches among the shrubs raking and weeding.

2

Afterwards no one ever came to know how he found his way to the Baron's estate. For all that he might have landed from the moon. Certainly Schwarzbauer had come from some remote and mysterious land, a distant region where the sun shone summer and winter, its furnace heat baking the earth, tanning humans to a cinder-black hue. Wherever the nameless place, whatever his antecedents, one grey autumn day he suddenly appeared at the Baron's, a fully-grown foundling, nameless, abandoned and lost.

On her way back to the manor with an apron full of swedes for the evening supper, Elfriede came on him as he lay inert and concealed beside a bed of tea rose shrubs. In the fading afternoon light the cook would have barely noticed the huddled figure lying on the ground had her ears not caught a low moan. Startled, she looked towards the bushes at what appeared to be a heap of colourless mud-stained clothes.

As she stared, straining her eyes at the bedraggled pile, in the shade of the foliage her dim gaze suddenly fell on the lineaments of a human face, indistinct and benighted, as though it had been pushed up from the depths of the black earth, was moulded with the same primal matter. A face such as one that Elfriede had never seen on a fellow being. With a strangled cry she stepped back, scattering the swedes on the ground, and fled in the murky light towards the manor.

Barely conscious, wakefulness that came and went, the body limp and the long limbs lifeless, the enormous frame slipped and tumbled and it was some time before Otfried and the Baron managed to heave it on to the wheelbarrow, carting it laboriously up to the woodshed behind the manor.

Stretched out on a mattress and covered with a rough blanket, inhaling with the imperceptible breathing the resinous smell of freshly-cut pine from the logs of winter wood neatly stacked along the walls, the fugitive lay comatose, drowned in a slumber that seemed to have permeated every muscle and limb.

Old doctor Streckenbach, a descendent of the barber-surgeons of old, who had attended to the maladies of the Monfleury family, without memorable success, for almost half a century, arrived late in the evening. He lingered over the prostrate figure but could decipher no particular malaise. Without a sure prognosis, the future appeared uncertain. The doctor shook his head, picked up his worn leather case, looked down at the patient with stoical compassion like a priest who had proffered the last rites, and slipped out into the night after taking leave of the Baron.

Fearful and confused, Elfriede had watched from the doorway. When the doctor had gone and, resigned for the worst, Otfried and the Baron turned indoors, later in the night with the house asleep she lit a lantern, stole into the shed, and sat down by the supine figure. With trembling hand she touched a damp sponge to the face, gently wiping away the stains of earth, all the while her ears alert, her eyes keen in the dim light for the merest sign of life.

Short, stumpy, well past middle age, Elfriede had entered service at the manor as a girl and never gone away, not a day's absence as she rose at first light, cleaned and scrubbed, polished, cooked and served, moving through the kitchen, the pantry, the halls and the hallway of the mansion with silent bustling gait, the peasant girth shapeless in half-a-century-old hand-me-downs from Baroness Gertrude's wardrobe. Her muted life had never known a retreat, a home of her own, the joys and sorrows of a family, the fluttering heart of motherhood. Hardly had she ever been much beyond the boundaries of the estate.

Herself an orphan, now this wind-stirred autumn night she looked at the giant of a man, the fondling she had stumbled on among the shrubs. Something, unknown and never before felt, stirred within her, awakening a sense of possession. A desire to hold and keep. It was she who had found him, so that however alien he was hers, to nourish and care for. She did not, could not parse the feeling, it rose and reached out from her innermost being, like a tendril silently groping in the dark, seeking out the light of day.

When early next morning Otfried and the Baron looked in, they found Elfriede sitting on the floor beside the stranger, a bowl of warm barley in her hand as she trickled little spoonfuls through the barely parted lips. They enquired if he was still alive. Elfriede looked up, her eyes fatigued from sleeplessness yet bright and content as wordlessly she nodded her head.

For almost three whole days the giant slept, soundless, uncomplaining and motionless. Then on the fourth, suddenly released from the mortal slumber, Lazarus-like he was restored to the land of the living. Elfriede was with him, as she had been every spare minute since that first night, nursing, cleaning and feeding.

As she lifted the spoon to his lips, a hand rose from the blanket and closed around her wrist. Startled she drew back, spilling the liquid. A cry of panic rose in her throat as she tugged to free herself. But the long, prehensile fingers held on, would not let go. Stricken, she looked at the large sinewy hand, sculpted in ebony, immensely strong, wound around her pallid, veined wrist. And lifting her gaze she saw his eyelids flicker and open, unveiling two large infant eyes, serene and innocent, as though opening on the world for the very first time. The fleshy lips parted, whispered an incoherent word, a sound of gentle supplication. The fingers freed Elfriede's wrist and the palm came to rest on hers, as if meaning to consign to her care something secret and precious.

"We ought to tell the authorities," said the Baron and was perplexed by his mother's stern refusal. "But Maman…," he protested, only to be cut short by a severe glance. No, Baroness Gertrude had other plans for the fugitive guest.

Old gardener Ulf, whose expert hands had over the years returned the rose garden to its former glory, had died some months ago. One afternoon cutting flowers for the house, he had felt unwell and sat down on the gravel path by the shrubs. Later in the day

Elfriede had come on him lying on the ground clutching a bouquet of white roses to his bosom. It was the Baroness's constant lament that the gardener had unreasonably departed before completing the season's pruning of the bushes. Now she had divined in the strange creature who had mysteriously appeared on her land a replacement for old man Ulf.

"But this chap, he might know nothing about gardening," the Baron insisted.

"How like you, child," the Baroness rebutted dryly. "Sometimes, Armin, you are as tediously punctilious as a book-keeper! He'll learn. The man has a human brain, I expect."

"He doesn't understand a word," the Baron persisted. "He can't speak!"

"There is not the least reason why he would need to speak."

"Besides, he doesn't even have a name!"

"He shall have one," the Baroness concluded decisively.

And a name was given. Baroness Gertrude christened the stranger Schwarzbauer. It was an odd name and Gretchen thought so during a visit shortly after the gardener's arrival. "Simple, dear," the Baroness explained. "He's black and he's a peasant. Schwarzbauer! I expect they are all peasants where he comes from."

The woodshed was repaired, renovated and partitioned in half. The small room was sparsely furnished with a bed, an antique chest-of drawers, a table and a chair. Otfried dug up an ancient wood fire stove from the cellar. Elfriede made curtains for the window from a worn table cloth. And the Baron found an old radio with a brown bakelite case, one of the several Invictas his father had bought after the war. Installed in his new abode, Schwarzbauer went to bed with the smell of parsley and thyme from the kitchen garden and woke at dawn to the long choral chirp and chatter of birds in the woods behind the shed.

Wordlessly Schwarzbauer fitted into the household and became a fixture on the estate as if he had been there forever. A peasant he may well have been in his previous life, for he took to his work with alacrity, digging, hoeing, raking, pruning with the skill of a horticultural expert. And he was tireless, lying on the ground to weed the beds, burrowing among the shrubs from morning to dark, putting away neatly the gardening tools at the end of the day, carting away the dead leaves, cuttings and faded blooms in the wheel barrow in which he himself had been gathered up.

Sometimes, doing the rounds of the grounds in her wheelchair, thinking that the gardener might be idling among the bushes or catching a nap, the Baroness would flourish her walking stick and bring it to rest on his bottom with feigned severity and he would look up with a wide boyish grin, baring a mouthful of perfect teeth that set off against the dark of his skin glistened a marble sheen. He did not mind the friendly chastisement, for he sensed that it was to this craggy old woman that he was to be beholden for having come through to the still waters of the harbour of his new life.

Otfried found in Schwarzbauer a kindred spirit, for while the latter could not speak the tongue, Otfried himself was a man of rare words. His family had been in the service of the Monfleurys ever since no one could remember when. His father Gottfried had served both Baron Armin's father and grandfather, accompanying the latter to the Western Front during the Great War, master and servant both returning from the hostilities intact in life and limb, save for their eardrums, ruptured by the close booming of giant cannons.

Ever attired in a wine-coloured, brass-buttoned jacket whose frayed collarless neck had been ably and invisibly mended time and again by Elfriede, in his diverse roles of butler and handyman, majordomo and seneschal, valet, nurse and much else, Otfried padded about the house and the grounds with measured steps, wordlessly going about his task, a tall lean figure of indeterminate age with a sparsely dressed head of copper-coloured hair and modest features whose entirely inexpressive set gave nothing away. Only at table in the kitchen, when Elfriede placed the food before him, did the mask take on a slight expression, of satisfaction and contained pleasure.

Unnoticed by the household, unobtrusively Elfriede's life too had undergone an imperceptible change. Tireless as ever, she went about her daily chores, but now her days were often longer. To the subdued bustle of her rounds she had added the task of seeing to Schwarzbauer's needs, modest as they were; dusting and tidying his little room in the woodshed, mending the wear and tear the rose thorns inflicted on the few pieces of clothing given him; serving him, placing an extra morsel on his plate and sitting by him at table, proffering a quiet smile of encouragement as he ate and looked up occasionally to meet her motherly gaze. Language barred speech, it would be some time before he could venture forth with the first uncertain steps into the world of words. But it did not matter. Nor did she pause to reason, to ask why. Somehow Elfriede felt an odd sense of fulfilment, that late in a life so uneventful, devoid of episode and excursion, she could at long last lay claim to the welfare of a fellow being.

3

Now the Baron trips lightly down the steps as the Professor brings the car to a halt on the gravel driveway. Immersed in this green retreat, with only his mother, music and books for company, the Baron greatly looks forward to these visits of ours, which over time have taken on a monthly regularity. Our day-long stay provides him with the Professor's amiable company, a sort of easy intimacy having grown between the two men over the years. Our visits, as well, lighten the burden of his mother's attentions, if only for a few hours.

The Baron greets the Professor, then turns to me with a broad smile. "Albert, old boy," he says patting my back heartily, "we have a surprise for you today!"

I wag my tail in uncertain appreciation. The mysterious announcement makes me wonder. The peace and quiet of a settled life, days that flow into each other with the placidity of a country stream, have made me averse to surprises. It might only be that Elfriede's baking skills have improved, which would lessen the risk of my ageing molars being loosened from their roots by the biscuits that I am usually offered at lunch. Or perhaps the gruel might be a little less watery. Little imagining my reticence, the Baron chuckles and with a final pat on my head remarks "Nothing ruffles old Albert's aplomb!"

Ever dressed in a green and purple tartan smoking jacket with a black cravat around the neck, slight of build, boyishly handsome with a head of light hair, the Baron bore scarce resemblance to his heavy-jowled, beetle-browed ancestors whose portraits lined the walls of the mansion. Ever amiable and good-humoured, there was nothing especially baronial about the Baron save perhaps the long procession of names with which his mother had chosen to burden him at birth.

His father, a mild-mannered country gentleman even less baronial in mien and girth, thought that it would suffice to christen the infant Armin Alexander. Baroness Gertrude thought otherwise, dredging up the given names of several generations of her Teutonic warrior ancestors and fashioning them into a chain which she placed around the baby boy's frail neck. Later not even the Baron himself could remember the long string of names. So that Armin Alexander Karl Theodore Manfred Reinhard Sigmund Waldemar came to be called simply Armin, both at home and at school.

Despite various liaisons, affairs brief and some less so, the Baron had in time become a confirmed bachelor. "Not large enough to house two ladies," he had once said to Gretchen looking at the mansion with an air of neglected melancholy, recounting then of a visit to the estate by a Spanish lady he had met during one of his travels. From the very first day the presence of the comely guest had abruptly and unexpectedly wakened in Baroness Gertrude a keen, almost passionate interest in the Spanish Inquisition and the bloody deeds of the Spanish Conquistadores in the Americas, both of which became almost the sole and loudly censorious subject of conversation at every meal. Baron Armin never heard from the young woman again.

The weighty matters of existence, life and death, wealth, name and fame, these the Baron found mostly tedious. Instead he had a considerable penchant for the insignificant, quixotic and whimsical odds and ends, the minutiae of history, details so miniscule that the most punctilious of scholars omitted them even as footnotes. The shelves of his study at the mansion were packed with rare literature on the unsung figures of writers, artists and composers, journeymen overshadowed by the great names and consigned to obscurity and oblivion. So that he could reel off erudite details, facts and figures so trivial and inessential that occasionally even the Professor looked at him with bemused curiosity.

With his personal encyclopaedia of trivia at hand, the Baron could readily recite Napoleon's supper menu on the night before the battle of Waterloo, explain why the Emperor's nephew Prince Napoleon was called Plon Plon, why Wagner wore silk underwear and Brahms disliked bicycles, how St. Patrick ended up in Ireland and why he was poor at grammar, the name of the nun Casanova shared as mistress with the French Ambassador, the street in Paris where Pascal talked with God for a couple of hours.

At lunch one day, when Otfried leaning over the table to serve appeared to have emitted an indecorous sound, the Baron casually remarked that the wounded and maimed from the Crusades who were treated at the legendary Medical School of Salerno were actively encouraged to pass wind at will.

The Professor looked up from his dessert. "I think I may have missed that bit of news," he said with a quiet smile.

"Eicere zephiros quosdam, quasi crimen putatur.
  Tamen qui eos retinent, periculum adeunt
    Spasmi, hydropisis, colicae et vertiginis.
      Haec saepius infelices exitus
        Sunt curiosa tristis urbanitatis"*

* Releasing certain winds is considered a near crime
  Yet to suppress them is to risk dropsy, convulsion, colic and vertigo
    This too often is the unhappy outcome of a sad discretion

the Baron recited from memory, adding with a chuckle, "Imagine, Ernst, those limbless Crusaders sitting around in the orange blossom scented gardens of Salerno breaking wind all day long!"

The Baron's propensity for the minor follies and foibles of men did not sit well with everyone. Less than amused, Carin Breitfuss, the new Head Librarian who was to invade our lives shortly, viewed it as a sign of eternal adolescence, facile and infantile. "Well, yes," she once remarked, "one can doodle on the edges of real life if you can afford not to have to put in an honest day's work to earn your keep."

As so often, Fräulein Breitfuss's acid pronouncement was out of place. A gentle spirit, preferring the turtle to the hare, the Baron had merely retreated from the hectic dash through life's obstacle course.

4

"Freude! Freude! Come along, lad. Here's someone to meet you. Freude!"

Neither the Professor nor I could see who the Baron was addressing. After a moment, suddenly, it appeared from under the mayflower bush beside the steps. Taken aback I shut my eyes briefly, for it was a sight such as I had never beheld.

Familiar with the various breeds of my race, over the years I thought that I had seen them all, squashed face pugs, sullen boxers, sad flap-eared spaniels, ever-frisky foolish Dalmatians, silly little Maltese bitches sporting ribboned bows on the head peeping out of ladies bags. Then there was music teacher Forkel's outlandish pet, an immensely tall creature with a head the size of an orange, who seemed to walk on folding stilts with the shrunken head held aloft and with never a glance at her fellow canines. It was rumoured that seated by her master as he played the piano, Forkel's Florenz raised a long leg each time he struck a note.

But I had never laid my eyes on a creature such as the one that now stepped forth. It was as if after a long day's toil in his workshop, our Maker had found Himself with bits and pieces, leftovers that he had decided to somehow put together. For it was the oddest specimen, a pointer's snout stuck to a poodle's head, a terrier's body with short setter's legs, a frightening pit bull tail that stuck straight up in the air and swung to and fro like a metronome.

Rump raised high, paws skidding and sliding on the gravel, with a hobble and a limp the creature steadily advanced towards us. Sheathed as it was in the strangest of coats, there was not the least sign of a bone nor the ripple of a muscle, for the grey moquette-like fur looked stiff, as if stuck on with glue.

The Baron clapped his hands, saying "Come along, Freude."

Freude! How humans delighted in giving their pets the most far-fetched names. Frau Gärten the florist had a miniscule Chihuahua she called Othello, widow Beck's moth-eaten tabby went by the grand name of Charlemagne; and then there was Montevideo. But to call this ramshackle creature Joy! In truth it looked anything but joyous, the stiff little paws scratching at the ground to gain a precarious toe-hold, the curious mismatched head nodding dangerously as if about to come unstuck.

Abruptly then my thoughts were arrested, for sniffing the air I could detect no odour, no tell-tale sign of the creature's presence. And thinking to have lost the one attribute that had remained intact, the sense of smell, a wave of sudden panic came over me.

"Freude, say 'Hullo Albert!'," the Baron commanded in an especially loud voice as the strange being stopped at his feet.

What happened next sent my head into a spin. Bewildered out of my wits, I backed away and would have bolted the scene had not the Baron said, "Albert, here's a new friend for you. Freud! Say hullo to Albert!"

It was not unusual to come across feathered creatures imitating human speech; albeit it has always been beyond me why the Maker should have bestowed the precious gift on the least intelligible of species in his kingdom. One was all too familiar with Montevideo's inane chatter. And once going into the hardware store with

Gretchen, for no reason at all a blackbird perched inside a cage had addressed me in unutterable language, words that had made Gretchen blush visibly.

Now at the Baron's stentorian order, the little button eyes lit up, glinting a peculiar and unhealthy yellow, as though a bulb had been turned on inside the skull. And the tiny head nodding even more precariously, a small, scratchy metallic voice came forth: *"Hullo Albert!"*

A canine uttering human words! Though somehow not entirely persuaded that this weird creature belonged to the kingdom of the Maker's creation, I retreated in consternation. Amicable and even-tempered at all times, I could not now help a growl. The warning shot, which I fear came out more as a moan, in no way deterred the new-found friend as, slipping and limping, laboriously he came forward towards me, all the while repeating *"Hullo Albert!"*

With another growl and half a bark that stuck in my throat, backing off frantically, my paws skidding on the gravel, loosing my balance I tumbled over. And then it was all over me. Flat on the ground, my legs in the air, shocked and atremble, I shut my eyes tight as the frightful creature heaved itself onto my belly, prodding me with the tiny rubber-hard nose, sinking the claw-like paws between my ribs, all the while hulloing away in a tinny metallic tone that grated in the ear painfully. Abruptly then, the umpteenth *"Hullo Albert!"* trailed off in a barely audible screech and the little fellow collapsed in a heap, lying on my tummy like a dead-weight.

I opened my eyes to see the Baron pluck Freude off me. "Oh dear!" he said cradling the seemingly dead creature, "I'm afraid our friends from the Land of the Rising Sun have sized the battery too small." He looked down at me as I sat up with a hangdog mien, adding brightly, "It's alright, Albert. An hour's recharge and your friend will be as frisky as ever." Heaven forbid! We had enough frisking for the day, I thought.

The Baron and the Professor made their way up the steps into the mansion. Following lamely on their heels, I could not help feeling suffused with a secret shame. What would my ancestors, indomitable hunters in the wild, have made of the sight of me prostrate and cowed, trampled underfoot by a bizarre specimen a fraction my size and weight. An inglorious spectacle, if ever there was one!

"Here we are," said the Baron as we stepped into the hallway. And then he did something so shocking that it froze me in my tracks. He flicked back Freude's collapsed tail, extracted a small plug on a lead from the creature's bottom and bent down to insert it in an electrical socket beside the hat-stand. Expecting shooting tongues of flame, a puff of smoke and a heap of ashes, I shut my eyes, thinking that the poor little creation deserved a more gentle farewell than this instant cremation. But there was neither flame nor fire. Freude sat there by the wall, still and lifeless, eyes hooded, the small poodle head fallen forward in repose, looking much like the children's furry toy pet that Adolf occasionally displayed in the window of his antique shop.

5

Washed-out, limp and confused, nagged too by the shame of the sorry spectacle I had offered, I went out, back down the steps, and ambled across to where Schwarzbauer was at work under the oak tree. The sun now risen in the sky spread a warming light on the meadow, the patches of daisy and cowslip glowing a crisp white and gold. I shook myself to life again, filling my lungs with the morning air fresh with the smell of new grass and young green.

Bent atop a tall ladder, Schwarzbauer was intent busily trimming the thick curls of ivy that had wound themselves around the mammoth trunk, foolishly attempting to strangle the giant oak. The gardener's face broke in a smile of gladness as he caught sight of me. Hurrying down from his perch he knelt on the ground and opening wide his arms enfolded me in a joyous embrace. "Ah, Albeer!" he repeated, his warm breath in my ear as one outsize hand gently caressed my head.

From our first encounter soon after his arrival, we had become bound by an odd bond, he welcoming me each time we visited the Baron as one would a long lost friend and I beside him most of the day as he toiled in the garden. Occasionally, pausing in his labours, he would sit up and draw me to himself, one arm encircling me, holding me close as he laid my head on his mighty chest.

He had no words and I was without tongue. But each time, at the sight of me, his face lit up with an almost incommensurable pleasure, a radiance so hearty and heartfelt I had seldom known in another human of my acquaintance. Adrift from his moorings in some distant place, immersed in the solitude of an alien land, beyond the reach and care of those who had sired and nursed him, familiar faces, loved ones, it was as if he longed to lavish on another living being the warmth and affection locked away in the storehouse of his heart. So that holding me close, rocking to and fro, he found in the wordless embrace a joyous release from the mute hours and days of his life.

The clank and rattle of Baroness Gertrude's wheel chair coming over the air, Schwarzbauer looked about in mild alarm, briefly planted his lips on my head, picked up the pruning shears and nimbly gained his place on the ladder, setting to work on the stubborn ivy, snipping and tearing, occasionally looking down to where I sat at the foot of the tree, calling my name softly so as not to interrupt our silent conversation.

In front of us Hubert's forbidding castle reared its dark head, the bartizan perched precariously at the corner as if about to topple over at any moment, the hollow eyes of the embrasures peering out blindly, the weather-worn fanged gargoyle heads protruding like black excrescences. The same pestilential ivy that Schwarzbauer was now busy decimating had taken firm possession of the walls, clinging to the rampart, creeping up to the crenelles and girding the merlons. Nature reclaiming its own, the Baron observed with a shrug.

6

Once years ago Baron Armin had taken Gretchen and me on a tour of the castle, a dim nightmarish journey that had haunted me in the depths of my sleep for several nights afterwards.

The main entrance being permanently shut, we had gone in through a side gate. But even before we entered the postern, the Baron raised our goose-flesh with a small hors d'oeuvre of horror. Family lore had it, he recalled, that Hubert displeased with the mild, even friendly look of the gargoyles had the stone mason trussed and hung head down from a corbel. Without sustenance, deprived of food and water, exposed to the intemperance of a severe winter, yet the wretched soul managed to survive for several days. But as life ebbed and the gelid body hung motionless, famished ravens and crows swooped down from the bleak hibernal sky to pluck gobs of dying flesh from the freezing carcass. Release finally came when, picked clean by the preying volatiles, the skeleton slipped its chains and clattered to the ground in a heap of bones.

"Please don't look at me like that!" the Baron said cheerfully seeing Gretchen's expression. "One can choose most things in life, not one's ancestry!"

We went down dark corridors and dim passageways, the daylight outside struggling to enter the twilight chambers through small windows of thick Lusatian glass stained dull with age. Up in the drum tower, Hubert's high oak canopy bed still sat along one wall. There the rogue warrior had breathed his last with his infant son's tiny arms wound around his neck. "But for that little boy I should not be here today!" the Baron observed with pensive cheerfulness. We looked down through the narrow windows at the moat, filled in over time and now a mere grassy dip in the ground; and beyond, the long undulating meadow, the rose garden at the far end, and all around the verdant sea of the evergreens.

We followed the Baron down steep stone steps into the netherworld, the bottlery with ancient wine barrels stacked along one wall, the air close with a hint of sour mildew, a large kitchen with an oversize oven because Hubert's only alimentary passion was freshly baked bread, a rarity in the long years of his murderous wanderings in the wilderness. Another short flight of the narrowest stairs led to the servants quarters, tiny monastic cells rough-hewn from enormous blocks of black stone, dark and dank, a bleary glimmer of light hovering uncertainly around the tiny barred openings set high in the wall.

And then the Baron led the way down an endless winding passageway so narrow that Gretchen had to walk almost sideways so as not to graze her shoulders against the rough corrugation of the stone walls. Painfully navigating the closed and airless space, a heavy damp seeping through the head-high ceiling robbing breath, stooped and hemmed in, unreasonably panic gripped the heart at the thought of being entombed in this sepulchral labyrinth that had never seen the full light of day and from which there was no return. Which, said the Baron, was precisely the fate that awaited those who had passed through this stone maze.

Abruptly the passage led into an open space. With some effort the Baron lifted the door made of heavy wooden blocks and set in the middle of the floor. A cold musty odour met us as we peered down into the tenebrous murk of the oubliette, a small square space with a narrow slit in the outer wall which let in a faint halo of daylight. The flooring was laid with a single unworked slab of rock, uneven and jagged; heavy iron rings set high in the wall hung at intervals. Apparently there were several such dungeons with no exit other than the trapdoors in the ceiling.

The inmates of these death-infested prison-cells were rarely tortured, said the Baron. Hubert built his castle late in life and after the quotidian sight of mutilated limbs and bloody carcasses over half a lifetime, in old age he had little stomach for the hacking, quartering and impaling of bodies that had once come so easily to him. So that those who crossed his path were simply led down into the oubliettes, shackled to the wall and abandoned with hope of neither redemption nor release. Locked away in the crepuscular cells, unheard and unseen, over days and weeks the victims slowly perished in gnawing pain, despair and agony. Occasionally Hubert's men would descend into the fetid gloom and remove the putrefying maggot-ridden corpses to make space for other damned souls.

It was with some relief that we came out into the open space of the bailey. A single gnarled crab apple tree stood in solitude in the centre of the inner courtyard, now unkempt and overgrown with tall grass, the walls blanketed with moss and lichen. A dull, hesitant light descended from the square of sky above. But away from the suffocating airlessness of the purgatorial lower depths, here at least there was the breathe of life, fresh air odorous with the smell of green. Gretchen asked how long ago the castle had been abandoned by the Monfleury-Pischendorpfs.

At the time of his great grandfather, said the Baron, when the manor house had been built. The family seat since the time of Hubert, the move from the castle was made unwillingly, with heavy heart. And the cause was none other than Hubert himself.

7

Over time there had been the occasional sighting, a frightened valet rushing in to say that a leering shadow had been seen lurking in the passageway, the cook claiming that freshly baked loaves had been spirited away by a mysterious hand in his very presence. Little notice was taken of the intermittent reports. The plan of the castle was haphazard and eccentric, chambers laid out in a disorderly fashion, narrow meandering corridors that often led to nowhere; daylight came in diffidently. Not surprisingly, the shade and shadows of the dusky interior offered the odd glimpse of a fleeting apparition, a spectral face, a phantom hand.

Besides, dim of sight and on the threshold of fumbling senescence, old cook Fessler often mistook barley for millet, salt for sugar, and on more than one occasion imagined that he had already prepared dinner, so obliging the master and his family to dine on stale bread and cheese. More likely than not the bread he claimed had been spirited away had not been baked at all. As for valet Ott, it was no secret that he was more than a little feeble in the head. All in all, little credence was given to the sightings. Making light of it, great-grandfather Wilhelm said that a castle worthy of its name always had a resident spirit.

But soon after the bicentennial of his death, Hubert had apparently decided that he had lain low long enough and the time had come for a reunion with the family. The once rare visitations became increasingly frequent. So did the laments and complaints of the servants. For some months it became almost a daily occurrence.

One day a young scullion bolted from the kitchen, never to return, after having seen Hubert's head floating in the steam rising from the cauldron of boiling water. A day later the footman claimed that he had come on Hubert sitting upright in one of the carriages, the stern apparition then imparting a sound slap on the intruder; indeed, the footman's right cheek bore the bruised imprint of several fingers. And not a week afterwards, crossing the mezzanine one evening, valet Ott fainted clean away and, in falling to the floor, broke an elbow; speechless for days, he could only whimper with eyes fixed to the ground.

But it was mostly the women servants, repeatedly importuned, harassed and molested, who were subjected to a crescendo of terror. One of the chamber maids making up the beds for the night found between the linen Hubert stretched out fully undressed. Petrified by the sight of the rampant body, the cry of horror frozen in her throat, the catalepsy released its hold only when Hubert's protruding eyes turned on her and his arms opened to welcome her into his embrace. With an agonized shriek of terror the poor woman fled the chamber.

Daily tasks began to be neglected as, stricken with dread, the women moved in pairs; so that four hands worked where only two were called for. But even the added precaution offered little protection against Hubert's offending presence. As the household slumbered in silence one rainy autumn afternoon, the quiet was rent by the piercing shrieks of two of the maids, who rushed into the Great Hall with hardly a stitch of clothing on them. Apparently Hubert had waylaid them in the passage to the buttery and, falling on the pair, stripped their garments so thoroughly that on escaping from his clutch one was left only with the girdle around the waist and the other a sock on the left foot.

One woman servant, who tended the garderobes, thinking to use the ruse to obtain a stipend, announced that she was with child, by Hubert of all people. Subsequently it was found that the child had been fathered by one of the stable hands and the failed blackmailer left the household in a huff.

Almost the only person to be unfazed by all the clamour was old retainer Manfried, great uncle of Baron Armin's Otfried. In over half a century of service at the castle he had seen and heard it all, armour-clad figures standing in the barbican at midnight, women's whispered voices coming from the wardrobes, prolonged moans echoing in oubliettes that had not held a victim for centuries. It was beyond Manfried what the fuss was all about. Besides, he maintained, it was proper that the ancient master of the castle visit his old abode from time to time.

His peace and quiet disturbed every other day, great grandfather Wilhelm turned to the pastor for help. Perhaps the clergyman could perform some ceremony to purge the castle of the undesirable presence, evict Hubert once and for all. A man of stern character and severe doctrinal orthodoxy, Pastor Adolphus shook his head. Family records showed that Hubert had died without receiving the anointing of the last rites. The clergyman declared that without this viaticum, Hubert had not been provided for his last journey. Unable to travel far, it was likely that he was condemned to inhabit the castle and its surrounds through eternity. Pastor Adolphus's learned verdict depressed great grandfather Wilhelm no end.

It got so that the household was thrown into perennial turmoil, with maids rushing down the passageways with ear-splitting screams, kitchen hands tossing food in the air as they fled ashen-faced, the butler glancing over his shoulder as he raced through the corridors with dishes to serve at table; the loud nervous neighing of the horses in the stables at the dead of night.

The household increasingly in turmoil, daily habits came to a near halt. Constantly on the lookout, ever on the edge, high-strung and with failing nerves, the members of the staff began to fall ill. And it was not long before one by one they began to desert the service, some not even returning for their wages. Nor could replacements be found, word having got about of the phantom visitations. Bed linen lay unchanged for days, clothing remained unwashed, the table was set with crockery that bore traces of past meals.

Finally, when the family was left with only a handful of servants, Manfried and cook Fessler, Jutte the mute orphan girl who great grandmother Conradine had taken in to help with her needlework, and valet Ott who sadly appeared to have become equally mute, Baron Wilhelm decided enough was enough. The construction of the manor house, which had been in the air for some time, was begun in earnest and a year or so later the family had moved out, leaving Hubert to his own devices in the abandoned castle.

"An odd piece of curiosity," said the Baron turning to Gretchen who had listened to the haunting tale with sceptical wonder, "Hubert never once appeared before members of the family."

"Perhaps he didn't want to frighten his own," thought Gretchen.

"Don't you believe it," the Baron laughed heartily. "Finding the larder empty, the man would have stewed his own aunt!"

8

On the way out we stopped in the Great Hall. Patches of reluctant light coloured red and green filtered in through the tall stained glass windows which depicted a veritable array of mythical fauna, ogres and leprechauns, satyrs and centaurs, hog-headed dragons, winged reptiles. Shorn of trappings and furnishings, the enormous chamber was entirely bare, save for the large portrait of Hubert above the stone mantle of the fireplace.

The image matched the nefarious deeds the Baron had hinted at. From a stout barrel chest and heavy shoulders robed in a fur-trimmed coat rose an oversize head, a short blunt nose in the large square face, fleshy lips curving downwards.

But it was the gaze of the large bulbous eyes brooding with a pensive malignity that made one look away. The artist had made some attempt to attenuate the expression of unrelieved ill-will, with a brush-stroke here and there to lighten the swarthy colouring of the grim countenance. But the touches at improvement were faint-hearted, for any significant departure from the true likeness might have led to the painter being dropped through the trap-door into one of the nightmare dungeons.

"Not a pretty sight," said the Baron, adding "It was Hubert's young wife who gave the family a human face."

Painted on the far wall was a giant mural of Hubert's coat-of-arms, similar to the one on the gate at the entrance to the estate but in greater detail, and a deal more truculent. Blood dripped from the dagger-sharp fangs of a long-snouted canine head, a ferocious canis lupus covered in the blackest pelt, one gauntleted hand with savage claws clasping a tall broadsword. In heavy lettering the crimson banner carried the motto SANGUINE AUDAX.

"Sanguine audax! Bold in blood!" the Baron guffawed. "Old Hubert could have left out the bold bit, just put down BLOOD as his motto!"

We came out into the still haze of the warm summer afternoon. To leave behind the tenebrous atmosphere of the castle and breathe again the unsullied air, set eyes on the uncorrupted green of leaf and grass and the unblemished blue of the sky, was like returning to the land of the living.

Gretchen sighed and sat down in the spreading shade of the great oak. "Hubert the Horrid. Why the 'Horrid', Armin?" she asked.

"As the Romans used to say, *De Mortuis Nil Nisi Bonum*. Speak no ill of the dead. Obviously the Romans didn't know Hubert!" And joining Gretchen on the old wooden bench he recounted the tale of his ancestor.

HUBERT THE
HORRID

1

Hubert was born the bastard offspring of the Duc de Monfleury and a chambermaid from Alsace.

Ignored by his father, unloved by his mother, there was no place for the misbegotten child in the seigniorial manor. Placed by his mother in the care of an aged relative in the uplands of the Ardennes, Hubert never saw either parent again. Much later and far away, in search of ancestral roots, he was to anoint himself Hubert von Monfleury-Pischendorpf.

Early on the orphaned boy showed signs of the traits that were to become later the hallmark of his ferocity on the fields of blood. Not for him the childish amusements of knucklebones, tag and queek, even less rag-ball and stick or gathering acorns in the woods. Unkempt and unchecked, he soon became the terror of the neighbourhood, lobbing off the tails of cattle, dropping cats in wells, tearing out the feathers of live birds he had trapped in the woods.

These more than mere boyish pranks reached a denouement when, at a country wedding, as the bride stepped through a cotillon, Hubert set fire to her bridal veil. Hapless and shedding lonely tears, the aged grand-aunt looked on as her young charge was mercilessly thrashed in the public square and forbidden ever again to enter the village.

But it was not the hurt of the smarting flesh nor the humiliation that wounded the impenitent boy. His one regret was that the only torment inflicted on the young maiden was merely the temporary loss of her golden tresses. Neither then nor later could Hubert ever admit to a wrong.

Shorn of communal bondage, outcast and solitary, he now spent his days in the wooded uplands. Walking great distances through the dense forests to the east, sleeping out in the open, hunting, trapping game, he honed those skills of stealth and survival that were to serve him well in the sanguine years ahead. Occasionally after dark he would steal into the village to visit the ancient aunt, bringing her game, venison, provisions taken from farmers' barns during night forays.

Oddly enough, and unusually for him, Hubert showed a peculiar tenderness towards the old woman, as though clinging to the last fleeting vestige of a mother's warmth he had never known. Only once ever again was a similar sentiment to burgeon in his heart, when in old age he was to shower his girl-bride with a gentle solicitude that no one had ever known him to harbour. Perhaps not even he himself.

2

The echoes of the early skirmishes and the first pitched battles of the Thirty Years' War had begun to sound over the land as Hubert came to manhood. And now with the death of his aged aunt, he cut his frail moorings. Footloose and bereft of the only human bond he had ever known, he left behind him forever the scenes and haunts of his boyhood, the small stone house of his infancy, the rolling hill country, the forbidden village. Moving ever eastwards, he crossed the vast forests of the Ardennes, irresistibly drawn like a beast of prey towards the clangour and gore of the fields of death.

Tossed up by the fortunes of war, fugitives and deserters, the wounded and the maimed had begun to roam the countryside. Vagrant bands preyed on the land, descending on hamlets and homesteads, harassing the peasants, molesting the women. The rape and pillage and slaughter, the gutted villages and abandoned towns, the pestilence and the burning hunger, these were yet to come.

Hubert fell in with one such rag-tag group. The motley collection of the bruised and dispossessed roamed aimlessly over the great northern plains, random predators propelled by hunger; stealing cattle, requisitioning poor booty from cowed peasants, occasionally giving vent to pent-up fear and despair, torching a homestead, abusing the womenfolk.

Hubert repeatedly changed one band of rabbles for another. But he soon tired of their petty thieving, their flatulent appetites, their verminous bodies, the foul odour of their breath. Most of all, he despised their cowering terror when faced with even a minor figure of authority, a burgomaster with a rusty musket, a mounted dragoon with halberd raised.

One vernal evening, resting under a spreading oak, watching a ragged group squabbling over a rotting shank of ewe, it came to him that his fate and fortunes lay elsewhere.

The Baron paused in his narrative. With a far-away gaze, as though peering through the mists of time, he said "Sometimes I think, dear Gretchen, that destiny is something others make for us. We are merely at the receiving end," he added smiling down at her. "Had Monfleury kept the bastard child in his household, Hubert would very likely have become just another member of that teeming multitude of young men who thronged the corridors of palaces, neither peasant nor nobility, simply parasites whiling away lives of idle dissipation. And then I would not be here now talking to you. Again, had the old grand-aunt not died when she did, probably Hubert would not have travelled east and joined Wallenstein's forces; becoming merely a professional cattle rustler who one day would have found himself hanging from a gibbet. Then, too, I would not be with you here this fine summer afternoon!"

3

Wallenstein, Duke of Friedland, was raising a large army for the Imperial cause and the name of the great condottiere drew men from north and south, from all walks of life, peasant, tradesman, mercenary and vagrant.

For the very first time, Hubert found himself in the company of men driven by a purpose, whose past was as varied as the babble of tongues they spoke, whose future held only the promise of battle, plunder and death.

From the start Hubert distinguished himself with a measure of reckless courage that left his companions-in-arms in awe and made him conspicuous to his superiors. And it was in the battle of Dessau, where the Protestant army was routed, that for the first time Hubert's savage ferocity surfaced in all its unrelenting malevolence. As Mansfeld's troops lay thick on the field at the end of the battle, Hubert set out alone in the fading light, stepping over the bodies on the bloodied ground, seeking out the wounded and hacking off their limbs, till the Silesian twilight filled with the dim, strangled cries of life ebbing away in agony.

It became a rite of horror. After each engagement, Wallenstein's Danish campaign, Stralsund, the great battle of Lutzen, silent and tireless Hubert would go out among the fallen, his ears alive to the moans and whispers among the corpses, setting then to his bloody task, severing an arm here, hewing through a leg, slicing off a cheek. It was as if some primal fury deep within him sought wordless release in the blood and torment of others. And in time it earned him the sobriquet that would follow him for the rest of his days: Hubert the Horrid. It became legend.

To be sure, in the years ahead he was to commit acts far more heinous than the simple dismembering of the living. He would earn other appellations, names that gripped men and women with terror. But then and ever after, even when the War was long over, the gore of the battlefields washed away by time and Hubert lay aged and infirm on his deathbed, he remained Hubert the Horrid.

The atrocious mutilations were seen as acts of indomitable courage. Silent and taciturn by nature, he gave away nothing of his past as he gathered around him a band of awed and loyal followers, who in the time to come were to become the hardy and obsequious companions of his long predatory years in the wilderness.

Meanwhile, the Thirty Years' War had dragged on for a decade and a half, covering immense territories, from Bohemia to the Baltic, drawing almost all the nations of Europe into this infernal cauldron of religious strife, alliances made and alliances broken, territories conquered and lost and reconquered. And all the while, the victorious and vanquished armies left behind them an unending trail of desolation, fallow lands without harvest, scorched lifeless villages, plundered towns; and hunger and disease that were soon to herald the onset of plague and death on a scale never seen before.

Wallenstein, suspected of treachery and the unwarranted ambition of taking control of the Holy Roman Empire, was removed from command of the Imperial troops. He handed over the army and, taking with him several hundred of his choice officers and men, retired to the capital of his Duchy of Friedland, there to while away his exile in idle splendour.

Unschooled and untutored though he was, thanks to his sanguinary deeds on the battlefield, Hubert had risen through the ranks. Chosen by Wallenstein himself to command his personal escort, Hubert inspired and nurtured a fierce loyalty in the hundred odd men under his command, a fealty greater than that owed to their Lord and Master.

"And here" said the Baron, seating himself beside Gretchen, "we have a curious episode. One of those minutiae that puts flesh and bones on the great figures of history."

4

Wallenstein was both glutton and gourmet. During the long campaigns of the war, he often missed the high and magnificent tables kept by his two wives, first Lucretia Nikossie von Landeck and, then, Isabella Katharina, daughter of Count Harrach. Now marking time in exile, longing for the splendours of the feasts of times gone by, Wallenstein cast about for a cook who could whet, satisfy and sate his palate. The head of the kitchens, Stanislaw Zyka, had fallen into disgrace after having served a venison stew with an excess of oats and had been assigned to the stables where, as his master remarked, "You should find diners galore with a passion for oats!"

Hubert was despatched with a dozen of his man and a generous purse to France to persuade, seduce or else abduct one August Moulinot.

At one time Moulinot had been one of the legendary names in the constellation of French gastronomy. Mentor of the celebrated and ill-fated Vatel, for long years in the service of the Comte de Gobineau, Moulinot had fed both nobility and royalty, not least the King, to resounding applause. But a bitter dispute with his patron over the combination of tripe with truffles had led to the parting of ways. Headstrong and resolute, Moulinot had retired to the countryside around Strasbourg. There he now lived quietly with his widowed daughter, in oblivion and in turn oblivious to the world, cultivating the one great passion of his ageing years: a richly variegated herb garden.

More than the promise of riches, it was perhaps the remains of a vanity from the years of his prime that induced Moulinot to accompany Hubert and his men back to Wallenstein's capital. Received as a celebrity, at once both guest and servitor, the Frenchman set out to conjure up repasts that left his patron not only sated but also bewitched. Sadly it was but a short interlude.

Gustavus Adolphus and his seemingly invincible Swedes had now swept far south into the German heartland, advancing on Munich and marching into Bohemia. And once again the Emperor had to resort to Wallenstein, calling him into the field to raise a fresh army to oppose the Swedes' unrelenting impetus.

Much of Wallenstein's wealth had been acquired through his marriages. Ever frugal in matters of money, if not in his tastes, he had a reputation for thrift. His farewell to Moulinot however was an unusually generous one. He gifted the old man with a treasure that would have lasted half a lifetime, and more. Little did he imagine then that it would be his last bequest. Nor could the master cook know that he would not live to enjoy these late, abundant fruits of a lifetime's labour at the kitchen fires.

Once again Hubert and his men escorted Moulinot, homewards now, to his herb garden and his daughter Jeanne. Skirting the path of the Swedish army, they first rode south. Then working their way northward, a mere day's journey from Moulinot's home, the party settled down for the night in the woods overlooking the village of Chatherault.

There was neither rhyme nor reason for what took place next. At daybreak Hubert and his companions set on Moulinot in his sleep, severing his head and dismembering the lean body. They buried the parts in a shallow grave and, close by, the gold and silver as well.

It could not have been greed. For why then undertake almost the entire length of an arduous journey and not be done with it the first night out? In any case, Hubert never returned to recover the treasure. Nor could it have been Moulinot's demeanour, for mostly he was inoffensive, except occasionally with the high and the mighty. A simple act of blood, then; for which Hubert had a singular predilection.

"The only solace in this senseless episode," the Baron added, "was that old man Moulinot was laid to rest in his native soil, albeit not entirely intact and in a shallow grave."

The rest of Hubert's journey down the years, as recounted by the Baron, was a tale of treachery and betrayal, an endless odyssey of murder, rape and pillage through a wasted land. Yet, there was worse to come.

5

Wallenstein had left behind him the last exile of his life and the sumptuous table sans pareil offered by Moulinot. At the head of his new army he engaged Gustavus Adolphus at the great battle of

Lutzen. The Swedish king was slain, but Wallenstein and his Imperial forces were defeated.

The Duke retreated to winter quarters in Bohemia and from there, intending to desert the Emperor's cause, he carried on secret negotiations with both friend and foe, Saxons, Swedes, the French. The Emperor's patience worn thin, he signed a secret warrant removing Wallenstein from his command. It was a veiled signal to those who felt that the time had come for the great captain to leave the scene and it sealed his fate. Hubert was present at the scene of treachery.

Wallenstein was lodged in the burgomaster's house in Eger, his personal safety overseen by Hubert and his men. Hours earlier, unknown to him, several of his trusted officers had been massacred by dragoons under the command of the Irish general Walter Butler. Neither could he have imagined that Hubert had been corrupted by Butler and his Scottish colonels with prodigious offers and promise of laisser passer.

Soon after midnight Hubert withdrew his guards, leaving Wallenstein alone and unprotected. It was the signal the English Captain Walter Devereux had been waiting for. With a number of fellow officers he broke into the burgomaster's house. Unopposed Devereux rushed up the stairs, flung the bedroom door open and ran his blade through Wallentein who, roused from sleep and unarmed, was given neither quarter nor mercy.

With the silent cognizance of a beast in the wild hearing a distant sound, Hubert recognised the enormity of his crime. He realized, too, that the Judas act of selling his Lord and Master would not pass without extreme consequence, for there were many in the ranks of the Imperial troops whose devotion to Wallenstein would demand mortal retribution.

That very night Hubert, at the head of several dozen of his most trusted men, left Eger, riding hard through the night and the following day to gain as great a distance as possible from the scene of the crime.

Moving south, keeping out of sight of the scattered Imperial garrisons, finally on the third evening they made camp on a wooded rise above a small hamlet. Hubert looked down at the silent farmhouses, the scorched timber of the torched barns, a broken dove-cote here, the lifeless chimneys, the parched earth all around; and stripped of their bark to assuage the pangs of burning hunger, the leafless trees keeping watch like gaunt sentinels over a land where life and the living had one day suddenly vanished. Overhead in the darkening sky the shrill cry of a raven in flight rent the evening air.

Hubert knew there was now no turning back, neither renewal nor redemption. His life had never known permanence, not at birth nor in youth. And now with his hands steeped in blood and stained with betrayal there could be no sanctuary, only the curse of unending vagrancy and malevolence.

"This last chapter is strictly for adults," the Baron said patting Gretchen's hand playfully. "Fit for Albert's ears alone!"

6

Like an apoplectic fever, the endless war dragged on in fits and starts. A mortal exhaustion had set in, with both victor and vanquished prostrated. The Four Horsemen had ridden over the land, leaving behind a bleak landscape of silence and emptiness, shuttered towns and gutted villages, with never a birdsong at dawn, the rattle of a miller's dray, the diurnal call of the owl, the tinkers cry, the chime of the church bells for the matins, the ringing laughter of young girls on a country road. It was as if Creation itself had been emptied and a pall fallen on the void, shutting out the clear light of day, shrouding the world in a miasma rising from the depths of some infernal region.

It was over this hellish landscape that Hubert and his men roamed for long years. Living off a land that, untilled and unsown, could offer neither grain nor fruit nor flower, they fell on the living few with the ferocity of beasts uncaged. At times they would enter a deserted village, meaning to ransack the homes, only to find the plague dead still at table or abed in the houses or heaped in a tangle of bodies in the village square, the putrescent flesh filling the air with a sickening sour vapour. Elsewhere, breaking into a homestead, they would come on a family huddled together, bedraggled figures of yellowed parchment skin hung on bones, with the breath of life fast ebbing. The poor creatures were well beyond pleading for mercy and, mercy denied, Hubert's men fell on these living dead, slaughtering them like so many sheep in the fold. Nothing earned, nothing gained, they were like avengers from the bowels of Hades come to remove the last human traces from the face of the earth.

"And the worst is yet to come," said the Baron pensively.

"Could there be anything worse than what Hubert had already done?" Gretchen asked raising her violet eyes.

"Oh yes!" the Baron nodded emphatically, "There is no limit to the evil in man. Sometimes I think that Lucifer in his fall from grace dragged the whole of human kind down with him."

7

In winter they would quarter themselves in the thick of the woods and forests, within reach of a village or hamlet. Made insane by the bitter cold and gnawing hunger, crouching in the thicket like animals in the wild they would wait long hours in utter silence for the children of the village to wander out to collect firewood.

Occasionally a father would venture forth to look for his little girl; a mother for her boy. It was a futile search, for the children never came home again and, more often than not, neither did the parent. Replete and replenished, Hubert and his men would break camp and move on to the next settlement, towards yet another carrion repast of innocent flesh.

There is neither record nor could there be count of the numbers of new-born and young who succumbed to the frenzied flesh-lust of Hubert and his companions. Certainly a long, interminable winter's quartering and feeding of several dozen men with ravenous appetites called for an abundant supply. And of such winters there were many.

Over the months and years word spread across the desolate land of the sudden appearance from the woods of ogre-like men who fell on stray children, the little ones never being seen again. The tale of the sightings and of the lost gripped with unspeakable terror a countryside already irremediably ravaged by famine, disease and death. It seemed to the wretched survivors as if God's wrath had not yet run it's course.

And so was born the dread legend of Hubert the Hungry. Peasants uttered the innominate in hushed tones, as though the mere utterance of the unnameable would conjure up the beast at their doorstep. Mothers clutched infants to their breasts, at night fathers tied their young offspring to their beds; tiny bells were fashioned and hung around children's necks, with the women rushing out with heart-rending screams if the faint jingling ceased for an instant.

And even long after, when memories had paled and only the aged could dimly recall the war and its endless devastations, mothers putting recalcitrant youngsters to bed would whisper the bogeyman name in their tiny ears: Hubert the Hungry!

8

So many interminable winters, endless seasons and years of vagabondage, of plunder and carnage. Now well into his forties, Hubert had begun to feel the weight of the incessant fugitive nomadism. The years of febrile slaughter had taken their toll. The surfeit of blood-letting and the quotidian sight of the human anatomy in all its gore had dulled his purpose; a sense of weariness had begun to permeate his spirit.

The great war was drawing to an end, bringing to a close the remnants of the medieval order. Wallenstein and Gustavus Adolphus had been long dead, no new warrior prince or paladin had appeared on the scene. And with the silencing of the musket and the sheathing of the sword, order and authority began to return to the land. Timidly the countryside woke from its lengthy slumber, the ploughman appeared in the fields once again, smoke rose lazily from homestead chimneys, woods came alive with the twitter of birds at twilight, and once again the bustle of life began to sound in the streets and towns.

With each passing day the world grew smaller for Hubert and his band. The nocturnal irruptions, the pillage and sack, the murderous raids were beginning to be things of the past. Now the peasant wielded a menacing pitchfork, the once cowed tradesman a good flintlock. Now, too, the company had grown. Hubert and his men were trailed by numerous women taken by force, violated and abducted, over the years of rage and rampage. And the woman had borne children.

Many of Hubert's companions had grown heavy and tired, now family men nearing middle age. Still capable of gross acts of violence, but the fires in their eyes had dimmed, the malevolence muted. Hubert saw reflected in their shrinking spirit his own secret and unspoken longing for a reconciliation with life and the living.

The cumbersome company, now perennially short of provisions, moved laboriously, purposeless and without destination, wandering aimlessly towards the more clement south, keeping to the solitary paths in the backwoods, away from sight. Hubert had never trusted in providence, even less in prayer. What he had, he had willed and earned, for well or ill. But there were times now when, fitful in uneasy sleep in the early hours of the morning, he felt an unseen hand tug at his sleeve, as if meaning to lead him out of the wilderness of his lost days.

Early one March the company encamped at nightfall in a coppice. Hubert, as was his wont from the days of his youth in the forests of the Ardennes, rose at daybreak. Wandering out to study the lie of the land, he climbed to the top of a wooded rise. And there he stood spellbound. In the space of an instant, he knew he had reached his journey's end and found the resort of his last resting place.

There in front of him opened out a vast green, an undulating meadow carpeted with the flowers of this early spring and enclosed all around by a dark virgin forest. At the far end, proud in its regal solitude, stood a giant oak, looking for all the world as if it had been there since the Creation.

"And that is where we sit now," said the Baron gently touching the ancient trunk behind them as though it were a sacred relic. "It has never been a mere tree, rather Hubert's Oak, the name given it then and carried down the generations." The timbre of his voice was tinged with a quite pride, as if wordlessly acknowledging the oak to be the true patriarch, rather than Hubert. And the Baron's tale then wound its way towards the twilight years of his ancestor.

9

There was little human presence in the area and even fewer settlements, a handful of scattered hamlets at some distance beyond the dense forests; the nearest town a good hour's ride away. Decades of war and upheaval had broken up estates, thrown into confusion tenures and titles, holdings lost ownership. With neither occupant nor claimant in view, Hubert took possession of the land and parcelled out large tracts among his men. But in fact the land was owned.

Johannes Abendroth, a very minor and impoverished nobleman, had been a trusted retainer of the previous Emperor. As reward for the long and loyal years of attendance, the great monarch had bestowed on the faithful servitor the titles of a vast sweep of virgin forestland in the southwest, the region of his origin.

With neither the means nor the age to do justice to the Emperor's liberality, Abendroth merely retired to a modest mansion in a small hamlet on the outskirts of his estate. Some years later his only son, intending to build one day a manor in keeping with the family's noble origins, cleared a swath of land in the forest, sparing only an ancient oak. But soon after the young man perished in one of the late battles of the War. The family withered even further, Abendroth's wife and daughter-in-law succumbing in the last days of the plague. Now half blind, the aged retainer lived in quiet senescence with his young grand daughter, a pretty child of six with burnished red hair.

Hubert's reputation had preceded him and, though dim of sight, the old man was not hard of hearing. Not wishing to depart the world afortime, Abendroth readily acceded the tenure of the lands, not in perpetuity but for Hubert's lifetime. In earlier days Hubert would have refused the condition with his broadsword drawn. But now returned to the land of the living, he knew that cunning alone would suffice to win the day.

On leaving the retainer's modest retreat, he was taken aback when on the doorstep the little girl, having heard from one of the maids the dreadful sobriquet, looked up with the smile of the innocent and said: "Are you hungry, Hubert?" Startled, Hubert froze in his tracks. In that instant something broke within him, like the release from a brimming dam a floodtide engulfed his senses. Bending down to brush the tiny fingers with his lips, he whispered words the child could not understand. It was a vow he would not fail.

10

Hubert's men had shed their past and turned their hand to the land. Mostly of peasant stock, they prospered. Ever faithful and beholden to Hubert, now their seigniorial lord, they paid their tithes and as always were his to command. By right of the tenure ceded by Abendroth, gradually he extended his control to the outlying villages, and beyond. He conducted his affairs with a firm hand but refrained from violent coercion, of which there was little need; his name alone sufficed to cajole and persuade. And times had changed.

The war over, peace had brought order and renewal. Tilled, ploughed and sown once again, the land awoke from its long slumber and offered generous and abundant fruit. Trade prospered anew.

Hubert's life had never known such halcyon days. His fortunes grew, he was lord and master of all he surveyed and, in time, he built his castle by the oak tree. But he had aged, half a lifetime of brute murder and mayhem had taken its toll. The detritus of the past weighed heavy on his spirit, at night the visitation of the faces and the mangled flesh of times gone by left him exhausted. Breathless in sleep, sometimes in the darkest hours before dawn he imagined the surrounding forest closing in, each branch and tree a figure of the multitude he had hacked and slaughtered with neither mercy nor quarter. Weary in spirit, in the solitude of these waning years he longed for a harbour.

Finally in his sixtieth year, he kept the vow he had solemnly taken and secretly nursed ever since. With the wordless acquiescence of old man Abendroth, for he was by now both blind and mute, Hubert took Ludmilla Beate Franziska to wife. She was but fifteen, lithe in limb and a full head taller than her spouse, and already pregnant with a beauty that was soon to blossom in all its radiance. The bride brought her virginal grace and a fecund womb. She also brought Hubert, as her marriage dower, the tenures and rights in perpetuity of all the lands, which he already possessed but was to own henceforth.

In the fugitive years Hubert had sired a score of children. In the turmoil and turbulence of the times they were scattered like so many straws in the wind, leaving no trace in his memory. Now Ludmilla gave him two daughters in quick succession. He doted on the little girls, nursing and caressing them, attending solemnly to their childish whims. And yet.

On marriage to Ludmilla, Hubert had assumed the title of Baron Hubert von Monfleury-Pischendorpf, the adjunct taken from the name of the locality. He now longed for a posterity to carry the name and his memory. But it was late in the day. Aged and ailing, prayers unanswered and hope in recession, when he had almost resigned himself to the oblivion of history, miraculously Ludmilla gave birth to a son, an heir. Perhaps for the very first time then Hubert uttered the Lord's Prayer from the depths of his heart.

One vernal evening, after evensong, placing her new-born in Hubert's arms as he half-reclined on a bolster, Ludmilla stood at the narrow castle window and looked out on the awakening season of the trees in new green. Dusk silently drew a pale mantle over the immense flower-bedecked meadow. She smiled as memory reached back to that first, child's encounter with Hubert on the steps of her grandfather's poor manor and his whispered words in her tiny ear. Now she was a woman in the fullness of youth and the startling splendour of her beauty. The burnished red hair drew to itself the last light of day and like the fleeting touch of an unseen hand a silent breeze brushed her face. Hearing the infant's soft gurgle, she turned her head.

There was an odd stillness in the room. Hubert's palm lay open on the bed, the eyes shaded in the lowered head. The child's arms were entwined around his neck, as the tiny head nudged and nestled against his cheek. Possession and endearment. Once Hubert would have given his life for a moment such as this with the man who sired him.

11

The baron fell silent. Gretchen followed his gaze as he looked pensively at the low turrets of the castle. "Thank you for telling me," she said taking his arm.

I had listened in amazement to the Baron's tale, awe-struck at what humans were capable of doing to each other. What astounded me quite as much was their perseverance: a war lasting thirty years! In comparison we canines were less than amateurs, our hostilities lasting but the space of a mere moment: a growl or two, a snarl with bared teeth, the odd measured bite, and then with a backward glance the combatants went their own way.

The afternoon shadows had lengthened. In the distance, by the rose garden, Otfried was lazily parambulating Baroness Gertrude in her wheel chair, the faint crunch of the wheels on the gravel wafted by the warm air. I followed in the wake of Gretchen and the Baron as they strolled over the green towards the manor. Somewhere in the woods an owl hooted idly.

THE DEATH OF
FREUDE

1

Lunch at the Baron's was a curious affair. In the large wood-panelled dining hall that gave out onto the terrace, Baroness Gertrude sat at one end of a seemingly endless table, the Baron at the other. The Baroness was at times hard of hearing, which made normal conversation between the two patchy and inconclusive. There was some ground for suspicion that she heard only what she wished to hear. Whatever the cause, her deficiency was however obviated by a contraption fitted under the table long ago by the Baron's grandfather, whose hearing had been impaired by the monstrous cannonades of Big Bertha during the Great War.

A narrow brass tube ran under the ancient wood for its entire length, with a small horn protruding discreetly at each end, into which the diners were meant to direct their words. Ingenious though the invention might have been, it did present an embarrassing inconvenience for those sitting in the middle of the table. When spoken into at the same time, the voices collided inside the tube, setting up a muffled resonance that could be mistaken for digestive and other intestinal sounds, which quite disconcerting for the guests.

Lunch at the Baron's was also plain and essential. Elfriede's skills at the stove rarely went beyond boiled meats, hash, and the odd bake. Unfailingly, there was an abundant supply of swedes and cabbage, local produce from the vegetable patch behind the kitchen.

All in all, one had the impression that the fare had not changed much since the time of Hubert the Horrid who, however, would have swiftly drawn his broadsword at the sight of the portions, which were miniscule, the Baroness tending a sharp eye on the extra piece of potato or morsel of meat that might fall on the plate of the fortunate guest. After a day at the Pischendorpf's, it felt as though one had not been fed since childhood. What was missing from the table was, however, amply made up for by the Baron's warmth, wit and easy-going manners and Baroness Gertrude's quirky ways.

Today Elfriede had stretched her culinary art to the limit and there was roast for lunch. Even before she had waddled in with the meat, sitting by the terrace door I had caught an inviting whiff, but my heart sank when she set down the silver platter on the table. The roast would have sufficed to feed at most a couple of new-born infants; which meant that there would be no trace of it when I was taken to the kitchen for my lunch.

Roast being something of a rarity in the manor, the Baron announced triumphantly into the mouthpiece, "Roast, Maman!" as almost at the same instant the Baroness cried "Roast, Armin!" into her horn. The outcome of the simultaneous entries was that Otfried, just then bending over to place the dish on the table, seemed to have made an unseemly noise.

Otherwise it was a quietly pleasant meal. Elfriede came and went wordlessly, setting down the cabbage at one end, the Swedes at the other, the potatoes with the Professor in the middle. Otfried sauntered from one end of the table to the other at his usual silent somnambulist pace serving the meat; a trifle slower and the diners would have found themselves at dinner. "Otfried's favourite pastime" said the Baron benevolently, "is to wander around with a roast!"

"We do so miss your Gretchen," the Baroness said, to liven up the table.

The Professor fell silent and looked down at his plate.

"Indeed, we do, Maman," the Baron voiced into his mouthpiece.

"We do all miss each other," the old lady added inexplicably.

It was a warm airy day outside. Under a pellucid sky the rolling green mantle of the meadow, speckled yellow and white, lay hushed in the noon silence. Inside Otfried padded about serving. I listened to the quite voices at the table, waiting for my turn in the kitchen. And little Freude's bottom was still cabled to the power socket feeding him his mysterious nourishment.

2

Lunch over, the Baron and the Professor adjourned to a small table that Otfried had set out with a couple of glasses of a pale liquor and a chess board. My own lunch had been of a disconcerting brevity, consisting as it did of some sort of pale gruel, along with a couple of bone-shaped biscuits that Elfriede had extracted from a large tin printed with happy canine heads. The biscuits must have been baked at Hubert's time, for I almost left my ageing teeth on them.

I stretched out nearby, behind the Baron's chair. The afternoon sun coming off the immense green tinged the air with a soothing light. Otfried had parked the Baroness in her wheel chair under the old cherry tree in blossom, where she now sat dozing with a blanket over her knees. Looking out through the balustrades I thought I could just make out the dark shape of Schwarzbauer quietly moving about among the flowering rose bushes, weeding and raking.

The two men above me conversed in quiet tones, the Baron drawing on his pipe, the Professor occasionally sipping from his glass, the game proceeding at a leisurely pace. Half listening to them as I looked out on the stillness of the verdant landscape, once again I heard mention of the curious name that often came up during their recent conversations.

"The problem with Heidegger..." the Baron was saying.

I had never seen the person, he had never visited our house. He may well have been a mutual friend of theirs. Whatever the connection, the gentleman appeared to have a problem that simply refused to go away.

"The problem with Heidegger…"

"Largely of his own making," the Professor remarked setting down his glass.

"I'm not so sure," the Baron mused. "Victim of the times one lives in."

"Willing victims, Armin," the Professor dissented dryly.

They spoke of the man as though he had knowingly contracted an incurable malady. But the drowsy hour was on me. I shut my eyes and the calm of the temperate air carried me away to reveries of other days. Dimly in my mind's eye, through a distant haze I saw Gretchen treading the green as she silently wheeled the Baroness, the burnished gold of her hair strangely iridescent under the blue of a sunless sky.

3

I must have dozed off, for suddenly coming to, I felt an odd furry hardness against my nose. Opening my lids I found a pair of eyes lit up with an unnatural light looking down at me, while a squeaky metallic voice repeated "*Play Albert! Play Albert!*" It was little Freude come to life again!

The sun was still high in the sky, as if it liked basking in its own light. The Baron and the Professor had left the table and were now strolling down on the green, doubtless still worrying over the nature of Gentleman Heidegger's illness. Baroness Gertrude dozed on in her chair under the cherry blossoms.

I stretched out idly, pretending to return to my sleep. But Freude would have none of it. He went on nudging me, his nose tickling my belly, all the while emitting the same two tedious words, "*Play Albert!*" Obviously my peaceful rest was at an end. I got to my feet and nudged him away. He tottered, then awkwardly regained his balance.

There was no shaking off the pestiferous little creature, his two-word idiom repeated so incessantly that the ears went fuzzy. In truth, limited as it was his gift of speech was somewhat more ample than mine and I might have felt a tinge of envy had he had some semblance with my canine kind.

As I strolled indoors into the dining hall and stood behind a door, it occurred to me that Freude might just be a mere contraption. For suddenly he had lost me and, befuddled, turned his head this way and that. I realized then that his Maker had forgotten to endow him with the sense of smell, that vital attribute that made of us hunters in the wilds. Not that I had done a great deal of hunting of late, in the wild or elsewhere.

I felt sorry for the poor little orphan. It seemed a peculiarly cruel joke visited on my kind and an affront to nature. Soulless as it was, what should I call the creature, a thing, an object, matter? Yet it moved, emitted odd sounds, replicated a curious bark, had a touching gaze. Freude reminded me of a bird I had once seen at a country fair Gretchen had taken me to. It sat on a little swing inside a cage, twittered and sang better by far than any bird I had ever heard in the woods; then, as we listened enchanted, abruptly it stopped, fell off the swing, broke it's neck and a whiff of smoke rose through the heap of pretty feathers. I'm not sure why, but I found it heartless. Curious the human attempt to replicate the real and the living!

Now Freude walked beside me as I sauntered down the long terrace, keeping pace with his awkward gait. I turned, and he turned, rotating on one hind leg. My pace increased, so did his, with a whirring sound as though murmuring wheels had been set in motion inside him. I broke into a trot, so did he, with a hobble, a waddle and a jump, the whirring wheels going ever faster and louder. I ran, and he followed, leaping forward, bouncing off the floor like one of those balls Gretchen used to throw at me to fetch in my younger days.

Freude no longer begged to play, for we were now playing, running the length of the terrace, then turning back, he with a small squeal of innocent delight and a grating screech from his innards. Tongue out and panting heavily, I did not know how much longer I could keep up this mad running to and fro. My breath grew short and I feared for my health. But such was the little fellow's joy as he hopped, capered and leapt that I was loathe to rob his hour of merriment. And then the foolish child took one leap too many.

4

Galloping towards the far end of the terrace, Freude's gambolling turned to a frantic rush and, as we reached the finish of our race, he leapt clean through the balustrades and sailed into the air with legs flailing. Then, like a dead weight he plunged straight down and the next moment I heard a dull crashing sound, followed by the tiny tinkle of metal fragments bouncing on stone.

I stood still for a moment to gather my senses before rushing downstairs and out the front door. There was not the least recognizable sign of the poor body, smashed to smithereens, the head half gone with one eye loosely hanging from a thin wire, the frisky tale now dangling lifeless from half a hip; broken fragments of the little legs, tiny wheels, a small green board with silver pin drops, innumerable minute odds and ends lay scattered on the steps. The fetching little black nose had rolled right down to the bottom and sat dispossessed on the gravel.

The sight had petrified me. I stood there alone for how long I could not tell, my eyes fixed on the gory scene, so to speak. Then I came to, awareness flowing in and with it a cloudy sense of guilt began to seep into my mind. I looked around at the empty afternoon. Not a soul about, I stood there for a long moment, desolate and grieving. Side-stepping then the remains of Freude, I went down the steps and in a daze silently trod the gravel path, slowly making my way towards the rose garden.

My mind was now permeated with a painful sense of wrong and grief. Had it been my doing that little Freude now lay shattered in a myriad fragments? I had once heard Matilde say of a man who had taken a life that the mark of Cain was on him. I did not quite know who Cain might have been, but wondered if his mark was to be branded on my front henceforth.

On reaching the rose garden I found Schwarzbauer at his indefatigable labours crouched among the shrubs. On seeing me his face lit up, he crept out, sat down by the side of the bed and, putting out his sturdy arms, drew me to him. "Oh, Albeer," he sighed wearily, laying my head on his chest.

The afternoon shadows had lengthened. In the distance, beyond the undulating green, the Baron and the Professor were still deep in conversation under Hubert's Oak. Otfried was idly wheeling the Baroness back to the mansion. An untimely cricket chirped somewhere.

In the quietude of the fading afternoon, ensconced in the warmth of his arm, I could hear the slow throbbing drumbeat of his mighty heart as, rocking me gently, Schwarzbauer sang a plainchant whose words were unknown to me but which stilled my troubled heart, assuaging my guilt, comforting my grief, the yearning threnody calming my spirit like a lullaby with a restive child. Of all the fond and poignant moments of my life, this among a few others would stay with me and which I would carry to the end of my days.

5

Freude was laid to rest later the same afternoon.

The sun was low in the sky when the cortège set out from the mansion, winding its way down the gravel path towards the rose garden. Parambulated by Otfried, Baroness Gertrude led the procession in her ornamental wrought-iron wheel chair. I brought up the rear, behind Elfriede, the Professor and the Baron.

The Baroness in person had supervised the arrangements for the burial. For herself she had chosen a long black shroud-like dress that covered her from neck to toe. From the powerful odour of mildew emanating from the garment, one would not be amiss in thinking that more likely than not the ancient raiment had sat in some forgotten cupboard in the cellar since the time of Hubert. A dark stole trimmed with fine lace hid her gaunt features, the only visible sign of life evident from the fidgety movements of the thin long prehensile fingers sheathed in black silk gloves. Certainly not an apparition to be encountered in the dead of a moonless night, I thought.

The Baron had attired himself a trifle more appropriately for the solemn occasion, shedding the ever-present mauve and green tartan smoking jacket in favour of a black one trimmed with blue cord. Otfried was his usual self in the frayed, maroon collarless jacket with brass buttons. Elfriede had merely draped herself in an old mantle that barely hid her gravy-stained apron. Indeed, following on her footsteps, I caught a distinct whiff of roast, a distraction perhaps not quite in keeping with the occasion.

Neither was I spared the vestment of bereavement. A black velvet armband, worn by the male mourners, was slipped over my neck; the tight fit proved irksome, making me rotate my neck continuously.

6

The sky was tinged with mauve and red as in grieving silence, save for the rattle and crunch of the Baroness's wheels on the gravel, we approached the rose garden, now a vast acre of darkening colours in the dying light. It was then that I heard the music, a faint dirge like melody, so languid and heavy that the sound seemed to be laboriously freeing itself from the bowels of the earth. There was a familiarity about it, and after a moment it came to me. "The Call of Valhalla" Gretchen used to call it, teasing the Professor when occasionally he played the piece.

The music grew louder, scratchy and uneven, as we made our way down the lanes through the endless beds of roses, the fading light redolent with the scent of the flowers. Finally we came to the site of Freude's last resort on earth, in the dead centre of the garden, a round clearing circled with rose bushes laden with the seasons first pristine white blooms.

Schwarzbauer had dug a small shallow grave in the middle. Now he towered above it, leaning on the shovel, his night-black face glistening bright with sweat. Bare to the waist save the leather work apron, for some odd reason he too wore the mourner's velvet armband around his neck. Nearby on a three-legged table sat the music box, a large brass horn erupting from its interiors and emitting the mournful dirge with a loud rasping hiss.

We stood around the open earth, the Baroness holding in her lap a large tin box with Freude's remains. I could not but help notice that the box brightly painted with canine heads looked very similar to the one from which Elfriede had at lunch extracted my meagre ration of the almost wooden, bone-shaped biscuits.

Heads were bowed in silent and solemn prayer, when abruptly the music began to slow, the dirge turning to a sort of sluggish growl. "Wind the machine, you fool!" the Baroness hissed. Then coming to sudden life she raised her silver-knobbed stick and thrust it with shocking violence between Schwarzbauer's buttocks. Eyes widened in disbelief, he gave a muffled cry, shot up on his toes and teetered for a long moment on the edge of the grave, as though about to plunge headlong into the dark earth. Miraculously regaining his balance, he stepped back, rushed to the table and frantically wound the shiny handle protruding from the music box.

Hissing and grating, the painful musical lament finally came to an end. Raising his hands Schwarzbauer brought his palms together but the forbidding figure in the wheel chair lifting her menacing cane brought an end to his attempt at further applause. Now at a brusque nod from the Baroness, the Baron stepped up to the graveside. With outstretched hands, he gazed up at the tenebrous sky and in loud vibrant tones that tore the sombre silence, he launched into an oratory whose first few lines threw my head into a spin:

Nos qui vivimus, mortuorum desiderio tenemur;
sed mortui desiderio num tenentur nostri
qui vitam agimus ad obscuras Stygis undas?[*]

101

The Professor nodded in approval. Elfriede's mouth fell open, while Otfried gaped in wonder. I thought that the Baron had finally taken leave of his senses.

"Stygian waters!" the Baroness snorted. "Armin!"

"Yes, Maman!"

Sharply called to order, the Baron looked crestfallen. Clearing his throat he reverted to our familiar tongue, but maintained the oratorical flight.

"Dimly there, on the far shore," he resumed in the same tone, shading his eyes to view better a distant horizon, "who do we see but our dear little friend frolicking on the empyrean green! Ah yes, dear Freude, precious child, play on, frisk and gambol to your heart's content, until the morrow when again we shall meet under the celestial canopy of eternity…"

Apparently not desirous of encountering Freude or anyone else under the celestial canopy any time soon, the Baroness raised an impatient hand, interdicting further suggestions of such imminent meetings.

"That will do, Armin," she said severely, inviting then the Professor to step forward and say a few kind and appropriate words. "For the little one," she added with what curiously sounded like half a sob.

Tall and upright, the Professor bowed his head. In a voice unusually mellow, he recited the rhythmic invocation with words that left almost the whole company dumbfounded:

Όπως η μέρα ακολουθά την νύχτα
και η νύχτα την μέρα
έτσι η χαρά το πένθος
και ο πόνος την χαρά.
Επίσης ο ζωντανός στέκει
και εντωμεταζύ ο νεκρός κείτεται,

αλλά αυτός θα ανασταιθεί
και οζωντανός θα τεντώσει.
Μέχρι εκείνο τον καιρό ησύχασε
λίγο νέε φίλε:
εάν ο θεός το θέλει,
θα ξαναβρεθούμε ακόμη.
Πού; πότε;
ο άνθροπος δεν μπωρεί
να ξέρει όπως, πού και πότε.
Έτσι, μέχρι τότε
σε χαιρετώ, να αυαπαύεσαι,
αγαπητή ψυχή, αντίο.*

* As day follows night, and night day,
So joy follows sorrow, and sorrow joy
So, too, the living stand and the dead lie
So, too, the dead shall rise and the living lie.
Until then, rest a while, young friend
We shall meet again. Where? When?
To us is not given to know
The how and where and when
So until then, fare thee well and adieu.

It may have been the long day and the sorrow that comes from the sudden end of so young a life. For the Professor, too, appeared to have taken leave of his senses. He might as well have read aloud the exotic menu of a restaurant in some far-off country. The words and their sounds could not have been more outlandish had he been a visitor from another world. The incomprehension was absolute.

Elfriede gazed pitiably at the sky, as though beseeching divine intervention to spare the sanity of the eminent gentleman. The Baron alone looked pleasantly around with a composed and entirely satisfied air. Oddly enough, Schwarzbauer too appeared quite comfortable with the Professor's measured verses.

The Baroness looked up helplessly at her son. "Greek to me,

Maman," the Baron whispered. "The tongue of the gods!" Ever in awe of the Professor's vast learning, the old lady now nodded in approval, satisfied that the noblest of tongues had been employed to see the "little one" off.

Schwarzbauer began to shovel in the earth as the gloam descended and around us the vast expanse of the garden darkened to the green of night. In the chill air the company made its way back to the mansion, the black ominous shape of the Baroness shuddering in her chair, Elfriede in a hurry to return to the kitchen where she had left the beets on the stove.

At the tail-end of the procession I paused for a moment to bid silent farewell to Freude and caught the tall dark figure of the gardener stealthily laying a large rose on the heaped earth.

Months later, on a subsequent visit, the Baron took us to the hallowed ground. It was mid-summer now and the rose garden was in riotous bloom. Amidst the medley of colours Freude lay under a slab of white marble. The Baron read aloud the inscription in gold on the square headstone embellished with a tiny canine figure that, alarmingly, bore a close resemblance to me:

FREUDE
child of a day
Mourned by all
loved by none
Requiescat Beatus

CARIN BREITFUSS

1

One early spring evening the cold wind sweeping outside unexpectedly blew a sea change through our lives, which would never be the same again.

We were at Martha's for dinner. As was the custom by now, the Professor sat at his corner table and I by his feet. It was a dull night in the restaurant, a sole unfamiliar face sat at the far end looking out of the window at the clear wind-swept sky. Martha had just set down a plate of her celebrated trotters with sour beets and the Professor had taken the first mouthful when, suddenly, a breath-catching apparition loomed over us.

She was infinitely tall; or so it seemed from where I sat. The legs rose endlessly towards a slender rounded body topped by a head of tossed rust-red hair with a curl here, a loose ringlet there. The sea-green eyes with the sparkle of emeralds and the full mouth were set in a neat angular face that flowed down to a long slender neck so fine and clean that it might have been turned by a master potter's hand. The ever so slight, almost imperceptible upturn at the end of the nose gave an impish, even wicked air. All in all, she was what humans called seductive.

She spoke the Professor's name. The voice was low, a touch hoarse, perhaps inviting. "I am Carin Breitfuss, the new Head Librarian."

The Professor managed to swallow the first mouthful of sour beets, rose to his feet and took her hand. She apologised for having interrupted his dinner.

"Won't you sit down. Have you dined?"

The Head Librarian needed no further persuasion. "I have, thank you." With that she joined the Professor.

"Oh, by the way, this is Albert."

"The famous Albert!" She stretched out a hand full of long tapered fingers, the nails painted violet. But they stopped short of contact. I briefly wagged my tail a couple of times in greeting. It may have been my canine sixth sense: I felt there was something distinctively artful about the young lady.

"I see we have most of your books in the library," said Fräulein Breitfuss with the brightest of smiles. "I'm afraid I had already read some of them."

Renowned though he was, a legend in his field, yet the Professor could not help that fleeting instant of human vanity. Raising his eyes from the plate, meeting her gaze with a smile I had not seen in a long while, he said, "Well then, it seems we have met already! So to speak."

Uli came to fetch me for my supper in the kitchen. While I chewed on a trotter, he wondered who the young lady might be. "I suppose someone visiting a relative," said Martha absent-mindedly, cleaning out the oven. "She'll be gone by tomorrow." Good and simple Martha! The young lady would not depart on the morrow, nor the day after. She had come to stay and she would turn our lives topsy-turvy.

2

When I returned to the table, it was time to leave. Fräulein Breitfuss had taken a house not far from ours, widow Slusser's wisteria-choked cottage, and the Professor offered to walk her back.

On the way out, passing the mantelpiece above the large stone fireplace, the Head Librarian's gaze happened to fall on the notorious dentures. She stooped forward for a closer look and stepped back even faster. "Grief! What on earth is it?" she queried dumbfounded.

"Oh that!" the Professor said with a smile of dismissal.

"The dentures of the Head Mother of the Mothers of the Fatherland," explained Martha who had come out to bid us goodnight.

"The mothers of what?" Confused and disconcerted, Fräulein Breitfuss peered at the neat, shiny set of dentures under the bell jar and read aloud the epithet in bold letters devised by Dr. Hammes and taped to the bottom of the jar: THOU SHALT NO LONGER BITE THE HAND THAT FEEDTH THEE.

"The Professor will tell you all about it," Martha laughed as she saw us out.

The wind had died down. In the cold pristine air the stars shone with crystalline brightness. We took our usual way home, skirting the woods. Below us the sleep-laden town lay silent.

With the familiarity of long acquaintance, Fräulein Breitfuss had slipped an arm through the Professor's. "What mysteries in your little town! You must tell me about those dentures," she insisted snuggling close to him.

"I don't think I ought to," he demurred. "It's a trifle risqué. You'd best ask Albert!" he added glancing back at me.

"Oh, I'm not a minor, you know. Well over eighteen! "

"I hadn't noticed!" There was an unusual lightness in his tone, a quite gaiety.

"Do tell me," she pleaded with a girlish air, half laying her head on his shoulder. Awkward with this unexpected intimacy, he gave in and told her of the incident of the dentures of the Head Mother of the Mothers of the Fatherland.

3

A year or so ago a bevy of old ladies had descended on the town, said the Professor. They had rented the small hall in the Municipality for their annual meet. A curious congregation of dilapidated women all dressed in a singular uniform of brown shirts and black skirts; black, too, the extravagantly knotted ties around their necks, as were the shoes and the kerchiefs in their shirt pockets.

The black caps with pointed visors atop greying heads, hair packed in a bun, gave them the appearance of some extinct bird in an ancient volume on ornithology, the auk or dodo or similar. What however stirred a degree of agitation in the town was the red armband with four arms joined at the elbow, the hands bent inwards, set on a round field of white. The same motif adorned the front of the caps. The ancient ladies styled themselves Mothers of the Fatherland.

When not in closed door assembly in the municipal hall, they were everywhere. For no visible purpose, least of all purchase, they crowded the shops and stores. Udo the butcher showed them his prime meat. They inspected baker Gersten's fresh bakes. They trooped into Frau Gartner's flower shop, old man Himmel's tiny bookshop, Farber's haberdashery, but especially Adolf's Antiques, where the only genuine antique was possibly the decrepit Adolf himself.

Mid-mornings they streamed out of the Henschel Gasthaus and spread out like locusts, congregating in groups of twos and threes on the pavements, around the churchyard, in the park. And oddly they did not walk as normal humans do, rather they raised their knees with each step, though not excessively, as their frail bones would surely not have tolerated extreme callisthenics.

The people in the town gawked, as if these withered creatures had fled some famished zoo. "Mothers of the Fatherland!" Dr. Hammes exclaimed watching a gaggle of the ancient ladies hobbling along with raised knees. "More like Grandmothers from Fairyland, I should think." The Burgomaster thought they should simply be quarantined. The Baron who had come into town on some errand suggested a more extreme measure: "Round them up en masse and put them on a train to Siberia!"

4

On the last evening of the jamboree the Head Mother, distinguished by red epaulettes on the shoulders, and two of her lieutenants dined at Martha's. From the moment they took their place at table, their manner was unbearably haughty and insolent. They addressed Uli as "boy," which soon degenerated to dolt, and finally lout and half-wit.

The green check table cloth had to be changed because in the summer heat a midge had fainted near the salt cellar. On resetting the table, Uli dropped a knife on the Head Mother's foot; which provoked a sharp yelp and a skeletal hand raised to deliver a sound clip behind his ears.

The ladies ordered "vin rouge." Not much of a linguist, Uli thought the lady meant meant the very best and fetched a bottle of Keller's celebrated Mittel-Rhine; for which he was told off in no uncertain terms, the Head Mother designating him a "nit-wit." Uli unaccustomed to such rude and demanding clientèle became flustered and handed out the menu cards upside down; receiving then a round of further abuse and told to fetch someone who was not a half-wit.

Martha was renowned for her kind and generous hospitality. Ever willing to oblige, she spared no effort to coddle and please her diners. Perhaps the only thing that put her back up was when Uli was mistreated by a guest, which rarely happened.

Now when she presented herself to the Mothers of the Fatherland to take their orders, it did not take long for hostilities to commence.

"Good woman, is this meant to be a menu?" the Head Mother waved the card scornfully.

"It says so. If one can read it right," Martha riposted with hands firmly planted on ample hips.

The intensity of the Mother's spectacled glare would have reduced a lesser spirit to ashes, not Martha. "We'll have the Huhn Fricassee," said the Fatherland's Mother peevishly.

"I'm sorry, but the last portion has just been served to that corner table," – where the Professor sat with me at his feet and received the ill-tempered scrutiny of the three Mothers.

Mindful that a client was ever a client, Martha then said in conciliatory tones, "I have some good Aachen Bratwurst. Would you like that?" The Head of the Mothers nodded dismissively. After Martha had departed, one of the Lieutenant Mothers scoffed: "Imagine, Brünhilde! A restaurant where they serve dogs fricassee."

Uli now appeared with the "vin rouge." Unaccustomed to lacquered corks, he began to fumble with the opener. "Leave the bottle alone, oaf!" the Head Mother barked as she snatched the waiter's friend from his hand. "Go and get the Aachen Bratwurst the fat waitress promised."

Slow in the head he might have been, but Ulrich was the friendliest of lads, ever kind and gentle and never an angry word. He had taken the Mothers' incivility and abuse in his stride. Now though he was truly incensed by the disparaging description of his own mother. "I'll give you your Aachen sausage. And more!" he muttered under his breath going back to the kitchen.

Martha heaped the sauerkraut on a large round pewter dish and arranged a good number of the short fat Aachen bratwurst all around. In the centre she placed a deep bowl of mustard. With his mother's back turned, before taking the dish away, Uli niftily unbuttoned his trousers and slipped his member among the Aachen Bratwurst. It's off-pink perfectly mimicked the colour of the sausages.

The Mothers' craggy faces lit up as Uli placed the heavy dish at the edge of the table. Like mummies suddenly come to life, they could not wait to get at the food. The Head Mother spooned a generous helping of the sauerkraut onto her plate. Greedily she helped herself to a first sausage, to a second one, a third, and then, spooning up Uli's member, which had been quietly nestling among its kind and now refused to be removed, falling back flaccidly on the dish, she paused narrowing her sight, not quite able to make out something she had not set eyes on for a very long time.

It couldn't have been more than the merest fraction of an instant before recognition dawned. The shock must have been considerable. The Head Mother's puckered mouth opened wider than it ever had, the head jerked back with a violent spasm, and out flew her dentures. The aim could not have been better. Describing a perfect trajectory the flying object landed in the bowl of mustard and sank out of view. There followed the most blood-curdling of screams as flailing hands dislodged the platter and flying Bratwurst rained down on nearby diners. Then in a frenzy of knees knocked against table legs, raised skirts revealing shrunken shanks, ankles twisted amidst the fallen chairs, the three shrieking crones rushed out into the night.

Later Martha recovered the dentures from the mustard bowl, washed, dried and polished them. Neatly wrapped in a brown paper packet, they were safely stored in a drawer. Months passed without anyone laying claim. Finally, they were put on show on the mantelpiece, under a bell jar. Later Dr. Hammes devised a suitable epithet for the deceased dentures: THOU SHALT NO LONGER BITE THE HAND THAT FEEDTH THEE.

Neither the Head Mother of the Mothers of the Fatherland nor the Fatherland's other Mothers were ever seen in town again.

THE BAUTEMPLE

1

The arrival of Carin Breitfuss created something of a stir in the town, the men agog at the sinuous gyrations of her shapely and slender body, the brisk scissor-like movement of her infinitely long legs, the head of burnished red hair tossed back with energy and impatience. Women stared at her with wonder and disquiet. The idle and the curious looked on, supposed and conjectured, spun surprising tales of her origins and her past, filling in imaginary biographies with minute suspect details such as the real colour of her hair, the slight upturn of the tip of the nose.

"East," declared widow Fruehauf firmly. "Yes, she's from somewhere in the East. No doubt about that."

"Oh, you and your East!" said Frau Daecher, whose husband ran the hardware store. "Next you'll be saying that Albert here comes from the East. And that the sun also rises in the East."

"The young lady must come from somewhere," said Matilde dryly, as the three women stood outside the butcher's looking at the cuts in the window.

Adolf of Adolf's Antiques presented himself punctually each morning outside his shop, which he preferred to call "emporium," at about the time Fräulein Breitfuss passed on her way to the Library. Unusually alive, trying to look debonair in his dark suit shiny with age, his hearty "Good day!" was dismissed with a pursed smile and the briefest of glances. Unable to draw the graceful attention of the young woman yet once again, he would peevishly retire indoors to immerse himself as usual in his study of "The Occult in the Orient."

Much to Adolf's chagrin, Udo the butcher fared better. Cheerful as ever but somewhat awed by Fräulein Breitfuss's towering presence which wafted into his shop the perfume of jasmine, occasionally patchouli and lavender, Udo felt he had begun to establish an encouraging degree of intimacy as he guided her through the selection of meats, helping her choose between the sirloin and the tenderloin. Hands touched over the purchase or payment, and the fleeting contact with the velvet smoothness of the long tapering fingers made Udo sigh in silence.

Entering the butcher's one day Frau Adler, the bank manager's wife whose permanent expression was a scowl, looked after the Head Librarian as she left the shop. "What does she have," she wondered aloud with an accusatory scowl, "that we don't?"

"She has tenderloin," said the butcher innocently, knowing well that Frau Adler preferred to answer her own queries.

The gossips found Carin Breitfuss haughty, and much too attractive to be a mere librarian, albeit a head librarian. "Women like her do other things," Frau Bader insinuated distastefully. "Things that librarians don't!"

Short, stout and square shouldered, resembling more a cupboard than an angel, Frau Engel was even more peremptory. A library was no place for a woman with long nails painted scarlet, she said, adding with sincere outrage, "There are other places for women who paint themselves scarlet."

But Frau Krause, who had known longing and pain, thought that the young lady sought among books what life and love might have denied her. And for once Montevideo kept his council and remained quiescent.

2

Whatever the mysterious antecedents that had driven her to us, for the first week or two the presence of the new librarian suddenly turned the people in our town into the keenest of readers, hungry for books, reviews, magazines. Mornings and afternoons they trooped to the library, singly, in pairs, their intent gaze falling everywhere except on the monumental shelves packed to the ceiling, as though searching out some hidden and invisible presence.

On her feet all day behind the counter, registering the loans, Frau Botticelli, the Assistant Librarian, was taken aback to see the steady stream of word-hungry visitors wandering aimlessly between the shelves, steadily peering through the glass into the small office where Fräulein Breitfuss sat working at her desk. "Dear me, we'll be out of books if this goes on much longer," she sighed handing Herr Egger, the poultry farmer, a giant of a man with hands the size of dinner plates, a slender volume on home-care and home-cooking. "No pictures," said the farmer indifferently turning the book in his hand as though handling an unknown object.

The pilgrimage brought not only Herr Egger, Gerber the fishmonger, Adolf on repeat visits, Pastor Schaffgott who maintained that most books were the devil's work. Fiedler from Fiedler's Electricals also came, as did grocer Glockner, Schicketanz the municipal clerk, supposedly the local trombeur da femmes, who wore a reddish toupee and considered himself something of a ladies' man, often boasting that no female bastion was entirely safe from his assault.

Frau Bader, Frau Engel and widow Ansel also looked in, but more to keep a close and severe eye that no impropriety was being committed by the new Head Librarian between the narrow shelf-lined passages. While engaging Frau Botticelli in absent-minded talk, they cast censorious looks on the menfolk wandering around idly among the labyrinths of learning.

The Baron came and had a private audition with Fräulein Breitfuss in her office; much to the chagrin of Henschel of Henschel's Gasthaus. Staring through the glass at the cordial encounter, the old man complained peevishly. "The rich and the famous," he said squinting through his dim vision, "they lay their hands on everything." Frau Botticelli consoled him with a volume on birds' eggs and nests. Henschel's interest in fowls and winged creatures in general was a genuine one; at the inn he often served his guests pheasant, duckling and guinea hen with ham.

3

Sad to say that, rejecting the many would-be suitors and admirers, Fräulein Breitfuss had set her sights elsewhere. The consequences of her choice would be far-reaching and no less regrettable. Afterwards I sometimes wondered why events occurred, why the world could not stand still, letting be, letting a being live undisturbed in the quietude of one's days.

And so the Professor and I found Carin Breitfuss at every turn of the road and at every other hour of the day. Or else she found us. Each day, morning and evening, our paths crossed as if by some preordained design, possibly the lady's own design.

On her way to the Library, passing our gate from widow Slusser's cottage, she would wave with the sunniest of smiles. Such radiance seemed quite unnatural at that early hour of the day. It did however have an unfortunate effect on the Professor, for a few mornings later he walked down the garden, exchanged brief pleasantries and, much to my dismay, invited the young lady in for breakfast. "Oh, thank you! I'll come in just for a moment," Fräulein Breitfuss accepted, without hesitation and with an eagerness that bordered on the indecent, I thought. And at that instant, my canine sixth sense felt a whiff of the days to come.

"I'll have some green tea," said Fräulein Breitfuss, scrutinizing the dining room with a cold eye. She took in the long watercolour above the sideboard, a field of wheat and barley under a pale cloud-littered sky.

"Local artist?" she enquired with a superior smile.

"No," said the Professor. "My wife. Gretchen was fond of watercolours."

"Oh! Very pretty." Fräulein Breitfuss nodded dismissively. "It's really a wonder that so few of the great names in art ever dabbled in watercolours."

"We have black tea," announced Matilde. "That is tea without milk. But no green tea."

"Thank you," said the visitor with an amused air, "I'll have what you call tea without milk."

It was the parting shot in many such skirmishes in the weeks and months to come. Matilde never quite accepted the young lady's often haughty tone, but most of all seemed silently to resent the gradual expulsion of Gretchen's spirit, the light and lightness that had filled the house and our lives over the years.

4

Soon Fräulein Breitfuss appeared to be everywhere, omnipresent wherever the Professor and I happened to find ourselves. When not at breakfast with us, and the Professor and I were out for a stroll in the park, she would come striding across the green in her long black skirt and jacquard waistcoat over a mauve turtleneck sweater, hair tossed back in the morning breeze. "Good morning, everyone!" she would greet, light and carefree like a school girl, slipping her arm through the Professor's. With a cursory glance down at me she cheekily added, "The ubiquitous Albert!"

There was something unnatural in her tone and manners, claiming and possessive, as she held on to the Professor's arm and we walked her towards the library. Odd to note, too, that ever sober and reserved the Professor appeared to lend himself easily to this silent air of intimacy, amused and pleased by the attention, as though basking in an unexpected ray of sunlight.

In the evenings now we went less often to Martha's for dinner. When we did, it was usually in the company of Fräulein Breitfuss. Mildly curious, perhaps a touch sceptical, Martha looked on benevolently. With her the young lady was courteous and compliant, accepting her suggestions, complimenting her culinary skills. With

Uli however she was more than a little patronizing, dismissing his attentions as one would that of a child. "Does Albert eat with you in the kitchen?" she inquired with mock-wonder when as usual Uli came to fetch me for my dinner.

"Did you know him well?" she asked the Professor enquiring after her predecessor at the library.

"Dieckhoff," said the Professor putting down his fork. "A good man. Perhaps a trifle lost. But then…aren't we all?"

"Frau Botticelli says he was something of a poet. One of those amateur scribblers, I expect. Or was his work actually published?"

"Neither scribbler nor Poet Laureate. Just passionate about verse, very fond of the likes of Rilke. 'In those small towns, gathered around old houses that sit and jostle…' That sort of thing. One often saw him with the Collected Works in his pocket."

"Why Rilke?"

"Why not?" the Professor smiled to himself, probably recalling the silent, remissive figure of the former Head Librarian. He had come to like the young man during his time with us. Always courteous, punctilious at work, forever dressed in an open neck shirt under a worn brown corduroy jacket, the dark eyes sunk deep in a pale face seemed to look out on a world shadowed with pain. Soft-spoken, he spoke little, but each of Dieckhoff's measured words seemed weighed down with the burden of thought. The Professor had been intrigued by a reticence that seemed to muffle the voice of some inner struggle. But he was grateful to Dieckhoff for having kept Gretchen company at a time when he had often been away.

"Why Rilke?" he mused. "I think Dieckhoff too was oppressed by the transience and tragedy of experience. Gretchen at any rate was very fond of him."

"Yes, I'm told he was a frequent visitor at your place," Fräulein Breitfuss remarked casually. "The other day I found among some papers he had left behind a poem dedicated to some woman. A lover perhaps. It went something like 'Of the multitude in heaven, the one that descends in the solitude of the night, angel and beloved…' I can't remember the rest. Does anyone know why he left so suddenly?"

"Not really. But odd. He was gone within days after Gretchen's death."

The Professor fell silent. He glanced down at me and then, abruptly pensive and drawn, looked out at the bright evening outside. And with him I briefly relived the awful moment of her going, when the heart and the house were hushed, as though never to breath again, wake again no more.

5

Courtship among humans intrigued me not a little. It was a long time ago, age had now blunted both desire and memory, but if I could recall right the matter for us canines was much simpler. A sight, a smell, the immediacy of urge, we mounted and mated, and it was all done in a jiffy. But humans seemed to circle each other in a curious sort of dance, each a prey of the other, closing in, only to draw back momentarily from the kill, then to start the dance anew. It all looked like a ballet in incognito, unmeasured and uncertain, the outcome unpredictable. So it was with Dr. Hammes and Nurse Ulrike. So too, at first, with the Professor and Fräulein Breitfuss. The courtship of Matilde was perhaps similar, but the pace a deal slower, spanning years. I only hoped to live long enough to see the outcome.

Our garden was tended by old man Bauer, who lived outside town and came in twice a week, to weed and prune, mow the lawn, train the creepers at the side of the house, plant the annuals. At the end of his morning's labour, he would go and sit by the kitchen door on a stool put out by Matilde. Hands on knees, wordless, motionless, he sat there watching the housekeeper, the dull brown eyes in a face weather-beaten by a lifetime out-of-doors following her as she moved about the kitchen.

Every now and then Matilde gave a brief sideward glance at the short-cropped grizzled head. There was in the gardener's stillness and gaze a sense of loss and longing, as though dimly through a mist he saw himself seated beside another kitchen door looking at a loved and familiar figure. Outliving his wife and daughter, perhaps he had lived too long, adrift now in a world of solitude and silence.

"It's hard," he said at length, laying a hand on my head as I sat by him, "living alone. Old people should live together. At least there'd someone to bury you when you're dead."

Matilde ever her laconic self said, "No one's dying as yet. And it doesn't matter who buries you!" Yet, the forlorn hunched figure of the gardener must have touched her, for handing him his mug of beer, she remarked in quiet jest, "There's time for that. We're not in a hurry to be buried, are we?"

The lightness of her tone drew Bauer out of his funereal thoughts. He smiled up at her wanly, took a sip of the beer, opened his mouth to speak, thought the better of it, fell silent, then lamely blurted out, "I wish you could see my nursery."

So it went, old Bauer seated by the kitchen, ever on the threshold of giving voice to his heart's desire, ever hesitant and reticent, retiring into the solitude of his days. And Matilde seemingly comfortable in her companionless life, ever busy and bustling, perhaps holding at arm's length and out of sight whatever the ache and emptiness of a solitary life. I wondered if Bauer's courting of her would ever come to fruition.

6

Fräulein Breitfuss's unremitting courtship of the Professor instead soon bore ready and ample fruit.

The absence of Gretchen had left us in a void, in a world with neither sound nor echo, a home without the jostle of voices, mirth and laughter. Ours had been a house of music, Gretchen's lilting song as she sat at the piano or moved through the rooms, the Professor's absent-minded humming as he searched for a book on the shelves; even Matilde's murmured intonation in the kitchen of some tune from the days of her youth. Then one day the music stopped and the voices were stilled.

Then, when she was gone, when occasionally the Professor played a record or sat for a desultory moment at the piano, the notes seemed to drift aimlessly through the bare rooms as though in search of a departed guest. Then, too, one day slipped into the next, endlessly, in an uneventful sequence, time standing still and the world seemingly far away. Occasionally Herr Vogel the school teacher or Dr. Hammes came for lunch or dinner, the Baron looked in or we drove to his estate for the day. But save for the usual morning walk with me and evenings at Martha's, the Professor worked long hours in the study; while I wandered in the woods or dozed in the garden, kept Matilde company as she moved through her morning chores.

Now the sudden eruption of Fräulein Breitfuss in our midst rudely threw open the shutters of our lives, letting in light, voices and movement. The abrupt interruption of our comfortable oblivion was not a little jarring. Unexpectedly the pace of our lives quickened, as if the clock had begun ticking anew, the hands on the move once more.

Once again the Professor hummed to himself as he looked through his papers. His pace as he walked was livelier, there was purpose in his movements, his voice fuller when he spoke to Matilde, their usual morning reparteé more brisk and tinged with good cheer.

Although never neglectful of her chores, Matilde herself appeared to be aware of the fresh air wafting through the house. Our visits to Frau Gärtner's florist shop were more frequent, punctually now the cut flowers in the dining room were changed. She had Bauer trim and clean some of the potted plants for the living room, reserving for the Professor's study a hibiscus in bloom, a living memento Gretchen had lovingly nurtured into a prosperous shrub. Spring was not only in the air, it had entered the house and our lives.

One morning, rubbing French polish on the sideboard, pausing in her labours to wipe a damp brow, Matilde looked down at me, breathed a sigh and said, "A woman's work never ends! When another woman comes into the house."

7

It was customary for the Professor to look into the library once or twice a week, briefly consult some heavy tome, exchange a word or two with Frau Botticelli. Now his visits became more frequent. Entire hours passed as I sat outside on the steps waiting for him.

The Library was the architectural pride of our town. Set in extensive grounds, tall and unusual, head and shoulders above the Kaiser's orchid lady's glass conservatory, it was quite out of proportion with the reading habits of the local population. Donated to the town by merchant Schenkel it was more a landmark, less a seat of learning and knowledge.

Owners of a sizeable acreage bordering the Baron's estate, the Schenkels had forever farmed the land. Their great ancestor had been a trusted companion of Hubert the Horrid during the long years of wandering in the wilderness. When the lands seized from old Abendroth had been parcelled out among his followers, Hubert had rewarded his loyal comrade-in-carnage with a large tract by the river.

Both farming and dealing in seeds, in time the Schenkels had prospered moderately, bought up titles to adjoining lands, raised cattle, built a large family farmhouse. Born in the same mould but breaking out of his peasant lineage, Hermann Schenkel left the land to his brothers and extended the trading to grains, wheat, barley, millet. Short and sturdy, dark watchful eyes in a round rubicund face, he made his way in the world with the measured caution and patience of a man of the soil. Never one to give short measure or go back on his word, trusted in the trade, by mid-life he had put together a small fortune.

The bane of Schenkel's life was that he could neither read nor write. Able with figures but untutored, he signed notes and documents with an undecipherable scrawl, which changed each time he put his hand to paper. It had sufficed to take him through life, garnering wealth and success, and probably it would have seen him through to the end of his days, had it not been for an obtuse municipal official who, examining the merchant's application for the extension of the barn where his grains were stored, lingered long over the snail's trail signature Schenkel had affixed at the bottom, turned the sheet this way and that, and at length looked up with a bemused air.

"I'm afraid we don't have in our office experts in Egyptian hieroglyphics," he said with a half smirk. "Perhaps you could be so kind as to read this for me."

"It's my name!" said Schenkel dumbfounded. "Hermann Schenkel."

He was cut to the quick. Confused and wounded in his innermost being, he made his way out of the Municipality. While his brothers tilled and ploughed, worked the land under sun and snow, he himself had come a long way from the cold farmhouse of his birth, the mud of the fields, the straw and manure littered courtyard, meals at the rough wooden table in the kitchen. He had gone out into the world, travelled, seen towns and cities, met and dealt with men from all walks of life. Once he had even greeted the Iron Chancellor in person; and ever since a portrait of the great man had hung in his house, for that brief encounter with Bismarck was in a way the high-water mark of his life, the distance he had come from the room above the cattle shed where he was born. Now to be jeered at by a petty clerk in a small municipal office!

More than mere anger, he felt a hurt that lingered in his mind for days and weeks, like a bruise refusing to heal. For him it was late in the day, too late to take to books and schooling. But a nascent thought took root in him, nagging his spare evening hours, that others should not be so affronted by the impertinence of officialdom. One day months later, gazing across a large open space, an acre of vacant ground, of a sudden it came to him: he would gift the town a proper library; where people might come to read, write, learn, drink from the fount of knowledge.

No expense would be spared, cost what it might. He had the resources and there were no heirs, none to inherit the trade, the money, the properties. The library would be the child he never had and he would lavish on it only the best, travertine and black stone, marble, hard woods. And the innumerable shelves of teak and rosewood rising to the ceiling would carry the weight of the wisdom of the world.

"An Alexandrian library!" the Burgomaster exclaimed when the merchant outlined his plans. Not versed in history, ancient or otherwise, but familiar with the name, Schenkel was surprised and impressed. "He too put up a library, did he?"

The local builder's draughtsman was charged with drawing up plans for the building, with the firm recommendation that it should represent what it was meant to be: "a temple of learning". It was the earnest young man's first commission and he set to the task with purpose, scrupulously pouring through encyclopaedias, volumes on architecture ancient and modern, jotting down detailed notes of temples past and present, Egyptian, Hellenic, Roman.

When finally presented with the detailed sketches, Schenkel chose the model of the Roman, with a wide flight of steps running up to a raised platform from which sprouted several stout Corinthian columns. At the top of the façade the broad triangle of the tympanum was to carry a frieze of flowers surrounding an open book inscribed in bold Gothic relief "SCIRE EST VIVERE". Schenkel peered at the writing with the sight of the blind. "Latin," said the young man proudly. "Knowledge is life!"

The land was acquired, construction began, the foundation and base were laid, and within months the structure took shape like the hull of an enormous ship in the sea of green of the surrounding open land. Work began on the façade and, mounted with laurel-wreathed capitals, the stout columns rose to the sky true and bold. And then late in the spring Schenkel's grand project suffered an unexpected setback.

A dignitary from the Emperor's court happened to be visiting the Monfleury-Pischendorpfs at their estate. The nobleman, a minor Margrave descended from a cadet branch of the Bombsdorfs, had always insisted on kinship with the Kaiser, claiming to be a distant cousin. Indeed, in Court circles he was good-humouredly known as "The Cousin". A large ruddy-faced man with a bull-horn moustache and a haughty stare, he considered himself one of the last guardians of the Teutonic heritage, as also a connoisseur of art and architecture, not least the lone living expert on Ostrogothian proverbs.

Coming into town one day in the company of old Baron Pischendorpf and catching sight of the now almost completed temple façade of Schenkel's library, abruptly and inexplicably The Cousin flew into a paroxysm of seemingly uncontrollable rage. Schenkel, busy on the site supervising the erection of the tympanum inscribed with the Latin motto, was summoned.

Following a cursory introduction, The Cousin drew himself up to his full height and flourished a glove in the air. "I engage in duel only with my peers!" he informed Baron Pischendorpf solemnly, before turning to Schenkel and enquiring in a booming voice, "Might I ask, sir, what is the purpose of this abhorrence?"

Taken aback, confused and wilting under the fiery gaze of the dark protruding eyes, Schenkel was at a loss for words as he gazed up at the stranger's oversize bristle-covered head, the face flushed with crimson outrage.

"Sir!" The Cousin orated, "Even the history books of the untaught tell us that our forefathers not only conquered Rome but also put an end once and for all to their gods and temples and effeminate licentiousness." He turned in subdued outrage to the Baron. "And what do we find now, millenniums later? A new Roman conquest! A Roman temple no less on the verdant plains of the Fatherland. An abomination! Intolerable! The Kaiser shall hear of this."

Towering head and shoulders above the merchant, The Cousin leant forward, lowered his voice and in a subdued baritone charged with dark presage said, "My good man, even in your rustic backwoods you must know that at this moment we are under siege. Encircled! To the north and east, even in the south, the foe is in waiting. Ready to march on us, tear us apart, dismember the Fatherland. No! Not at all a time to lend oneself to pernicious foreign influences, Roman temples and the like." Regaining his full, commanding stature and turning to the Baron he added in an off-hand but ominous tone, "Neither the Kaiser nor I would want to see any one of our sons of the soil pass for a traitor."

Befuddled, stunned by the menacing tone, helpless and speechless, Schenkel looked after the towering, leather-coated figure as the visitors retreated. It was not so much the veiled charge of treachery that disconcerted him. That the Kaiser should hear of his misdeeds, whatever they were, was unthinkable. He of all people, whose reverence for the Emperor coursed with the blood in his veins! That evening, at home, he stood long and alone in front of the portrait of Bismarck, as though in penitence for a wrong he could neither fathom nor recall.

8

As the most loyal of subjects and, not least, patriot, it was unbearable for Schenkel that he should in any way offend the Emperor. And he saw that The Cousin had not been far wrong, for within months the dire prophecy appeared to come true. The storm of war had begun to gather. One fateful day, then, a mad man's revolver-shot at the passing carriage of an Archduke set fire to the tinderbox. Large armies began to amass to the East and the West. Foreign powers were poised to fall on the German lands and dismember the Empire. The Iron Chancellor alone would have known how to deal with this encirclement, Schenkel thought. But the great man had been long dead.

Men were called to arms and work on the library was suspended. The materials, the precious wood, stone and marble were placed in storage. The services of the draughtsman-architect were dispensed with. His work besmirched, his dream of scaling the architectural pantheon shattered, soon after the young man enrolled in the army, left town, was sent to the Western Front, never to be heard from again.

With the reverberating din of battle in the distance, the slow reversal of his country's fortune's after the first heady victories, the steady trickle of the melancholy return home of the wounded and the maimed which swelled in ever greater numbers with each passing day and week, Schenkel saw the world he had known silently crumble around him. His faith in the Emperor was still unshaken, but now there were voices of defeat, hunger was in the air and in homes that had always had their fill, grains were in short supply, his trade languished. Some evenings wandering around the site of his unfinished library, he gazed at the temple façade and the immense raised platform behind as though looking on the silent, petrified ruins of the land from which he had sprung and so loved.

Finally one late autumn day the cannons fell silent. Schenkel woke to a world he could no longer recognize. The Emperor was gone, the nation taken prisoner. In the sudden hush that had fallen like a pall over the land, he saw the grim faces of defeat and humiliation; silent figures of men and women moving slowly, listlessly through the daily task of living. Travelling through towns and villages in a vain, half-hearted attempt to revive his business, he looked at the bedraggled children in the streets, pale and famished, and the sight hardened his resolve.

There would be better days, the nation would rise once again and, as in the times of the Iron Chancellor, once again take its place among the mighty of the earth. And when that day came, Schenkel thought, in that new and renewed world it would not do to be untutored, unlearned as he had been. "Knowledge is life." The young draughtsman's Latin motto often echoed through his head.

His wealth much diminished in the aftermath of the war, nonetheless Schenkel resolved that cost what it might the library would be completed, the last labour of love even if it meant

126

impoverishment in the waning years of his life. Plunging with renewed vigour into the work of the building, he had the site cleared, materials were brought out of storage, and he turned to the Baron to help procure the services of an architect to review and redesign the main body of the library.

For well or ill Hubert had been a warrior and the House of Hubert had maintained the tradition, his descendants down the centuries taking up arms at the service of any potentate able to protect and enrich the family. A Monfleury-Pischendorfp had distinguished himself in the battle of Sadowa and in the military circles of the new German nation the family name carried a discreet resonance. Not surprisingly, when the Great War came, old Baron Pischendorpf offered his services to the Kaiser, served nominally on the Western Front and returned home at war's end with his eardrums shattered by the monstrous cannonades of Big Bertha.

A small horn held to one ear, he turned his head this way and that, trying to catch Schenkel's words as he outlined his plans for the library. Finally the Baron nodded and asked his aged retainer Gottfried to fetch a magazine from the mansion. As the curiously slender, pianist's fingers of a large hand turned the pages, he told Schenkel of a group of young men in Weimar who could help put up a construction in keeping with the times. "They call themselves Bau…something," he remarked vaguely, showing the merchant the photograph of a commodious chair made of steel tubing and strips of leather.

"A chair!" murmured Schenkel perplexed.

"Oh, they make tables as well," the Baron assured, turning the page to a picture of a plate of glass on three short tubular legs. "We'll have one of these Bau people down from Weimar to look at your library," he promised.

Before taking his leave Schenkel timidly enquired after The Cousin. The Baron nodded his head and after a long pause said gravely, "I fear the gentleman has fallen into uncertain company."

Gottfried was summoned again and asked to fetch a newspaper. The Baron turned the sheets until he came to a page with a large photograph. It was a city street scene, of a ragged crowd gathered around an open truck with a dozen men aboard, all dressed alike, black ties and long sleeved shirts with broad armbands printed with a black circle enclosing what looked like a jagged streak of lightening. Schenkel could distinctly make out the figure of The Cousin standing in the middle, towering above his companions, the large dark eyes glaring out at the crowd with an odd ferocity, one arm raised stiffly at an angle as though in august salute.

"A rabble band," the Baron said with an air of mild distaste. "All dressed in brown like puppet soldiers. Brownshirts. They go about haranguing people in the streets. I'm afraid our friend is in the thick of it," he added sadly.

Schenkel peered at the dull, ochre-tinted photograph. "What do they want?" he asked with a puzzled brow.

"Heaven only knows,"said the old nobleman distantly, looking out over the rose garden bathed in the silence of the late afternoon light. "One day heaven will tell."

9

Architect Schneck was a man of few words and when he did utter the odd sentence, it was as though he spoke to himself, for his own benefit. The self-communication baffled Schenkel and he waited with awed attention for the stray utterance that might come his way. He was impressed, too, by the urbane sartorial elegance of the grey tweed jacket and paisley-speckled mauve bow tie. Keeping a discreet and respectful distance, so as not to disturb the profound meditations of the architect, he watched the solemn figure as through the cold afternoon Herr Schneck stood still in front of the Roman temple façade of the library, occasionally paced to and fro, studied the tympanum with the Latin inscription, gazed up at the sky, lowered his eyes and hastily scribbled in a tiny black notebook.

After a second full day of observation, contemplation and determination, finally the Bau-architect made his pronouncement.

"We'll keep the temple front," he remarked indifferently. Schenkel eagerly stepped forward. "Certainly!" he exclaimed in full agreement with the expert appraisal. But Herr Schneck was not in the least interested in a second opinion, he had aired his irrevocable judgement on the matter and that sufficed. "We'll see to the rest," he added with a light wave of the hand before wandering off towards the green.

Over the next few weeks Schneck came and went, brought other men, a Bau-assistant and a Bau-supervisor from Dessau. Together they climbed the front steps, clambered over the base, studied, surveyed and measured. Schenkel watched from afar as the architect, ever attired in the tweed jacket and mauve bow tie, the angular face as solemn as ever, gave perfunctory directions to his two Bau-men.

The commission had been a costly one but he did not grudge the expense and expenditure, biding in patience to be shown a drawing, an outline, a mere sketch of the completed edifice. None came his way, not even a simple description. Only once, noticing Schenkel's silent forbearance, the architect made a firm declaration that sounded definitive and not subject to review: "We of the Bauhaus are not given to wordy proclamations!"

It was several months before construction started in earnest. A large workforce was summoned, proving a solace to the hardship and misery of the ever increasing numbers of the jobless. In the town Schenkel came to be seen as something of a benefactor, men in the street doffing their caps in deference and gratitude as he passed by. It gave him a sense less of pride, more of fulfilment. To give back something of the abundance received, he thought as he sat by the silent bedside of his ailing wife.

People came to watch as work on the building proceeded rapidly, the long lateral walls of the immense rectangle rising to the height of the laurel-wreathed capitals, the concrete then sprouting massive iron girders angled to follow the triangular slopes of the tympanum. To the wonder and dismay of the onlookers long slabs of the heaviest green-tinted glass were laboriously hauled up, positioned and slotted between the girders, filling the yet to be finished interior with a light sea-green illumination.

The draughtsman's original plan for the library calling for marble vestment on the outside, a large quantity of pale gold Siena marble had been ordered. Now when Schenkel timidly raised the matter with the architect, Schneck looked at him coldly. "We of the Bauhaus are not given to surface embellishment," he said. Briefly baring his teeth in a replica of a smile, he added, "We don't design imitation Taj Mahals!" Repulsed, Schenkel retreated wondering about the unfamiliar name. Eventually the marble was laid as flooring for the library.

One evening when the workmen were gone, the architect and his assistant retired to Henschel's Gasthaus, Schenkel stood at the site amidst the machinery and materials of the building yard. He gazed at the now almost completed structure, massive and monumental, the last fading light caught and held by the vast sloping glass plates of the roofing.

After a long moment he extracted from his pocket a large folded sheet, spread open the crisp paper, looked up at the building. His thoughts worked back over the years, in his mind's eye he saw once again the face of the young draughtsman, eager, radiant with the hope of youth. The Bau-architect had merely realized what the young man had dreamt and set out on paper, only the materials had changed, concrete in place of stone and marble, glass rather than slate. If only! Had he not lent such a credent ear to the bark and bombast of The Cousin, the young man might not have perished in the fields of blood, the promise and passion of youth buried with the unknown dead. In the silence of eventide broken by the distant twitter of birds Schenkel slowly trudged home weighed down with a sense of dull remorse.

10

"Seven thousand remainders from a printer in Ulm," said Mayr. "Then there are two bookshops shutting down in Augsberg. And a large private collection belonging to…I'm afraid I've forgotten the name."

"Everyone selling off books!" Schenkel wondered.

The school teacher peered over his glasses. "Goethe and Schiller don't go with a hungry stomach."

"But knowledge is life!"

"So is bread," Mayr concluded dryly, going back to the long list of purchases he had made over the past few weeks.

Mayr had retired from teaching years ago and retreated to his small stone house on the edge of town. There, widowed and childless, he lived out a sedentary existence, working on the one passion he had nursed through most of his adult life: a biography of the great Vandal chief Gundamund.

Rarely leaving the house, save for an occasional stroll by the river, shut in the small study crowded with books on the one and only subject, morning and evening he worked tirelessly, studying, making notes, drawing charts, pouring over maps, meditating. As he proceeded to garner material and thought the time might have come to put pen to paper, abruptly Gundamund disappeared from view. Mayr had followed on the tracks of the Vandal warrior as he departed Magna Germania, led his men to the regions of the lower Danube and set on the Romans, and then history seemed to have simply misplaced him.

Perplexed, the school teacher ran back and forth through the chronicles of the Visigoths and the Ostrogoths, the doings of the Silingi and the Hasdingi, leapt years and decades to follow the trail of the Vandal kings Rhaus and Raptus and their depredations on Roman soil. But Gundamund had vanished in thin air.

Mayr abandoned his tranquil retreat. Restless and anxious, he travelled, visiting city libraries, archives, delving into documents, burying himself for days in dusty tomes. He called on historians, consulted authorities on the period, discussed with several writers who had authored works on the Vandals or their contemporaries. All to no avail, the whereabouts of Gundamund remained as mysterious as that of the Holy Grail. Then when hope had dimmed to almost a flicker, a glimmer of light showed at the end of the tunnel in the person of a Professor Emeritus from Heidelberg.

A certain Gundamund, recounted the Professor, does in fact make a brief appearance some years after Mayr's Gundamund had routed the Roman legions. A shepherd in the countryside around Ravenna, this Gundamund had succoured the Roman general Stilicho during his flight from the Visigoths down the Adriatic coast, a Samaritan gesture which had secured him a footnote of immortality. The teacher found the anecdote repulsive. The vision of the great Gundamund wrapped in shepherd's garb and herding sheep around a hillside was simply preposterous.

Mayr left the lisping professor and made his way home. Dejected and embittered, he sat in his study listlessly moving about the papers on the desk, as though sifting through the ashes of a lifetime's passion. Nothing now remained, he felt, save to while away the hours and years waiting for the end.

It was about this time that Schenkel called on the teacher and made the offer to work on the bibliography of the library, the interiors having now arrived in the final stages of completion. Heavy at heart, emptied of wit and spirit, at first Mayr demurred. Schenkel persisted, and was persuasive. He needed for the task, he said, someone learned and knowledgeable, familiar with books, and he could think of none better qualified than the teacher.

He gave Mayr a free hand and ample funds. Once convinced, the old teacher plunged into his labours with a vigour and vengeance surprising in one who only weeks earlier had sat morbidly invoking his own mortality. It was as if with his renewed spirit he meant to cock a snout at Gundamund for his truant disappearance. He consulted encyclopaedias on books, drew up an index of writers, ancient, classical, modern; compiled lists by subjects and categories; set out a guide of magazines and reviews to which the library might eventually subscribe; ordered catalogues from publishers.

Mayr took to travelling, visiting bookshops and booksellers, libraries, the small bespectacled figure surprising suspicious publishers with the volume of his orders. Times were hard, the country was racked with trouble and strife, the gaunt anxious faces of men and women in the streets spoke of hunger and exhaustion.

Money was short, increasingly worthless, and Mayr found huge stocks of remainders with printers and publishers, booksellers shutting shop and their contents put on the block for a song, private collections often to be had for a modest consideration, disposed of in desperate haste, without the loving passion that had brought them together over a lifetime or more.

Cash in hand, Mayr bought, at times buying almost by weight, like buying up an entire jumble sale, the good and the indifferent, the bric-a-brac with the odd Sèvres or Meissen. Not surprisingly, more often than not there were doubles or triples of the same title. And for some there were dozens, even hundreds of copies. Dieckoff once complained that the library had no less than ninety copies of "Tales of Terror from the Land of Ur" and as many as two hundred odd of "Infelicitas Animalium" by a Mrs. Mildred Horton-Smith of Milwaukee. And then, obviously, there were several hundred volumes, some erudite, others mere tales and legends, on the Vandals, the Goths and the Ostrogoths.

The station master was overwhelmed as trains that had never deigned to halt at his small station now stopped and disgorged wagon-loads of innumerable heavy wooden crates dispatched from the four corners of the country. The platform strewn with the voluminous boxes at times obstructed the path of passengers alighting and boarding. On one occasion Frau Gesselschaffer, the slaughter house supervisor's wife, who was carrying some prime cuts to her daughter in the city, unable to work her way through the labyrinth of crates failed to board her carriage and vowed never to touch a book again; albeit the only publication in her house was the journal of the Meat Traders' Association.

Occasionally, too, a crate would break, strewing books over half the platform, the air redolent with fresh printers ink. One day Schenkel, coming into the station to oversee the cartage of a newly-arrived stock, found a freckle-faced little girl gazing intently at a book at her feet as she silently bit on her flaxen pigtail. Schenkel stooped down, picked up the book, and held it out. A small pale hand reached up timidly to receive the gift.

A week later crossing the green Schenkel found the girl alone on the park bench by the lake, intent on the book on her lap as her lips read in silence the caption under a colour plate showing a fez-capped caterpillar drawing on a hookah atop a giant mushroom. The child looked up and said, "He has something important to say to Alice." Schenkel gently smoothed her pale gold head and resumed his errand, his heart suddenly buoyed with the joy of an elation he had never known. He carried that rare moment with him through the remains of his life.

11

Surprisingly architect Schneck was up to his word and it provided an occasion for one of his grand pronouncements. "We of the Bauhaus," he declaimed, tugging at a wing of the mauve bow tie, "march in step with Time," adding with philosophical solemnity "What is man without Time?"

"And what is Time without man?" posited his Bau-assistant with like solemnity, much to the architect's annoyance.

The last workman left the site a calendar year after work had commenced and Mayr took the better part of another twelve months to catalogue the tens of thousands of books he had assembled. Schenkel had hoped that the school teacher would accept the honour of becoming the first Head Librarian, but Mayr had other plans for his declining years.

He handed over to Schenkel the vast array of pristine book-lined shelves and a voluminous bibliography he had meticulously compiled with almost a medieval calligrapher's hand. Retiring then to his small stone house by the river, shut in his retreat, once again and for one last time he set off on the trail of his lost Vandal warrior. The silent pursuit lasted through the remaining years of his life. Perhaps in the end he did find Gundamund, concealed somewhere in the folds of the hills gently rolling down towards the waters of the Adriatic. But then it was too late in the day for the school teacher to chronicle the elusive wanderings of the Vandal. Gundamund remained lost in the mists of history.

It was Bau-architect Schneck who finally came to the rescue and sent down from the capital a Frau Steiner to fill the post of Head Librarian. Meticulous, considerate as ever, Schenkel rented rooms for her in widow Winkel's rambling, bramble-covered house on the main road out of town, granted her a generous emolument, and gave her access to the fund he had set up for the upkeep and running of the library. For some reason, perhaps simply the peasant instinct when watching clouds on the horizon, Frau Steiner inspired in him the trust he had always sought in his fellow men.

Rebekha Steiner was familiar with books, and knew book-keeping too. For several generations the Steiners had owned and run a prestigious antique bookshop in the capital, at the corner of a quiet street off Hauptstrasse. While her brother, a twin but younger by bare minutes, travelled around the country and abroad in search of collector's items, Rebekha kept shop, dealt with customers, managed the accounts.

There then came the day when a group of men in brown shirts led by a fierce giant of a figure with a large close-cropped head entered the shop and went on a silent and diligent rampage. Huddled in a corner, brother and sister watched in terror as shelves were torn off the walls, bookcases overturned, the air filled with the tintinnabulation of shattered glass raining down on precious and priceless volumes trod underfoot.

When the fury seemed to have abated, a member of the band emptied a large can of its liquid on the books piled high in the middle of the shop. Clad in a long black leather coat, sturdy legs shod in knee-high matching boots, The Cousin stepped forward, glared from under his caterpillar eyebrows at the clasped figures in the corner, uttered a hoarse cry resoundingly echoed by the rest of the group with arms raised forward in stiff wooden salute, lit a match and let it fall on the damp heap. The conflagration was instant, the tongues of flame leaping up and out as though fired by the force of the words on the burning pages.

135

The brown-shirted men were gone with the speed at which they had arrived and done their work. Now a small crowd had gathered and watched in awe and fear as the fire engulfed the interior of the shop, the shattered glass frontage a kaleidoscopic wall of heat like the imagined molten gateway to the netherworld. In the crush and confusion Rebekha suddenly found herself alone, her brother nowhere in sight. It came to her then that he had stayed back to salvage a rare manuscript locked away in the safe earlier in the day. In frenzied despair she rushed towards the infernal doorway screaming out his name in a voice that seemed to die in her throat, the gasping call finding answer only in the crackle and burst of wood and glass.

12

Schenkel had aged and bereavement had added to the burden of the years. Shortly before the inauguration of the library, his wife's long illness had come to a merciful end. In the weeks before she finally succumbed, he would sit by the bedside holding her hand, frail and light as a feather, the same hand she had given him a lifetime ago at a country wedding.

Bent over the fading life in the penumbra of the shaded light, in hushed tones he described to her the tall luminous cathedral windows of the library, the row on row of hardwood shelves darkened to a clear tan, the waxed glow of the clear gold Siena marble flooring. The words reached her dimly through the nebula of pain and, momentarily struggling back from the closing oblivion, she would open her eyes to whisper with halting breath, "You'll take me to see it, won't you, Hermann?"

When she was gone, laid beside his brothers in the small cemetery on a silent rise behind the woods of the Pischendorpf estate, Schenkel felt emptied and astray, like a craft let loose from its mooring, afloat and adrift yet motionless on the waters. A sense of weary loss came over him as his mind halted at the milestones of a long lifetime's journey. All gone now, king and country, his brothers, the woman who had patiently accompanied him down the years, rejoiced with him, shouldered the burden of his pain.

And now looking around at the troubled land, strife-ridden, sunk in misery and hunger; listening to the bark and clangour of strange new voices rising in a tide of anger and malice, Schenkel was filled with foreboding for the days to come as, again with the peasant's instinct, he watched the darkening horizon. In his dim vision even the library had begun to appear a monument to waste and futility. Listless and despondent, he let go only when Frau Steiner reached out to him through the gloom and led him by the hand into an aura of light and warmth.

Rebekha Steiner was in her mid-forties when she had left behind her the ashes of her life and taken up Schenkel's offer to run the library. Handsome yet, the beauty of youth still lingering in the finely chiselled features, the large dark eyes looking out on the world through the merest veil of age and pain, the gentle voice still carried the ring of better days, the quite smile kind and full, tinged perhaps with a hint of melancholy.

They came from worlds apart, Schenkel from the open fields and the rough-hewn living of the countryside, Rebekha from the closed spaces of books and music, the refined conversations of urban drawing rooms. Schenkel watched in silent wonder the finesse in the least of her gestures, listened to her soft-spoken address, as she took him by the hand and offered hers in wordless sympathy. In another place, at another time, the solitude of each might have found solace in the other, in a union of affection, perhaps intimacy. But Schenkel knew his place in the order of things, he came to respect her, admire her person from a distance, grateful to have found in this woman come from afar the companionship of a sister. And she saw in this simple soul not the brother she had lost, no not that, rather a friend and benefactor who asked for nothing in return.

13

At the far end of the library building architect Schneck had created a sort of large pavilion, a hexagonal space all wood and glass, meant for exhibitions, meetings, chamber music concerts. There Rebekha would join Schenkel as he sat in a commodious, cushioned wicker chair, to read to him through the long winter afternoons when there was scarcely a visitor to the library.

Like a child taking in the words of a tale told by the mother, he listened to the soft cadenced voice as she lead him through worlds he had never imagined, journeys across oceans and continents, from castles in Ruritania to the burning plains of India, the crystal-laid banqueting tables of the rich and the lightless hovels of the poor, magical cities and mythical figures, Uruk and Gilgamesh.

One day Rebekha took courage in her hands and read him a page from a small red cloth-covered book, a gift in girlhood from her father, a work she treasured and which had been her constant companion for many years. In the great Florentine's poetic dream of love imagined and love lost, she had found solace and renewal in her new life. There were no castles nor men on horseback, neither battle nor romance. It surprised her when he asked to hear it again. When she had done, he looked up and timid as a child said, "Will you read it one more time?" And she did. "…*She was called Beatrice by many who knew not what it meant to call her this…*"*

Touched, her heart brimming with a strange gladness, Rebekha took his hand and held it for a long moment..

She sat by him and read, eyes shut he listened, thinking sometimes how little he had lived, how little he had known of men and their deeds. How true were the young draughtsman's words.

* "…fu chiamata da molti Beatrice li quali non sapeano che si chiamare…" ´
VITA NUOVA – DANTE ALIGHIERI

Scire est vivere! Knowledge was indeed life. He was glad then, and grateful, that providence had allowed him to build and gift the library. The architectural mèlange had inspired a local wag to dub it "The Bautemple." He preferred that to the official name of Bibliothek Schenkel. A temple where generations to come could walk the pastures of the mind.

One early spring afternoon Rebekha left him to attend to people in the library. Out on the green there were children's voices in the distance, tiny figures darting under trees in new leaf. He picked up one of the books from the neat pile on the trolley beside his chair. His fingers moved over the page, as though scanning the words, imprinting on his mind what his eyes could not decipher.

When the visitors had left, Rebekah tidied the counter before hurrying back. There was an odd sense of repose in the silence of the pavilion. In the green twilight seeping in through the glass roof she saw him slumped forward, head resting on his chest. She knelt by the chair to take the book he held in his hand but could not prise the fingers open. The slim cloth-covered red volume held tight in his dead grasp, he would not let go, as though wanting it to keep him company on the long journey ahead.

THE CAPTAIN

1

The Captain made his fateful appearance in our midst about the time Fräulein Breitfuss had become a frequent visitor to our house. Much too frequent, I felt. He was introduced as a step-brother. She called him Ebi; or perhaps it was A-B. Human names have always been such a muddle to me.

Captain Eberhard Hunger was a tall, slender young man. A mass of unusually blond hair and pleasant features made for a mild, boyish appearance. The trim beige-coloured moustache was almost imperceptible, unless at close range. He seemed to posses a limited supply of clothing; for on every single visit he wore the same blue uniform with a black tie and a brief multi-hued stripe on the chest. The braided hat under his arm was a permanent fixture, except when he sat at table. At a glance, he must have been some years younger than his sister.

Captain Ebi smiled a great deal but hardly ever spoke. Indeed, he never spoke at all. A nod and a quiet smile were his response to all queries and comments. One of the few occasions when he exercised his vocal chords to any extent was at table one day when Matilde served him a third helping of her Kaiserapfel dessert, to which he responded with "Very good. Thank you" before plunging his spoon into the contents of the plate. There was one other time when he became surprisingly loquacious. Out in the garden one afternoon, he stooped to pat my back, adding "Good boy, Albert!" I could not quite make out the cause for such effusion on his part.

The Professor's attempts to engage the young man in

conversation ended with him talking to himself. "I understand officers are extremely well paid nowadays," he said amicably. Captain Ebi raised his gaze from the plate, smiled and returned to the cherry flan. "Obviously, being stationed away from home must be a costly affair," the Professor persevered. The Captain was engrossed in chasing an elusive cherry around the plate and looked up with a smile only after the pursuit had borne fruit. "In our days life in the army was rather spartan." The Professor might as well have spoken in an empty room, for Captain Ebi was now busy brushing away an errant crumb from his uniform. Matilde was a deal more successful in provoking a response. "Oh, thank you!" he said moving his head away as she readied to serve him yet more flan.

And yet, I did notice that when alone with his sister, Captain Ebi became surprisingly voluble, quite captain-like, even brusque. She would at times hang her head as he poured forth a stream of angry-sounding words. The petulant flow ceased only when she reached out to take his hand and place it gently against her lips. Once, though, I was more than a little appalled to see that when leaving our house after dinner, right outside the front gate his palm came to rest against her cheek with no mean force. Half sobbing, Fräulein Breitfuss wrapped her arms around his neck and said "You mustn't mind him, darling!"

2

They were a very close pair. Inseparable from the moment he arrived in town to the hour of his departure, she never let him out of sight, almost as though fearful of losing a precious possession. Always and everywhere they walked arm in arm. Even at the merest distance, her anxious, protective gaze cocooned him. "Secret twins!" Dr. Hammes remarked one day watching them as they strolled in the park.

"Poor darling!" said Fräulein Breitfuss. "He lost his mother when he was only four."

"So did you," Dr. Hammes concluded.

For a brief moment she looked nonplussed. Recovering, she said brightly, "We are not twins, of course. I am older. And I'm afraid I've spoilt him."

Spoilt him she had. Although now he could walk on his own, she continued to indulge him. On occasion she and the Professor drove to the station to pick him up on arrival and, accompanying them in the car, I had noticed that Captain Ebi never had with him a single stitch of luggage. At most he carried under-arm a battered leather briefcase, from which when by himself he often extracted small items of foodstuff, a bun, a pack of crackers, a half-eaten candy bar, a bag of crisps. One of the first times, sitting out in the garden, he had offered me a tiny tail-end of half a bread stick he had found in the briefcase. I had politely declined, thanking him nevertheless with a wag of my tail. But his departures were gift-laden and he boarded the train with a cascade of boxes, packets, bags.

"Poor darling!" Fräulein Breitfuss would tell the Professor, "I just had to get him a pair of those shoes. He wouldn't know how to buy one."

Or else "Poor dear, he so badly needed a raincoat. But he'd never know where to get one."

"In a shop, I expect," Dr. Hammes observed drily.

Once speaking of the doctor she remarked that as a person he was not very "simpatico." Whatever the word meant, here tone of voice did not sound entirely complimentary. He often seemed to be in her way and I had the curious impression that she grudged the Professor the doctor's friendship.

The Professor himself appeared to suffer Captain Ebi's arrival. His appearance invariably subtracted Fräulein Carin's presence, save for the odd dinner in the house. "The young man does get a good deal of leave," he said to Dr. Hammes one day. "Underemployed, I should think," the doctor remarked. "We don't go to war quite as regularly as in the past. Young people were kept busy then!"

Even in the early days, before they became entwined in a

seemingly inextricable intimacy, the young lady's temporary absences appeared to have a deleterious effect on the Professor, making him moody and restless, often shutting him off for the entire day in the study. Greatly missing our daily walk in the woods, I would set off alone to visit Gretchen, to sit by the cool white marble slab under which she lay; and wishing that Fräulein Breitfuss and her Ebi would simply disappear into thin air. Little did I imagine then that not only would the pair not dissolve in the atmosphere, they would in fact manage to consume the quiet autumn of my life.

FRAU BOTTICELLI

1

Udo's gaze falling on some svelte young lady out in the street as he arranged his cuts in the window, he would sometimes remark that certain dreams could come true, to which Matilde rebutted dryly, "Not that sort of dream!" What the good-hearted butcher perhaps never imagined was so could certain nightmares. By some singular, and unmerited, twist of fate it fell on me to experience the latter.

In truth I had sensed the looming hour of doom ever since she had set foot in our house. Yet the sanguine nature of my canine heart, ever hopeful, ever trusting, had obfuscated the actual vision of the dread moment. She now came and went, sat at the breakfast table, dined with us at Martha's, whiled away late evenings with the Professor in his study, wound her alabaster arms around his waist as we walked in the woods. Like the slow darkening of rain clouds on the horizon to a distracted eye, the growing familiarity of her quotidian presence lulled my otherwise keen nose to the peril of things to come.

Even before that dread dawn that like unexpected flood waters altered forever the lazily winding flow of our lives, the young woman's creeping tentacles had begun to encircle and take imperceptible possession of our daily habits, minor household matters, small details that went unnoticed.

Out in the garden one morning, while Bauer trimmed the spread of ivy on the side of the house, Fräulein Breitfuss remarked on the hollyhocks along the fence. Planted by Gretchen years ago and now gone to seed, aged and flowerless, they stood in a row like tall spears, mute and purposeless. "A bit phallic, aren't they?" she said turning to the gardener. "You'd do well to cut them down."

Afterwards, sitting by the kitchen door, Bauer scratched his grizzled head and mused, "All my life they've been hollyhocks. Now the fräulein says they are called phallic or phallux. Or something. Must be a modern name."

"You tell her you can tell a hollyhock from a phallux," Matilde told him sternly, handing him his mug of beer.

"I can tell hollyhock from phlox," the gardener assured her. "But not phlox from phallux."

A few days later Matilde herself had a brush with Fräulein Breitfuss, a minor duel but one of many in the early days, when the newcomer sought entry and the housekeeper barred the way to the hearth. Later, when the young lady had taken firm possession of the Professor's heart, and limbs as well, the skirmishes between the two women gave way to a détente, that was not quite cordial, an armed truce in which each held and kept her ground, yielding nothing of essence, merely biding time to see the other off over the horizon. The sentiment was certainly true of Fräulein Breitfuss, who perhaps would have even given one of her dainty fingers to see Matilde set sail for the New World, or any other world for that matter.

The subject of this particular round of sparring was nothing more than the heavy, colourful curtains around the bay window of the dining room. "Decidedly baroque, wouldn't you say?" Fräulein Breitfuss remarked picking up with two fingers an end of the heavy jacquard cloth with the same enthusiasm she would have brought to removing a dead rat.

"No," said Matilde pausing in her dusting, "we got it from Farber's haberdashery."

"Haberdashery!" Fraulein Breitfuss laughed, though it was more a loud snigger. "I thought they had removed the word from dictionaries ages ago."

Unperturbed, Matilde applied the duster to the sideboard as she said, "Farber had it specially ordered."

"Farber's of Fifth Avenue!"

"No, you'll find the place near Frau Gärtner's flower shop, if ever you want to look in."

"Thank you. But I think I'll forego Herr Farber's à la mode expertise."

Matilde arrested her duster and looked quizzically at the young lady, perplexed by her contrariness so early in the day. In a reconciliatory if not motherly tone she said. "That's a very nice dress you are wearing."

"Not dress, Matilde! Tailleur," Fräulein Breitfuss corrected mockingly, smoothing the lapel of her mauve-pinstriped grey jacket. And in a hiss surprisingly charged with peculiar vehemence, she added, "And it didn't come from Farber's haberdashery!"

Not content with having put Matilde in her place, that of the professional duster, she threw a distasteful glance in my direction. "This creature should be out-of-doors," she remarked with an odd sense of spite almost. "And put on a diet!"

The behaviour of humans was at times a conundrum to me, but it was a rare day to come across such unreasonable temper, malice without cause. Certainly ill-will such as hers would not help one attain what Dr. Hammes called the celestial heights. "Man comes trailing clouds of glory from God's heaven," the good doctor had once said in jest to Gretchen. "But there are serious doubts that many of us will make it back to the celestial heights!"

2

My habits were governed by the careful training imparted to me by Gretchen in my puppyhood and, regular as a metronome, I had kept to them ever since. Dawn saw me out through the hatch in the door of my little room at the back of the house, across the rear garden and out the gate up into the woods for my daily needs. When done, I would wander and roam as the light of the rising sun turned the green canopy overhead translucent, the resin of pine and the musk of the betulian oil of the birch coming alive and permeating the air with the first warming sunlight.

An occasional scurrying hedgehog but mostly squirrels darted about me. The benevolence in their eyes as they looked on reminded me that long gone were the days when I would bound forward towards the waving tease of their furry tails, which somehow always managed to elude my chase. Age had dulled sight, weight had made me earth-bound, live and let live I was now content to watch their play and pranks as they slid up and down tree trunks and described somersaults off the branches.

Down the slope from the woods, below me the town stirred from its fitful sleep, with a bark here, the odd voice, a vehicle starting up reluctantly in the distance. The pristine silence of the early hour now broken by the chorus of birds atwitter in the trees, I retired to my bunker-den for a brief forty-winks before going back to the house to climb the stairs and wait by the bedroom door, waiting for Gretchen to wake and call me in.

Waking, she would call my name, and I would nudge the door open to go and sit by her bedside, to be greeted by her soft, drowsy "Good morning, Albert!" a sleep-laden hand reaching out to caress my head. The Professor usually slept on, soundless and motionless somewhere under the duvet. The morning dimly filtering in through the drawn shades, sitting in the warm stillness, looking at Gretchen's face nestling in repose amidst the tousled gold of her head, I sometimes thought that should my Maker one day take it on Himself, by whim or purpose, to turn me into a human, I should still want to be where I was, here crouched by this bed, the gentle weight of this loving touch resting ever so lightly on my head like an unspoken benediction.

And that blessed hand was on me till the last, the dreadful end-days when she lay in the darkened room, shutters drawn and a shaded light on the far side of the bed. Day and night became one, seamless time, as the doctor came and went, the nurse like a ministering angel in white moved through the dim air, the Professor hunched motionless on a chair, and Matilde coming to fetch me for supper and sleep.

I was made to wait outside as Dr. Süssmayr medicated and

147

Nurse Kuhn washed and cleaned, but always, each fading day, mornings and evenings I would hear the beloved voice, feeble and flickering like a candle in a draught, asking for me to be taken in. Then I would sit by the infirm bedside, as I had sat on all the mornings of my life.

Inert, the splendour of her still youthful body wasted by the long season of pain, one enfeebled hand would helplessly graze across the bedclothes, working its laborious way towards me, the dormant palm resting on my head with the infinite weightlessness of a feather in the wind. And forcing her mind out of the nebula where consciousness and sleep melded, forcing her eyes open to the twilight room, she would slowly turn her face, the sparkle of her violet eyes now spent, lustreless, to spell my name in a child's murmured whisper, the lips parting to trace the memory of days gone by when the splendour of her smile lit the house and our lives.

That evening she would not let Matilde take me away. Her voice was oddly stronger, she seemed to have wended her way back from faraway places, finding herself again in the home she loved, once again among those she cherished. Sombre, yet there was a newfound serenity about her as she spoke, slow and halting, to the Professor, caressing his face as though to imprint and store away his lineaments in her memory.

When he had gone, to rest in the guest room where he now slept, she lay back in quite exhaustion. Matilde had already gone and when late in the evening Nurse Kuhn too had left to spend a rare night at home, in the nocturnal stillness only her whispered breath lingered in the room, like the unseen presence of a spirit hovering in the air. Crouched by her bedside, lulled by the pale silence, I slowly drowsed towards sleep, towards dreams that remained with me but which afterwards I could not recollect.

First light was seeping through the shutters when I came to with a start, called to wakefulness by the song of a voice that rose of a sudden from the depths of sleep, then as suddenly receding in ebbing echoes. In the chiaroscuro of the mute dawn I found my chin resting on the bed, pressed down on the sheets by the dead weight of her cold hand. The whispered breath of the unseen spirit had departed the now orphaned room.

3

The Professor was not the earliest of risers and after my morning sally into the woods I often drowsed by the bedroom door, until I heard him stir, when I would go in and wait for him to wash and dress before going down to breakfast. Some days when the Professor lay in a while longer, with a glance at the hour Matilde would playfully chide us, saying "Will it be breakfast or lunch, gentlemen?"

Today settling down by the door, I was startled to hear voices in the room. Never had I heard the Professor talking on his own, nor had he ever exhibited vocal imitations of the human female. My ears pricked up in alarm and just as I thought I might nose my way in to look into the mystery, the door opened to reveal a sight that quite robbed me of breath.

Shocked out of my six senses, I gazed haplessly up the infinitely tall legs, smooth as turned ivory, as they rose endlessly above me, a faint brush of burnished gold at their conjunction fading away towards the belly as it sloped up and out in a slight pout. Bare save for a flimsy silk gown printed with wild orchids and open down the front, the lithe figure stood above me glaring down with an odd smile. It was a moment before I recognised Fräulein Breitfuss.

Odd how the appearance of humans changed when fully clothed. And odd, too, how in moments of stupor and drama the mind played truant and wandered off after facile thoughts, for it occurred to me that I too might have looked different had Gretchen clad me in youth in a coat and shod my limbs in trouser legs. A hat I could not have worn.

She glared down at me for a long moment before calling out to the Professor. "I think your Albert here fancies me!" she said with a sort of wicked mirth closing the gown and shutting out the intimate view.

"That makes two of us," came the Professor's sleepy voice muffled by a yawn.

"The way he looks at one, a proper lecher this creature of yours!"

"Tel le maître, tel le chien!"

"More like tel le chien, tel le son maître," Fräulein Breitfuss laughed shutting the door behind her.

Now both Gretchen and I were orphaned from the room. Mourning our banishment I went down the stairs and out in the garden, to wait for Matilde to arrive. In the keen spring morning, I felt the cold air of change on my face.

4

She had come to stay, and she stayed. In the days and weeks that followed, her presence became pervasive as she spent mornings and evenings, and nights, in the house. Her hand worked small, imperceptible changes in the daily routine of our lives. Matilde now came in later, we ate at Martha's less frequently as Fräulein Breitfuss often saw to dinner herself, the quality of my fare declined as increasingly I was fed out of tins.

Farber's flowery curtains in the dining room were finally seen off, replaced by light white gauze hangings. The heavy brocade across the French window of the living room suffered the same fate. The old leather pouffe on which Gretchen used to put up her feet while watching the picture-box was retired. The sterile hollyhocks in the garden were cut down, Bauer still puzzling over Phlox and Phallux.

I often found the young lady contemplating Gretchen's watercolour landscape above the sideboard in the dining room. Her expression left little doubt that she meant to be rid of it. Piecemeal she seemed to be bent on banishing Gretchen's spirit once and for all. Objects and furniture were reordered, the Professor's habits reformed, with books put away in their place on the shelves, papers tidied and piled neatly. Accused of inviting insects indoors, Gretchen's hibiscus in the study was relocated back in the garden.

The one change that was disconcerting and baffled Matilde particularly was the disappearance overnight of Gretchen's picture in a square silver frame that had sat in one corner of the Professor's desk in the study for as long as one could remember. It was a black and white portrait of Gretchen in her youth, against a backdrop of scudding clouds, her gaze turned skywards, the long strands of fine hair streaming in the wind. An exhaustive search by the housekeeper failed to turn up the photograph. On Matilde enquiring after the mysterious disappearance, the Professor murmured blandly, "It'll be somewhere, I expect." Somewhere it certainly was, only the mysterious hand that had whisked it away knew of its whereabouts. The picture and frame never reappeared again.

The lunch and dinner menus were reworked. Matilde looked on askance as the strips of bacon wound around the roasting pork shoulder were removed. "Cholesterol," Fräulein Breitfuss explained with mysterious brevity.

Matilde turned the word over in her mind for a moment. "No, can't say I've ever made that for the Professor," she confirmed, adding "Never heard of the dish."

Fräulein Breitfuss gave her a half-smile of compassion. "Well, now we have. And oh, while we're about it, you might want to make the ragoût with a little less lard. Bad for the heart."

Matilde looked nonplussed. "Whose heart?" she asked with genuine concern.

Later, on the way to the library, Fräulein Breitfuss said, "Matilde ought to cut down on the cream and lard. I told her they were bad for the heart."

"Whose heart?" the Professor asked absent-mindedly, leafing through Rebekha Steiner's biography of Hermann Schenkel.

5

"Well, it seems you have a new mistress now, Albert," Frau Botticelli mused rubbing my head as we sat on the steps of the library. "New master too," she added cryptically, drawing on her usual cigarillo.

Certainly, the Professor's day had changed, the old set routine of the long morning hours in the study replaced by long morning hours in the library. The small reading room was set aside exclusively for him and there, under the watchful eye of the Head Librarian, like a school boy at his homework, he laboured diligently among his books and papers. Fräulein Breitfuss would go in from time to time and, putting her head next to his, speak in quite, intimate tones.

The Professor's private cove did not go down well with some of the regular visitors to the library, especially Frau Adler who occasionally in the afternoons brought her son and sat the little boy in the small room with a comic book while she searched the shelves for romantic reading material, her favourite being those with dark, handsome strangers assiduously courting and conquering pale young maidens in distress.

"I thought this was a public library," she remarked with her usual scowl, staring through the glass at the Professor bent over his books.

"It is," Fraulein Breitfuss retorted with a not dissimilar scowl. "Which is why we can't choose our public!"

Crabby and churlish as ever, Henschel of Henschel's Gasthaus, who only very occasionally came to the library merely to consult some volume on game and game hunting, though it was thought that the sole purpose of the visits was to extend his unreciprocated attentions to Frau Botticelli, asked that he too be allotted a private room. Frau Botticelli laughed. "You should be able to find one at the Henschel Gasthaus!" she half whispered in his ear. Henschel was not amused, but he did appear to savour the fleeting brush of her lips against his ear lobe.

6

So whole mornings I sat between the towering columns of the Schenkel library, looking out on the world, the park with the pair of swans idling in the lake, the orchid lady's glass dome beyond the line of trees bursting through the green like an enormous soap bubble; the squat, massive stone façade of the church beyond the grounds of the library darkened by age and topped with a cross that drew to itself the bolt of every summer lightning, as though continuously sanctified by the fiery finger of heaven.

Between one brief doze and another I watched the slow procession of familiar faces down in the street; the butcher's little blue van with Udo at the wheel pulling up abruptly to keep pace with Lulu the chambermaid from Henschel's Gasthaus as she walked down the pavement with a peculiar swing of the hips. Frau Bader and Frau Engel sauntered down the road, eyes cocked towards the library, their mind's eye no doubt lit up with the unspeakable images of the Head Librarian's doings with male visitors between the serried phalanx of books. Now nearing her centennial anniversary but still able to walk and talk, old widow Ansel clung to their arms as she hobbled between the two gossips, but too far gone to entertain hearsay and malice, she was content merely to let her toothless gums suck on a soft toffee.

Ilse Krause went past twice each morning, on the way to the shops and then back to her little cottage by the station, the never absent wicker basket sprouting leek and salad and a loaf of dark bread heaped over the ever present Monty nestling somewhere under the shopping. Unusually one morning I was roused from my light slumber by a strangled croak of "Fat dog!" and opened my eyes in time to catch the head of the insolent fowl swiftly duck back into the basket.

There was a time when I certainly would have rushed down the steps and removed clean the impertinent bird brain from the rest of the creature. The wisdom of age, not least the weight of the years, counseled otherwise, for so precipitous a leap could well have ended with a broken neck. Montevideo must have got wind of my bellicose sentiments, for on Frau Krause's return journey he kept entirely out of sight; albeit I thought I heard a dim cackle of glee rising through the greens.

And sitting there, on a rare occasion I saw Madame Gaugué with her spaniel Agnès. A noble woman of sorts, I had heard it said, fallen on hard times, one day years ago she had appeared from nowhere, found refuge in our town and, in time, married the station master. It was an odd match, the union short-lived.

High-born and lofty, high-cheeked, tall and elegant, her fastidious manners kept everyone at arms length, the refined olfactory sense of the sharp nose finding unpleasant odours everywhere. Unable to bear for long her hauteur, the flare of her nostrils at his approach, the disparaging look at table as he chewed his meat, a mere year after the wedding the dispirited spouse threw himself on the railway tracks in the path of the early morning milk train from Mainz.

The widow reverted to her maiden name, wore the habits of bereavement for ever after, going about town in elegant black taffeta set off with a silver brooch, and procured herself a more compatible companion, Agnès. The pair could be seen occasionally, upright and sedate, aloof as royalty, strolling in the park, seemingly unaware of the presence of other humans, or living beings for that matter. It was there that I first set eyes on Agnès.

She was in her early youth, a radiant creation, the russet and white fur giving off the same sheen as that of her lady's silk dress, the fine coat moving in smooth unison with the lithe undulations of her young body; the fetching ears falling gracefully to frame a small head set with large eyes bright that shone with an ineffable sweetness I had never before seen in one of our kind. Yet, as she tilted the dainty head to take in her surroundings, there was a curious contemplative distance in her look, as though observing from above things and beings of a lower order, perhaps something of the same haughtiness with which her mistress looked out on the world.

Memory dimming, my recollections were now vague, fogged by the passage of time. Yet I could remember how the blood rose and the limbs stiffened at that first sight of Agnès. I was then in my high youth, full of truant energy and lusty vigour, rampant at the vision and odour of so divine a creature. I could not now tell if I had pursued her, mounted and mated. Perhaps. The lost moments of life leave behind them a trail of regret. I had none, my tail ended where it did. Perhaps after all she had been mine, if only briefly, if only once.

Time had worked its change, I saw now, watching the pair slowly make their laborious way down the road. The haughty air of the head held stiff gone, the sedate upright walk turned to a half limp, gaunt and bent Madame Gaugué shuffled forward with halting, uncertain steps, eyes cast down, the shine of the black taffeta dress, hanging rumpled and shapeless on a skeletal frame, turned to a drab metal-grey.

And Agnès, grown stout in the rump, top-heavy, keeping laboured pace with her mistress, the once dazzling sheen of her coat turned to a dun brown and off-white, she looked what in fact she had become, a pitiable old bitch. Sensing my presence at the top of the steps, briefly she turned her head to look up towards me, a dull melancholy hazing eyes that had once sparkled like water in sunlight. It was a fleeting glance, for she looked away almost immediately, as though shamed by the ravages of age and time she wished to conceal herself from the cruel gaze of day.

7

With Fräulein Breitfuss's exotic efforts in the kitchen, with little cream and even less lard, dinner at Martha's had become almost a rare occurrence, and I saw far less of Uli. This morning on an errand for his mother, it was a joy to see him bound up the steps of the library. Arms around me in a happy cuddle, rubbing his chin on my head he said, "Albert! Sorry I couldn't come for our walk. Two wedding parties in the restaurant this week."

For some odd reason, perhaps no reason at all, several young couples in the town had suddenly decided on tying the knot and Martha's was the usual venue for the lunches and dinners after

Pastor Schaffgott in the dark interiors of the church had severely admonished the newly-wedded couple against wayward thoughts. I hoped the minor epidemic would soon be over, for I missed Uli coming to the house to fetch me for our weekly walk down by the river, by the willows past the stone house where teacher Mayr had lived.

Strolling along the bank, looking at our images mirrored in the emerald sheen of the moving yet motionless water, Uli would pick up a twig and conduct himself as he broke into hushed song, curious lyrics set to a tune then making the rounds:

Albert here, Albert there, Albert everywhere
But where, Oh where?
Ulrich here, Ulrich there, Ulrich everywhere
But where, Oh where?

With a final flourish of the baton, he would stoop down to caress my head, before once again taking up the ditty. Uli they said was dim-witted, but if dim-wits meant the never-failing cheer and warmth of a guileless heart, then one could only wish that a few more humans were slower in the head.

Late mornings I was joined on the steps by Frau Botticelli, who came out for a few puffs on her cigarillo. We sat together, the tapering fingers of her veined hand quietly smoothing my back. In silent contemplation we looked out on our small world, familiar sights, known faces, the year's first swallows encircling in flight the orchid lady's green glass dome. Frau Gärten from the flower shop went by with an outsize bouquet of red roses lightly speckled with mayflower, which camouflaged her head, giving her the appearance of a floral being.

Pastor Shaffgott hastened past, headed for his church, no doubt to admonish yet another wide-eyed wedding pair for varied temptations past and future. The severe look of disapproval he cast in our direction could not have been meant for me, for obviously I was free of wickedness. The dart was aimed at Frau Botticelli, who had last visited the church for her christening and not seen the forbidding interiors since. As likely, the Pastor's disapproval extended to Frau Botticelli's little cigarillo, its slightly acrid burnt leaf odour tickling my nostrils as the faint wisps of smoke rose in the air.

8

It was with the same curls of grey smoke, the same pungent smell of the stubby little cigar that he came into her life. Bent behind the counter, sweeping the floor, she had not heard him enter the shop. The sharp odour reaching her, she raised her head, and there he was. Much later Wilhelmine once told him that at first sight he not had looked much like her man of destiny. "Ah, but *I* found my fairy princess!" he had laughed, pressing her finger tips to his lips.

Ever gracious and courteous with women, his description when first he set eyes on her that afternoon was more the compliment of affection. Dressed in a blouse a size too large for her slender shoulders, a heavy maroon skirt that fell to her feet, the long auburn hair unkempt and tousled, Wilhelmine resembled neither a fairy nor a princess.

Nor indeed, standing there meek and hesitant, did Botticelli cut the figure of destiny Wilhelmine or any other young woman might have awaited in patient expectation. Short, round-shouldered, a finely-shaped head topped with dark hair combed back in waves, shod in dull green corduroy trousers worn at the knees and a woollen sweater of indeterminate colour that buttoned up to the neck, he would have passed for an honest workman but for the full lips silent yet pregnant with eloquence, but too for the large eyes bright as an infant's.

Wilhelmine stared at the unfamiliar face for a long minute, uncertain, vaguely alarmed. She came to with a start when finally he spoke. Perhaps it was a greeting but in a tongue she had never heard before. "Signorina," he said, lips parted in a quiet smile, "vorrei parlare con il titolare." The even timbre of his voice, a soft tenor, was soothing, reassuring almost. Wilhelmine shook her head, smiled back timidly and raised her hands. "Oh pardon! Fräulein!" Shaking his head in turn, in courteous apology, he now broke into her language, speaking slowly, inching forward hesitantly, as if the words had been learned by rote.

She understood him now, nodding her head in encouragement to urge him forward, as one would with a child reciting lines from memory. And with a child's simple diction he told her of the purpose of his call. The words lagged behind, but his voice was now full and firm, his expression confident and his gestures surer as he reached into a large straw hamper on the ground, extracted and placed in a neat row on the counter several wedges of gold-hued cheese that gave off a rich aroma of honeyed milk. Lastly he drew out a long string of small sausages dusted white with flour and neatly winding it around one muscular arm placed the garland beside the cheese.

He looked up at Wilhelmine, eyes bright with innocent pride, the round face lit up with the joy of a master of the house receiving a welcome guest for a banquet. And even as she looked on, surprised, taken in by the wordless eloquence of his presence, he flicked open a tiny penknife, sliced a small sliver off one of the wedges and held it out towards her. She drew back, diffident, he nodded in encouragement, inviting her with the guileless, expectant smile of a child. She raised her hands, showing him the grime on her palms from the cleaning.

Nimbly reaching out over the counter, he proffered the morsel, gently pressing it between her lips. Taken aback, she looked at him wide-eyed as the cheese crumbled and dissolved in her mouth, filling her palate with a smooth medley of cream and honey, depositing tiny crystals on her tongue and releasing a faint aroma of apricot and ripened quince.

That evening, supper over, Wilhelmine placed a quarter plate with small shavings of Botticelli's cheese on the table in front of her father as he sat in his crippled chair. She watched as he slipped tiny crumbs into his mouth, uncertain and weary, the tired eyes meeting her gaze in silent query. She knew him, could gauge his thoughts, the cautious set of his mind. "Not to worry, father," she said with quiet reassurance. "The man said we could pay him after it's all been sold."

His mouth moved wordlessly, savouring the taste. When the meagre portion was gone and Wilhelmine reached out to remove the plate, he nodded and looked up with a modest expression of pleasure. Yet she read in his eyes a hint of doubt, as if to ask who in this town, in times such as these, could afford such luxury.

9

For some odd reason, or reasons known only to himself, each time he came into town from his estate, Baron Pischendorfp stopped at the store, if only briefly, buying some trifle, a box of matches, a small pack of candles, a bar of soap, items for which he had neither need nor use, which on his return would be handed over to old butler Gottfried who dispensed with them as he saw fit. If Wilhelmine happened to be out, having momentarily left the shop in the charge of little Fritz from next door, the Baron would leave, bowing out through the low doorway without a purchase, without tarrying.

Her girlish heart free of doubt, simple and uninquisitive, Wilhelmine never queried the Baron's visits, never stopped to wonder why one such as he, a man endowed with name and wealth, should call with such regularity at her little shop which had so little to offer, even less to attract. Yet he came, punctual at mid-afternoon, often alone, occasionally with his small son Armin. Then he would linger, courteous and affable, glancing at her with a smile, turning his gaze to the meagre store on the shelves as if searching for something that had gone missing, turning back to her with a look as though she had been suddenly removed to a great distance. It was but a mere moment, for hastily he would pick some small article, place it on the counter, and search his pockets for the small change.

She would now have been about Wilhelmine's age, perhaps a trifle younger, in her late teens. And in his mind's eye, she would have been Wilhelmine's mirror twin, the same fine auburn hair, the same neat and high brow and pale oval face set with large brown eyes flecked with gold, the very same narrow waist rising to slender shoulders. But his little Renate had gone when a mere child and, as her name would have it, here she was, reborn, in the replica of a young shopgirl in this poor grocer's store. The pain of loss spent, subdued by time, the memory was renewed each time he came into the shop.

Once strolling together in the rose garden, he had come near to mentioning Wilhelmine to his wife. But Baroness Gertrude was a woman severe in her sentiments. Unlike the Monfleury-Pischendorpfs, she had not come from a house of spurious nobility founded by a marauding fugitive such as Hubert the Horrid. Her antecedents went much further back, in a direct line of descent, to the Knights of the Teutonic Order, a great ancestor having fought in the battle of Novogrod in 12-something and perished in the frozen waters of Lake Chud, a grandfather who had stood in the vicinity when the king was crowned emperor of the new German nation.

Renate then was for her a child who had come in their midst and left soon afterwards. More than remembrance it was a bare fact, a paragraph in the chapter of her life which, unlike her husband, she had apparently firmly relegated to the past. For Gertrude there was only Armin, her little boy, in whom coursed the ancient blood of her fathers, who lit the hours of her day, nestled in the folds of her sleep. The Baron kept his council and never mentioned Wilhelmine nor his visits to the little grocer's shop.

Today Wilhelmine, made bold by the familiarity of the Baron's regular visits, took courage in her hands and timidly drew his attention to the wedges of cheese displayed under glass, which she said a stranger had brought from the south. In imitation of Botticelli's seductive skills, she broke off a generous piece and held it out for him to taste. The Baron turned it over in his mouth, sucking on the morsel like a child with a lozenge. Recognition suddenly dawned, his face lit up and turning to his little boy he said "Do you know, Armin, your grandfather once had a whole round of this given to him by someone they used call The Cousin. Heaven knows why they called him that!" He paused in recollection, "It comes from, yes, Parma I think"

Reassured, put at ease by his willing good cheer, Wilhelmine asked "Will you take some?"; surprised at the same time by her own audacity.

"We'll take it all!" the Baron laughed. "But imported foods don't come cheap, I expect. We'll have to break into Armin's little piggy bank, won't we?" he added running a hand through his young son's head. "Please put it aside, I'll have someone pick it up tomorrow."

The ice broken, the diffidence gone, the Baron left melancholy and yet light at heart, thinking he had heard in Wilhelmine's words the shy melody of Renate's voice, had his little girl lived and come of age. And Wilhelmine herself, quietly elated, was pleased that she could tell her father that the entire stock of cheese was gone, could dissipate his unspoken doubt. And she was pleased too that she would not have to turn Botticelli away. For some reason, which she neither fathomed nor questioned, she wanted him to come again, bring the strangely warming ray of his presence into the dull round of rote and routine in which her life moved, in which each day was much like the one before and the one to come.

10

When that afternoon Botticelli and his Tuscan cigar walked through the door of the shop and into her life, Wilhelmine was not yet twenty, a tall awkward girl, shy and retiring. Plain in appearance, pale and unadorned, negligent in clothes that did little justice to her slender figure, elsewhere, in another walk of life, the pencil-drawn brows above clear eyes set in a clean oval face, the light chestnut hair trimmed and dressed, she would have made an attractive young woman. But motherless since childhood, with a father who had dragged himself from the end-days of the war crippled in the leg by a shell on the outskirts of some nameless village on the Russian steppes, Wilhelmine had come to womanhood aforetime, without the way stations of play, carefree mirth and girlish laughter. Nor had the lost years of adolescence allowed room for the small frivolous vanities of maidenhood.

A soldier-ancestor returned from the battle of Sadowa had set up shop near the old mill, the business had prospered and several generations of Gesslers had lived in comfort off the earnings. Stocked with choice foodstuffs, legs of ham from Prague, bottled herrings marinated in wine from the north, smoked venison, rare cheese from across the border, Beaufort and Roquefort, sweet wines, Màlaga and Madeira, and more, the store garnered an affluent clientele, the local gentry, the doctor, lawyer Stuffer a veritable glutton, the Monfleury-Pischendorpfs whose steward stopped by weekly to place generous orders.

By the time Wilhelmine was born, trade had long withered, impoverished first in the harsh aftermath of the Great War and, later still, for scarcity of provisions during the second upheaval, when her father was called to arms, leaving his sickly wife to tend to the shelves emptied of all save bare necessitates. Then, with the grey desolate silence of defeat and disarray that hung like a pall over the land, with her mother gone, a little girl sat in the corner with the stub of a pencil working on a torn page of brown straw paper she watched as her father, silent and embittered, limped about the shop arranging, counting and rearranging the meagre stock, not Beaufort and Roquefort but foreign foodstuffs still, the diet of the victorious armies, small square tins of corned beef, tall cans of powdered egg, bars of chewy chocolate candy.

Morose and reticent, often in severe pain, increasingly Gessler absented himself from the shop, to sit in the small patch of garden at the back in fair weather or else retire upstairs to lie by the window staring out for long hours at what had once been a prosperous part of the town, now the solitary cobbled street sprouting weed, the decaying houses bereft of menfolk perished in far-off fields and inhabited by bedraggled women, children lean with the pallor of hunger.

He was not yet sixty but the thinning head of hair turned chalk white, a face creased with lines that sank deep into the flesh, the pained, invalid's movements, not least the eyes still and unseeing, as though forever frozen by some dread sight, gave him an air of senile age and decrepitude. And like an infant for whom the immensity of the world is enclosed in the mother, for him the vision of life had narrowed to the figure of his daughter.

Barely in her teens, it fell on Wilhelmine to tend to the shop, to procure the scarce provisions, serve the trickle of customers, put away the meagre takings and parse the accounts. Already though times were changing with the slow but sure recession of the shadow that had loomed over the land, giving way to a flickering dawn that held the promise of life and renewal. As if released from some secret store, foodstuffs gradually reappeared, flour, sugar, eggs, not yet abundant but proof that the everyday amenities of living could still be had, at a price. Bread was less dark, less leaden, meat still scarce but tasting of heaven.

Gessler watched, silent and absent-minded, seeing only his child and not the young girl who in the spate of a mere year or two had become an able keeper of the shop and its trade. The shelves were fuller, more people came and went, the takings were still small but the till rang more often. Soft-spoken and gentle yet Wilhelmine had learned to drive a bargain, but it was done with grace and quiet; her eye tutored to catch a short measure, which she always recovered with the charm of a timid smile.

She had a young lad bring in fresh produce from the countryside, beet, carrot, cabbage and turnip in winter months. A sturdy youth, tall and agile, with a frame meant to work the earth, hands roughened by the soil, he was perhaps a year or two older than Wilhelmine but quite as monosyllabic, the slight stutter giving his expression an air of faint anxiety. After each consignment young Bauer would linger in the shop, as though readying himself to give voice to a thought that weighed on his mind. Yet each time the words failed him as he looked around helplessly, finally coming out lamely with some purposeless afterthought: "Next week I'll bring some crab apples," or "We'll be putting down leek this winter."

In time, with familiarity, finally he made so bold as to ask if Wilhelmine ever went out, if she liked dancing, or perhaps she might like to visit their farm. Nothing came of it. The courtship was half-hearted and elliptical, much too vague in speech and hesitant in intention for Wilhelmine to notice. A lifetime later, old gardener Bauer sometimes trudging past the library would look up straining his dim vision and on occasion caught sight of her sitting on the steps, the now heavy-set face wreathed in curls of smoke. There was no salutation, nor recognition by Wilhelmine. Somehow she had always been above him, beyond his humble reach.

11

Wilhelmine was largely untaught, her childhood schooling interrupted early, first by her mother's death, her father's infirmity and the burden of household chores and, later, the tending of the shop to earn the family's keep. Propelled by necessity into adulthood, subtracted from the company of those of her age, her busy days shuttered within the walls of a silent house, she had not learnt nor had the occasion for children's games, running free amidst the guileless giggle and titter of young voices, grooming dolls and playing at little mother. A sort of mother in earnest, housewife and nurse, she had little time for the play and pastimes of the innocent.

From early age Wilhelmine had a singular inclination, that for the written word. Over time it became her tutor and companion, the source of her learning and the world in which she sought refuge from the cares and tedium of her everyday life. As a child she would sit by the window in the shop and in the pale afternoon light streaming in through the glass, intent on a fragment torn from a newspaper or magazine, moving a tiny finger under the lettering she would lisp the sound. Sometimes when a recalcitrant word eluded her grasp, she would quietly call her father who, hobbling over and putting his head next to hers, would read it aloud, tell her the meaning, kiss her on the cheek and return to his work touched by this small fleeting moment of intimacy.

Gessler's own schooling had been minimal. Family circumstances and adverse times had dissuaded the family from providing ample learning, nor had his proficiency as a boy gone beyond mere reading and writing. Not surprisingly, then, like others of his station in life he nursed a solemn respect, if not quite reverence, for learning and the learned. His fond, caressing gaze on Wilhelmine as she sat in the corner perusing and parsing words, scribbling on scraps of paper, he imagined that one day she would go on to higher things, work with books among people of another order, move easily in the realm of the mind.

One afternoon taking her hand he limped slowly up to the library and asked for the loan of a child's storybook. His mother had occasionally read him the odd story, but when he put down Grimm's Tales on the counter, the librarian solicitously suggested with a gentle smile that "Perhaps it might be a bit too grim for the child's age." She fetched from the shelves a little book with pastel illustrations of pixies, fairies and elves, bent down and turned the pages for the little girl to see. Wilhelmine nodded her pleasure and looked up at the kind lady whose tender smile seemed to caress her with a motherly warmth.

It was the gateway to a new world for Wilhelmine as her little feet tripped and skipped towards the library each week, laboriously climbing the broad steps up to the mighty columns fronting the tall hardwood doorway. Inside, in the suffused light filtering down through the glass plates of the roof, in the still quiet peopled only by the mute inhabitants slumbering on the pages of the endless rows of books, she would wander between the shelves keeping the librarian company, the little hand nestling trustful in the warm clasp of the lady's palm.

One day Rebekha Steiner sat Wilhelmine down in the little reading room and, heads bent over the open book, together they read aloud the fabled antics of Aesop's creatures, the little girl pausing to giggle over the colour plate of the fox suspended mid-air under a cluster of grapes, the tiny mouse atop the elephant's mighty hump. It then became an afternoon appointment that Wilhelmine never missed. Once or twice a week, in the empty winter afternoons when there was barely a soul in the library, she would sit in the little room nestling in the warmth of Rebekha's arm as they read together, the child and the woman, an infinity of time between them, brought together by a motherless home and half a lifetime of retreat and solitude.

A quarter of a century after Schenkel had gone, now in her sixties Rebekha Steiner still ran the library, managed the funds of the trust he had set up, looked after the maintenance of the building, the upkeep of the grounds. The position had served her well, her gratitude and loyalty to Schenkel had been amply rewarded, assured her survival. Living in obscurity in an out-of-the-way small town, holding a post coveted by none, her ancestry and antecedents unknown, somehow, perhaps miraculously, she had avoided the malevolent eye whose ferocious reach had decimated those of her tribe.

Sometimes now coming awake at first light, half asleep and casting a fleeting glance at the distant seasons of her life, her mind conjured up dimly the figure of her brother, torchlit like a column of fire among the crackling flames. It seemed to her then that he perhaps had been the first, the precursor of all those others of his kind, the multitude that had later followed and perished in the atrocious furnace of a loathing both fathomless and inexplicable.

But Rebekha rarely dwelt on the past, on the pain and loss of the life left behind in the ashes. Waking this dawn her thoughts turned to Wilhelmine. She found herself filled with a pleased wonder, surprised at how, silently, imperceptibly almost, the child had come in and taken up the long-vacant spaces of her heart. She could only marvel at so precious a gift in this fading season of her life.

12

True to his word and punctual in his promise, Botticelli returned a fortnight later. Neither bold nor hearty, he almost tip-toed into the shop like an intruder in the dark, the spent cigar limp between his lips, his eyes wandering, uncertain. He started when with hurried step Wilhelmine walked around the counter, going towards him with a smile of gladness and greeting.

"Gone!" she said brightly. "All gone"

Botticelli drew back startled. "Gone?" Puzzled, his brow creased, searching out a word that had momentarily escaped him. With a swift gesture as if snatching away something, he asked, "Taken? Stolen?"

Unusually for her, Wilhelmine broke into brief girlish laughter. "No! Sold! I've sold all your cheese. The sausages, too!"

The large bright eyes stilled, he stared at her for a long moment, suspended between credulity and disbelief. "Sold," he said slowly savouring the word like a tasty morsel. Coming, then, to sudden life his sturdy arms closed around her and he swept her off her feet, lifting her high above his short stature. Letting go, setting her down, he planted a resounding kiss on her cheek.

"O bella fanciulla! Meraviglioso! Meraviglioso!" he repeated with boyish elation as Wilhelmine, flushed and surprised, gently disengaged herself from his arms. No one had ever held her so, she had never felt the close press of a man's body, lips so firm and full on her virginal cheek. His sudden burst of joy, the strong clasp of his arms around her lithe body, the flavour of his lips on her skin bathed her with a confused glow, the pallor of her face turning to a warm blush.

She watched through the window as, sleeves rolled up the sturdy forearms, he opened the back of the van, rummaged inside and slowly, carefully filled the hamper with pieces of cheese, strings of sausage. Wilhelmina was struck by the grace of his movements, supple and measured as those of a dancer, so unexpected in one such as he, short of height, roundish in frame. And through the glass she caught, faintly, the slow lilt of the melody he whistled as he went about his work. Wilhelmina felt as though she had known him forever. She did not ask, nor could she tell why.

13

Regular as clockwork he came once a month, summer and winter, in fair weather and foul. Unaware, somewhere in a deep recess of her consciousness the calander turned and the clock ticked, keeping count of the days to his coming. Sometimes, with the snow lying deep on the cobbles and the grey winter afternoon fading, serving customers as they came and went she would glance out to catch sight of the old coloured van, quietly anxious that he would not come. But he always did.

He would bring in fresh stock, she would settle his account. Arriving early, he would linger in the shop, an hour or two, longer on summer days when evening came late and he could leave unhurried. His travels around the country improved his language, he spoke with greater ease, not quite fluent yet but without the hesitance and halting reticence of his first visits. Sometimes he would trip on a word, mangle a phrase, and then he would laugh, and she with him. It made for companionship, she was at ease with him, and he with her.

He would tell her of his travels, recounting his adventures on the road, his misadventures with customers and shops in this town or that city. In time he told her of his country, his home, the town on a great lake set between towering mountains. One day he showed her a postcard photograph and Wilhelmina peered in wonder at the slightly faded old print of tree clad hills, dotted here and there with small red-tiled houses, rising up to long mountain chains cradling a seemingly endless plain of water that curved and turned and vanished out of sight.

In time, too, he told her of his hopes, the dream on which he had set his sights and his heart. Wilhelmina listened, touched by his faith, swept up by his boundless certitude, feeling herself a part of the vision as with arms stretched and the giddy enthusiasm of a lovelorn youth he described the scene. He conjured up a promenade on a water front strung out with the flower-bedecked gardens of villas and mansions of the high and wealthy who idled away long summer months in the balmy air of the becalmed lake. And there, behind a long plate glass front, he would have his spacious, high-ceilinged emporium, the window set out with a display of choice foods, a dozen variety of cheese, legs of ham, glacèed chestnuts, dark chocolate with hazelnut cream filling, bottles of rare wines; smart and knowledgeable assistants serving at the counters, discreetly suggesting, guiding the fastidious clientele, the gourmet and the gourmand, offering what only the palate of the affluent and the few could savour and appreciate.

Flushed from the soaring flight, a little out of breath from painting the dazzling canvas, at length Botticelli lowered his arms, coming down to earth. "One day," he said quietly, adding with a pensive smile, "I'd like you to be there."

"Oh, I'm not sure I'd be allowed into a place like that," Wilhelmine said with coy cheerfulness. And they both laughed, like children when the elves and fairies dance away from the vanishing land of make-believe.

There were times when the weather broke, hastening the evening, bringing the sudden downpour of a storm to come, or the first silent floating flakes of early winter snow. Then Botticelli would put up at the Henschel Gasthaus, staying there the night and passing by in the morning to see Wilhelmine briefly before leaving town. One such afternoon, when Botticelli had tarried mending a punctured tyre and billowing waves of dark clouds loomed in the autumn sky, the first wind rising and raising the dead leaves in a swirl over the cobbled street, without thought or intention Wilhelmine asked, as though she had always done so, if he would come for dinner to the house.

He looked up in surprise from where he sat fitting the tyre. Lips pursed, he nodded, but uncertain, hesitant. "May I?" he asked, seeking assurance, seeking comfort in the wisdom of acceptance, as if on the brink of a momentous decision. His instinct for the unseen and the unsaid was a distant voice that seemed to whisper that it was a turn that would change the course of things. The whispered oracle voice was right.

14

In the year and more that he had come and gone, he had never been beyond the shop. There had been no occasion to enter the house, nor had he set eyes on her father. Now here he was, seated across the table facing the old man, Gessler's pale watery eyes on the stout bottle of wine he had brought, shifting then to Botticelli himself, holding him in a still, wordless gaze that expressed neither query nor curiosity, if anything perhaps a sort of vague wonder that his Wilhelmine had brought this stranger into the house, to his table.

As Wilhelmine finished in the kitchen and readied to serve the dinner, Botticelli's attempts at conversation appeared to fall on deaf ears, his still modest command of the language faltering, the words laboriously strung together failing in coherence. Gessler's head occasionally gave the merest nod, only once his face uncreased with the dim pleasure of a smile, when Botticelli's disorderly speech expressed admiration for Wilhelmine's acumen and work in running the shop. Gessler seemed to mellow then, emerging from his stillness to thank Botticelli as he poured the wine, going quite so far as to raise the glass before a taking a sip and emitting a small sound of contentment.

It was a quiet evening, the homely repast wholesome and simple, for Wilhelmine had not had a mother to teach and train her in the ways of the kitchen, nor had her busy adolescence left time to hone her skills at the stove. She served the two men, helped herself sparingly, spoke to each in turn, gentle and kindly with her father, amiable with Botticelli, bringing the table together in the manner of a family that dined together each evening. It confused Botticelli, for this was not the Wilhelmine he had seen and known these many months.

He looked around the room and saw the remains of better times, the solid furniture carved and polished, the heavy brocade drapes now faded with age, the fine china on the table, the weight and feel of the cutlery in his hand. He himself came from a different order, rustic, laborious, rough-hewn in manner and living, his family table never spread with such fine linen albeit the floral patterns now dulled with wear.

Out of the corner of his eye he watched Wilhelmine as she moved about, removing the dishes, bringing in a small cut-glass bowl of fruit, patting the cushion on the bulky leather armchair by the sideboard where her father would recline after his meals. It surprised him. No longer was she the shy, awkward girl he had often seen in the shop. Here she was mother, housewife, keeper of the home, brisk and assured, a whole grown woman at ease with herself and with her world.

And there and then, in the span of a fleeting moment, like a chrysalis giving sudden and miraculous birth to the iridescent wings of a new life, Botticelli felt within him the first timid flutter of something light and ineffable. Until now theirs had been a friendship of sorts, amiable and casual, with neither earnestness nor afterthought. Or so it had been for him. Without notice, now of a sudden Wilhelmine, the woman his eyes beheld, became a vision in his mind, setting in motion thoughts, the first far echoes of nascent desire.

When later they went down the stairs and she saw him out at the front door, Botticelli was oddly subdued, confused by the indefinable stirring within. Thanking her quietly, awkward and hasty, he briefly pressed his lips to her cheek. She watched from the doorway as he went out into the night and down the street, the still quiet broken by the hollow dragging steps of a drunk on the far pavement.

15

The dark past now rapidly receding into history, with changing times and the certain promise of better days, Botticelli's business prospered. His journeys became more frequent, he took to touring and visiting clients at fortnightly intervals rather than once a month. He extended the range of supplies to legs of ham, smoked meats, wine. And some months later he got himself a new van, still painted red, white and green but with his name printed large on the sides.

Now, too, fair weather or foul, on each visit he stayed back, putting up for the night at Henschel's Gasthaus and in the evening dining with Wilhelmine and her father, bringing to the table not only bottles of wine but also fine slices of cured meat, boxes of dry figs, almond biscuits. Imperceptibly he had slipped into the Gessler household, almost a family member, at ease with his surroundings, solicitous with the old man, gentle and courteous with Wilhelmine.

Her father had come to accept Botticelli, as one would a neighbour or some long-lost young relative, looking at him with a sort of pensive benevolence as he sat across the table. Time had stopped for Gessler years ago, the hands of the clock merely presented a mechanical feat, so that he would enquire after Botticelli before he arrived or soon after he had left town, asking "Is your man coming this evening?" Wilhelmine shied away from the possessive, merely nodding her head timidly.

Wilhelmine was punctilious with the accounts, settling Botticelli's bill to the last penny. Increasingly he took the payments with a kind of awkward reluctance, hesitant, embarrassed almost. "Please give it to me later," he would say. "Later when?" she asked levelling her gaze. "Afterwards." She ignored his lame procrastination, pressing the money into his hands.

Trade was trade and she had not forgotton the vision he had conjured up that afternoon, of his grand emporium by the lakeside that was to cater to the refined gluttony of the rich. Once she told him as much and, touched, breaking into a soft smile, he reached to brush her cheek, saying "You remember?" "One always remembers good dreams," she said smiling down at him. She thought the words came from her reading, the one constant passion she still nourished through this new distraction that had made its way into her heart.

She asked her father but he gave no sign of assent, nor did he object. He lived his days in her penumbra and she could do no wrong wherever she chose to shine her light. So the room behind the shop which had lain damp and empty was given to Botticelli to store his stout rounds of cheese, hang the legs of ham and store the wine whose sales had gone fourfold in a matter of months. "That way you don't have drive all the way home every few days," Wilhelmine said. And in one corner of the shop she placed a small table with drawers where he kept his papers and accounts. Seated there of a late afternoon, before the shop closed, doing his sums he would watch her move about, tidying the shelves, putting things in order. If only! he thought to himself, feeling the weighted throb of a melancholy heart.

16

This year the summer was long, as though the sun had decided it would banish the seasons and shine on forever. As early as April the weather had turned clement, the days radiant, the evenings mellow, fragrant with the burst of new leaves, flowers blooming fast and busy as if answering some secret and hurried call.

It was the summer of Wilhelmine's twenty-first year. She had come of age. But the call of her heart had taken her beyond mere chronology. Still shy and retiring, certainly, for nature had gifted her so. But like a plant taking sure root, her inner self had found the strength of a courage she had not known before, discovered intent and purpose beyond the caring for her father, keeping house and managing the shop. She had not known men as companion, friend or lover, the sinuous whisper of desire, the vigour of an arm encircling her body. These were still beyond her imagining. What was newfound was an awakening, the silent recurrence of a distant longing that had neither colour nor shape nor sound. It was not a visitation in the dark of the night or in the depths of her sleep; rather, a slow, soundless unfurling, much as a flower wakes to meet the first light.

Rebekha Steiner noticed. She knew Wilhelmine, had known her since childhood. Had they not come from such disparate walks of life and so distant in time, she would have been a second mother to the young girl. Mother she had not been, but mentor of Wilhelmine spirit, tutor and distant guardian of her mind. So that one day in the library, as Wilhelmine sorted through books to take home, Rebekha looked at her in intent silence, saying then "You are happy, Wilma." Wilhelmine looked up in surprise, understood, pressed her lips in a timid smile and nodded. Rebekha did not ask why, merely caressed the auburn head with her ageing hand. She loved Wilhelmine, only as one who is not but could have been the mother that loves a child.

A week later, hurrying towards the library, in the haze of the late afternoon light Rebekha saw Wilhelmine standing by the lake in the park, with Botticelli beside her, his arm resting light around her waist. When next Wilhelmine came to the library to return the books, she asked gently, "Is that your man, Wilhelmine?" Emboldened by her newfound strength, she looked into Rebekha's eyes and nodded assent, without hesitation, timourless, yet not without a flutter in her heart which soundlessly asked: Is he, is he your man? "I think he is," she added softly, lowering her eyes. Tried by the chimera of life's blind saraband, Rebekha glimpsed the faltering moment and reaching out to take Wilhelmine's hand she almost whispered, saying "Be happy, dearest!"

With his stock stored at the Gessler house, returning home only occasionally, no more than once a month, Botticelli came into town oftener than he ever had, filling his van every few days and staying overnight on each visit. Regular as a boarder he dined at the Gessler's table and, afterwards, arm in arm with Wilhelmine they went out into the bright twilight of the lengthening summer evening, looking into the shop windows that now displayed the small comforts of life, strolling in the park, sitting on a bench by the little lake watching the eternal pair of swans duck and pirouette in their tireless ballet.

He said Wilhelmine was too long a name, too much of a mouthful, and called her Wilma. He was Enrico, she called him Rico, which was what went in his family. They made an odd, even unlikely couple, she tall and willowy, he a good head shorter, stocky and compact. She still wore her mother's clothes, loose-fitting and floral-patterned, sartorial vestiges of another age. He was smarter now, a white open-neck shirt with collars spread like bird's wings over the lapels of a trimly-cut light jacket, trousers to match.

People in the town gawked, the gossips gossiped. There had not been another familiar stranger in the town since Ilse Krause's sailor man. Ilse's sailor being a sailor had drunk, caroused, mingled with the men in the beerhouse, recounted atrocious and uproarious tales, made people laugh and cry into their beer mugs, in time he had become a mascot of good cheer and jollity. Not so with Botticelli, he was a shade more sunburnt, his hair much too dark, he confined his presence largely to the Gessler house, coming and going almost in stealth.

There was something vaguely suspect about him, thought Frau Klagges the most suspicious of the gossips. "He'll make off with the girl one of these days," she confirmed. They had seen Wilhelmine since childhood, apparent concern for her safety was paramount in their thoughts. Frau Schiedermair who always wore a single pea-hen feather in her hat, and had done so ever since she had capped her oblong head with a hat, was categoric: "Then she'll be sold!" "And sold well!" exclaimed Frau Klinger whose task it was to round off whatever the thesis and add the finishing touch.

Widow Ansel was different. Not a particularly regular member of the gossip circle and often a dissident one, the wisdom of her concern came from her true life story, her husband having gone off some years ago with a Macedonian lady and drowned in the Aegean soon after. In the shop one day she stared at Botticelli's Parmesan wedges under the glass. "Foreign," she muttered to herself; looking up then and contemplating Wilhelmine thoughtfully, in motherly tones she added, "I think, dear, it's best to stick to one's own kind." The veiled alimentary allegory was not lost on Wilhelmine. She nodded with a submissive smile as widow Ansel asked for a small piece pointing at the stout roll of Kochwurst.

Heedless of the prying eyes and censorious looks of the gossiping crones, her guileless nature unable to admit the unkind voice of the wagging tongues, Wilhelmine went her way comforted by her father's benevolent neutrality, sustained by Rebekha's motherly contentment for her new-found felicity. And she was oddly happy that Botticelli had even found a friend, with little Fritz from next door keeping him company as he came and went, helping him unload the van, his boyish babble loquacious and ceaseless, as if they were equals and had known each other for ever.

One day watching the boy and the man as with play and laughter the two scrubbed the side of the van, unawares, like the tide soundlessly lapping the shore, Wilhelmina found her thoughts touched with a vague, indecipherable longing for a home with voices, the sound of running feet, play and mirth.

Theirs was friendship and companionship. They held hands, he wound his arm around her slender waist, smoothed her auburn tresses, held her briefly against him. She stooped to rest her head against his, caressed his cheek. There was ardour in their touch, patient longing in the fleeting kisses, desire in wait in the press of their bodies. But they were not intimate. Wilhelmine sometimes felt that something unsaid, doubt or reserve, held him back. Her womanhood silently sought possession, he appeared to hold back, masking passion with affection and tenderness, marking the distance with grace and respect.

One warm summer night, returning after a long stroll in the town, standing at the doorway to bid him goodnight, abrupt and unthinking Wilhelmine said, "One day you'll not come back!"

Botticelli was taken aback. He looked up, querying her expression. She had never before questioned his good faith, never doubted nor demanded, and he had let things be, complacent in the warmth and comfort of their friendship, almost as if shying away from wading into deeper and uncharted waters.

"Why do you say that?" he asked with innocent surprise.

"You'll not come back," she repeated. She said it quietly, meekly even, without plaint or force, as though stating a mere fact, a prescience that was certain, that one day would come true.

"Never!" Vehement in denial, he seemed to be cut to the quick, wounded in his pride, his honour put to the test. "Never!" A sense of bravado overcame him. Brash and heedless, unthinking of the entanglements of his own life he said, "Alright! I'll ask your father, if that's what you want. I'll ask him!"

And when he did, the old man was neither surprised nor concerned, as if the question had to do with some everyday matter, mundane and without weight. His dim, watery eyes looked past Botticelli, towards a nebulous distance where his sight sought nothing in particular. At length, he lowered his head, fixing the cutlery on the table in a contemplation that appeared to call for immense effort. "You are a good man, Enrico," he murmured, then raising his gaze and nodding with certitude he added, "You'll take care of her."

17

Wilma and Rico became man and wife on a late summer day. Much to the dudgeon of the Pastor, they were married at the municipal office, for Rico was of Roman faith and Pastor Steinitzer was unyielding in his Lutheran creed.

Presiding over the brief ceremony, blind in one eye and with occasional double vision in the other, old Burgomaster Huschke was disconcerted by the sight of two grooms, Botticelli being doubled by his straining retina. Troubled by the thought of sanctioning a bigamous union, he drew out the short civil sermon to reiterate that marriage was a bond between solely one man and one woman, and no more, and would have gone on repeating the severe limit set out by law and custom had he not turned his head and caught sight of Rebekha Steiner who was to give the bride away. Satisfied then that it was a double wedding, the two grooms each having a bride, he pronounced the twin couples man and wife.

Only Rebekha and little Fritz were at the station to see the newly-wedded off. As Wilhelmine leant out of the carriage window to wave and the station slowly receded, with beating heart she felt the past fall away, a lifetime, her childhood and maiden years vanish in the haze of the afternoon light.

As the train steamed across the vast plain, nestling in Rico's arm, looking out through the wide window of the carriage, catching glimpses of towns and cities, long swathes of forest green, Wilhelmine was filled with wonder, thinking how little she had seen of her land, the enormous spaces gifted by the providence of nature, inhabited sparsely by man and his works.

To be sure, the fleeting landscape of water and woods, spires and hamlets, fields of corn and barley bathed in the gold of the afternoon sun, these she had read of in books, imagined and seen distantly as in a vision. And as in a dream, too, she felt the warmth of her husbands body as he held her close, the strong arms girding her waist, hands entwined. She felt his breath in her hair as he spoke to her, the brush of his lips against her ear. The vista of the world racing past outside seemed to echo the geography of her new-found life, with sensations and stirrings read of and culled from books but till now unknown to her, unfelt and novel.

It was a long journey, half a day and the better part of a night, first across an endlessly flat and even country, giving way to an undulating land of meadows and pastures and then, when darkness fell, over wooded hills and through mountains looming stark against the indigo blue of the night sky speckled with the merest pearl sliver of a nascent moon, to descend finally through rough-hewn ground broken by lake and river. At break of day, stealthy and imperceptible the salt of the sea wafted through the carriage and Rico caressing her head as it rested on his shoulder said, "Soon now. We'll be there."

Wilhelmine thought that it could not be but a dream as the train rattled over the causeway and with sleep-laden eyes she looked out at the watery city grow to life, the morning light casting a silken sheen on the lagoon out of which rose clusters of buildings with tiled roofs, towers and steeples and domes in the distance bathed in dull gold, magical and miraculous. The whistle blew and Rico's head pressed against Wilhelmine's he said this was the dream he had meant as his wedding gift.

Awed and entranced, warm and secure in the intimacy of his nearness, watching the sea and the sky and the flight of seagulls, white and weightless, like so many prayers from heaven, swoop down to skim over the water, she asked: "Can anyone gift a dream?" Bold and playful "I can!" he said. Spoken in jest but he was right, she thought. An ethereal vision such as this could only be given, bestowed and entrusted, to be stored away and cherished.

18

They lodged at a pensione not far from the station, overlooking a quiet canal whose still waters mirrored the lichen covered walls of houses that turned and wound away out of sight. The lady of the house, a stout matronly figure with large grey-blue eyes, dressed in black, opened the Venetian shutters, then at the far end of the room a door to a tiny balcony that gave onto the canal below and the morning coming off the water filled the room with a suffused light. Concerned and motherly she eyed Wilhelmine.

"So thin!" she exclaimed turning to Rico. "We'll have to put some meat on those bones!" she laughed, her voice high, melodic with the cantilena of a lullabye. "Now you'll want to be left alone," and with all the lightness and grace of an operatic dancer she almost tip-toed out of the room.

"People here don't talk. They sing!" Rico said, secure and at ease with himself in a familiar world, as he held his bride in his arms, in the embrace of a homecoming. This moment, in the unfamiliar world of this strange and radiant city afloat on water, through the miasma of ardour and the ache of longing, oddly Wilhelmine felt that she too had at long last reached her mooring.

She knew the city, peopled only on the pages of books. The traveller who had wandered infinitely towards the ends of the eastern world and returned a decade and a half later only to find the door of his home barred. The melancholy story of the man and the boy entwined in the mysterious longing of a fatal passion. And Rebekha had played to her on the gramophone in the library the briskly sensuous and scintillating music of the red-headed priest.

But she had never set eyes on the sea, nor breathed its salt. Now escaped from the narrow confines of her home and the small town of her birth, released from the heart's empty echo, standing on the moated edge looking out towards the open waters, the great dome of the church across the bay, the steel prow of a gold and black funeral gondola ploughing soundless through the rippled surface, she was filled with wonder at the artefacts that man's hand had so laboriously moulded into a second Creation.

Turning away then, hand in hand they strolled across the immense square guarded by winged lions on columns and facades, giant bronze figures that struck the hour in the enamelled clock tower, little round tables set out row on row on the worn stones of the patterned floor and the ceaseless swerving and sweep of the flocks of pigeons alighting and dispersing like torn pages in the wind. Wilhelmine was filled with an elation, replete and wordless, that her spirit had never known, neither as a girl nor as woman.

Lunch was at the pensione, with the signora fussing over her, heaping her plate with the motherly encouragement of "Mangia! Mangia!", turning to Rico with her sing-song enquiery "Are they all as lean and starved where she comes from?" which he graciously translated for her as "She wants to know if everyone is as beautiful where you come from." Wilhelmine looked up at the lady with a faint blush, for compliments were not given out with such ease where she came from.

In the evenings they set out for the quieter interior, away from the throngs of visitors, down the dimly-lit cobbled lanes of the quarters where the people of the town lived, the vine-covered balconies hung with washing, the twilight chirping of birds in cages hung from windows, cats padding stealthily by the walls. Sure-footed, Rico navigated the winding streets, under archways and over small stone bridges, coming out into a paved square lit with small shop windows, and led the way into some tavern unexpectedly alive, redolent with smoke and voices, talk and easy laughter.

Sat at a corner table for two, surrounded by labourers still in their overalls, the loud company of sturdy workmen with hearty appetites, served by a bustling red-headed young girl who sang her words, came and went with a smile here, a banter there, they dined off abundant plates, Wilhelmine vainly protesting the portions, Rico laughing as he lifted the carafe to pour generously the pale red wine, saying "More meat on those bones, as the signora said!" Emboldened by the spirit of the place, the air of good companionship, she shook her head vigorously, asking "Would you prefer me as round as her?" He reached to take her hand, kissing the fingertips. "No," he said both solemn and tender. "Just as you are!"

There was passion in his possession, certainly, strength and ardour when on the first day of their arrival and for the very first time their bodies had met and entwined, released from the bondage of a desire so long denied and held at bay. Yet there was a sort of gravity, reticent and thoughtful, even as he took her, held her slender, supple body tight, as though something in him refused the total abandon of mind and spirit that the pounding flesh called for.

Wilhelmine could neither see nor divine, for her part she could only yield, hastening towards a fulfilment longed for and nurtured over so many seasons. Afterwards, in the days that followed, when the first timidity was gone, when the landscape of his body had become familiar to her eyes, the efflorescence of her desire encircled him without modesty or reserve, so that she clung to him, liquescent and demanding. He lent himself to her urgency, meeting the cry that rose from her body. And yet, secreted within, aloof and inscrutable, there lurked the same elusive spirit, the same withdrawal from unreserved surrender. An uncertainty of will or intent sparked by some distant pain or guilt seemed to linger like drifts of mist in some obscure recess of his mind.

The days flew by, the week of their stay was almost over. On the last day but one, he took her to the Lido. Summer's end and the holiday crowds had mostly gone. Strolling along the promenade, passing the straw-hatted men and parasoled ladies, Wilhelmine gazed out over the open waters towards the haze of the shoreless horizon, mesmerized by the immutable blue of the sea, new and mysterious to her eyes, as was the ineffable happiness of her new-born life.

She glanced at Rico. Unlike his usual self, the accustomed lightness and gaity absent, he looked thoughtful, the dark pensive eyes shaded with melancholy as he looked out wordless at the becalmed sea. She took his arm, drawing him to her. "What are you thinking? Will you tell me?"

"Oh! Nothing much."

"Tell me about the nothing much!" she insisted smiling. "Are you worried?"

"Just the future," he said quietly, humbly almost.

"Oh! The future comes to us. To all of us, Rico."

"Perhaps it has already," he said, his voice oddly tired, seemingly burdened with a weight that pressed down on his spirit. But living as he did mostly in the realm of hope, gloom did not come to him easily or for long. Abruptly brightening, he wound his arms around her. "Enough of this!" he exclaimed. "I have something special for you."

During their stay he had bought her small gifts, lace doilies, an embroidered table centre-piece, a collection of tiny animal figures moulded from mere droplets of crystalline glass. Now he led the way through the quiet back streets, turned to an ancient wooden doorway and ushered her into a darkened interior.

Coming in from daylight, blinded by the sudden darkness, Wilhelmine shut her eyes for an instant. When sight returned, she found herself in a twilight world lit with the luminous red glow of a dozen small fires around which hovered dim silhouetted figures, their soundless movements agile and sure, the gestures imbued with the grace of an age-old ritual, as though these men had been here forever, going through the same immemorial motions.

As Wilhelmine's eyes grew accustomed to the half-light, she now saw clearly the large hall with high, grated windows, the men at work, twirling and twisting a thin translucent rod over a furnace here, blowing through a tubular length there, wielding tongs with expert and gentle hands, the shaping of a burning goblet as if created by the sacred fires of heaven, the moulding of a slender swan-necked vase burnished with the fiery red of molten lava.

Rico had spoken to a tall, elderly grey-haired man and now beckoned her to his side. Spellbound Wilhelmina watched as the end of the glass rod caught fire, turning the colour of an angry sun, and then the wizard hand reaching out, nimbly working a pair of tongs, artfully teasing and drawing at the fierce matter to mould fine long petal shapes, gently forcing to turn a curl, impress a vein. A slight nod from the old wizard summoned a bright-eyed lad who with a swift sleight of hand embellished the slender curling petals with a purple fairy dust, when the miraculous blossom of man's ingenuity was returned to the furnace.

Long after, half a lifetime and more, when the memory of that brief week in the city of waters had faded to a nebulous recollection, when the beating heart had stilled and the winter of time robbed the last warmth of an already spent passion, the crystal iris still stood in its white ceramic vase on the small table by Wilhelmine's bed.

Some rare morning now, waking early, the sleep-laden eyes catching a misty glimpse of the fine, wrinkle-edged purple petals, her hand still reaches out between the empty sheets, as it had on that last Venetian dawn, finding then the touch of fulfilment.

19

Outwardly Wilhelmine's life changed little, if at all. She still tended the shop, nursed her father, managed the household. Rico's demands were few and modest, clothes to be washed and put away, the odd button to be sewn, a pair of shoes to be taken to cobbler Freitag for new soles; an extra place at table, setting out a glass for his grappa after dinner.

Wilhelmine took for herself and Rico the bedroom at the back of the house, which had been her parents' and had lain empty and shut since her mother's death. It was a large airy room that opened out on a green at the end of which stood the old mill. On warm evenings Rico often sat on the window sill with his little cigar, watching the light fade over the western sky, the mill silhouetting to a dark hulk.

Old Essler put to bed, her chores done, Wilhelmine would join him, her arms around his neck as occasionally he proferred the cigarillo which she drew on with an excess of zeal, pouring out between a cough and a hiccup a long stream of smoke that caught the night air and drifted out into the dark. Sometimes they sat there long, close and touching, but silent. Oddly, Rico who had once been voluble and spirited had become less so since their marriage, not quiet taciturn or morose, but often reflective with a hint of melancholy, as though at a remove from where he found himself. Wilhelmine noticed and quietly wondered.

She knew so little of him, his family and antecedents. In the early days he had shown her a faded postcard of the town he came from, the red-tiled houses, the oleander fenced villas on the waterfront, the vast lake flanked by tall mountains, the site of his erstwhile dream of an emporium filled with the finest produce man's palate could savour.

Once, before their marriage, sat by the fireside in the evening after dinner, he had extracted a small photograph from his wallet of a grey-haired elderly woman stood in front of an old stone farmhouse and looking away from the camera, the ageing lineaments bearing a recognizable resemblance to Rico's, the same large dark eyes, the same full lips, the rounded chin. Herself motherless since almost infancy, Wilhelmine felt touched by an odd tenderness as she looked at the image of the old lady. Reaching out she took his hand as he lightly pressed the picture to his lips before putting it back in the folds of the wallet.

Then again, once he had mentioned an elder sister, married and gone far away across the seas with her man. Maddalena he had called her, Magdalene to Wilhelmine, she liked the name but Rico carried no image of her. And save for a passing mention of a father killed when he was a mere child, by "your people" he had added quietly, without vehemence, there was little else. But it was not in Wilhelmine's nature to pry and delve, look back or beyond. It did not matter. She had taken him as he stood, for what he was and what he meant to her. One day she would see his mother, she thought, the house he was born in, the streets he had roamed as a boy.

For herself it was a time of grace, fulfilment such as she had never expected nor imagined. Her heart satisfied beyond measure, replete, she could not have asked for more, would not have asked for other than what she had. Behind the façade of her daily life, her father, the shop, the house, the landscape of her inner self had changed beyond recognition, no longer timid and retiring but bold and assured, as if with Rico's coming into her life she had stumbled on the hidden storehouse of a spirit that had dwelt within unknown to her. And with the release of the genie came the dawn of her womanhood, amity and intimacy with her own body, freeing her and setting her off on a journey of discovery, of desire and the secret interstices of its fulfilment, of the mind's longing and the ache of the flesh enmeshed inextricably. Lying in Rico's arms, her breath subsiding, Wilhelmine sometimes felt that heaven could grant nothing more nor greater.

20

Rico came and went as before, driving his van and plying his trade, stopping over for a day or two, rarely an entire week. At intervals he would be away a whole fortnight to fetch fresh stocks, visit his mother. Wilhelmine missed his presence then, absent-minded as she served her customers, idly wandering about the house in the evenings as if in expectation of coming on him of a sudden. Her father abed, she would light one of his Tuscan cigars, sit on the window sill looking out at the night and the silent congregation of slumbering clouds pale in the light of an early moon. Turning then in bed at dawn in somnolent search for the comfort of his presence.

Rico's tos and fros did not go down well with the gossip circle, now vexed by his refusal to play the part of the foreign scoundrel assigned to him. His refusal to abduct Wilhelmine, to sell her off subsequently, had come as a sore disappointment. Frau Klagges was impenitent, still hopeful for the worst. "That man will do it yet. Give him time, dear," she assured Frau Schiedermair who adjusting the pea-hen feather in her hat added, "No doubt about it, none at all!" Frau Klinger rounded off the allegation exclaiming, "Any night now!"

Unknown to Rico and Wilhelmine, their union had caused a bitter rift between the tattling ladies and widow Ansel, which led to a parting of ways. The widow recalling the happiness of the early years of her marriage, before her husband had eloped with the Macedonian lady and drowned in the Aegean, wished the young couple well, her benevolence raising a snort from Frau Klagges as she hissed "From you of all people! Some of us never learn." For quite some time after, crossing paths in the street, the two women looked away without the least sign of recognition. By way of benediction widow Ansel even bought a small wedge of Rico's cheese, although it strained her household finances not a little.

The weeks and months added up to an entire year and with Rico still refusing to abduct his spouse, the aggrieved ladies found in his absences fresh cause for complaint. "A man and wife are meant to live together," Frau Klagges asserted severely. "Each and every day of their lives. Together!" added Frau Siedermair trying to straighten the broken pea-hen feather. "And die together!" Frau Klinger nodded in conclusion with such vigour that it caused a painful crick in her neck.

Death did indeed visit the Essler household soon after. Wilhelmine's father had not been keeping well and that winter, a long cruel season of icy rain, snow and unremitting cold that chilled the marrow, pale and gaunt the old man lay in bed day after day, inert and oblivious. There was no discernable malady, neither pain nor sufferance. Without remedy, adrift in an unknown region, his eyes rested quietly on Wilhelmine as she held his hand sitting by his bedside, as though with the wordless gaze he wished to take his leave, relinquish his place in the family now that his Wilhelmine was secure in the care and protection of a man of her own. In life Essler had never known the language of attachment and affection, never had the words of endearment to match the intense love he bore for this his only child. It was an abundant vein that had remained hidden and unmined.

21

Freed of the encumbrance, for loving him as she did concern for her father's well-being had always burdened her mind, Wilhelmine now came into the entire possession of her life. With his death the past fell off, receding to memory and remembrance. She could at last turn her gaze ahead, attend to the future. The house was hers and she could choose to make of it the home she wished. Rico was no longer the live-in husband but lover and companion in his own right.

Once again Wilhelmine's life experienced a sea-change. Rico's demands were few and none at all during his regular absences, while her father's needs had been many. With him now gone, she again had time for the world of the mind, a passion that had fallen into neglect since her marriage. Once again she had time to keep Rebekha company, talk of the books she had read, wander among the shelves of the library leafing through those yet to be read, listen to Rebekha recount fragments of the past, her Berlin childhood, her father's passion and reverence for antique volumes.

With Rico she could not share the intangible, the taste and texture of the immaterial. The hieroglyphics of the realm of the mind meant nothing to him. Earthbound, he understood matter, felt and savoured the primal sentiments that moved man. But as with Wilhelmine's father, his modest upbringing had imbued him with respect for the written word, the world of learning and the learned. Seeing her engrossed in her reading he would busy himself elsewhere in the house. In the evenings dutifully he would wait for her to finish the page, the chapter before claiming attention and possession.

Wilhelmine now lived in two separate but somehow contiguous worlds, both enclosed in her being, complementary, each nourishing the other. Her mind succoured and satisfied, she sought in Rico love and only what the living could offer, the fulfilment of the yearning of her body. Careful not to draw him towards regions unknown and alien to him, she in turn gave generously only that which he could comprehend, care, intimacy and amity.

It was a year of immense grace, days and nights so perfect, each offering its separate fulfilment, that had time and the world stood still and Wilhelmine gone down the days to the end of her life, she would have wished for nothing more nor different, not a single hour changed, not a single page altered.

"Wouldn't it be wonderful, Rebekha, if things stayed as they are?" she said one day. But Rebekha knew better. "All books would then end with the first chapter!" she said lightly. "Besides, you would soon tire if the world stood still." Wilhelmine shook her head girl-like in denial but not quite convinced. And in silence each thought of the changes in her life, the intricate and labyrinthine paths that had brought them here, sitting close together on the steps of the library, looking out at the becalmed summer afternooon.

22

It was in the third year of their marriage that Rico's absences grew noticeably longer as going back to replenish his stocks and visit his mother he was away for weeks, on occasion an entire month. Wilhelmine waited, worried, missed his coming and going each day, missing too the sturdy hold of his arms around her each time he entered the house.

When finally he returned, in her celebration of his homecoming she forgot the brief abandonment, welcoming him without complaint or reprove, offering him the small accustomed comforts of home, the familiarity of her body. Rico proferred no explanation but afterwards, the ritual of passion performed and desire consumed, seeing in her eyes a look of silent query, vague and distant he would murmur about difficulties at home, problems with suppliers, a half-hearted litany of which he himself seemed little convinced, nor was it meant to convince. Wilhelmine did not press him, content and grateful that once again he was with her, her inner self wanting the world to hold still, unchanging and perennial.

But Rico she noticed had changed, of late almost shying away from her at times, distancing himself not from her presence but withdrawing from the unspoken intimacies of shared lives. It baffled her. As though rebuked by some furtive guilt or shame, as if seeking atonement, he preferred courtesy where previously there had been closeness, deference in place of nearness. And when Wilhelmine took him in her arms, drew him into herself, at times he met her with a passion that seemed tinged with the melancholy of regret, perhaps remorse.

That last autumn, Wilhelmine unable to read, decipher Rico's malaise, herself disquited, watching as if from afar the decay of their love, increasingly felt a sense of helplessness. There was no apparent cause, there was nothing she could ask or ascertain, nothing for which she could take him to task. Outwardly, in their daily lives, he was still very much the man she had known, attentive and thoughtful, undemanding. He held her as he always had, close and enfolding, tenanting her body and spirit with the same ardour and abandon, so that breathless in the night, she clung to him, thinking to hold him and the world still, quiescent and secure.

At the door, seeing him off as he left once again, something impalpable overcame Wilhelmine. Abrupt and unthinking, she asked, "Shall I come with you? I'd like to see your mother."

Startled, Rico looked up at her, pausing then as if trying to find a way out of her gaze. "What about the shop?" he asked hurriedly. "You can't shut it."

"We can!" Trying to make light of it, she added "It's ours after all."

Rico lowered his eyes, apologetic, grieved almost. "No, not now," he said softly. "You know she's not well."

She took his hand and held it against her cheek. "Take care and come back. Soon. It doesn't matter if you can't get all the things. There's enough here."

She could not tell afterwards how long they held each other in the pale autumn morning sun. And as the van sped off down the street, little Fritz from next door, who had grown almost to her shoulder and was friends with Rico more than ever, joined her at the doorway. "He'll be gone a long time," he said in his still squeaky, child's voice. "I wish he wasn't gone at all," Wilhelmine almost whispered in a prayer of bereavement.

23

Rico was gone a full month, and then another. Wilhelmine had expected him back for Christmas but the Infant was born and the day gone and a flurry of snow had ushered in the new year and still he had not come, nor sent news. Distraught and lost Wilhelmine turned to Rebekha.

"He's ill," said Wilhelmine. "He needs me."

"He's with his people."

Unusually, and for the very first time since they had known each other, Wilhelmine turned on her sharply. "And I?" she asked with vehemence almost, the rage of desolation. She broke then, as Rebekha took her hand. "I'm sorry, I didn't mean that. Please forgive me!"

Wilhelmine laid her head on Rebekha's shoulder and wept fitfully as the aged hand caressed her. Long ago, in another life, Rebekha had known men, had loved and been loved in return, had hoped then for the familiar world of marriage and home. It had not come about, betrayed by the times she had fled in loss and distress, taking with her only the shards of her dreams. This though was different and, like a helpless mother with an afflicted child without hope of healing, she could not find the words to comfort, reassure, hold up a lantern to light the path ahead. As Wilhelmine sobbed in her embrace she could only offer the warmth of her affection and a prayer from the heart.

It was a long winter, longer than any Wilhelmine had known. Each morning she rose and resumed the rounds of her daily life, the hands of the clock moved, the dates on the calendar came and went, but it seemed to her that time had wearied of its own motion, permeating her with the same weariness as she kept the shop, checked orders and accounts, fed herself indifferently at the empty table, laid down her comfortless spirit on the vacant bed. Through the ebb and tide of love's misery, the interminable days of waiting, hoping and hope betrayed, Rebekha soothed and sustained her, drawing her attention away towards the world of imagination, books, music, drawing her into the unrevealed folds of her own life.

People in the town noticed, word was out that Wilhelmine's husband had not been seen in months. Passing in the street the curious peered through the shop window. The regulars who gave the shop custom and knew Wilhelmine were now kinder, more gentle, as though commiserating with a grief in the family, as in the aftermath of her father's death. Not so Frau Klagges, who declared with utmost satisfaction, "I told you so. Never trust these strangers!" "No, never! Never!" concurred Frau Siedermair who had replaced the broken pea-hen feather with one from a guinea-fowl and now flaunted the novelty by continually turning her head this way and that. "Safer to trust a snake," Frau Klinger declaimed, pronouncing the last word on the subject with the authority of an expert.

24

It was the last day of March, a gusty afternoon, the brisk wind carelessly shredding the lightly clouded sky, the late winter chill still loitering in the air. Wilhelmine looked at the small envelope, addressed in a poor hand, the lettering disorderly. She shut the shop, ran upstairs and sat on the edge of the bed, staring in trepidation at the irregular lettering on the grey square of paper, unable to tear it open, almost as if of a sudden she had lost the sense of movement. Long minutes later, when the flush of panic had receded and her breath had slowed, she extracted the letter, tearing off a corner for the envelope was a size too small.

"*Carisimma…*" Wilhelmine had learnt small fragments of Rico's tongue, random words, names of objects, phrases frequently uttered by him. But it would not suffice to read, understand the contents of the letter short as it was.

She took it to Rebekha, who knew several languages, fluent in two or three. They sat in the little reading room to the side, which had become a sort of retreat for Wilhelmine when she came to the library. Rebekha read through the letter in silence, put down the small lined sheet on the table and looked up. Wilhelmine pale and expectant, her eyes imploring, reached and took her hand, holding it fast and firm. "Please tell me," she pleaded in a small voice. "Is he well? Will you read it to me?" Rebekha nodded, picked up the letter and read, softly, gently, as though the words had the power to wound, translating line by line and pausing inbetween.

"Dearest,

    I ask your forgiveness for not having written earlier. You will have been worried and this has saddened me much. I had wanted to write but things are very difficult here, many problems in the family. I cannot explain them now, the situation is very complicated.

You have always been very good to me, given me much. I have not forgotten and will never forget. I want to be there with you, as we have been in these years. One day, if God so wills, when things are better I'll come back to you.

Look after yourself. I always think of you.

Kisses and an embrace from your

Rico"

A couple of people had come into the library and Rebekha went to attend to them. Wilhelmine looked out at the faint, almost colourless blue of the afternoon sky swept clean by the high March wind. She had wanted the world to hold still, she thought, and now her prayer had been amply granted. But it was the stillness of atrophy, like the gaunt winter trees outside, still leafless, which the wind could not move or shake. She had wanted the promise of unchanging fullness, not this limbo of waiting in the dark.

She wiped the slow tears and picked up the letter. She had understood the words, but not their meaning. She understood there were problems, his gratitude, his desire to be with her. She could not grasp the measure of their significance. The why and the when escaped her, left her empty-handed, suspended between hope and the acheing desolation of finality.

Rebekha returned and was surprised when Wilhelmine asked if she would read the letter as Rico had written it, in his own words. The language might be beyond her, but like the untutored ear hearing music she would catch the tone and the timbre, the melody of his voice, the beat and motions of his body as he had held and loved her.

"Carissima,

Ti chiedo perdono per non averti scritto prima. Sarai stata preoccupata e questo mi ha reso molto triste. Avrei voluto scriverti ma non è stato possibile, le cose qui sono molto difficili, moltissimi problemi in famiglia. Non posso spiegarti ora, la situazione è molto complicata.

Sei stata sempre buona con me, mi hai dato tanto. Non l'ho dimenticato e non lo dimenticherò mai. Vorrei essere li con te, come siamo stati in questi anni. Un giorno, se Dio lo vorrà, quando le cose miglioreranno, tornerò da te.

Abbi cura di te. Ti penso sempre.

Baci e un abbraccio dal tuo

Rico"

25

"I'll go to him," she said.

She was weary of standing still on the shifting sand under her feet, weary of the waiting and uncertainty. Drained of will and intent, her mind ached. Emptied of the strength, the energy that the care and call of everyday life demanded, she felt worn and aged. Dulled in body and spirit, she drifted through the days in the grey haze of a stupor that shut the door on the world outside. Enervated, she had abandoned the constant companionship of her life, books, reading. She now saw Rebekha only occasionally and then she was mostly silent, absent and morose, half listening, refusing to be drawn out, released from the twilight within which she had shut herself away. And in bed at night, sprawled and leaden, an arm enclosing the space where he would have been, she wept without tears, with a sort of inturned pity.

Late in April one day she went to Rebekha and told her that she would go to see him. The release of spring, the awakening earth and the warming sun, seemed suddenly to have infused her with a new-found strength, freed mind and body from the long winter hibernation, recalled to life her former persona. Inexplicably, she felt bold and willing to look life in the face, undaunted by what the morrow might bring.

"Yes, I'll go," she said, the firmness of tone surprising Rebecca. She would go and find him, bring him back cost what it might. She had resources, her acumen had made a success of the shop which had garnered a large clientele; Fritz worked for her as garçon after school hours, running errands, making deliveries. Until his departure Rico's trade too had prospered. She would fetch him back and they would build a life anew, not on the remnants of the past. No more of the vagrant travelling days for him, no longer would he be a mere bed and breakfast boarder. She would have him by her side each night and, with sights set on the horizon, she saw a home with voices, the laughter of the young, infant arms around Rico's neck as they strolled through the evening lights of the town. Yes, she would go to him, she decided, stubborn and resolute.

"Are you sure?" Rebekha asked perplexed. "It's a long journey. Shall I come with you?"

She shook her head, thanking her for the kind offer. At the station to see her off, anxious and with an odd foreboding, Rebekha held her for a long moment. "You'll look after yourself, won't you?" Wilhelmine boarding the carriage smiled down reassuringly. "I'll do that. And I'll be back sooner than you think!"

There was such certitude, so much radiant hope in the voice that it troubled Rebekha. She who had sailed through uncharted waters, come perilously close to the reefs and shoals, looked into the abyss, knew all too well life's wild reel between the swell and the deep. Now as the train pulled away she could only pray that this child of her heart be spared the plunge into the chasm.

26

The night train went south and Wilhelmine dozed fitfully. Only once, lulled by the dull monotone of the tracks, did she graze into sleep for a short hour or two. And in that brief oblivion, her mind restless with excitement and apprehension, she dreamt of a pursuit across a mountain pasture, with Rico walking ahead in the distance and she hurrying in his steps but inexplicably held back, unable to reach him, his advance and her strained progress at a constant equidistance; the soundless chase finally, abruptly raising a sheer rock face before her.

Startled into wakefulness, Wilhelmine sat up in her berth. In the break of daylight outside she saw the train run along the water-edge of a wide lake still as a mill-pond, encircled by the snow-capped heights of dawn-blue mountains, an occasional chalet-like house along the shore, a tall pole with a flag, a white cross on a field of red, aflutter in the chill morning breeze. And a while later a grey-uniformed, tall handsome man with a trim moustache came by to ask for her papers, departing wordlessly with a touch of the braid-ribboned cap in salute.

An hour later, as the morning grew, skirting gorges and ducking under tunnels the train descended through the wooded hills of narrow sunless valleys towards more fertile land inhabited by square, red-tiled brick houses, tapering factory chimney-stacks and the winding tarred roads of towns and villages. And then, under the limpid sky, the early sun came to rest on a vast expanse of water flanked by green mountain ranges that marched in serried ranks toward the horizon. Nearing journey's end, the beat of her heart quickening, Wilhelmine thought of that other journey, waking at first light with Rico at her side and the train steaming across the causeway over a lagoon towards a magical city of dreams. It now seemed so long ago.

The faded picture postcard that Rico had once shown her now sprang to life. The villas and mansions with their palm fronted gardens were still there, the wide curving promenade along the lakefront waking to the day's first bustle, and across the broad avenue lined with beds of early bloom a long row of canopied shop fronts. Recalled by memory Wilhelmine turned her gaze towards the imaginary site of the emporium of Rico's vanished dreams, in its place now the long glass plate window of a pastry shop.

She crossed the street to a row of small cars parked neatly along the kerb and approached the last one. Leaning against his vehicle the wiry figure puffing on a cigarette wordlessly directed her to the head of the queue even before she had spoken. The driver, a quiet elderly man with greying sideburns, looked at the piece of paper Wilhelmine held out, thought for a moment, his face then lighting up with recognition he said, "Ah, si! Brunate." Wilhelmine got in as courteously he held the door open, handing her back the cloth bag with which she had travelled, which contained a few clothes and small toileteries.

They set off through the town, not quite as elegant and polished as the lake front, the scars of war still visible here and there, the new grey box-like, anonymous edifices already risen where the rubbles of ruin had been. They went down a straight main road, turning left into a long sloping avenue lined with the gardens of older houses, small villas and mansions with oleander flanking the gateways and wisteria climbing the open terraces. Then the ascent began in earnest.

The fresh morning air faintly perfumed with leaf and flower wafted in through the open window as the car took the turns and wound around hair-pin bends of the ever winding road. The town fell away, the lake now a vast flat breadth of glass silvered with the glaze of mid-morning light.

Impatient and yet suddenly diffident, Wilhelmine watched the towering landscape, her sentient heart aflutter, doubt and apprehension crowding her thoughts. Her new-found spirit failing, her boldness abruptly vanished, she wondered if he would be displeased by her unexpected and unannounced arrival. Would he turn away? Or would he stride out and his outstretched arms close around her, as always? Would he whisper her name, his breath lingering on her skin, as on those far-away nights in the enchanted city of waters?

Still climbing, the engine straining with a noisy whir on the steeper rises, past small houses crouched here and there on the hillsides, clumps of evergreens, early Alpine bloom, they came to a broad stretch and the car pulled up on the side of the road. The driver opened the door to let Wihelmine out, indicated a stone-paved path sloping up the hill, took the payment counting the money out of Wilhelmine's hand and nodded respectfully.

Wihelmine walked slowly up the path flanked by the low branches of chestnut and pine. Here and there leaves grazed her head. A little further ahead the path levelled out to flat ground. Through the overhanging foliage she saw a wide open space, an unfenced garden with a handful of young trees, cheery and peach. Set back from the uneven green was an old stone house with shuttered windows and leaning against it a newer double-story construction of bare brick and mortar, the open windows and the front door painted a dull grey.

In front of the entrance, under a spreading apple tree sat Rico on a cane chair with an infant in his arms and a fair-haired little girl at play at his feet. A stout young woman with long dark hair severely drawn back and tied with a ribbon fed the infant from a small white enamel cup. Wilhelmine could hear the voices but at this distance and in the open space not the words. And as she watched, an old lady in black, the mother whose portrait Rico had once shown her, emerged from the stone cottage and stood by until the feeding was over, gathered up the silent new-born from Rico's arms and cradling it in hers paced about the garden slowly. The young woman then sat herself down on Rico's lap, winding an arm around his neck and laying her head against his. The little girl at their feet nursed a small cloth doll in silent play.

There was talk, the occasional laugh, but Wilhelmine could not tell if it was he or the woman in his arms. She could not hear, did not hear. The world was hushed and the scene played itself out in silence. She stood still, shielded by the shade of the chestnut branch, the risen sun now bathing the garden and the houses in a warm light that filtered down through the spring green of the trees in new leaf.

She must have stood there a long while watching the quiet family scene. Or perhaps it was mere minutes. She could not remember. At length she picked up the bag and turned back down the slope, the path finally letting her off on the main road where she had alighted. The taxi was gone, she had not asked the driver to wait.

She had not expected to call on his services quite so soon.

A fortnight after her return she posted him a note, a handful of bare lines. She thanked him for his letter, thanked him, too, for the short years of happiness. She wished him and his family well and hoped his children would take after their father, his kindness and goodness of heart.

She never heard from Rico again.

27

A year later Wilhelmine sold the shop. It was a going concern and it sold well. But she kept the house and sometime later Rebekha moved in with her. There was ample space, Wilhelmine kept the bedroom that had been Rico's and hers, Rebekha moving into her father's, with yet another to spare, which had been her childhood room. She made small changes, paint was renewed, furniture rearranged, the heavy drapes came down giving way to lighter, airy cloth, letting in light, banishing the shades and shadows of the past. The two woman settled into a home all their own.

Now approaching her mid-seventies, running the library single-handed weighed on Rebekha. The library itself had been turned over to the Municipality, Rebekha still managing it's affairs. She took on Wilhelmina to assist her with the day to day work, place orders and subscriptions, register loans and returns. Wilhelmina knew books, eyes shut could guide people to the various sections. Now under Rebekha's tutoring she learned cataloguing, indexing, filing, gradually relieving the older woman of the labours behind the scenes. Running the shop had given Wihelmine a sense of method and order, she was quick to learn. And she liked this new world, devoid of the measuring, weighing and bargaining of commerce.

Wilma to the few friends and intimates, Wilhelmine to the library public, she kept Rico's name, it was hers by right. Occasional strangers, newcomers unknown to her found it curious, odd that in a town like ours she should carry a name such as this, peculiar and out of place. "No relation I presume of *the* Botticelli?" said the new school teacher. It was said in gentle jest and Rebekha smiled.

Wilhelmine herself held nothing against the past. It had been her choice and she had erred. Young and untutored in life's intricate labyrinth she had gone down a blind alley. And she held nothing against Rico, apportioned neither blame nor betrayal. He had not lied, nor misled her. If at all, his sin of omission was hers as well, for taking him as he was, she had not queried, not looked beyond his warm and heartening presence at his antecedents.

But the nights were hard. She often wished that daylight would linger until dawn. She drew out the evenings, sitting with Rebekha in quiet conversation after dinner, reading by her bedside until the aged eyes shut in repose. And then, in the solitary night, supine and restless in her bed, suspended between sleep and wakefulness, reason and fortitude gave way to mourning, her body slanting towards the empty space to embrace in spirit a presence that had fled. Even later, when the balm of time had soothed and softened the ache of his absence, some mornings waking early she would fall back on the sheets heavy and listless, to lie then and gaze motionless at the purple petals of the crystal iris in the white ceramic vase.

28

In time Rebekha relinquished her post and Wilhelmine was appointed Assistant at the Schenkel Library. Formally untrained and without official qualifications, she could not hope for more, aspire to a higher position, nor in truth did she ever. Content at work, regarded by the public, she retained her place as over the years Head Librarians came and went.

Rebekha lived with Wilhelmine till the end. Mother and more, sister and friend, she guided Wilhelmine in her work, nursed her through her early solitude, expending on her all the love that her heart had stored away through the better part of a lifetime. Aged and frail, the outside world increasingly shut out from view, she waited for her Wilma each evening. And each evening Wilhelmine's homecoming was a small celebration of serenity, warmth and comfort. When finally Rebekha's long life of retreat and survival came to an end, Wilhelmine was by her side, mourning the farewell more than she had the death of her father or the loss of Rico.

Now in the prime of her life, sombre and graceful, a woman of some beauty, Wilhelmine might have had other men, admirers, suitors to court her, lovers to fill the void of her empty nights. But she had already known yearning and fulfilment beyond measure and, brief though it had been, she thought it would suffice for one lifetime. Not wishing to tempt fate once again, she ignored the compliments and overtures, steadfastly espousing her widowhood over the years.

So now in late middle age here she sits on the steps of the library, the willowy figure turned to matronly girth, the fine auburn hair sharing her head with strands of silver, the heavy-set face wreathed in the blue wisps of the habit bequeathed her by the only man she has ever loved. Stubbing out the cigar-end and rising to go back indoors she sighs and laying a hand on my head looks down kindly as she says, "Old Albert! You seem to know everyone's secret. One day you must tell us something about yourself."

I would, gladly, had I had a tale to tell.

SLEEP

1

Our town, said Carin Breitfuss, had slumbered for some several hundred years. Upheavals, wars that had changed the fate of entire nations, floods, famines and plagues had come and gone. Ignored by history and untouched by man's march through time, revolts, reformations and revolutions, monarchs beheaded and Popes exiled, our town had drowsed through them all. "This place," said Fräulein Breitfuss, "might as well have been on Mars or the moon"

She had looked through the archives and found merely a single recorded event worthy of some note. This concerned the occasion when once Hubert the Horrid had ridden into town with his men, tied the presbyter to a pole, lobbed off the sexton's left ear lobe, whipped the bailiff, hung the burgomaster head down from a gibbet and made off with his wife.

In the singularly eventless chronicle of the town there was another episode, a minor one, when a farmer's wife was found with a freshly laid egg in the folds of her skirt. Accused of having laid the egg herself, the poor creature was dragged to the town square to be immolated at the stake. A timely confession by her husband saved the day, the farmer claiming that of late his spouse had been inclined to sleep in the barn with the chicken rather than attend to her conjugal duties in the marriage bed. The elders had then ordered the culling of the entire stock of the carnal poultry, the fowls being served up at the ensuing public feast. "Hardly an event to take one's breath away!" Fräulein Breitfuss remarked dryly.

"If I'm not mistaken," said school teacher Vogel dredging his memory, "there was another occasion when the town distinguished itself. A diplomatic incident of far-reaching consequence."

That, he recalled, was the time when the son of the famed Atürk Pasha charged with an ambassadorial mission by Sultan Suleiman of Constantinople had lost his way en route to the Emperor's court and wandered into our town. Dismayed by the peculiar wardrobe of the strangers, not least the loose silk pantaloons and pouffe-like headgear, and fearful that the company might well have been a band of evil genie let loose to end man's days on earth, the notables of the town encouraged by the presbyter locked up the young nobleman and his retinue in a cellar. Days later news of the capture reaching the Court, a furious Emperor despatched a body of dragoons, who liberated the disconcerted envoys and departed post haste, but not before soundly flogging the burgomaster and tying the presbyter to a pole.

"Well, yes," said Fräulein Breitfuss with a disparaging smile "perhaps an episode worthy of taking its place beside the defeat of the Turks in the Battle of Lepanto."

"It is of course for historians to decide," commented Herr Vogel with sombre reflection. "But it may well be that the retreat of the Turks from our continent commenced with that incident, which I personally tend to consider of immense significance."

The Librarian tapped her pencil on the table impatiently. "Now Gentlemen…"

"I should quite like to hear your view on the matter," Herr Vogel insisted.

"My view on the matter," said Fräulein Breitfuss with sharp brevity, "is that locking people up because of their baggy pyjamas is an act of dubious intelligence! Now Gentlemen …"

Herr Vogel persisted in following his singular train of thought. "If one considers the depredations of the Turks at the gates of Vienna …" he began.

"Herr Vogel, if you please, we shall be taking up the depredations of the Turks at the gates of Vienna and elsewhere in due time," the Librarian said with severe exasperation.

This first encounter set the tone for the mutual antipathy between the librarian and the school teacher, the one considering the other a bumbling bore who invariably clung to the irrelevant minutiae of whatever the subject with the tenacity of a terrier; while Herr Vogel saw in the young lady a shallow creature with a desirable figure but quite headless, which was perfectly in keeping with his general opinion of women.

2

This afternoon Fräulein Breitfuss had invited to the library some of the more prominent figures in town. By virtue of his position Burgomaster Schultz was there, as were Dr. Hammes, the Baron, Herr Vogel, the Professor obviously, and I with him. The eminent company now sat in the small reading room while the Head Librarian explained the reason for the convocation.

The anonymous past could not be undone, she said, but it was her firm intention to place the town if not on the map of the world at the least in the civilized human circle. She picked up a slender volume titled HERMANN SCHENKEL AND THE BAUTEMPLE and briskly leafed through the pages.

"As most of you may be aware, Hermann Schenkel was the benefactor who built the library and donated it to the town. It was meant to be, in his own words, a temple of learning, a fount of knowledge. As motto he had chosen SCIRE EST VIVERE, knowledge is life."

"Scire est vivere," muttered Herr Vogel to himself. "Two infinite verbs as subject. Curious to say the least."

Fräulein Breitfuss disregarded the school teacher's cavillous musing. "As it happens," she continued, "in all these years the library has been able to promote neither knowledge nor life. How could it, given the abysmal reading habits of the inhabitants. Schenkel might as well have built his library on the Pampas!"

Of the tens of thousands of volumes in the library, it appeared that the one book forever out on loan was "Tarzan and the Apeman." "Fortunately we have some two hundred copies," Fräulein Breitfuss added with a wry face. Burgomaster Schultze who had picked up from Frau Botticelli "Tarzan and the Apeman" on his way in for the meeting placed an arm over the cover of the book and looked sheepishly out of the window.

"And there are no prizes, gentlemen, for guessing the second most popular work with adult males."

"Tarzan and the Apewoman," Dr. Hammes suggested, adding hastily "Culled from my observations. Obviously!"

"As for the ladies of the town, the perennial favourite is 'The Scarlet Woman and the Dark Stranger' series," the Librarian announced with a despondent air.

All in all, it was a dismal picture. The inhabitants needed to be shaken out of their age-old lassitude. Accordingly, the librarian announced her intention to launch a series of events that would take the fount of knowledge to the populace since the populace refused to come to the fountain on its own.

Herr Vogel looked up with renewed interest. "Mohammed and the mountain! It so happens that this proverb …."

Fräulein Breitfuss cut him short unceremoniously. The first of the series, she announced, would the projection of a film in the library and it was to be hoped that the screening would attract a sizeable audience. She asked the assembled company to lend a hand in promoting and publicizing the event, the first of its kind in the annals of the town.

Burgomaster Schultz espoused the cause without hesitation, revealing with unabashed enthusiasm that he had a been a keen cinema-goer since infancy, having seen each of the early Tarzan films at least a dozen times. He had also seen the later versions, in colour, but these could not hold up a candle to the early black and white ones. Face glowing with boyish excitement, he confessed to his blood racing at the sight of Tarzan swinging from a liana at some dizzy height while the deep-throated ululation rang through the forest.

The Baron reproduced a soft imitation of the cry, with the Burgomaster joining in with considerable vigour. Transported to childhood and unable to resist the primordial call, Dr. Hammes added his voice to the duo, but in a more musical tone. The Professor desisted, while Fräulein Breitfuss looked on askance. For myself, I was too well mannered to set up a howl in a temple of knowledge!

3

Peace and harmony reigned in our house. A casual visitor would have certainly thought that we had all lived together in benign and loving accord over a lifetime, with never a sharp edge nor an unkind word. The impression would not have been out of place.

Fräulein Breitfuss had ingratiated herself with Matilde with a single stroke of shrewd perspicacity. The praise heaped on her Sauerbraten at dinner one evening had overwhelmed Matilde. The red wine vinegar steak stew had always been the pride of her culinary art but never had it been acclaimed with such fervour. At first she had received the accolade with an air of suspicion. But the shower of encomium raining down on her was so profuse that she had let go.

The barbed exchanges and armed stand-offs were now, apparently, a thing of the past. The peremptory disposal of Gerber's flowery curtains in the dining room and the mysterious disappearance from the Professor's study of the silver frame with Gretchen's portrait were forgotten, or presumably put aside. Matilde had even adapted her skills to the rationed amounts of lard and cream advocated by Fräulein Breitfuss, going so far as to pass on the homily to Bauer. "Bad for the heart?" responded the gardener puzzled. "Whose heart?"

The phlox and phallux controversy long over with the disposal of the hollyhock stems, Bauer himself had been won over heart and mind. Seduced with the gift of a tattered copy of "The Uncommon

Gardener," one of the several hundred in the library, and impressed beyond measure with the young lady's horticultural expertise when Fräulein Breitfuss one day easily identified a double petunia, Bauer now executed with deference the least of her suggestions, bordering the flower-beds with pansy, training sweet-peas along the fence, lobbing off one stout arm of the wisteria that was threatening to invade the living room through the bay-window.

"She's a lady-woman," he said one morning sitting at his accustomed place by the kitchen door.

Matilde oiling an old revolver, an heirloom from the time of the Great War that had belonged to the Professor's grandfather, smiled down kindly at the gardener. "Why, have you met many ladies who are not women?"

Bauer took a sip of the beer and pondered the conundrum. "I've met ladies and I've met women." With furrowed brow he added "But it's hard to tell one from the other."

4

In announcing to the public the projection of a film at the library, Fräulein Breitfuss employed a shrewd ploy that would involve the entire town. A notice was set out at the entrance inviting suggestions for the choice of the film, the written title to be handed in at the counter to Frau Botticelli. The response was overwhelming. It was also not quite what the librarian had expected.

Within a week Frau Botticelli had collected several dozen slips. But Fräulein Breitfuss good intentions had gone terribly awry, any expectation of intelligent popular participation dashed beyond hope.

"What in heaven's name is wrong with people in this place?" she exclaimed in exasperation. "Does it surprise you, Ernst, that these same folk almost burned a poor woman at the stake because she was found with an egg on her?"

"That was some time ago, Carin," said the Professor looking up from his book.

Stretched out on the carpet by his feet as he sat reading, the long legs entwined, Fräulein Breitfuss had been going through the slips with the suggested titles. As the slender fingers sorted through and discarded the strips of paper, she accompanied each with a sigh, a moan, a groan, a smirk, a titter, a laugh, occasionally an exclamation that might have helped Bauer tell apart ladies from women.

"Listen to this, Ernst," she said with a girlish laugh. "'The Rise of the Mummy'! And this one. 'Aladdin's Seven Wives'."

"Did he really have that many?" the Professor remarked in a distracted aside.

"Well, it seems he does. All seven of them. Must be the choice of that terror of womanhood Schicketanz at the Municipality. And this! "Jezebel's Tomb". Where on earth did people see these things?"

"There used to be an old cinema near the station, The Metropole." The Professor put down his book. "Carin, why not simply show 'Tarzan and the Apeman'. I'm sure you could find a copy."

"Really, Ernst!" And with a high, girlish laugh she slithered up the sofa, her sinuous figure winding itself around him as her lips fastened on his neck, as if meaning to devour his flesh.

Rarely had I been privy to intimacy between humans, but on the few occasions I found the sight peculiar if not somewhat alarming, what with the entanglement of legs and arms, the frenzied hurry to shed clothing, lips seeking out lips with a sort of primitive hunger, the flushed contorted faces and strangled breath. On the whole an awkward spectacle. What was more disturbing was that the Professor should lend himself to a performance of the sort under the gentle gaze of Gretchen as she looked down from the water-colour portrait above the mantelpiece. Fortunately, the phone ringing, Gretchen and I were spared the brazen display.

"Frau Botticelli," said Fräulein Breitfuss returning and regaining her composure. "I've often wondered where she got that curious name." Leaning then against the Professor, she turned her eyes on me as I drowsed by the fireplace. "Do you think Albert's ever been love?"

The Professor smiled fondly. "Oh, I should think our Albert's above that sort of trivia."

5

"Something experimental and avant garde," said Fräulein Breitfuss. "Something to wake the good citizenry from their centuries-long sleep!" As it turned out, the title alone of the final choice was likely to extend the lengthy slumber.

She had got Frau Botticelli to locate on the shelves a monumental encyclopaedia on film-making, an equally voluminous tome listing all the films ever made since that first two-minute reel of a man frantically pedalling a bicycle against an indistinct background; various reviews and magazines.

Locked in the library after hours, the two women had combed through the endless pages. Occasionally they came across some of the titles submitted by the public. "The Rise of the Mummy" was there, along with a dozen other mummies performing various antics wrapped in white bed sheets. It was also discovered that several decades ago the Jezebel series of films had enjoyed a certain notoriety owing to body-clinging chiffon gowns worn by the ladies playing Jezebel, whose thinly-veiled depravations had moreover filled audiences with awe and shock. Aladdin and his wives were absent from the various listings; while there were Tarzans galore, represented over half a century and more by muscular but largely mute actors with intimidating, Herculean torsos.

Finally Fräulein Breitfuss came on an item she thought would shake the audience out of its somnolence. Considered by eminent critics something of a masterpiece of its genre, it ran for several hours and in its time had drawn the censorious gaze of the authorities owing to the presence of a semi-nude figure recumbent on a bed. But the excellence and the high-minded nature of the work could not be in doubt, one esteemed French critic extolling the film for having *distilled within the space of a few hours the quintessence of the existential dilemma of modern man."* Fräulein Breitfuss read out quotes from other similar paeans.

"This should wake up the good people! Wilma, please call and ask if they have a copy at the Frankfurt Filmmuseum," she said with brisk satisfaction as Frau Botticelli looked on doubtfully but kept her thoughts to herself, as she always did. The title of the film was brief and explicit: "SLEEP".

Burgomaster Schultz lent his official weight by having outsize hoardings put up in the park and elsewhere, announcing a marathon film show at the library, with the title printed in bold shocking red. The public was invited to pick up the admission passes at the library counter, since seating was limited in the hexagonal pavilion at the far end of the library building.

The town responded with unaccustomed enthusiasm, the passes snapped up within the first couple of days. Word had somehow got out of an unclothed figure reclining on a bed, which fired the fancy and imagination of quite a number of citizens. Expectation ran high, for it was thought that the rumoured scene could not be the only one of its kind but merely the prelude to more provocative and tumultuous happenings.

Adolf who had finally made the acquaintance of Fräulein Breitfuss came out of his antique shop to engage her in brief conversation as she passed on her way to the library. "Sleep. Certainly an eventful title!" he remarked, his eyes gleaming through the thick lenses. "Come and see for yourself," she responded with a mysterious smile. The antique dealer rubbed his hands in silent glee as he went back indoors to resume dusting the ceramic ocarina.

At the butcher's, Udo attempted a roundabout route to glean advance news on the piquant scene. "The figure on the bed, is it a single bed or a double one?" he asked with an air of disinterest as he trimmed the chops. "Single or double, beds are for sleeping, Udo," Fräulein Breitfuss informed in a matter of fact manner, to which Udo nodded gravely, as if receiving the wisdom of the ages.

No less curious but prudish and prurient, a number of elderly ladies censored the choice of the film outright, maintaining that the title alone would contribute in no small measure towards encouraging promiscuity. "Mark my words!" said Frau Bader, "The person on the bed won't be alone for long." Frau Engel nodded in severe agreement. "Beds attract company!" she remarked with intimate conviction. Old widow Ansel, unable to comprehend the drift of the talk, merely looked at the evening sky and asked if it was already time to go to bed.

6

Extensive search in the library store room had unearthed an ancient projector. It was from Schenkel's time, a massive piece of equipment in cast iron with heavy levers, large bakelite knobs, a powerful lens, and able to accommodate outsize reels of film. It had been little used except in the early years when occasionally Party officials had come to town and held conferences in the library, showing hour long reels of gigantic rallies with million-strong crowds, helmeted soldiers marching across vast squares holding aloft flags and standards, leaders haranguing the rapt onlookers in shrill voices.

Herr Metzler now ran his hand over the dark green paint of the projector with the care and reverence with which one might touch a sacred relic, gently worked the buttons and levers with their shiny chrome finish, one finger lightly tracing the raised inscription "Strobe & Schuster" on a silver metal plate at the base. "These were the very best," he said in a voice charged with a melancholy sentiment.

For well over half his life Metzler had been the projectionist at The Metropole. Thousands of films had passed through his hands, he had cut, spliced, joined, occasionally censored on behest of the cinema owner. He had mounted and projected innumerable reels of mummies, Jezebels, Aladdins and Tarzans, but apart from a few frames he had never seen a film in its entire length. The contents were of no interest to him. He was enamoured solely of the details of the process, the quiet whirr of the machine, the silent unwinding

211

of the reel, the beams of flickering light that brought alive fable and fantasy. The projection started, he would sit by the machine stretching out his tall wiry frame on an easy chair, watching the endless strip of celluloid pass through the pinch rollers, wind around the idler wheels, snake its way up towards the dazzling luminescence and come to life. In later years, drowsing off occasionally as the audience below gaped and cringed and laughed, he would be woken by cries of "Metzler! Metzler!" as the reel came to an end and the hall was plunged into night-black darkness.

A man of few words, his sombre face adorned with a trim moustache, the snow-white hairline refusing to recede despite his seventy odd years, Metzler was called out of his retirement by Fräulein Breitfuss's marathon film night. The projector positioned in its place in the pavilion, on running trials with an old documentary on the edelweiss and other Alpine blooms, Metzler was startled to discover that the ancient machine suffered from a singular eccentricity. At random intervals the pulley would seize, the whirring fall silent and the projector would come to a halt, leaving the edelweiss fixed on the screen like a slide. No more than half a minute later, stealthily and with not the least warning, the take-up reel would be on the move again, as though the machine had merely decided on a brief pause from its labours.

After the tenth such stop-and-go, Metzler switched off the power and sat looking at the projector for a whole hour. Such machines, large and small, he had known since his youth and he had worked them in a variety of circumstances, under an open sky, with a backdrop of heavy shelling and gunfire, under an air raid, in a smoke-filled back room with jostling foreign soldiers watching improper images on the screen. Never once had he encountered a projector that seemed to have a will of its own.

The next morning he took the machine apart, checking the valves, the circuits and contacts, the gears, shafts and levers. All was well and in order. He double-checked. He oiled, fitted back parts, screwed down the cover. The machine looked and sounded as though it had just left the premises of Strobe & Schuster, albeit the partners and their workshop had long since perished under an errant bomb. And then it came to him, his mind suddenly deciphering the mystery of the enigma.

Fräulein Breitfuss looked in. The fault could not be put right, he told her. The defective component could be changed, she suggested. There was nothing to replace, he said, everything was in order.

"I don't understand," she said impatiently, glancing at her watch.

"Age," said Metzler, adding with sombre conviction, "It happens to people."

"This thing is not people, Herr Metzler!"

"Age. It comes to things and people."

Fräulein Breitfuss looked at the projectionist curiously. "You're not telling me this machine suffers from organic disorders!"

Not quite sure what the Librarian meant, Metzler nodded. "We all do," he said. "Ladies pause at a certain age. Machines too," he added laconically.

7

Matilde declined Fräulein Carin's invitation, saying she preferred to sleep rather than watch others do it. Martha was of the same mind, saying she preferred her own bed to watching those of others. But Uli was game. "Albert's coming with me, Ma, and we'll tell you all about it." Uli was my constant companion at public events and after dinner we set off for the library.

Most people in our town went to bed with the birds, even though few had garnered much wealth and even fewer the proverbial wisdom. By sundown much of the populace appeared pale and exhausted and with the onset of evening it was not an uncommon sight to see people in the street yawn wearily as they made for home at a somnambulist pace.

For sure there were hardier souls, at Eichel's beer-house, at Henschel's Gasthaus. But these places were seen by many as locales of dubious entertainment, if not quite coves of wickedness. They were open late, ladies in garish dresses went in and emerged only hours later. The sight alone of chambermaid Lulu's wanton posture as she stood on the steps of Henschel's drawing on a cigarette would have sufficed to fire the imagination of the likes of Fraus Bader and Engel, lighting up in their minds unspeakable scenes of degenerate revelry. Indeed, the ladies were often thoroughly outraged merely at the sight of Lulu's restlessly swivelling hips. Fortunately, fast asleep in bed with heads tightly bound in curlers, seldom had they had occasion to encounter the boisterous and unsteady revellers who tumbled out of Eichel's at midnight.

Tonight the two women had decided to make an exception, renouncing the chaste comfort of their duvets and taking on the onerous task of guarding against the loosening of public morals. Seated at the back of the pavilion, still as waxwork figures, their watchful gaze swept the scene, taking a silent census of people who had come in to watch the suspect spectacle. "We're not here to watch the film," Frau Bader had affirmed severely on the way in. "Not at all," Frau Engel had echoed, "we'd rather go blind." They were there as guardians of propriety and to record for future memory the names of those who lent their presence to such an unseemly representation.

Entering the pavilion with an urbane air, Adolf the antiquarian made a courtly bow, but his fulsome obeisance was entirely ignored as the two ladies stared fixedly ahead, their sights locked on Udo and Lulu as the pair sought seating towards the front to have a closer view of the happenings on the screen.

As their eyes swivelled like periscope sights, meticulously scanning the pavilion from side to side, of a sudden both the women visibly stiffened and held their breath, Frau Engel near to fainting, as a group of workmen from the local foundry entered and stood above them exhaling heady fumes from one of Eichel's stronger brews. Frau Bader loftily requesting them to kindly move on, one of the group, a short barrel-chested young man with hirsute arms, looked down menacingly, released a powerful burp in her direction and employing the rudest of terms told her to be "Off!" In a fit of near apoplexy Frau Bader collapsed against her companion.

It was something of her coming-out night and Fräulein Breitfuss could be seen flitting about the pavilion, greeting a familiar face, stopping for a word here, flashing a smile of welcome to one and all. It was especially pleasing for her to see the foundry workmen, for it was precisely this segment of the populace that she meant to uplift from its cerebral lethargy. She spent several minutes in their company, bending forward brightly to exchange a word or two as the burly men looked on with vacant smiles, their gaze curiously fixed mostly on the smoothly rounded curve of her stoop.

She looked radiant, with clothes to match, a round-necked mauve cashmere sweater under a trim gun-metal jacket and a navy-blue skirt with folds and flares in the right places; the fine red shoulder-length head of hair falling in curls and waves. Even Uli noticed her bright, seductive presence, sighing "I wish she'd come to eat at our place more often."

The Bader-Engel duo had a different opinion. Recovered from the shocking impertinence of the foundry workers, taking in the scene with beady eyes, their gaze froze at the sight of the Head Librarian. "Just look at those scarlet nails," the former muttered through her teeth. "The devil's colour!" pronounced Frau Engel through the little lace-trimmed kerchief which she still held to her nose against the lingering noxious odour of Eichel's potent brew.

Despite the late start and the promise of a marathon showing that would stretch into the early hours, the pavilion had almost filled up. Bank manager Adler had come, for once without the praetorian presence of his scowling wife but surprisingly in the company of his head-clerk Schiefferdecker. This was something of an event in itself. No one could recall ever having seen the clerk anywhere other than at the bank, the emaciated frame hunched hermit-like behind the counter, as though not wishing to disturb with his presence the clients and visitors who entered the premises. Almost invisible to sight, he processed cheques and drafts, loans and payments with the mute presence of a spirit and the alacrity of a snail moving backwards. There were those who suspected that Adler locked the clerk in the safe at the end of the working day, putting him back at the counter at opening hour the following morning.

Burgomaster Schultz was there of course, in the company of Frau Gärtner the florist. Their laughter and talk appeared to suggest a sort of unwholesome rapport, which did not sit well with the custodians of propriety who exchanged looks that hinted at a thousand improper tales. Despite the absence of Tarzan and his primal cry, the Burgomaster was in high spirits. In all the years he had held office, and he had held the mayoral seat seemingly for ever, largely owing to the utter disinterest of the inhabitants of the town in aspiring to any kind of office, high or low, in his time as mayor it had ever been Shultze's ardent wish to promote joy and well-being, laughter and happiness.

He had done his utmost, placed new benches in the park, retired the ageing swans in the lake and brought in an animated new pair, planted a maypole on the green. But the town lived on the edge of the known world, finances were limited, circuses, fun fairs and folk dance troupes found greener pastures elsewhere. Apart from bringing in a handful of minor, undistinguished artistes for a late summer spectacle, almost the only major achievement of Herr Schultz's long tenure went back some years, when he had successfully managed to lure a stray Russian lady painter into town to display in the park her water colours of the Urals: though even that had ended on a sorrowful note, nature conspiring to ruin both artist and her works with an unseasonable deluge.

Municipal clerk Schicketanz had turned up and now sat in the middle of the pavilion peacock-like, the wine-red jacket and matching bow-tie making him conspicuous as he peered at the female members of the audience. Clearly he had come not so much for the enrichment of his mind as to set his sights on future conquests, not that the sum of his past conquests amounted to anything more than leering at the ladies who called in at his office for certificates, registrations, odd notarial work. Then, cavalier-like, he would offer them a seat with a flourish and spend the next several minutes groping on hands and knees under his desk for an object, a pencil, a rubber-stamp, that he unfailingly managed to drop in the presence of female visitors. On one occasion his search between the pastor's wife's feet had lasted so long that an inadvertent movement of the comely lady's knee had dislodged one or more of his front teeth.

The Professor sat in the rear with Dr. Hammes and the Baron, the trio quietly conversing as the announced hour approached. The Baron had it in mind to bring his mother, but Baroness Gertrude had declined out of hand. "And what would I do there, Armin?" she asked dismissing his invitation. She had last been to a cinema several decades ago and it had been quite enough for her. She could still recall with dim horror her vain efforts to restrain the unabashed glee of her husband at the sight of the swirling, raised skirt of the buxom young lady who had pranced and pirouetted her way through the hour and a half of "The Dance of the Viking Maiden".

Uli and I had settled down comfortably at the back, under the projector. For the past several minutes Uli had been laboriously trying to make sense of the short programme note that Frau Botticelli had handed out at the entrance. He read through the first lines but, ending the paragraph, time and again he came up against words that baffled him. He read them aloud, he read the words singly, he read the sentence backwards: "man modern of dilemma existential the of essence the hours few a of space the within distilled…". And still it made no sense. Once again he read it as set down on paper: *"…distilled within the space of a few hours the essence of the existential dilemma of modern man"*. But the meaning remained elusive.

Uli appealed to Metzler who sat behind us on a deckchair he had procured somewhere, running his hands gently along the base of the projector as if to soothe its nerves against the coming ordeal. The old man pondered the words. "Distil…essence," he repeated. "Something to do with making perfumes. Anyway, it's not for us to understand such things."

Handing back the paper he looked at Uli. "Young man, you may be too young to be here tonight,"

"He's younger than me," Uli protested pointing at me where I sat by his feet.

The projectionist studied my ancient face for a moment and nodded. "Oh." Satisfied he went back to tinkering with his machine.

8

Unusually the old projector had a built-in alarm inside its massive innards to warn the audience of the start of the show. At the stroke of the hour Metzler pressed the warning button and set off the loud whine not dissimilar to that of an air-raid siren. The lights dimmed, the projector started up stealthily and after a lengthy countdown of circled numbers the flickering beams of light flashed **SLEEP** in bold black lettering across the screen. A murmured groan rose from the pavilion.

Burgomaster Shultz's garish hoardings in the park had conveyed the illusion of a film in riotous colours and as certain kinds of scenes were best seen in colour, the audience suffered a passing moment of disappointment. But it was brief, as without much ado, shorn of the tedious list of names of actors, authors, caterers, carpenters and electricians, the film plunged into the heart of the matter.

The screen filled with the image of a somewhat dimly lit windowless room sparsely furnished with a narrow bed and a cane-bottomed chair beside it. The faded beige wallpaper was printed from ceiling to floor with the motif of a willow tree overhanging a Chinese pavilion, with a boatman holding a pole and adrift in his tiny craft on the surrounding lake. A naked bulb hung over the bed. Inanimate and soundless, the room might have been there ever since humans first bent branches overhead and houses came into being.

Several minutes passed as the image remained printed on the screen, the even whir of the projector and the expectant breathing of the audience the only sounds to break the becalmed silence in the pavilion. Abruptly then, as the sound track came alive with a rasping hiss, the door at the far end of the room creaked open and a short balding figure with a hat in his hand came in. Soundlessly shutting the door behind him, he walked towards the bed and set down his hat on the chair. Bending forward and stretching out cardigan-clad arms he tried the bed, pressing his palms on the white sheet until the springs emitted a low twang.

With deliberate slowness he began to undress, first the cardigan which he gently placed over the curved back of the chair, then the check shirt, the buttons loosened from their eyelets with fastidious care, the shirt itself quietly draped over the cardigan. He looked down at his naked torso, lightly running a hand over the thick curly mat of hair on the chest. And now as he contemplated his trousers and his fingers reached for the clasp of the belt, the audience came alive, with muffled gasps, a titter here, a whisper there, a wheezy cough, a stifled "No!" from either Frau Bader or her companion, or both.

Heedless of the dismay among the onlookers, the figure on the screen proceeded to undress at his own leisure, drawing out the belt from the trouser loops, winding it around one finger and placing the coiled leather on the chair, beside the hat. Next, sitting on the edge of the bed, he undid the shoe laces, removed the shoes, rolled down and out the short socks which he deposited inside the shoes which in turn he neatly placed under the bed.

He stood up and, accompanied by loud gasps, a nervous squeal and a stifled scream from the rear of the pavilion, shamelessly he let his trousers down, revealing a paisley print pair of shorts. It was more than enough for Fraus Bader and Engel. And when one of the foundry men suddenly bawled "Take it off!" the cup brimmed over and the good women leapt from their seats, stumbled down the aisle and rushed headlong into the night.

Oblivious of the puritan flight, the figure on the screen scratched his somewhat rotund stomach, performed brief callisthenics raising and lowering his arms a time or two, turned his head this way and that to ease the muscles and opened his mouth in a loud and prolonged yawn, revealing a neglected set of dentures. Finally, picking the trousers off the floor and meticulously arranging them over the headboard, he laid himself down on the bed and shut his eyes.

With the recumbent figure on the bed perfectly motionless and the room returning to its previous stillness, the ancient projector thought it time to take a pause. The low whirring ceased, the reels came to a halt. But the image stayed on the screen, the audience unaware that the motion picture had been converted to a slide-show. Nor were they any the wiser when after the brief respite the machine started up again.

9

It was perhaps after a quarter of an hour of patient expectation, with the man on the bed engulfed in sleep, the regular breathing coming clearly through the scratchy soundtrack, that the audience began to show signs of restive weariness. Heads moved about, feet scraped the flooring, bodies repositioned themselves in their seats. There were murmurs, groans, whispered exchanges.

The foundry men in the middle of the pavilion were the most restless of all, letting off imitation sleep sounds, snorts and snores, breaking into short bursts of laughter, occasionally punctuating the silence with words that would have paralysed the senses of the Bader-Engel pair had they not fled the scene so precipitously. As the sleeper continued comatose, with the occasional twitch of a leg, an arm, the restrained animation of the foundry party grew louder, until the young man with hirsute arms suddenly shattered the peace with "Where is she? Bring on the lady!" Following suit one of his mates barked "Throw the bum out!" A third joined the chorus to make a truly unreasonable demand, chanting repeatedly "We want our money back!"

In the semi-dark Fräulein Breitfuss was seen leaving her place in the front row. Her head momentarily illuminated by the flickering rays from the projector, she crossed the pavilion to where the unruly foundry men were seated together. What she said no one heard but mysteriously she managed to quell the outbreak; although during the secret parley she did give a couple of sharp squeals as though bitten by an insect in some particularly tender spot.

A moment later the group rose from their seats and trooped out noisily, casting aspersions and worse on the way to the entrance. Not content with the lamentable show of incivility, the hirsute young man stuck his head back through the door and released such a barrage of scurrility that had it had ears to hear the old projector would have gone into a permanent pause.

When the echoes of the shocking words had died down and quiet returned once again, the audience became aware that the reclining figure on the screen had begun to snore, the sound-track emitting an irregular and intermittent canine growl, which abruptly subsided giving way to a hoarse groan like a bellow being emptied of air. The growl and the groan alternated for quite some time, gradually producing a soporific effect in the audience.

Heads nodded here and there, Schiecktanz had abandoned his rakish posture and slumped in his seat like a prostrated satyr. Adler had deserted head-clerk Schiefferdecker, who sat tilted forward leprechaun-like, about to fall off his seat like a dead weight. Further down Burgomaster Schultz slumbered peacefully with one official arm around Frau Gärtner, the comely florist's head pillowed on his shoulder. And upfront Udo and chambermaid Lulu were so closely wound together that those few who could occasionally lift their heavy lids preferred to watch the seemingly endless embrace rather than the happenings on the screen.

Uli had a mind to leave but enervated by the lack of events on the screen and seduced by the somnolent atmosphere in the pavilion, he had stretched out on the chair and begun to drowse, and I with him. Behind us Metzler had wearied of the play-pause antics of the projector and was now fast asleep on the deckchair, his own occasional snore joining that of the cadaverous sleeper on the screen, occasionally too standing in for the silenced sound-track when the projector decided on a pause.

First light had begun to seep in through the tinted glass of the roof when the impatient twitter of an early bird broke my rest. Uli too had been woken by the thoughtless chatter of the feathered creature and was rubbing his eyes to make sense of our whereabouts. In the brightening dark of the pavilion one could make out the odd figure here and there slumped forward or reclining in the seat, heroic souls who had finally yielded to the demands of the nocturnal hour. Metzler's tall length was still dormant on the deckchair, the seraphic expression of the trim moustache betraying some secret dream in the land of projectors. And the Strobe and Schuster machine itself had gone into a permanent pause, the screen illuminated with the single still frame of the recumbent figure who seemingly had passed onto eternal slumber.

Uli and I gained the exit carefully picking our way through the disorderly rows of chairs. The early May morning met us with the refreshing balm of a cool breeze, the pristine air faintly redolent with the smell of leaves and the nocturnal effusion of late spring flowers. The town was still fast abed. Not a soul about, we slowly crossed the green, Uli breaking the vernal hush as he crooned the tune of an old cradle song Gretchen sometimes recited walking in the woods, whose words went something like:

> *Babes in the wood*
> *Rise up and sing*
> *Rise up and play!*
> *Night is far gone*
> *Sleep is fast abed*
> *Rise to the new day!*

MR. SÈAMUS O'MALLEY

1

Mr. Sèamus O'Malley arrived in town in an ancient bottle-green van. The crumpled corduroy suit which clung to his meagre frame was of the same faded colour. The emaciated face hung with a long unkempt beard of an indeterminate orange hue was topped off with a narrow head sprouting long sparse strands of a darker orange. With his drowsy, half-shut eyes, he gave the impression of a hermit just woken from years of unbroken slumber.

Mr. O'Malley was accompanied by a Mr. Seosamh O'Reilly, who introduced himself as the artist's agent, "but above all friend and comrade-in-arms." Of a stouter build and prosperous around the middle, Mr. O'Reilly on the other hand was dressed in happier colours. The orange waistcoat under a green and black checked sporting jacket bestowed on him the look of a circus master of ceremonies.

There was a third occupant of the vehicle, who promptly leapt out and took up position between Mr. O'Malley's feet. "And this is Felicity," said Mr. O'Reilly beaming down at the supercilious tabby, "Felicity O'Malley." The arrogant feline cast a brief, defiant glance in my direction.

The Arts Committee had gathered in force on the steps of the library to welcome the visiting artist. Fräulein Breitfuss who spoke several foreign tongues introduced the members, starting with Burgomaster Schulze.

Mr. O'Reilly appeared taken aback. Letting go of Herr Schultz's hand hastily, he turned to his friend and comrade-in-arms. "Fancy that, Sèamus!" he exclaimed. "A buggermaster, no less! My word!"

An expression of glee briefly lit up Mr. O'Malley's drowsy face, revealing some very disorderly teeth. Fräulein Breitfuss was perplexed by the obvious hilarity of the visitors. "But surely you do have buggermasters in your country?" she asked earnestly, attempting to improve her mastery of the visitors' tongue.

Mr. O'Reilly passed on the query to Mr. O'Malley, "Do we have buggermasters in Donegal, Sèamus?"

"We may," replied Mr. O'Malley with a cryptic smile.

"We may. Indeed, we may. But it is not for us to know, dear Señorita."

"Wrong country, Seosamh," Mr. O'Malley prompted quietly.

Thereafter the other presentations went smoothly enough. The Baron was the last to be introduced. "Now," said Fräulein Breitfuss, "I would like you to meet a very special Member of our Committee, Baron Pischendorfp!"

"My word, a Baron no less!" Mr. O'Reilly pronounced with some awe. "Have we met many barons on our travels, Sèamus?"

"The Baron Café in Ballymore," Mr. O'Malley recalled hazily.

"Baron Pischendorfp is one of the patrons of the Exhibition," the Librarian insisted.

"Oh, truly! Well, then, how do you do Baron Piss-and-drop?"

"We do what we can," the Baron responded nonchalantly.

Brief pleasantries were exchanged. Fräulein Breitfuss remarked on their long journey.

"A long journey, certainly, Mademoiselle," Mr. O'Reilly concurred.

"Wrong country, Seosamh," Mr. O'Malley corrected from the background.

"Indeed, a long journey, Miss Brightpuss," Mr. O'Reilly resumed. "No, we never fly. Friend Sèamus prefers his feet on earth, the long and winding road, close to nature's handiwork. A hand greater than that of Michael!"

"Angelo," Mr. O'Malley added in an off-hand manner.

Introductions over, the guests were ushered towards Martha's for lunch. "Ireland!" Dr. Hammes said to the Professor in an undertone. "A wet island made even more damp by the tears of its history!"

2

Burgomaster Schulze had been much taken by Fräulein Breitfuss's idea of what she grandly termed "A Summer of Arts". The various events, he believed, would promote a tourism historically absent from our town, by attracting visitors from far and wide, even distant points of the globe.

If truth be told, save for travelling salesmen and the odd holiday-maker gone astray, no one ever came to our town unless obliged to do so; for there was neither art nor architecture, nor history, the only noteworthy showpiece being the orchid conservatory of the young lady who had been pleasant to the Kaiser, now visited by Dr. Hammes's daily stream of dumb patients. The library with its Roman temple façade was perhaps deserving of a mention. The only other real presence worthy of note was that of the Professor, with the occasional academic or expert briefly calling on us. Not surprisingly, Mr. Sèamus O'Malley was to be the very first artist of international repute to exhibit in our town.

The Burgomaster's meagre Municipal coffers would partly fund the events of the "Summer of Arts." The remainder was to be donated by the Baron to mark the 400th Birth Centenary of Hubert the Horrid. Old Baroness Gertrude protesting the redundant expenditure, the Baron had responded with "Maman, remember! Honour Thine Dead!" Impressed by the biblical sounding words recited in the Baron's solemn tone, she had given way. More than honouring Hubert or any other family dead, the Baron merely looked forward to the divertissement the festival would offer to relieve the tedium of a long summer.

The selection of the Arts Committee had gone off without a hitch. The Professor, Dr. Hammes, The Baron and Herr Schultz were obvious choices. Fräulein Breitfuss nominated herself Secretary. But the name of Herr Vogel caused considerable dissent.

"Why not Albert, then?" the new Secretary demanded pointing a peremptory finger towards the door beside which I had stretched out, the dry proceedings of the Committee having provoked an irresistible somnolence, so that I could barely keep my eyes open.

"Why not, indeed?" Dr. Hammes seconded the idea. "As his personal physician, I can vouch to Albert's superior intelligence."

There followed an interminable debate. It had always amazed me how, unlike us canines and other creatures of the supposedly lower kingdom who acted directly on an idea, humans laboured the same points over and over again, until they lost sight of the substance of the matter. The deliberations this afternoon were no exception.

The Burgomaster thought that Herr Vogel had a sound heart, to which Fräulein Breitfuss responded by stating firmly that she had not the least interest in the condition of the teacher's heart, sound or otherwise. A harmless soul, thought Dr. Hammes, apart from the fact that he saw the devil in every detail. The Librarian thought he might better see the Devil if he stood in front of a mirror.

"Oh, come Carin!" said the Baron laughing. "Obviously you've never met the Devil."

"I have now!" she shot back impatiently.

The Professor, I noticed, was non-committal. He had befriended the teacher, tolerated him with good humour, had in an odd manner even become fond of his quirks and endless digressions. But now he refrained from coming to his defence, almost as though fearful of drawing on his head the young lady's wrath. It was curious to watch the workings of the human female's hold on the human male. Very different from our canine tribe, where the female was of only occasional consequence. However, it was now heartening to observe male dominance prevail and overcome Fräulein Breitfuss's irrational feminine whims. Defeated by the fraternity of men, she finally gave in and the teacher was opted on.

Herr Vogel was a small, lean, fidgety figure, with thick lenses, argumentative and ever prone to delve into some of the more obscure minutiae of the universe. When occasionally he came to the house for lunch, there followed labyrinthine discussions with the Professor on certain extremely nebulous topics. In recent months all the talk had been about what the Professor called the Theory of Numbers. Numbers I knew: two chunks of meat were two chunks of meat, and no bones about it. But the Theory itself proved quite beyond my meagre canine comprehension and I quietly tip-pawed out to the kitchen to keep Matilde company.

Today the full Committee had been convened to take a final decision on the first manifestation of the Summer of Arts, an art exhibition. The Members had barely taken their seats in the smaller reading room of the library when Herr Vogel launched on a virulent denunciation of modern art.

"The Moderns! " he sneered. "A dot on the canvas, a couple of stripes, a dash of paint here, a splash there. Toddlers in kindergarten do better. Why, I read just the other day that at the Venice what-do-you-call-it …"

"Biennale," the Professor helped out.

"Yes, the biannual or whatever. There a canvas was recently exhibited with nothing more than a slash in it. Simple vandalism!"

"Italian Post-Modern," Fräulein Breitfuss informed him in a superior tone.

"The Italians. Oh, the Italians!" he grimaced with distaste. "All cherubs in skimpy diapers, angels ascending and descending, Virgin Marys feeding monstrous-looking infants!"

The Burgomaster had an ambitious idea: "What about Picasso? Certainly …"

Herr Vogel cut him off with a dismissive "He's dead. In any case, hugely overrated."

After a grand tour of human artistic endeavour almost from Babylon onwards, it transpired that for the school teacher only a certain Albrecht Dürer and a foreign gentleman by the name of Gainsborough approached anything that might properly be termed Art.

"Highly eclectic," Dr. Hammes observed.

Regrettably the modest means at the disposal of the Committee prevented possible access to Herr Vogel's protégées. The Professor finally came to the rescue, proposing to the visible annoyance of the teacher that the matter was best left to the Secretary's discretion. "Thank you, gentlemen," said Fräulein Breitfuss, beaming all around and extending a caressing hand on the Professor's arm.

3

One of the main problems for the Committee was the absence of a suitable venue for the Exhibition. "An open-air gallery," someone suggested. The Burgomaster hastily turned down the proposal, recalling the time when a travelling Russian lady painter had set out her water colours of scenes of life in the Urals in the park. A sudden torrential summer deluge had in no time washed the colours clean, leaving a score of empty canvases.

Penniless and devastated by the loss of her only source of livelihood, the poor woman had to be lodged and fed by the Municipality for several weeks. Put up at Henschel's Gasthaus and keeping the company of unsavoury travelling salesmen who spent the odd night at the inn, she had taken to strong drink, footing the bill for which had almost drained the finances of the Municipality.

"Yes, I do remember that," said the Professor, recalling that Gretchen had given the prostrated artist some of her old clothes. "One wonders whatever happened to her."

"I expect she simply went back to the Urals," Dr. Hammes mused.

Fearing another such burden on the meagre resources of his Municipality, the Burgomaster himself came up with a rather original idea. There was a spacious old barn on the outskirts of the town, once used for stocking wood, now fallen into disuse. The aged owner, Herr Holtzmann, had retired from the trade and lived not far from the barn itself.

When approached by Fräulein Breitfuss, the old wood merchant retreated into an obstinate silence and repeatedly refused to meet her. On her third appearance at his door, he sent out word to say that it was not proper that a man and a young woman should meet alone. Several of the Committee members then undertook a visit to the gentlemen. Craggy and ancient, the merchant was nonetheless sharp and sprightly.

Responding to the request with a dismissive, thick flannel-clad arm he said, "No, no, no naked ladies in my place!"

Reassurances that no image of unclad persons would be exhibited were futile and received with cynical complaisance.

"Artistic ladies are always nude, don't I know!" the old man nodded with the certainty of an expert.

On being told that, dressed or otherwise, there would be no ladies at all, he looked incredulous. "Then where's the art?" he wheezed, truly puzzled.

4

It was learnt from a joiner who had worked for Holtzmann that the merchant had a voracious appetite. "He could eat a whole horse," the carpenter said. That apparently was just what he had done one Christmas. Holtzmann had bought a nag from farmer Ackermann, which he and his wife had then consumed entirely over the festive season. The Committee members were impressed.

Martha's services were enrolled and a grand dinner organized in honour of the octogenarian; although she had never served horsemeat and had no intention of doing so now. I sat in the corner by the window as Martha and Uli went back and forth piling the table with a cornucopian repast.

The Committee took it in turns to compliment Herr Holtzmann on his health, his youthful appearance, his appetite. On the latter subject he did justice to the compliments, giving a mighty demonstration of his digestive prowess. In this he was partnered by the Captain, who was visiting this particular weekend.

The prodigious pair smiled, nodded conspiratorially and proceeded to attack the contents of their plates with a frightening vehemence that would shame any canine of my breed. After having rapidly demolished several Blutwurst the girth of an infant's forearm, they went on to devour rapidly the repeated helpings of the Rinderbrust Burgerlich with baked potatoes that Martha piled on their plates.

The aroma of the rich boiled beef tingled my nostrils so, that I could only pray that the gargantuan appetites of the two men would be sated enough to spare a morsel or two when Uli came to fetch me for my supper in the kitchen. Sad to say that in their mad rush to outdo each other, the delirious duo polished off the last of the succulent meat; so that good Uli could offer me nothing more than a single Blutwurst chopped up in soup.

When finally the wood merchant had drained the last of his beer, he smacked his lips, passed the serviette over his face several times, and said very simply "Wood"; proceeding then to prise out laboriously a tiny sliver of beef lodged between his worn molars.

The Arts Committee members had dined sparingly and were not a little anxious for a positive outcome. Holtzmann's monosyllabic pronouncement left them baffled. "Wood," he repeated. Seeing their quizzical looks, he explained that he would make the barn available on one sole condition. All exhibits were to be made of wood and related matter, leaves, bark, twigs. "Roots, too," he concluded, completing the botanical cycle.

After a couple of muffled burps, he added as postscript: "No naked woman."

"Wooden nudes?" Herr Vogel ventured recklessly.

His gaze fixed on the generous slice of Nusstorte on the Captain's plate, the old man shook his head emphatically.

And so it fell on Fräulein Breitfuss to search north and south for an artist who worked in wood alone. How and where she managed to unearth Mr. Sèamus O'Malley no one ever came to know.

5

The preparations for the Exhibition brought the Professor and Fräulein Carin ever closer. They seemed entwined, shadowing each other through the day. In the morning, when he sometimes went for a walk after breakfast, she was there. In the afternoons when she went to supervise the work in the barn, he was there. Often at dinner, at Martha's, they were there. They walked arm in arm in the street. In the park she wound her arms around him. Strolling through the woods she laid her head on his shoulder and he would smooth down her hair when the breeze blew it about. She would touch his face for no visible reason. They were so enmeshed that one day in the kitchen, after breakfast, Matilde said to herself, "They'll be needing a surgeon to separate them!"

When I accompanied the Professor outdoors in the company of the tenaciously sticky young lady, I hardly ever heard a word, for they spoke softly, as if the air might carry their voices to unwanted ears. She murmured, the Professor nodded; she laughed, he glanced at her with a quite smile. They looked as if they had known each other for many long years, had endless secrets to share. And I thought of Gretchen, her carefree gait, the joy of living in her eyes, the ringing crystal of her laughter.

Today, though, Fräulein Breitfuss was louder, almost ebullient, as we sat outside Holtzmann's barn watching the workmen paint the frontage a deep wine red. My canine nose caught a whiff of the vulpine in her forced laugh, the words sounding rehearsed and hollow, as unfolding a sheet of paper she said to the Professor: "You won't believe what I found in the history catalogue yesterday. Our good friend Dieckhoff seems to have been a regular Romeo. Listen to this:

'Dearest, I think and have thought endlessly, and the more I do so,
the more certain I am that life would not be life without you, and
even were it to be so, it would not be worth living. You said the

other day you had the love and trust of a good man, high and considered in the world. I could not better that. I could only give my all. But without you I have no worth, I am nothing at all. Shall I see you tomorrow? Ever and always yours, R.'

Romantic Reindhart! From what I've heard of the man, you wouldn't think he was capable of waxing so lyrical about another man's wife. I just wonder who the Juliet might have been. He talks of the husband being high in the world. You don't think it could have been the Burgomaster's wife?"

The Professor looked at her baffled and annoyed. "That's unkind, Carin. Did you know that Frau Schulze lost a leg some years ago?"

"I didn't. I'm sorry." Then with a nonchalant shrug she said, "Not that it stops the adulterous limb working."

The Professor looked away, seeming to lose interest in the subject. "She's over sixty," he remarked quietly.

"So are you!"

6

The work on the barn had been completed by the time Mr. Sèamus O'Reilly and Mr. Seosamh O'Malley arrived. With its timbered walls and low sloping roof, it may not have looked quite the venue for high and meritorious artistic activity. But it did on the whole present an attractive frontage, the wine red setting off the surrounding green and the trees along the narrow stream that wound its way down to the river.

The spacious interior had been spruced up and painted an off-white with a raised dais at one end fronting a seating for an audience of about a hundred; while the other half, partitioned off with a curtain running the width of the barn, was meant to serve as the exhibition area. A wide barn door at the far end gave on to the grounds: two sizeable side entrances gave access to the "Conference Hall," as Fräulein Breitfuss called it.

The ancient wood merchant was fetched. Great was his amazement to see his timber storage transformed into what looked more like an attractive country inn. At first he vigorously denied that it was his old barn, until his eyes caught sight of the long grey board above the main side entrance. He contemplated the sign for a long moment, lip-reading the bold black Gothic lettering. Silently he lisped it a second time, and then again, finally bursting out in a despairing cackle.

"But I'm not dead yet, am I?" he asked looking around pathetically.

"Well, I doubt it, Herr Holtzmann," Dr. Hammes reassured him unconvincingly.

The old man put out one flannelled arm towards the doctor; who took hold of the withered wrist, felt the pulse while gazing thoughtfully in the air, made an unnecessarily long count and finally gave his reluctant verdict.

"I believe you are still alive," said Dr. Hammes letting go the dead arm.

"But it says THE HOLTZMANN MEMORIAL CENTRE," Holtzman wheezed excitedly. "Memorial means dead. I've seen dead memorials."

"True, Herr Holtzmann," the Baron nodded with agreeable sagacity. "Memorial means in memory of."

"Whose memory?"

"Yours!" Herr Vogel said with, I thought, unnecessary cruelty.

"I told you, doctor!" the octogenarian cried. "I told you! I must be dead!"

"If you say so, good man," Dr. Hammes agreed, amicably taking the insistent would-be deceased by the arm and leading him inside.

Holtzman looked at the long curtain that concealed from sight the exhibition area. Suddenly his dim eyes came alive with a strange light. Fidgeting excitedly and babbling incoherent sounds, finally he found tongue.

"Ladies," he cried squeakily, "naked ladies! They are in there … hiding behind the cloth!"

The Baron drew the cord and the pale blue fabric of the curtain slowly gathered in folds at one end, to reveal the exhibition area, empty save for the presence of a black and white mongrel sitting contentedly in the middle of the newly laid wooden floor.

"Naked dog!" Herr Vogel said vindictively.

Deflated and disheartened, Holtzmann muttered something through his slow breath, turned to the company and with a despairing melancholy softly whispered: "No ladies! Where's the Art then?"

7

For several days since their arrival, and prior to the inauguration of the exhibition itself, not much had been seen of the artists, and even less of their art.

Lodged at Henschel's Gasthaus at the expense of the Art Committee, the artistic pair rose no earlier than mid-morning, nibbled at a late breakfast, ordered several bottles of wine from Henschel's cellar and left for the day. The green van had been seen noisily making its laborious progress out of town with Mr. O'Reilly at the wheel, Mr. O'Malley beside him cradling Felicity the arrogant feline. They had been sighted some way off, in the countryside, idling on the river bank. Fräulein Breitfuss maintained they were busy scouring the surroundings for natural material for their exhibits. Undoubtedly the hectic scouring called for prolonged hours of rest and refreshment by the river.

Arrangements had been made for the artistic duo to dine at Martha's. Punctually each evening they presented themselves with sizeable appetites, their one invariable preference for Martha's succulent Wiener Schnitzel washed down with generous libations of both beer and wine. Each evening, too, the dinner commenced with Mr. O'Reilly musing on the nature of the dish.

"I would say, Sèamus, these were cutlets."

"They are," Mr. O'Malley reassured his companion.

Invariably, too, they finished the meal with impressive portions of Kaiserapfel crumble, which once again raised Mr. O'Reilly's culinary curiosity.

"I wonder how they make these apples," he would say.

"They grow on trees, Seosamh" Mr. O'Malley explained feeding himself a good mouthful.

Martha, who usually attended to her diners in a housewifely manner, heard quite a few such exchanges and thought that their conversation was peculiarly devoid of artistic content. There was much talk of food and even more of drink, occasionally a low-toned exchange on women and female attributes, but hardly ever a word on the passion and agony of artists.

Dinner over, they took ceremonious leave of Martha, Mr. O'Malley kissing her hand with a gallant bow and depositing tiny crumbs of the Kaiserapfel crumble between her fingers; while his companion, less formal than the artist, planted a resounding kiss on Martha's cheek, blowing heady fumes of beer and wine into her ear.

The night being still young, they moved on across the park to Eichel's beer house, where over several stubels of Eichel's unfiltered Weissbier they made unreciprocated conversation with the locals; some of the natives looking oddly unhappy when addressed as "Fräulein" by Mr. O'Reilly, who merely wished to sharpen his linguistic skills.

Old man Henschel, whose Gasthaus had been a post-chaise hospice since the time of Hubert the Horrid, complained of the disorderly hours kept by the artistic couple. "They come and they go," he whined. "Going and coming at all hours. Ruin my reputation!"

Burgomaster Schultz dismissed the complaints out of hand. He would not brook a word against the visitors, who after all were almost the first foreigners in town since the time when the son of Atürk Pasha on an ambassadorial mission to the Emperor's court had inadvertently taken the wrong turning and wandered into the town square, where he and his retinue were promptly seized upon and locked in a cellar, the citizenry frightened out of its wits by the brightly coloured pantaloons and outsize turbans of what they took for ill-intentioned genie.

"Look who's talking! The devil calling the kettle black," said Herr Schultz indignantly, much to the puzzlement of all present. "If people only knew of the goings-on in that den. Once I even saw a young woman leave the place at six in the morning!"

Fräulein Breitfuss, too, was quick to leap to the defence of the O'Malley-O'Reilley duo. "Most artists tend to be Bohemian in their habits."

"Even when they are not from Bohemia," Dr. Hammes concluded.

But what could not as easily be glossed over was Henschel's grievance that Lulu the chambermaid had been repeatedly and intentionally exposed to the manhood of the two visitors. "They flaunt it," he said with a peevish melancholy bordering curiously on envy. But the flaunting did not prevent Lulu from continuing to enter their rooms frequently each morning. Gossip at the Gasthaus had it that Mr. O'Malley had not limited himself to the mere flaunting but had also actually entertained Lulu with his showmanship, Lulu herself taking some pride in having knelt at the maestro's feet.

8

Public funds having been employed for the "Summer of Arts," invitation to the inauguration of the Art Exhibition had been sent out to everyone who was anyone, which in effect meant everyone. And everyone came, it being an idle Sunday afternoon.

Gersten the baker and Udo the butcher were there, as were bookseller Himmel, the fetching florist Frau Gärtner, Adolf of Adolf's Antiques who came with an antique folding camera from his shop. Unusually, Herr Adler the bank manager, who was hardly ever seen away from his desk and spoke only within the precincts of his bank, also came, with his perennially scowling wife who today had decided to grace her large head with a small leghorn sort of hat and heels that resembled stilts.

Martha walked across the green looking as I had never seen her before. Sans her ever-present apron, dressed in a graceful flowery dress and with a smart hat adorned with a few cherries, she was the image of an attractive and prosperous matron. Frau Krause was there, the wicker basket in her hand bulging suspiciously; no doubt Montevideo was ensconced somewhere inside, dreaming his palm-fringed tropical dreams.

Everyone had come, except Herr Holtzmann, for whom a seat had been reserved in front of the dais along with the Committee members. No amount of persuasion or prayer had worked. The old man had taken umbrage with the naming of the barn. "They've made me a memorial," he muttered peevishly. "I'm not going to my own funeral. It's not right." There was some ground to suspect that the complete absence of naked ladies had made him lose all interest in Art.

As always, the Baron had driven into town in his ancient black beetle-shaped, open-top car, which was parked near the exhibition end of the barn. Much to my surprise, and pleasure, he had brought along Schwarzbauer, who was seated in the back in his leather work apron holding an enormous bouquet of white roses that the Baron meant to present to Fräulein Breitfuss during the opening ceremony of the Exhibition.

9

Seated on the raised dais with the Burgomaster on one side and the artist and his agent friend on the other, Fräulein Breitfuss formally introduced the artistic visitors to the public. The Burgomaster then welcomed the duo, highlighting the merits of their art, the immense effort and sacrifice they had made in choosing our town of all places to exhibit their latest compositions.

The occasion also marked, he concluded, the establishment of indissoluble ties between the two countries and it was his earnest hope that our town people would soon learn to sing the Donegal Dingle and other such melodies from the far-off island, so that we might offer a hearty welcome to the numerous visitors who would undoubtedly flock to visit the exhibition. "Today people fly, to Shanghai, for no reason whatsoever. They fly to Hawaii, why?"

The Burgomaster's mysterious digression was left hanging in the air; for greatly impressed by his enviable knowledge of the globe, the audience burst into eager applause. Ever a good soul, stout, hearty and down to earth, Herr Schulze was liked by everyone, except Adolf of Adolf's Antiques. And the Burgomaster's latest attempt to put our town on the map of the known world, along with Shanghai, Hawaii and other such exotic locations, was both sustained and lauded by the citizenry.

When the applause finally died down, without elaborating further on why people flew to Hawaii, Herr Schultz said, "And now it is with immense pleasure that I call on Herr Oh'Really to say a few words on the eminent, the great Herr Seamouse Oh'Milly!"

10

The post-prandial hour, following an extended lunch with generous libations of beer, seemed to have had a soporific effect on the eminent visitors. It appeared at first sight that neither of the gentlemen named was available for active participation in the conference. Head thrown back, eyes shut, overwhelmed no doubt by the Burgomaster's generous introduction, Mr. O'Malley seemed to have slipped into a meditative languor. The unstinting praise seemed to have affected Mr. O'Reilly no less. Head down and with arms crossed over the chest, he appeared to have fallen into a deep trance, which obviously affected his breathing, producing an irregular nasal sonority.

The Burgomaster looked baffled by Mr. O'Reilly's failure to rise to the occasion. Thinking then that the gentleman's immobility might be caused by his inadequate language skills, by way of assurance he added emphatically and with resounding loudness, "Genius knows no language. Chinese, Celtic, Greek or Tyrolean, greatness speaks for itself. I now give you Herr Oh'Really!"

With the booming mention of his name resounding in his ears, Mr. O'Reilly came to with a start. Rubbing his eyes and arresting a yawn, he rose to his feet slowly. A hearty applause initiated by Herr Schulze and taken up by the public appeared to make him aware of his whereabouts.

"Ladies and gentlemen, friends,' he said with a lazy drawl, staring fixedly at the air. "First and foremost, surely foremost, our heartiest thanks to his eminence your Buggermaster." His gaze rested on Herr Schultz for a long moment, as though attempting to recall a face seen somewhere.

"Few," he went on hesitantly, "very few, indeed none have had the good fortune of having a Buggermaster such as your Buggermaster, who without doubt must be the master of all Bugger…"

"Oh! Buggerthemaster," exclaimed Mr. O'Malley suddenly, before regaining his meditative silence. Despite the total incomprehension, the audience broke out in cheerful applause, Herr Schultz getting to his feet to acknowledge the ovation with a radiant smile.

"And, let me add," Mr. O'Reilly resumed when quiet had returned, "for add I must, so do allow me to add that truly it is an honour, and what an honour, to be so honoured. I repeat, for one cannot but repeat, that we are honoured, honoured beyond measure to be so honoured. Truly and similarly, it is an honour and, my word, what an honour to have with us here today an artist no less than Mr. Sèamus O'Malley! A round of applause please, if you will."

The request being incomprehensible to the general public, Mr. O'Malley acknowledged the respectful silence with a drowsy smile. Unperturbed by the unresponsive audience, Mr. O'Reilly resumed his vagrant oration. One hand moving about in his trouser pocket, as though quelling an irritating itch, he said, "Let us then, friends, come to the heart of the matter."

"As if the heart ever mattered," Mr. O'Malley observed stifling a yawn.

"From the day he departed his dear Donegal many a season ago, Sèamus O'Malley's art has stood out and apart, away from the namby-pamby brushes and paint-pots of the Picassholes and Warholes."

"Not to mention all the other holes," Mr. O'Malley added sententiously.

"I can safely vouchsafe, gentlemen…"

"And ladies," Mr. O'Malley insisted.

"Ladies always, first and last!"

When the appreciative clapping of the audience at the inclusion of the fair sex had died down, Mr. O'Reilly resumed the eulogy. "I can and do vouchsafe, ladies and gentlemen, and ladies again, that everywhere Sèamus O'Malley's work has been received with applause so thunderous, so deafening, that it still rings in the ears and down the years. From Cairo to County Clare, from Calcutta to the Klondike, from Muswell Hill to Montevideo…"

Through the thicket of chair and human legs, I saw Monty's head suddenly pop out of the wicker basket at the mention of his name. "Mon-tee-vee-dee-io!" he cackled loudly drawing out the word, proceeding then to demand sharply *Me Monty Who You?* Frau Krause's gaunt hand hastily stuffed the truant head back in the basket.

Nonplussed, Mr. O'Reilly inclined his head. "Begorrah, Sèamus, there's a ghost in this chamber!"

11

Basking in the warm noon sun, I sat by the side door of the barn, where the Professor had left me. As Mr. O'Reilly's talk proceeded, the elevated claims of Mr. O'Malley's artistic genius branding generations to come fairly incomprehensible to me, the attention of my nose was caught by a pleasant meaty aroma wafted by the quiet afternoon breeze. Sniffing the air, I thought the trail of the smoky, savoury smell led to the curtained-off area which displayed the artist's work, as yet unseen by the public.

Getting to my feet, I nudged my head past the blue cloth separé and was taken aback by the sight of the exhibit. Having lived as I had in a house with paintings and artefacts, Gretchen's water-colours, sculptures, moulded glass pieces in variegated colours, a brass head of one of our great minds in the Professor's study, I was accustomed to human artistic expressions. But a work such as that which now lay on the floor of the exhibition area I had never seen, nor could ever have imagined.

On the large white square painted in the middle of the new wooden floor lay a dry lichen-covered branch. Torn rudely off a birch tree, the limbs of the bough were unpainted and unadorned, except the topmost. The sturdy wooden arm was wound with what suspiciously resembled and certainly smelt of meat. Strips of bacon, my nose told me from the smoky aroma of the fatty streaks. Even more curious, the extreme end of the limb was hung with a small paper flag with red and white stripes, with a boxed corner printed with numerous white stars on a field of blue.

The air redolent with the appetising smell of fatty smoked meat, I thought it an attractive piece of work, certainly a novel type of art. As I breathed in the rich aroma by the lungful and marvelled at the boundless inventiveness of the human imagination, suddenly a fellow canine appeared at the rear entrance of the barn whose wide doors had been thrown open. It was the black and white mongrel Holtzmann had seen in his search for hidden naked ladies.

Tongue lolling, the wretched creature appeared excited as it sniffed the air with its head turning this way and that. Catching sight of me, it stood still for a moment, gave a hesitant wag of the tail and fixing the large submissive eyes on me lowered its head. Half-crouching then, emitting a low mournful whine, as though protesting my presence, slowly the urchin slunk forward like a thief in the night.

Behind me Mr. O'Reilly's oratory was now in full flow. "As the

Almighty is our witness," he thundered, "and may the Saints bless Him a hundredfold, and more, we are a band of brothers, brothers and fathers and cousins, living and loving in peace and harmony. Yet my friends, the message is clear, limpid as the moonlight in the bay. The human tree has withered, for a single branch has gathered to itself all the fruit, the chosen few have laid their hands on all the bacon…"

The shaggy black and white coat on the lean frame was all atremble with agitation and impatience as the intruder stood mesmerized in front of Mr. O'Malley's peculiar artefact. To my horror, then, it put out a pink tongue and gave the bacon a long hungry lick. After savouring for a moment what must have been a highly agreeable taste, it began to nibble greedily at the meat; in the process chewing up the paper flag. But the bacon had been wound tight around the wood and the flesh refused to yield to the increasingly frenzied attack. Finally, sinking its teeth into the meat, it battened onto to the dry wood and desperately pulling this way and that, laboriously tugging at the branch, the cur slowly moved backwards towards the entrance. The next moment both animal and exhibit were out of the door and gone from sight, leaving the white square bare save for a small broken twig.

12

Withdrawing my head from under the curtain, I looked outside. The mongrel and the exhibit were nowhere to be seen. Instead, Schwarzbauer had alighted from the Baron's car and holding aloft the enormous bouquet of white roses was striding towards the exhibition entrance with, oddly, Felicity the O'Malley cat close on his heels.

The gathering had listened with patience and perseverance but had understood little or nothing of Mr. O'Reilly's impassioned dissertation on Art. Now eager to get on with the afternoon's business and view the artist's much lauded but as yet mysterious creation, the audience rose to its feet with a resounding applause that all but drowned out the speaker's concluding words as he said "Like man art too is mortal, my friends. Here now, gone the next moment!"

Headed by the Burgomaster and the Committee Members, the small crowd moved towards the curtain. "I now declare the Exhibition officially open," Herr Schultz announced with the pride of a father presenting his first-born. Pulling at the cord with deliberate slowness, he gradually drew the blue curtain aside.

A single sibilant gasp rose from the visitors. Standing erect and towering in the middle of the white square was Schwarzbauer in his brown leather dungarees, the jet black sheen of his naked arms and shoulders set off by the mass of white roses held high as he bared his radiant set of teeth in the proudest of smiles. Beside him, on the floor, sat Felicity, perfectly still, as if made of porcelain.

Mistaking Frau Gärtner for Fräulein Breitfuss, Schwarzbauer stepped towards her with the bouquet of flowers. At which the fetching florist fell back, gave a short scream, swooned and fainted clean away, and would have dropped to the ground in a heap had not butcher Udo's meaty arms gathered her up.

In the babble that now ensued, the Baron directed Schwarzbauer towards Fräulein Breitfuss. She had however just sighted the O'Malley-O'Reilly duo slipping out quietly through the side entrance. With a hoarse cry of "Gentlemen, gentlemen!" she hurried after them, followed by the gardener, who was now determined on delivering the bouquet to the correct recipient.

Leaving the hubbub and confusion in the barn behind me, I padded outdoors, just in time to catch sight of the artistic pair trotting rapidly across the sunlit green towards the wooded rise, with Felicity leaping in step behind them. In vain pursuit Fräulein Breitfuss had broken out in a mincing run with shrill cries of "Malley! Reilly!" Close on her heels, striding like a giant, the roses firmly held forth, Schwarzbauer boomed "Madame! Madame!"

13

Having been paid in advance, the artistic pair saw no reason to tarry. Bags packed and ready, they departed as soon as they had gained Henschal's Gasthaus. Uli reported seeing the green van chugging past Martha's eatery in a billowing cloud of black smoke.

Henschel himself was glad to be rid of the "foreign gentlemen" but complained that they had removed a bottle of schnapps from the bar on the way out. Lulu the chambermaid grieved that neither of the gentlemen had bid her a proper farewell; especially "Herr Molly" who had made her so familiar with his artistic attributes. But she treasured the thin chain with a small enamelled-green shamrock that the artist had given her and for a long time afterwards the pendant nestled comfortably in the warm folds of her ample bosom.

It was also discovered that the couple had run up a bill of no mean size at Eichel's beer house, with Eichel threatening to sequester the old van should the pair chance to pass through town again. But neither van nor its owners were seen or heard of ever again.

A few days later, Henschel handed over to Dr. Hammes a small cardboard box with odds and ends that had been overlooked by the artists in their hurried departure. Lunch over, sitting out in the grounds with the Professor, the doctor went through the contents. He extracted a couple of faded, half-torn photographs from the jumble.

The first figured a much younger Mr. O'Malley and a far slimmer Mr. O'Reilly, each with a long drooping moustache, dressed in pink and white checked shirts and blue dungarees, heads sporting wide straw hats. The artist appeared to be playing a harmonica, while his friend held to his lips what looked oddly like a long comb half-wrapped in a strip of paper. Behind them a long dirt road flanked by ramshackle wooden houses stretched into the distance; above their heads a wooden sign with crooked letters read TEQUILA Y SEÑORITAS.

The second was a faded black and white postcard-sized memorabilia, of the duo in their youth, the lean faces topped by cloth caps, smiling uncertainly in the firm clasp of a large buxom lady in the middle, the trio posing in front of the Ballymore Baron Hotel, a large double-storied cottage with wisps of smoke rising from the chimney stack. The small inscription in an uncertain hand at the bottom read:

For Sèamus and Seosamh
May you conquer the world
Love
Caithleen O'Donnel

The box contained a few other oddments, bits and pieces from far and near. A small unframed mirror, with a bold print on the back that read: **STOLEN FROM INDIAN RAILWAYS**; a teaspoon from the Grand Hotel in Cleethorpes; an empty bottle of antacid tablets; two stained Whitbread beer mats. And a slender, dog-eared paperback with a garish cover, titled "FAMOUS FALLEN WOMEN OF IRELAND."

"One wouldn't have thought there were many fallen woman in Ireland," Dr. Hammes mused putting the collection back in the box. "Only martyrs fallen for the Cause."

NOBUKO DANCE
THEATRE

1

The arrival of the Nobuko Dance Theatre troupe did not auger well for the relationship and by the time the troupe departed something appeared to have broken between the Professor and Fräulein Carin. But it was the visit by Dr. Ochoa that caused irreparable damage, seemingly beyond repair or reconciliation. Relations between humans are so complex and contorted that one of my kind could not begin to ask the why, what and the wherefore of the matter. Nor could I, unusually and keeping in mind the well-being of my Professor, take comfort from the young lady's prolonged absence from the breakfast table.

For days he locked himself in the study. I sat outside, waiting in vain expectancy for our accustomed walk in the woods or a stroll in the park. Morose and irritable, he emerged briefly to wander aimlessly through the house. When Matilde enquired what he might like for lunch, his reply shocked me not a little. "What you will," he said curtly and made for the study. Matilde looked after him thoughtfully, a shade of sadness shadowing her matronly features. She returned to the kitchen with a sigh. I walked out to the garden to sit in the dull late summer sun.

His thoughts elsewhere, the Professor sat at table almost unwillingly, ate indifferently, in silence. Today the usual banter and elliptical exchanges with Matilde were absent. Only once did he raise his gaze, looked at me crouched by the door and said, "Albert ought to be outdoors."

"He's not the only one," came Matilde's tart response. "Will you be dining at Martha's or should I leave something for the evening?" she asked.

"Thank you, I think I'll be staying in. Please put out something for Albert as well."

I for one would have much preferred to accompany him to Martha's, for the fare certainly, but not least for the warmth of Uli's company while I ate in the kitchen. It was disheartening to have to dine out of a tin at this late age, when for the better part of my days Gretchen and Matilde had fed me from the stove. Fräulein Carin had wreaked havoc with our lives, but I had never imagined that she would come between me and my supper, as well!

To make matters worse, after several days of Fräulein Carin's absence from the house, the Captain arrived for a long weekend and the pair had been sighted walking arm in arm in the grounds of the library. The Professor grew ever more despondent, now hardly emerging from the study except for a brief, wordless meal.

Several days later Dr. Hammes came by and, on his firm insistence, the Professor dressed and we went for a late afternoon stroll. Usually the two men discussed varied matters but there was always an enclosure around their intimate lives. The doctor never enquired after Fräulein Carin and the Professor never touched on his friend's progress, or otherwise, with Nurse Ulrike. Today the talk was casual and desultory, as though a shadow had come between them.

"You don't look too well, Ernst," the doctor said. "Shall I come by tomorrow and give you a check. After all I do happen to know a thing or two about the human anatomy, as well," he added with a forced lightness.

The professor smiled wanly. "The lungs breathe, the heart still beats. That should be enough."

"It should. Clinically speaking," Dr. Hammes agreed reluctantly, accepting the Professor's refusal of his offer.

"Clinically speaking!" The Professor's small hollow laugh was at once both amusement and mockery. "Don't tell me Thomas that you've begun dabbling in the realm of the spirit, as well."

"I limit myself to the occasional cognac, thank you." Thinking he might have come too close to the bone, he changed tack and asked: "What did you think of the Nobukos' performance?"

"Oh that!" The Professor made a brief dismissive gesture. "I told Carin what I thought."

He did not elucidate further on the thoughts he had shared with Fräulein Breitfuss, until the doctor remarked, "I sometimes think that today we have among us several billion artists, at the least. Scribblers, doodlers, ham actors. A puppy managing for once to pee straight against a lamp post is declared an artist." Giving me an apologetic glance, he added, "No offence meant, Albert."

No offence at all! I had been trained in puppyhood by Gretchen not to urinate against lamp posts or other such objects of public utility.

Encouraged by a similitude of sentiments, for a passing moment the Professor became his usual self, voluble even. "I'm afraid, Thomas, we live in an age of universal brain damage. Art today is whatever one chooses to do, quite as often not do."

"The art gallery in place of the music hall and the circus." said Dr. Hammes drawing hard on his spent cigar. "Change of locale, same audience."

"Yes. Have you ever had occasion to watch the blank faces of the hordes trooping through the Louvre or the Uffizi? Most might as well be staring at a shop window filled with orthopaedic articles. Shout 'Art!' from a rooftop and the next morning you'll have a coach load of the same crowd from heaven knows where gaping at a dim white room with a smashed light bulb on the floor."

The doctor laughed aloud. "I expect the solemn faces would be equally awe-struck if you replaced the bulb with a leg of ham!"

"The acquiescence of ignorance!"

Dr. Hammes was pleasantly surprised by the tone of indignation, pleased that his friend appeared to have recovered from his prostration, if only momentarily.

As an afterthought the Professor added, "I ought to tell you though, Thomas, I've nothing against the Itos. A very decent couple."

"As decent as they come. But where on earth does Carin dig up these exotic sorts."

"I'm afraid you'll have to ask her," the Professor replied distantly.

The bizarre theatricals of the Nobuko dance duo had no doubt come between him and Fräulein Carin; not to mention the incident with Dr. Ochoa. If matters of such slight import could cause such division, happily then I could not see a radiant future for the couple. Obviously it grieved me to see the Professor cast down, abandoned and despondent. One could only pray that it was merely a passing cloud. Forgetting that some clouds came to stay and release a downpour on one's head!

2

As with Mr. Séamus O'Malley, Fräulein Breitfuss had unearthed the Nobuko Dance Company in some dim corner of the world. Unseen and unheard, they had been invited to perform in the "Summer of Arts" for an audience which would have much preferred to see an elephant stand on it's tail. So would I. In this at least the people in our town shared my limited horizons.

But the Art Exhibition and the Marathon Film Night had taught Fräulein Breitfuss nothing, carried away as she was by her position as arbiter of taste and culture. Her proximity to the eminence of the Professor, and not only eminence, had given her carte blanche to ride roughshod over other voices. She consulted the Committee members but briefly, giving a cursory description of the rarefied artistic merits of the Nobuko troupe; which she herself had never witnessed.

"Not quite as commonplace as a Tchaikovsky ballet or the Dancers from the White Mountain," she declared in the manner of an authority, "their Art might at first prove somewhat incomprehensible." So it did, from first to last.

Herr Vogel's attention however was caught by a passing name. "Who," he asked with a ferret's suspicious air, "are the Dancers from the White Mountain?"

"I think you will find," said Fräulein Breitfuss in a tone that was meant to be a decisive snub, "that the name itself says it all."

"But which White Mountain?" the school teacher insisted. "The one in the Caucuses or the other one near the Slovak town of Plišneck?"

"You take your pick, Herr Vogel," she dismissed the perfectly reasonable query with rude impatience. "Now, gentlemen, if I may go on…"

"One small question, Fräulein, if I may interrupt you," the Burgomaster said meekly. "Can one then take it that we shall be receiving a good number of wealthy tourists from Japan?"

"Oh absolutely, I should think!" Dr. Hammes cut in with the indisputable certainty of one of the less fallible of the ancient oracles. "There is no reason to doubt," he assured the Burgomaster, "that hordes of video-wielding tourists from the land of the Rising Sun will be travelling half way round the world to watch a performance they can catch from around the corner of their homes."

Thus assured, Herr Schultz beamed in expectation and let Fräulein Breitfuss proceed with her presentation of the outlandish dancers from the Second Municipal District of the Lesser Hokkaido.

3

Fairly extravagant arrangements were made to lodge and feed the Nobuko dancers. Fresh funds were called for, which were gladly coughed up by the Burgomaster from Municipal funds. After all, beckoning flocks of visitors from over the seas, it would finally put our town on the map of the world.

Light-headed and forgetful, Herr Schultz had apparently overlooked that the Art Exhibition had not drawn a single out-of-town visitor, save for an elderly Finnish couple who had taken the wrong turning off the main highway and almost immediately decamped terrified at the sight of Schwarzbauer's black robotic figure holding aloft the bouquet of white roses.

The Baron too came forth generously. In memory, he claimed, of the visit by the Imperial Emperor to one of our Kaisers. "Although," he mused, "what they had to say to each other, if anything at all, heaven only knows." Not least, he added, there was an affinity in adversity, a common bond that had led to both the nations going down in flames together.

The entire upper floor of Henschel's Gasthaus was reserved to lodge the members of the dance troupe, who would doubtless be numerous. Fräulein Breitfuss put in a special request that cherry blossoms be placed in vases in all the rooms. It being long past the cherry season, late crab apple flowers from Frau Trott's garden were inducted into service.

For the first evening all the tables at Martha's were booked for a grand gala dinner. Fräulein Breitfuss went through the cookery section in the library, to help Martha work out a menu suitable for the visitors. It was thought that celebrated though the dish might be, her trotters with sour beets was unlikely to tickle their palates. But while there were cookery books galore on the shelves, ranging from entire volumes on Victorian deserts such as roly-poly and spotted dick puddings to Hispano-Irish fusion cuisine and secret recipes from the Outer Hebrides, there was next to nothing on Japanese preparations.

Finally, patient search by Frau Botticelli turned up a slender volume by a Miss Emily Jane Hewitt, who had lived in the village of Kamakura, in the Prefecture of Uraga, at the time of the Mikado. Although not setting out clearly the purpose of her sojourn of several years, with merely a passing mention of the local Shogun's huge appetite for foreign meats, the little book on Japanese mores and manners did touch on local food habits, one item of particular interest being seaweed. Miss Hewitt described in meticulous detail the preparation of the seaweed, the drying, pressing, cutting in strips; then simply added that foodstuffs were rolled in the strips. Rolls of seaweed not being available, Uli suggested using toilet rolls, but was told off by his mother and despatched to the kitchen to finish the dishes.

4

The arrival of the Nobuko Theatre Dance Company caused some consternation. A solemn white-haired Japanese gentleman alighted, followed by a petite and considerably younger Japanese lady in a shiny green wrap which fell all the way to her dainty little feet. A substantial amount of luggage was unloaded, and then the train pulled out of the station. It was feared that language difficulties might have prevented the rest of the troupe from leaving their carriage.

Fräulein Breitfuss stepped forward and addressed the elderly gentleman: "Master Katsuro Ito?" She must have practised the mouthful in private and also got the novel mode of address from Miss Hewitt's little book.

"Hö!" said the visitor and made a deep bow.

Fräulein Breitfuss bowed. The old gentleman bowed again. She felt obliged to follow suit, after which Master Ito once again emitted the heavy half-nasal sound of "Hö" and bowed. She bowed, he bowed, then fearing that it could go on for the rest of the afternoon, she extricated herself with half a curtsy and turned to the lady, who said with a charming smile and a giggle "Katsumi Ito" and bowed. Fräulein Breitfuss bowed.

But before Lady Katsumi could repeat the performance, Fräulein Breitfuss enquired anxiously, "And the rest of the dance company?"

Katsumi Ito giggled sweetly. "Dance company?" she repeated with another giggle. "We dance company," she explained succinctly, with a charming smile and yet another bow.

It then dawned on all present, the Professor, Dr. Hammes, the Baron, that the Nobuko Theatre Dance Company in reality consisted of only the two Itos; although we never did find out whether they were man and wife, brother and sister, cousins, companions, or other. It was however learnt later that the Company had been named after Master Ito's grandmother, whose dancing, as well as a few other secret and celebrated skills, had greatly impressed one of the Mikados. Veiling their surprise and disappointment, the Committee Members stepped forward and were introduced by Fräulein Breitfuss.

Miss Ito was especially delighted as, looming over her, Dr. Hammes offered a surprisingly graceful bow. "Hams!" she said with the most girlish of giggles. Returning his courtesy, she tilted her silken head to one side, repeated "Hams! Like porku meat?" and tittered again with a fetching smile, before delivering another gracious bow. "There's worse, my dear," the doctor smiled with utmost charm, returning the bow.

All in all, there was a great deal of bowing, with Master Ito punctuating every other bow with his favourite expression, while with every presentation Lady Katsumi smiled and giggled in a most charming manner. On the Professor being introduced, the Master actually uttered a word. "Professor! Hö!" he exclaimed with reverence, before proceeding to the bending.

The station master, who had been standing behind us, felt he too ought to participate in the ceremony and took to bowing without having been invited. Trying to keep a count of the bows, I felt it was more than a little unfair that the visitors had to bend incessantly while the Committee members took it in turns.

I had been standing behind Dr. Hammes and he felt there was no reason why I too should not be presented to the visitors. With a broad sweep in my direction he said, "Albert!" Something about my appearance made Master Katsuro change his usual acknowledgement. "Hä!" he exclaimed going into a bow. The human gesture of courtesy being beyond my skills, I merely wagged my tail; but it was done with the warmth of welcome. Lady Katsumi merely mispronounced my name, said "Allber" and daintily covering her mouth went into small fits of giggle.

5

The gala dinner at Martha's did not turn out to be the affair it was meant to be. All the tables being reserved for the supposedly numerous dance troupe, the empty restaurant had a somewhat desolate air despite the radiant presence of a large bouquet of white cluster chrysanthemums in a cut-glass vase on the round table in the centre.

Martha had set the long table by the window for the chief guests and the Committee Members and there they now sat. An empty place at the table had been filled with a last-minute invitation to Herr Adler, the bank manager. A tall, lanky figure with thinning auburn hair, he ate quietly, said nothing and might as well not have been there. Only once did he attempt to engage the guests in conversation, muttering something vaguely about some place called Hiroshima, but seeing Master Katsuro's startled expression he desisted and the exchange died there. I sat in the usual corner, by the table where the Professor dined when alone.

Martha had foregone Fräulein Breitfuss's recommendation of seaweed wrappings. Instead, she served a main course of succulent beef cubes drowned in cherry-flavoured cream sauce with sliced wood mushrooms; accompanied by potato dumplings stuffed with parsley and chive. It was a hearty dish, washed down with wine, and aquavit in place of the rice wine requested by Fräulein Breitfuss.

The fare was only partially appreciated by Master Katsuro, as he carefully scraped the sauce off the meat and finely sliced the cubes of beef prior to feeding himself. With the dumplings, too, he discarded the potato and extracted the chive and parsley filling.

The table-talk was not particularly memorable. Language might have been a barrier, but somehow I had the impression that the dance duo were not given to ardent conversation. Master Katsuro slipped the slivers of beef into his mouth and looked at his fellow diners with the most benign of expressions. Lady Katsumi was rather more alive, putting away the meat at a steady pace, as also the dumplings after setting aside the chive and parsley.

"Do you eat much meat?" Fräulein Breitfuss asked solicitously.

"Eat much meat," the young lady giggled prettily.

"So do I," said the Burgomaster redundantly, tucking in with a controlled voracity, each mouthful followed by a long sip of the aquavit.

With the serving of the fruit, Master Katsuro became rather more animated. He watched with keen admiration as Martha personally peeled, stoned and sliced a plump juicy peach and placed it in front of him. With a soft "Hö" he bowed his head, then looked up at her with what must have been his first smile in decades. Turning to Lady Katsumi he uttered a couple of monosyllables, which she immediately announced to the table with a modest giggle: "Master Katsuro like Lady Kitchen."

Quietly conversing with the Professor, the Baron remarked good humouredly, "And it is to be hoped that Lady Kitchen too like Master Katsuro!"

"Like Lady Kitchen," the dancer insisted with a long, less than modest giggle.

Like her he must have, for the Master's eyes keenly followed Lady Kitchen's every movement as she came and went serving and removing dishes.

The dinner nearing the end, the Burgomaster proposed a toast to the guests. He had eaten very substantially and drunk even more of the aquavit. Fulfilled, and filled to the full, his large, good-natured face exuded conviviality and camaraderie, and a shine of damp. Rising with some difficulty and holding forth the glass, he announced in a booming voice that resonated through the empty restaurant: "A toast!" One by one the other diners rose with their glasses. Master Katsuro and Lady Katsumi looked alarmed, but after a moment they too got to their feet uncertainly.

"A toast to our friends from across the seas!" Herr Schultz declaimed in a loud rounded voice, holding the glass aloft. "May many of their kind follow in their footsteps and may they remain with us long! To our friends, Master and Lady Katz!"

With that he threw back the drink and, with a strangled cry of

"Banzai!" tossed the glass behind him. Martha's precious liquor crystal flew clean through the air and out the open window into the night. It must have landed squarely on the head of one of the strays that loitered around the restaurant after dark, for the night air filled with the most excruciating howl followed by a series of yelps as the wretch fled into the night in pain.

Master Katsuro looked amazed, the other diners disconcerted. Martha went to the window in the hope of catching sight of her prized crystal. And Lady Katsumi had the last giggle.

6

"Schöpping!" said Lady Katsumi with a girlish giggle. And shopping she went.

Much as Fräulein Breitfuss might have wished to accompany her, she and Master Katsuro were busy supervising the stage preparations at the Holtzmann Memorial Centre. Dr. Hammes would have happily steered the young woman around town but was away attending a conference on domesticating marsupials

For one reason or another, the other Committee members too were unavailable. The Baron was busy attending to Baroness Gertrude, who had come down with her annual cold and insisted on having her son at the bedside, saying "I could never forgive myself if I left without a last look at you." The Professor had hardly ever stepped into a shop in his life and would not have known what to do had he done so; besides he had work in hand to complete as Dr. Ochoa was expected to visit us shortly. As for Herr Vogel, he refused point blank, stating as a firm moral tenet, "I never go into a shop with a woman." So it fell on Matilde and me to chaperon the visitor during our morning round of shopping.

"Allber go schöpping, too?" Lady Katsumi asked sweetly, tickling me under the chin.

On the way to the shops, Lady Katsumi abruptly stopped in her tracks. "Change money?" she asked earnestly.

Matilde looked puzzled. "What for?"

The young lady drew out a few grey notes from her flat little handbag. Matilde turned the narrow slips of paper in her hand. "I don't think you could buy anything with these, my dear," she said peering at the illustration of a man in a housecoat. "Are you sure it's money?"

At that moment Lady's Katsumi's face lit up. "Banku," she said pointing animatedly at a low red-brick gabled building not far from the Library.

"Oh, the bank!"

"Banku," insisted Lady Katsumi, smiling.

And to the banku we went, Matilde slightly perplexed by the visitor's inability to read correctly such a large signboard.

Possibly Lady Katsumi was not entirely impressed by the dim, rather shabby interiors of our local bank. "Banku?" she asked uncertainly as we went through a double entrance whose doors opened on each other and sprang back on people's faces without warning. The décor inside was spartan and unexciting, grey walls plastered with old banking posters, a table and a couple of chairs, two counters adjoining a plain pine door which led to the Manager's office, a Venetian blind of green plastic slats behind the large glass window on the side assuring confidentiality.

"Banku?" repeated Lady Katsumi looking timidly at the gaunt gargoyle figure of clerk Schiefferdecker hunched behind the only open counter, the other being permanently shut.

It was surprising with what rapidity Matilde could master a foreign tongue. "Yes dear, Banku," she said reassuringly.

Schiefferdecker peering through glasses as thick as tumbler bottoms silently turned Lady Katsumi's banknotes in his hands for several minutes. "One didn't know they play Monopoly in Japan as well?" he mused thoughtfully, studying closely the figure of the housecoat-clad gentleman on the notes. "I think you'd better ask Herr Adler."

Matilde and I waited patiently after the visitor had been ushered in to see Herr Adler. Clerk Schiefferdecker worked unperturbed as we heard giggles and a series of sharp little squeals behind the Manager's door.

"It does take long," Matilde muttered looking askance.

"Oh, Herr Adler likes to put things through a thorough examination," the clerk remarked dryly.

And thorough the examination must have been, for when after a good quarter of an hour Lady Katsumi finally emerged smoothing her dress and clutching a handful of proper money, she looked flushed and flustered. "Good bankuman," she smiled to herself tucking the notes into her little handbag.

The first stop was at Udo's. After the daily procession of the usual customers, penny-pinching housewives and querulous old maids, the butcher was delighted to see a fresh face in his shop. "You're only selling meat, not Swiss watches," Matilde dryly rebutted the shopkeeper's effusion, poking an expert finger into a trussed piece of roasting beef.

Lady Katsumi surveyed the array of cuts under the glass and tilted her head with a fetching smile. "Me see your meat?" she asked Udo with a girlish giggle.

"Oh, would you really?"

"Udo!" Matilde reprimanded curtly, "Please remember the young lady is in my charge."

With a head full of reddish curls, a short nose and eyes blue as a clear winter sky, stocky and with forearms that hacked through ribs and collar bones with a single blow, Udo was easy-going and good-humoured. His lady customers accepted the sly and suggestive bantering, knowing there was neither intent nor malice in the words.

He now took the visitor through the array of loin, leg and shoulder, belly pork, ground pork, lean pork, chops, ribs, sirloin, undercut, brisket, liver and sweetbread; pronouncing each distinctly as though imparting a lesson to an apprentice. At the end of the row he pointed to a heaped tray. "Sausage, Aachen sausage," he added lifting a string of the pink tubed meat.

"Like sausage," Lady Katsumi giggled pressing one between her dainty fingers.

"I'm sure you do!" the butcher arched his eyebrows.

"That'll do, Udo," Matilde interrupted slapping down a piece of braising meat on the scale.

At the florist's, where Matilde was to pick up the white iris the Professor and I were to take to Gretchen the next morning, Lady Katsumi in her shiny green dress winged like a flighty butterfly, moving from bouquet to bouquet gently sniffing the cut flowers, her face lit up with a radiance that made her look like a child lost in a fabled garden.

Frau Gärten, a sweet gentle soul who had been widowed in her youth, when one sunny day her husband had laid himself down in the garden on a bed of gloxinia and never got to his feet again, found light and beauty not only in flowers but in all things around her. Enchanted by Lady Katsumi and her adoration of the floral display, she said, "Isn't she sweet? Just like a doll. Look at her skin, pure alabaster!"

"It's the seaweed they eat," Matilde remarked, momentarily quite as charmed by the slender flitting figure among the plants and flowers. "Fräulein Breitfuss thinks so."

"And what a beautiful costume. Kimono, they call it, don't they?"

"They can call it what they like," Matilde said returning to her usual self. "I'd never find my way out of one of those."

Lady Katsumi returned with a posy of red and blue anemones. With a bow and a guileless smile, she said, "For Ma Tilde," and held out the pretty flowers.

"Oh!" exclaimed the housekeeper, for once lost for words. She could not at all remember when last someone had offered her flowers.

8

Meat and flowers were fine for the house, but hardly mementoes that Lady Katsumi could proudly exhibit to friends on her return home. Matilde thought a small antique piece would better remind her of the visit to our town. Reluctantly she took the young lady into Adolf's.

Matilde had never liked the name, nor had she any great liking for the man himself. The name, she thought, did not do him justice, it was much too good. No one seemed to know the reason for this undercurrent of hostility. But widow Ansel, whose memory apparently reached back to prehistory, could remember that once long ago the antiquarian had assiduously courted Matilde for several seasons; only to decide in the end, when the young woman's thoughts had turned to the choice of her bridal dress, to forego the bliss of wedded life and a houseful of bedraggled children running amuck. As parting gift he had given her a slightly-chipped piece from his small collection of Meissen crockery. "At least I had Monty to console me," Frau Krause remarked sadly. "Poor Matilde only a broken mug."

"And what fair wind brings such lovely ladies to my den?"

"Den. You can say that again!" Matilde retorted dryly, avoiding the complacent gaze of her erstwhile suitor. Thinking, too, it was just this sort of windy elocution that had seduced her foolish youth.

Half-balding, thinner than a pole, silver pince-nez clipped firmly to a bony nose, Adolf went to great lengths to look dapper, which meant donning a charcoal grey, pinstriped, double-breasted suit that hung on him as it would on a metal wire coat-hanger and which had been worn without respite over so many summers and winters that the cloth had taken on a bright sheen that almost mirrored the surroundings. Matching the slim, weathered tie a paisley-print handkerchief hung limply from the breast pocket.

Matilde introduced Adolf to Lady Katsumi, who was about to make the usual bow of courtesy when something arrested her attention. "Adolf!" she exclaimed with a short giggle of astonishment. "Great leader Adolf?"

The antiquarian stiffened as Martha said sourly "Great leader Adolf dead!"

"Oh! Sörry! So sörry," Lady Katsumi grieved, but not quite convinced quizzed again, "Not Adolf San?"

"Neither son nor father," Matilde explained impatiently, adding for Adolf's benefit, "Some names are best forgotten."

"Some have greatness bestowed on them," Adolf said trying to make light of the matter. "Others are burdened with greatness at christening!"

The troublesome introduction over, Matilde asked Adolf to show Lady Katsumi some of his genuine antique items. "And none of the usual bric-a-brac," she said, adding briskly "We are in a hurry. These people are coming to dinner and I must get some fish. Fräulein Breitfuss wants me to make shushu."

Adolf carefully laid out a variety of small porcelain objects on top of the long glass case: a blue shepherd, a piano doll, an invalid feeder spoon, a decorated chocolate cup, a figurine nude lady dancer, a harlequin head tobacco jar, an elephant-borne hatpin holder. Quietly he added a ceramic clown with nodding head.

Rubbing his bony hands, he pointed a skeletal finger at each object, adding "antique" before the description. "…antique doll, antique feeder spoon, antique lady dancer…and this," he added pausing before the nodding clown.

"And this is what sailor Krause brought you once from China," Matilde interrupted. "Not antique! Nor that little lady."

Adolf straightened up, rapidly removed the clown and nude figurine to a drawer and declared with officious solemnity, "Antique inasmuch they have been here for many years."

"So have you," Matilde murmured under her breath.

9

The small dinner party given by the Professor in the house that evening, limited to Fräulein Breitfuss and the Itos, got off to a less than pleasant start. Inadvertently Lady Katsumi earned the Head Librarian's eternal hostility when, over drinks in the Professor's study, she became bewitched by the large water-colour of Gretchen over the mantelpiece.

The portrait was the work of the travelling Russian lady painter whose canvases displayed in the park had been washed clean by the sudden summer downpour. She had drawn Gretchen in light pastels, the cascading gold of her hair touched by a gentle breeze as her violet gaze fell softly on the onlooker. The likeness was so true, so utterly alive, that her presence filled our house, as though she had never gone away. In my heart I ever blessed the Russian lady each time Gretchen's eyes fell on me. It was also the one gaze from which Fräulein Carin averted her eyes.

Now with folded hands Lady Katsumi stood enchanted before the portrait cooing "Preety! So preety."

"Very."

"You Lady Mother?" Lady Katsumi ventured with a shy giggle.

"Neither lady nor mother!" Fräulein Carin hissed venomously. Leaving her guest perplexed and confused, she turned to the Professor who was showing one of his books to Master Katsuro. I would have gladly leapt to Lady Katsumi's side and shared her admiration had not Matilde at that moment called the company to table.

Irritated, and doubtless scheming how best to erase the last conspicuous vestige of Gretchen from the house, Fräulein Carin nevertheless forced a bright face. When the company had taken their places at table, she said addressing Master Katsuro, and him alone, "Master Katsuro, this evening we have a Nipponese menu. I hope you like it."

Old man Ito looked puzzled and batted his eyelids as if trying to look through a fog. "Like Nipponesemen?"

"No, no!"

"No like Nipponesemen?"

"The shushu is ready" said Matilde coming in with the chilled rice wine that Fräulein Carin had procured from mysterious sources. "This tastes of nothing," the housekeeper remarked setting the bottle down on the table. "They should make it from grapes."

"It's called sushi, Matilde," Fräulein Carin reminded.

Making her way back to the kitchen, the housekeeper shrugged her shoulders, adding under her breath "Too old to learn foreign things."

Despite her indifferent air, the housekeeper had lent ear to Fräulein Carin and together they had worked out the menu for the evening. Save for trout, occasionally salmon and herring, fresh fish was a rarity in our town. An ingenious solution was thought up by the two women.

I had sat by the kitchen door in the fading sun of the long summer evening as Matilde, quietly muttering and grumbling, drained and dried the roll-mop herring fillets, wound each around a large pellet of mushy, over-boiled rice and tied the roll with sewing thread. Garnishing the white of the rice with chopped bits of smoked salmon – decidedly not a favourite item with me, she proceeded to arrange the rolls upright on a large porcelain serving dish strewn with fresh cress. Undoing her apron, she looked at her handiwork, heaved a sigh and sat down heavily on the chair by the door.

"Don't you go in for this foreign stuff, Albert," she said in motherly tones quietly ruffling my head. "Stick to your own kind, that's what I say."

Matilde had been in our house forever, or at least as long as I could remember. She had been a bustling young woman in my puppyhood, quiet and firm with my youthful antics, but always warm and caring, a second mother. She and Gretchen went well together, never a brusque gesture or angry word between them. A lonely soul, she ignored solitude. Ever on the move, busy and orderly, nothing escaped her notice. Our home was her home, and yet there was an odd distance, as though she had locked her heart away in some secret recess. Now with Gretchen gone and the passing years, we had grown old together, her frame broader, her gait slower, the abundant head of hair greying to a dull white tied in a bun. And I sometimes thought that age had brought with it a curious air of nonchalance, as if she was willing to let life drift, taking whatever course it might choose.

10

"Here we are," said Matilde putting down the dish with culinary pride.

The diners peered at the contents with interest. "What is it Matilde?" the Professor inquired with genuine curiosity.

"It's what these folks eat. Shishu,"

"Shishu!" exclaimed Lady Katsumi breaking into a titter that turned to a helpless giggle as she repeated the word over again.

Fräulein Carin looked daggers as she served the roll-mops, stopping with the giggling lady. "You do eat sushi, don't you?"

"Eat sushi, no shishu," conceded Lady Katsumi, flushed and simpering.

Master Katsuro stared timidly at his plate, the herring rolls nestling in the cress flecked with shreds of salmon. After a long moment of contemplation, he uttered a quiet "Hö," looked up at Fräulein Breitfuss, made a bow with the head and silently took up knife and fork. Very carefully, with the patience and precision of a watchmaker, he removed the thread, undid the rolls, set the fish fillets to one side, discarded the cress, placed the flecks of salmon on the pellets of rice and began his repast. Lady Katsumi followed suit, but with less meticulous a craft.

Having watched the surgical operation, Fräulein Carin asked impatiently, "Does Master Katsuro not like fish?"

After a brief exchange with the elder, Lady Katsumi said in a matter of fact manner, "Like fish. No this fish." Then with a tinge of vengeance she added, "Old fish, no fresh."

"Interesting," the Professor declared looking up at Matilde who had come in to see the progress before bringing in the main course of poached trout. "You must make it again some other time."

"I suppose I could then use the herrings the old gentlemen has left on his plate," Matilde muttered not a little put off by the guests' eccentric table habits.

Contrary and vexed, Fräulein Carin had decided not to stay the night, and after she and the Itos had departed and Matilde tidied up and said goodnight, I followed the Professor into the study. He paused in front of Gretchen's portrait, gazing silently for a long moment at the image of a world now irredeemably lost, gone for ever. Passing a hand through the greying silver of his head, as though brushing back the thought, he sat down heavily to his papers.

Kind Matilde, thoughtful as ever, had spared me Fräulein Carin's newfangled culinary invention, instead setting out on my dish a fair portion of chopped boiled beef. Filled to the full, I stretched out by the idle fireplace. The warm summer night drifted in through the open window behind the Professor's desk.

Through weight-laden eyes I looked up at Gretchen. And meeting her wistful gaze as wisps of sleep floated through my head, in the still nocturnal hour I wondered why happy days came to an end, why loved ones departed aforetime, why others were left to mourn their going. Someone somewhere certainly knew the answers. Not I.

11

A ringing hush fell on the audience as the curtains parted and a wondrous sight came into view. Beyond the polished wooden floor of the raised stage was a backdrop in iridescent colours of a panorama that took the breath away.

On the horizon, under a pellucid sky of an infinite blue, a mountain peak in dense indigo rose majestically, gently sloping up towards the heavens, the crest crowned with a halo of snow of the most immaculate white. Luminescent emerald green terraces descended from the base and spread out in a vast plain like a sea of serenity. Crowding the foreground, contrasting the ethereal stillness of mountain and plain, was a veritable forest of cherry trees in riotous bloom, the sweeping cloud of pink blossoms filling the air with a roseate glow.

An audible gasp rose from the public as the curtains parted fully to reveal Master Katsuro at one end. Standing motionless in a voluminous black and white gown, the wide round gold-leaf embroidered lapel framing the small face, he looked like an image printed on the screen. Almost entirely bald, curiously now the crown of his head had sprouted a jet black brush of hair that swept up and turned neatly downwards to the nape. In front of him a thick shiny length of metal tubing hung from the angle iron of a tall stand. In his hand he held a short wooden rod with a knob.

But it was the sight of Lady Katsumi that sent a ripple of rapturous murmur though the audience. Unrecognisable now, her face was a mask sculpted from the whitest of marbles, two black strokes for eyebrows, cherry-red lips, the head crowned with a bouffant of shiny night-black hair drawn back to a large bun stuck with long red-lacquer pins sporting gold tassels. From shoulder to toe her body had disappeared in a vaporous patchwork of kaleidoscope hues, crimson and white, emerald green, topaz, the luminescent silk delicately printed with gold bamboo leaves. A high black and silver band girdled her torso. Like some fairy creature slumbering in the land of dreams she sat under a leafless tree swarming with crepe cherry blossoms.

As the public gazed speechless, after a long moment of pin-drop silence Master Katsuro's arm came alive as he almost imperceptibly struck the metal tube. The faint metallic resonance lingered in the air briefly before dying out. The public held its breath but all was still on the stage, the fairy creature still comatose.

"Is the lady dead?" Uli asked Martha in undertones. It being their evening off, the restaurant closing for a day each week, mother and son had come to take in the spectacle. They now sat at the end of a row in the back and I by Uli's feet.

The hall was fairly packed. People had come from out of town as well, it being rumoured that Japanese warriors would give an

266

exhibition of swordplay. It was also voiced that dainty young ladies versed in the art of pleasure would exhibit some of their skills onstage, which had brought in a sizeable group of farmhands from outlying areas.

Udo, who had displayed his meat and charmed Lady Katsumi, and had been in turn enchanted by her coy looks, sat with us, next to Matilde, gazing fixedly at the slumbering damsel under the cherry tree. Herr Adler, apparently bewitched by Lady Katsumi's performance in his office, was there too, his unaccustomed enthusiasm silently reprimanded by his wife, her eyes more on him than on the stage, dousing his eagerness with the most severe of scowls. The Baron had brought Schwarzbauer, who now stood arms folded and praetorian-like in the doorway, his towering frame all but invisible in the closing evening save the white of his sturdy teeth. And Frau Krause who was never absent at any event of any import was somewhere in the vicinity, Montevideo's occasional cackle from the wicker basket distinctly audible to my ears.

Old timber merchant Holzmann, still nominal owner of the barn-theatre, had come and sat behind us muttering and grumbling, fidgeting noisily in his seat, repeatedly asking even before the performance had begun the whereabouts of the ladies. With the stage curtain still down and no ladies in sight, he was vexed by yet another absence, complaining that theatres had cushions and he had none, crying out loudly in his squeaky voice "Where's my bottom-cushion?"; to which a wag in the audience responded with "My kingdom for a bottom-cushion!" The ululation and antiphon went on for quite some time until the curtains went up and the old man was rudely bid by one of the farmhands to shut his mouth for the rest of his days.

12

After Master Katsuro had struck the tubular gong several times, with the ebbing resonance the sleeping maiden under the cherry blossoms had come to life. Lithe and graceful, she now rose to her feet and, shading her eyes with one luminous-white hand, gazed fixedly at the horizon with its snow-capped peak. So engrossed was she by the sight that she stood there so for several minutes. Master Katsuro then applying himself to the sound machine with greater force, the young lady daintily flitted butterfly-like across the stage still shading her eyes and looking at the imaginary horizon above us, at which all heads turned to the back of the hall, only to see Schwarzbauer's disembodied teeth glistening in the gloom.

There followed a long series of such tableaux, each lasting several minutes, with Master Katsuro striking the tube and Lady Katsumi taking up varied postures, standing perfectly still, now gazing heavenwards, now leaning forward with arms outstretched, now lowering her head in dejection, covering her face in grief with one berobed arm.

"What does it mean, Ma?" Uli asked his mother in a whisper.

In the twilight filtering in through the open doors Martha peered at the printed half sheet. "Act. I: The Cherry Maiden's Wait for Her Lover," she read into his ear.

"The train must be late," Uli concluded, stretching out an arm to stroke my head.

Indeed, it did seem that the Cherry Maiden would have to wait a while longer yet, if not a lifetime, for the truant suitor. And in truth it did appear that the audience had not quite the patience of the lovelorn damsel. As her wait proceeded through innumerable still poses, the public appeared to become restive, the tedium bringing on loud yawns, the occasional figure tiptoeing out in the evening.

Understandably, after a day of hacking and chopping, Udo's ardour had given way to an intermittent somnolence, his drooping eyelids brought to life only by Master Katsumo's ever louder strikes on the tubular organ. And midway through the performance, with not a single sword-wielding warrior in sight nor any sign of the ladies of pleasure, the farmhands rose as one man and noisily made for the exit, heading no doubt for Eichel's beer house. And despite his wide-eyed admiration for the Cherry Princess, Herr Adler was forced to vacate the scene, firmly held by the arm and steered towards the rear door by his frowning wife.

Behind us Holzmann had been quiescent after having been told off by the farmhand. Now with the Cherry Maiden's endless scrutinizing of the horizon, with neither she nor the audience seeing anything worthy of note, he became restive, scraping his feet on the floor and muttering to himself about the missing pleasure ladies, his loose dentures clicking loudly each time he opened his mouth.

"I don't think the man's coming, Ma," Uli murmured.

"Just like any man!" said Matilde.

Both early risers, she and Martha got to their feet. Uli and I followed them out through the side entrance. "You can stay," Martha told Uli. "Tell me in the morning if the young lady's beau finally turned up. And don't forget to take Albert home."

Uli extracted a small rubber ball from his pocket and lobbed it at me, saying "Catch, Albert!" It flew over my head. Enervated by an hour with the Nobuko Dance Troupe, it was all I could do to stroll over and fetch the ball back. The crickets had begun to chirp and we stood in the cooling night air watching the steady trickle of dark figures silently slip out of the theatre. Ilse Krause hurried past, with Monty's beaks snapping idly inside the wicker basket.

There was not much of an audience left when Uli decided to go back and have a last look to see if the Cherry Maiden had finally located her paramour. Indeed the hall was almost empty, save for the Arts Committee members slumped in the front row, with the bereft Maiden still tripping around the stage in search of her swain, while Master Katsuro went on striking his tubular bell. Schwarzbauer's teeth no longer on display, he had relinquished his praetorian stance at the rear exit and now slumbered peacefully stretched out in the doorway. At the back, steadily wheezing and whistling through arrhythmic snores, Holzmann too was fast asleep, no doubt ogling ladies of pleasure in the land of dreams.

THE BOY CLAUDE

1

Hostile to none, easy-going and confrère with all, almost all, as is the inborn bent of my breed, I simply could not imagine why I of all living creatures should have been visited by the bane of the Boy Claude. The only answer could be that I must have sinned awfully somewhere along the way, to be so tormented for an entire high summer by the pestilential urchin.

My first encounter with the Boy was an infelicitous one. Out shopping one morning, leaving the counter at Gersten's bakery, Matilde and I followed out an elderly lady with a stout little, snub-nosed, freckled face boy. At the door, suddenly, the lad turned around, screwed up his plump face and shot an unhealthy red tongue at me. The old lady caught the rude act reflected in the glass door and, thinking that it was directed at Herr Gersten, fetched the offender a sharp clip behind the ears. The errant boy broke into an unnecessarily loud howl as he was firmly dragged by the arm out into the street.

"Once more, Claude," said the lady with the air of one who delivered on her word, "and you'll go without supper!"

Sniffling and dribbling, he nodded his head in apparent contrition. No sooner had his guardian turned her back when he scowled, pulled hideous faces at passers-by and reserved one last incivility for me. Pulling his mouth wide open with pink sausage-thick fingers, nodding repeatedly he stuck out the repulsive long tongue; reminding me of one those monstrous gargoyles in Hubert the Horrid's castle. Matilde raising her hand threateningly, he skipped off and rejoined the old lady.

2

Widow Winterhalder lived a stone's throw from Dr. Hammes surgery; though obviously it would not do to actually throw stones at the doctor's glass house. She had been a widow for as long as anyone in town could remember. Adolf of Adolf's Antiques once said that she was born a widow; as usual hardly anyone ever understood his cryptic remarks, least of all he himself. Whatever the chronology of her widowhood, the old lady had a daughter, Leni, who at an early age had gone off to the land of the Franks, where she had married a Frank. The lamentable outcome of the union between Leni and the Frank was the Boy Claude.

Each midsummer Frau Winterhalder's grandchild was sent over to spend his holidays with her. I had seen him the previous year loitering around town, making a nuisance of himself, honing his skills at delinquency. He would spend the long idle summer afternoons, when there was hardly a soul about, throwing pebbles at the pair of swans in the lake; snapping off a switch with which to behead an entire bed of flowers; urinating on the new park benches the Burgomaster had recently placed in the shade under the trees.

Once I even saw him gleefully pluck at the nose of an infant in a pram while the mother browsed through the old volumes outside Himmel's bookshop. The woman picked up the wailing babe and had almost quietened him, when the torturer suddenly reappeared with a beatific and adoring smile, at the sight of which the new-born gave out a cry of terror and almost leapt out of his mother's arms.

In an effort to halt the rot and the advent of another Hubert the Horrid in the making, hoping to convert his mind to the higher things of life, widow Winterhalder dragged the boy to the library and asked Frau Botticelli to give him reading material suitable for his age. The kind librarian sat him down in the small reading room by the side, spread out a variety of boys' books on the table, even gave him a toffee from her little store in the drawer under the front counter, patted his head and left him to make his leisurely choice.

Sucking loudly on the toffee, the Boy Claude leafed through the books hurriedly, tearing out a page or two here, a few there, and stuffing the crumpled paper in his pockets. Having ripped out the entire last chapter of "Westward Ho!", his pockets bulging with literary parings, he now set to work on the spoliated volumes with the stubble of a pencil, scratching out a word, an entire line, working the lead furiously over whole pages. In no time he had devastated a small portion of the library's children's section. Done for the day with his vandalizing labours, he then picked out one of the more weighty works, "Tales of Terror from the Land of Ur," and ordering the rest in neat stacks, he went to the counter.

"Goodness," said Frau Botticelli putting on her spectacles, "that's a big one! You must love reading."

She registered the loan, gave him another toffee from the drawer, caressed his puffed cheek kindly, and sent him home. As appreciation for her motherly ways, he turned around at the entrance and gave her a demonstration of his indefatigable tongue.

When the Boy Claude brought back the book after a few days, Frau Botticelli, pleasantly surprised, squinted down at him from behind the counter and said, "Goodness, child, what an eager reader you are. You've read it all, haven't you."

He looked up at her with the unsullied innocence of a lamb and nodded. Rewarded with a toffee, his cheek patted tenderly, with a skip and a hop he was out the entrance and down the steps.

Inside the library, putting away "The Tales of Terror from the Land of Ur," Frau Botticelli found the book oddly heavy. She opened it in the middle, gave a short scream and fainted clean away. The pages had been gouged out to make a sizeable niche and the librarian found herself staring not at the doings in the Land of Ur but the carcass of a large field mouse.

3

People in the town said that there had never been a summer such as this in living memory. Adolf the Antiquarian, who dabbled in a great many esoteric topics as also oriental astronomy, insisted that the sun was fast approaching the earth and that anyone living beyond the age of a hundred would not live to see the light of day. The catastrophic prophecy so shocked widow Ansel, who had recently celebrated her ninety-ninth year, that she left us a bare fortnight later.

Whatever the sun's inclination, certainly the midsummer days seemed to have caught fire. The grass turned a pale straw yellow, plants withered, the swans in the lake drowned themselves underwater, and people shut themselves indoors for several hours in the afternoons. Impervious to heaven's angry gaze, the Boy Claude seemed the sole occupant of the town.

Most days now after lunch the Professor and Fräulein Carin retired upstairs. Doubtless seeking relief for their heated bodies, they drew the curtains and shed their clothes. I myself stretched out and drowsed in the garden under the cherry tree, seeking comfort in what shade it could offer.

Not quite asleep nor awake, one heavy-lidded eye open on the empty street, I thought of other such days, the long afternoons in the woods with Gretchen, when the Professor was away, as she lay in Herr Dieckhoff's arms while he read to her and her hand softly brushed my coat. I often wished then that the Professor too could be with us, so that I might have around me those I liked and loved most. For I did greatly like Herr Dieckhoff, his quiet presence, the timid, almost melancholy gaze, the loving gentleness of the pale hand as it smoothed the gold of Gretchen's head. I wondered where he might be now, if ever he would return.

4

A couple of workmen in splotched white overalls appeared in the street carrying a long ladder. Out of breath, they paused in front of our fence. The one at the rear, short, stout and balding, looked me over and exclaimed "A dog's life! Just look at him. Fed, pampered, maybe even kissed now and then by his lady-mistress."

"That's a mouthful more than you get from *your* lady-mistress!" his mate laughed.

"You can talk! Want to change places, friend?" he asked addressing me.

"Not him, crafty old bastard!"

They picked up the ladder and went their way, leaving me to wonder idly on the inanity of their exchange, apart from the not entirely complimentary appellation thrown at me. How humans wasted their gift of speech, I mused, more often than not mouthing vacuous and tedious allocutions. Not having been granted the same faculty, I detected a tinge of envy in the thought.

The soporific hour dragged on and my eyes had almost shut when, suddenly, to my dread and disbelief, a familiar face appeared in sight. The Boy Claude! He stopped in front of the gate, screwed up his face and fixed me for a long moment. I crouched low, pressed my nose into the grass and would have willingly foregone my favourite supper, knuckles with dumplings, to make myself invisible. All to no avail, for in a moment the round baby face lit up with an evil light as, waving a short stick, he cried "Gros chien!"

Now, a year later, he had grown, mostly sideways. Fatter around the middle, the rotund face lodging small dark button eyes above puffed cheeks, the head of black spiky hair atop rounded shoulders, he resembled in miniature the creature in the poster outside Dresner's garage where occasionally Gretchen went to have the car tyres seen to.

"Fat dog! Fat dog!" he called making grotesque faces that had little of the human, sticking out and waggling a tongue that resembled a mildewed sausage.

"Fat dog! Fat dog!" he repeated waving the stick, hopping all the while on two stumpy legs that descended from mud-stained shorts like plump pillars of flesh. I sat still watching the buffoonery, thinking he would soon tire, which he did. Huffing and puffing, provoked by my passivity, he pulled a truly monstrous face, hurled the stick at me and skipped off; only to trip on the uneven pavement stones and fall flat on his face. With a howl of pain he raised himself on all fours and shot an odious look in my direction, as though I had somehow engineered his fall. I would have gladly obliged, had I had the wherewithal!

Our address now became a regular stop on his daily vandalistic expeditions. He would appear at the appointed hour, when the heat rose and good people retired indoors, stealthily creeping down the road to burst suddenly at our gate. To the tedious chant of "Fat dog!" he would begin pelting me with a variety of objects, a stone, a handful of pebbles, a broken ladies umbrella, once even half a cabbage. Old man Bauer, coming as usual to tend our garden, was mystified by the presence of the vegetable. "I can't remember planting cabbages," he said to Matilde, adding with a cryptic nod of the head, "You can't tell with these new seeds nowadays. Genitally modified, they say. Things come up by themselves."

Matters came to a head when one afternoon Boy Claude actually appeared with a broken babies' pushchair. With clearly evil intent he hurled the tangle of metal and canvas at me, missing my head by a mere inch or two. I thought it best to call it a day. Leaving him to his delinquent devices as tongue lolling he performed the usual jig of the imbecile, I went indoors.

The curtain-drawn interiors were dark, and silent. I stood for a moment in the hallway and shut my eyes, then climbed the stairs slowly to the Professor's room, where he had retired with Fräulein Carin after lunch. Not wishing to disturb their rest, I paused on the landing. The door was ajar and in the dim light filtering through the curtains I could see the young lady unclothed and astride the Professor on the bed, their breathing in unison resonating in the room with a muffled cadence as she rose and fell above him. It was odd that they should exercise themselves with such energy in the heat of the day. Fräulein Carin then gave a long strangled moan and slumped forward, lying motionless atop the Professor, as though life itself had ebbed away.

As she slowly fell away from him, her face turned to the door. Her eyes looked dull and spent, damp glistened on the skin. The Professor lay still and breathless, one arm loosely wound around her waist.

Then she saw me, as I sat crouched on the landing. Coming alive with sudden electric energy she leapt off the bed, bounded forward and shut the door with such violence that it made me jump.

There were voices in the room now, Fräulein Carin's loud and distinct as she said, "It's so eerie, when he looks up at me with my clothes off. Dirty old lecher!"

I heard the Professor's hollow laugh and words I could not make out.

"No, not the only one in this house," she said impatiently. "Seriously, Ernst, he must go. So unhealthy wandering about the house all day. He should be outdoors. You've got to take him to Dr. Schneidhuber's."

For some unknown reason I started at the sound of the name. I had heard it somewhere, I was certain, but it was so well lodged in some secret recess of my memory that I could not place it. I padded down the stairs and out the front door.

The Boy Claude had moved on to his next criminal rendezvous and I stretched out once again in the shade of the cherry tree. The languor of the warm air brought down the shades over my eyes and I had just begun to drift into a light torpor when the key turned in the lock and I woke with a tremor. Memory came flooding of one my very last visits with Gretchen to Dr. Hammes. That was where I had heard the name of Dr. Schneidhuber, the terror of the animal kingdom.

That night my usual dreams of distant greens and silent fields of corn and barley where I walked with Gretchen dissolved into a nightmare vision of Dr. Schneidhuber. I had never seen the grim legend in person, but now from the depths of an angry night his face rose towards me like a leering mask, a peculiar cross between Hubert the Horrid and the Boy Claude. Begging for mercy, cringing I shrank into an airless corner of my slumber; to wake with a whimpering cry, my body all atremble.

It was the one time in this long life when I would have willingly given a limb, half a leg, preferably my tail, to have the gift of speech, if only for a brief moment. I would have reasoned with the

Professor, for his was a reasonable spirit. I would have recalled his never-failing kindness down the days, his good-humoured forbearance of my impish high spirits when I was a mere pup.

But I feared it was late, the die had been cast. My most fervent protestations would have gained nought. Fräulein Carin had conquered the good man mind and body, spirited his soul away. Hard and obdurate, her eyes were unyielding when they fell on me, firm in her resolve to deliver me into the waiting, blood-stained hands of the diabolical doctor. Now more than ever my heart cried out for Gretchen, cherished keeper of my life, ever-loving mother of my days.

5

As the car sped out of town, I glanced out the rear window to catch a last glimpse of the faces and places I had known since puppy-hood. There on the left, next to Gersten's bakery, with the small blue van outside was the butcher's, stout Udo standing in the doorway in a white apron talking with Frau Krause, with never-absent Montevideo peering out of the wicker basket. Further on, beyond the chemist's, Herr Himmel was rearranging the old books on a table outside. Next door, Adolf was probably dusting his less than antique antiques before settling down for the morning with a volume on the wisdom of Oriental wise men.

My heart ached as the familiar scenes slipped past for the last time. There in the distance the tall temple façade of the library, the broad steps outside on which I had sat many a time watching the world go by and on which Frau Botticelli now stood drawing on her short twisted cigarillo, the dry, burnt aroma suddenly wafting through my memory. And the park with the freshly painted green benches; the pair of swans in their small world of the lake, gliding serene and satisfied through the reeds.

Goodbye to all this, then. And I had not had the time to take leave of those who had befriended me, in whose kindness and warmth I had basked down the years. Simple-minded Ulrich, a companion for all seasons with a rare goodness of heart. Dr. Hammes, ever ready to humour the least of God's creatures. The Baron, noble in mien and gait, whose good cheer at all times lightened the day. And Schwarzbauer, a man among men, lost in the wilderness of his own life, yet ever joyous, ever comforting.

Grieving the unsaid farewells, fearful of what lay ahead, I lost count of the distance we had travelled and came to only when the car turned into a tall gate with an arched metal insignia overhead that chilled the marrow in my bones. SCHNEIDHUBER PETWEIGHT CLINIC, Fräulein Breitfus read out the words with ill-disguised satisfaction. And as the car pulled up on the gravel front of a large dark brick building, my eyes fell on one of the most curious sights I had ever seen.

On a neat lawn by the side of the severe edifice a man in a green cap was cycling around leisurely. A sight hardly worthy of note but for the fact that behind the cyclist the tandem was fitted with two low saddles on each of which sat a corpulent dachshund with forelegs resting on short straight handlebars, while the rear legs somehow strapped to the pedals rotated in unison with those of the human cyclist. Humped forward, the canine riders looked neither left nor right but gazed intensely ahead.

"An hour's cycling is the best way to start the day," Fräulein Carin smiled maliciously glancing back at me.

A short bald man in a white medical coat now appeared at the entrance as we got out of the car. I noticed he had a slight limp as he came forward to meet us. But what impressed me immediately were his glasses, thick as window panes, behind which the two dark ferret eyes gleamed with a strange light. Greeting the guests, he put out a chubby square pink hand the size of the generous slabs of meat Martha served in her Sauerbraten.

"Schneidhuber," he said in a squeaky voice which seemed to come from behind him. "And so! this is friend Albert," he smiled down at me, exposing a series of irregular smoke-stained teeth. There was something in his tone, not quite sinister but less than cordial, that made me think this was one friend I could do without.

We followed the doctor down a long dusty corridor, the walls lined with old framed prints of odd-looking animal heads, and were about to go through a door when a most frightful canine yelp resounded through the building. The doctor turned to the Professor and said with an apologetic smile that reeked of falsity, "An impatient patient!"

It was a large office cluttered with papers, old books, a glass-topped table that had not been dusted in recent decades and leather covered chairs that had decidedly seen better days. The walls were fairly plastered over with mysterious graphs, figures of various animals, a chart identical to the one at butcher Udo's showing the various bovine sections; the poster-sized photograph of a bulldog so immense that the neckless head seemed a mere appendage. On the far wall a moth-eaten stag's head looked down on the untidy spectacle. I somehow felt the ambience did not bode well.

When the visitors were seated, rubbing his hands Dr. Schneidhuber beamed an unctuous smile. "Before Albert is entrusted to our cure," he said clearing phlegm from the throat, "I'm sure you would like to know something about our methods."

"It might be interesting," the Professor remarked dryly, one hand resting protectively on my head as I sat by his chair.

"It is, that it is!" the doctor addressed Fräulein Carin as he settled into the worn upholstery with a small heave.

The Petweight Method, he said, went back to the early 1900s and was based on the pioneering work of Mrs. Mildred Horton-Smith of Milwaukee, a humanist, vegetarian and great lover of plant and animal life. From her observations on the family farm she had deduced that not only erroneous diet and sedentary habits but also and mainly excess of satisfaction and happiness caused animals to gain disproportionate weight.

For a number of years the good lady of Milwaukee had carried out rigorous and controlled experiments on test groups of canines and felines, as also on smaller samples such as canaries. It was found that forced sleep deprivation, stress caused by uncertainty about the future, continuous change of habitat and environment, a general condition of instability and what Dr. Schneidhuber termed, between clenched teeth, a "regime of induced unhappiness," were all crucial factors whose systematic application in combined permutations resulted in positive and radical loss of weight. It was on the basis of these proven and indisputable findings that Mrs. Mildred Horton-Smith had elaborated her theory of *Infelicitas Animalium*, a seminal work that revolutionized the treatment and cure of animal obesity. As final proof of the pudding, the doctor added that strays and mongrels were never found to be overweight.

"As also stray humans," the Professor observed with pursed lips.

"Precisely so!" Dr. Schneidhuber exulted, his eyes behind the thick lenses glinting with satisfaction that his visitors had grasped the essence of the Milwaukeean elaborations. Quite as abruptly, though, he grew sombre and the shadow of a distant regret fell across his face.

Mrs. Horton-Smith, he said, had attempted to apply the same methods to human overweight. Controlled and confidential tests with the human young on her farm had yielded very encouraging results. Regrettably, the authorities in their ignorance had intervened, shut down the experiments and sequestered the farm. Thereafter, as is the fate of all pioneers, Mrs. Horton-Smith's name had been besmirched with absurd and utterly false accusations of cruelty and inhuman treatment. Acquitted at a subsequent trial, she had retired to a homestead in a remote corner of Wyoming, where until her last days she had applied herself to the study of inter-plant communication, as also discovering in the scarlet flowers of the Oswegotea mint a definitive cure for mammalian senility.

But the Horton-Smith theories had not passed into oblivion, Dr. Schneidhuber added animatedly. No, far from it. They had been taken up and re-elaborated in detail in the 1930s by the great Prof. Finke at the University of Ulm. Later, during the years of conflict, encouraged by the authorities no less, the eminent professor had himself carried out extensive and comprehensive trials on sizeable human sample groups with complete success. Indeed, so successful were the experiments that almost none of the surviving subjects ever again regained any weight at all.

"Mrs. Horton-Smith's ideas were entirely vindicated," the doctor remarked, his glasses gleaming with a quiet sense of triumph. Once again a wistful melancholy crept into his tone as he added with a sigh, "Alas, the world is often blind to genius. As with the great lady, Prof. Finke too spent his latter years in exile, in the rain forests of Brazil. Though even there, forgotten by an ungrateful humanity, he managed to carry out further clinical tests on the natives."

"But now," he said emerging from the brief reverie, "you may wish to see for yourself our practical application of the Horton-Smith-Finke elaborations."

With that he pressed a red button on the side of the table and in a moment a large, robust lady came through the door and greeted the visitors. She was introduced as Frau Leona Fleischer and, in truth, there was quite a lot of the leonine about her. A blond shoulder-length mane fell away from the large head, while the heavy-set face with round dark eyes gave her the air of one not to be trifled with.

"Leona, would you mind showing our visitors some of our main facilities," said Dr. Schneidhuber with a conspiratorial smile. Oddly, as she followed the Professor and Fräulein Carin out through the door, his hand darted out stealthily and tweaked Frau Leona's ample bottom.

6

We went down long, ill-lit corridors, our guide observing that the lighting was intentionally kept low so as not to excite the patients. Bright interiors induce hope, she explained, which in turn could adversely effect weight loss. Her manner was brisk and business-like, the voice low and hoarse.

"This," she said, opening a blue door, "is the Anti-Cellulite Steam Chamber."

It was a large damp space illuminated with blue lighting. Sizeable galvanised drums with a circular opening at the top were placed at regular intervals. Only one was occupied and it was an appalling sight. A black spaniel's head stuck out of the drum while thin wisps of steam drifted out of the cylinder through the tiny perforations in the lid around the poor creatures neck. The helpless eyes in the tilted head looked at me like a child in the last throes of wordless suffering, accompanying our exit from this chamber of torment with the low whimper of a life ebbing away.

"Do they suffer much?" Fräulein Carin enquired brightly.

"Not any more than one would in a Turkish bath," Frau Leona replied plainly. "Of course, it is an eight-hour treatment for five days the first week, with one small meal in the evening."

"They must be in pain," The Professor remarked putting out a protective hand to beckon me to his side.

"Well, yes." Frau Leona conceded in a matter of fact manner. "But more mental than physical. We have integrated traditional slimming techniques with the Horton-Smith-Finke methodology. Prolonged hot steam bath combined with a sense of isolation and claustrophobia."

"One doesn't often get that in the Turkish bath!" the Professor murmured.

A sort of convivial guffaw escaped Frau Leona as we turned a corner into another long dim corridor and stopped in front of a red door. "Here we have the Induced Psycho-Stress Unit, which combines strenuous exercise with a sense of instability. All the advanced equipment was designed by Dr. Schniedhuber himself, obviously in accordance with the Finke-Horton-Smith norms." She opened the door on a veritable bedlam.

The spacious hall was filled with the thin mewing of cats, the whimper, yelp and strangled barks of canines, the irritated chatter of a baboon, the nervous twitter of birds. There were cages of various sizes and shapes, each holding a patient undergoing Induced Psycho-Stress. A reddish glow filtered down from the high ceiling.

Immediately in front of us was a longish cage, barred on all sides with steel rods, with sharp metal barbs at one end towards which the conveyor belt floor moved at a steady pace. A rather round, haggard black collie walked endlessly on the moving belt without making any progress whatsoever; occasionally exhaustion slowed its pace and then it would drift backwards until the sharp wire barbs at the end dug into its flesh, making it leap forward with a pitiable howl.

A similar but smaller cage held a fat grey tabby which, prodded in the rear by the pointy metal ends heaven knows how many times, had abandoned the moving conveyor floor and now hung desperately by its claws to the side of the cage, eyes dilated with terror as it voiced hapless little sounds.

In another cage, open at one end, a decidedly overweight and aged poodle gave out a sharp yelp at regular intervals as it approached the opening and as regularly a large rubber ball swung back and struck its nose.

"The physical expenditure here is supplemented by a controlled dosage of pain and fear," our guide explained. "Factors which impede the accumulation of fat."

"Factors which also impede me from staying here any longer!" the Professor announced, moving back towards the door.

Unperturbed, with one hand on her ample hip, Frau Leona said, "Now next door we have the Weight Compression Vacuum Chamber."

"Please carry on, Carin." The Professor's tone was icy. "Albert and I will wait outside."

"But Ernst…," Fräulein Breitfuss had begun to say, when the Professor turned back down the corridor towards the entrance. My heart bursting, I followed him out. I would have followed this man to the ends of the earth.

7

The air in the car was heavy with a stony silence as we drove back. Not a word had been spoken since we left the SCHNEIDHUBER

PETWEIGHT CLINIC. I had looked back through the rear to catch a last glimpse of the mansion of horrors. Dr. Schneidhuber and Fräulein Leona stood at the entrance with a perplexed air, the doctor's right arm moving stealthily behind the matronly figure of his assistant.

Resurrected and returned intact to the land of the living, I hoped never again to see the thin-lipped, white-coated figure again for the rest of my days. And I never did. But there was the odd evening when Uli overfed and I overate, and then, tossing in restive sleep, from the nether depths of an infernal world peopled with truncated and mangled bodies of half-alive animals the round hairless head of the criminal doctor rose towards me like a knotted sphere of bone, the dense glasses gleaming with a smile of infinite malevolence. Fleeing desperately from the fiendish image, I would wake to the first light of dawn gasping for air.

The late morning light today was clear, the countryside becalmed under a limpid sky touched on the horizon with a faint brushwork of white. Unlike other times, the steady hum of the car failed to make me drowsy. I felt renewed, felt age and weight fall away, born again into a new world whose sights reached out to me for the first time: the high summer green resplendent under a generous sun, the ripening ears of wheat rolling away into the distance like a vast undulating sheet of gold.

But my renewal was in sharp contrast to the decidedly chill air inside the car. The Professor sat upright, almost rigid behind the wheel, staring fixedly ahead at the road. Fräulein Carin was frozen in her seat, head angled, looking out at the fleeting landscape. Not a word had been uttered since leaving the Clinic, nor a glance exchanged.

So we might have driven back to town, perfect strangers come together for some unknown reason. But then, abruptly, without the least notice or warning, in a tremulous voice driven by desperation and a sort of strangled fury, Fräulein Carin asked something that swung around the Professor's head.

"Would you marry me if I asked?" she said.

He turned to her sharply, a bewildered look on his face as he sought and met her eyes. For a seemingly never-ending moment only the hum of the car rose above the resounding silence. And in that long instant my new-found life ebbed away and my tongue felt parched at the mere thought of Fräulein Carin coming to live with us, her presence shadowing my days and nights. Confused and despondent, I knew in my heart of hearts that Gretchen's spirit which hung over us, watched and blessed us day by day, would finally be banished.

I was not alone in my confusion. Wordless and uncertain, at last the Professor looked away and set his gaze on the road ahead. But Fräulein Carin's query hung in the air, echoing, demanding an answer. Her breathing itself, heavy and insistent, declared that she impatiently awaited an answer.

"I thought," the Professor said finally, his voice mimicking a feigned and uncertain lightness, "it was for the man to ask!"

I heard his words with relief, yet wished he had not spoken. Spurned out of hand, her face crumpled into a mask not of anger but of bitter contempt as though looking on something immensely distasteful and drained of worth.

"How petite bourgeois!" she said in a voice charged with furious scorn. "All your name and fame and still tied to the petticoat of commonplace conventions!"

I feared the worst. Fortunately the Professor refused to rise to the bait. He sat perfectly immobile save for the slight movement of his hands on the wheel, eyes set firmly on the road. In all the years I had never heard such words hurled at him and it saddened my heart not a little to see a man so wise and good treated with such denigration and contempt. At another time, in my younger days, I might have bared my teeth and gone for her dainty throat.

The furious outburst now gave way to a measured asperity as she said, "Truly pitiable, Ernst, the way you live in the past. Clinging on to dead relics. Like this creature!" she added with a backward glance at me.

I found that offensive. Creature I might be, but certainly not dead, nor a relic yet. And the senseless woman could not see that neither the Professor nor I, or for that matter any living creature, could be anything more than the sum of our past.

"Blind! Just how blind can you be?" she went on, with a consuming bitterness that meant to hurt. "You cling to a past that you never saw. Perhaps you choose not to. If you only knew what your Gretchen…"

The Professor turned to her. "Please don't!" he said quietly but so imperative and absolute was his tone that she faltered and desisted, the words dying in her throat.

The town was in sight, faces and places that only hours earlier I had thought I would never again set eyes on. I felt an odd sense of tenderness, of homecoming from an infinitely long journey; realizing then how the heart stubbornly clung to the everyday and the familiar. But I felt, too, it would never be the same again. For sure I had eluded Dr. Schneidhuber's torture chambers, but something unseen had broken in our lives. There would be a parting of ways, when and in what manner I could not foresee. If only I had known!

8

Apparently our life resumed its usual quiet hum-drum course. I was taken to Dr. Hammes for my routine monthly visits and under the sunlit dome of the conservatory nurse Ulrike still feigned tender hurt at the doctor's cheerful complacency for their future. Gardener Bauer still scratched his head and worried about the appearance of the cabbage in our garden without any having been planted.

Adolf of Adolf's Antiques turned his hand at new antics. Much to the distress of Frau Krause, he announced that it was now official that the sun's rapid approach towards the earth would singe to death all fowls of the air; resulting in Montevideo being left indoors on sunny days; albeit it was hard to think of him as a fowl of the air.

Possibly not intending to perish in the imminent solar collision, sadly old timber merchant Holtzmann had passed away only a fortnight earlier, ascending no doubt to a Paradise made entirely of wood. The Captain however still came and went, but mostly came more frequently.

Fräulein Carin also came and went, but the visits were less frequent, her stays shorter and, with the passing of the high summer heat, certainly there was no reason for her and the Professor to adjourn after lunch and unclothe themselves. Now, too, she hardly ever stayed overnight at our house. The enchanted evening walks in the woods had also ceased.

"Breakfast for one or two," Matilde still insisted on asking. "One," the Professor would say in an off-hand way, in the manner of a distracted response at litany. Until one morning, before she could pose the familiar enquiry, the Professor said, "Breakfast for one, for the moment." Taken aback but hardly able to conceal her pleasure, Matilde went back to the kitchen muttering "No breakfuss for Breitfuss."

The fading summer afternoons were still warm and, while the Professor retired after lunch to the study, I strolled out to the garden to lie at my accustomed place under the cherry tree. And as life resumed in the post-Schneidhuber era, so did the post-prandial visits by the Boy Claude. I wondered when he would finally leave town to return to the bosom of his parents in the land of the Franks.

I had decided that I would pay no heed to the intrusion of the pestilential creature, even though each afternoon a veritable collection of the town's waste and debris rained down on my head, accompanied by the tedious jibe of "Gros chien! Gros chien!" Matilde was puzzled by the odd litter in the garden, an old shoe, a beer bottle, a pair of wooden coat-hangers, half a dozen fruit cans.

Gardener Bauer was even more perplexed, and not a little fearful; for while the appearance of the cabbage could have been a one-off freak slip of Nature, nothing could account for the appearance of carrots and beets, randomly strewn around the garden; unless of course for once Adolf had got it right with his prophetic proclamation of the sun's imminent arrival. "Carrots, beets. Without planting! Must be this climate change they talk about," he wondered nervously, inviting Matilde to share the large cellar under his house, which he intended to stock up with food and water. The housekeeper took the empty beer mug from his hand and bid him good morning.

I soon discovered that there was a decided limit to my vow of non-violence, my benign tolerance being sorely tried one afternoon when the Boy Claude appeared with a strange object in his hand. He stood at the gate with a malicious grin, shamelessly exposing a mouth full of uneven teeth stained dark with liquorice. Chanting then the usual inane jibe, he pointed the thin long barrel at me.

Out squirted a jet of a malodorous blue liquid, hitting me square on the nose and wetting my head. A second jet followed, then another, and several more, till my coat was entirely drenched and a burning itch from nose to tail took hold of my body. As I writhed and scratched and rolled over rubbing my back on the grass, the wretched bully doubled up with laughter, the toothy pumpkin face distorted with mad hilarity. It was an affront that the dignity of my age could not bear and I decided that the time had come for a just reprisal. Goodness might well be its own reward, but evil deserved other deserts.

9

A couple of days later, at the appointed hour, I sat outside our gate. In the distance, in the shade of the trees lining the road, I could see the young rapscallion's round pudding figure approach with a jaunty air. He was perhaps a small stone's throw away when suddenly he caught sight of me. Taken aback for a moment, he halted in silent contemplation of my presence before breaking out in a grin permeated with pure malice. Bending forward then in the stalking hunter's crouch when the prey has been cornered, he came towards me a step at a time, with the barrel of the spray gun steadily aimed at me.

I rose to my feet and walked away as the first jet of liquid splashed behind me. I heard him quicken his pace. So did I. The second jet fell wide. He broke into a sluggish trot. So did I. A few drops of the blue liquid caught the tip of my tail. I broke into a run. Huffing and puffing, he followed flat-footed. Although both of us were weighed down with considerable ballast, I could still outrun him, for it was obvious that he had not of recent won many trophies in major sports events, nor for that matter in minor ones.

We had now reached the last house and the end of the street; after which a short stretch of green abruptly dipped, sloping steeply down into the woods. I stopped at the edge, waiting for him to reach me. Thinking me cornered, he came forward at a frantic pace, the short stumpy legs moving ever faster. Propelled by his corpulence alone, he seemed to be out of control of his body as he came forward in a blind rush. Then as he came on me, I leapt aside.

Just as he tumbled forward, falling headlong down the slope, I saw to my horror the figures of a man and a lady in the shade of a tree, towards which the Boy Claude was hurtling at reckless speed. With a frantic cry echoing in the air, arms and legs flailing he landed on the unclothed man, who curiously had been lying atop the unclothed lady.

In the ensuing pandemonium, while the Boy Claude howled in pain, the man thrown off his fleshy mattress and the woman breaking into an ear-splitting scream under the weight of the Boy, I recognised the faces of the bucolic couple; but just could not understand why butcher Udo had come to the woods to convince the lady of the goodness of his meat. The young woman I now saw was chambermaid Lulu from Henschal's Gasthaus.

Finally, freeing herself from the prostrate weight of the rude intruder, still screaming she fled through the trees without her clothes, which lay scattered where she had lain. Udo picked himself up painfully, looked at the loudly sniffling figure on the ground, picked up a long twig and with a frightening roar set on him, whipping the Boy with all the energy he applied when hacking his meats in the shop. It was just too painful a spectacle and I turned back towards the house, my ears ringing with the pitiable cries from the scene of the flogging.

I never saw the Boy Claude again, save one last time and briefly a few days later. He was out with Frau Winterhalder as she did her round of the shops. One arm stiff in a sling, one eye black and swollen, strips of plaster adorned his face, while the legs were a mass of cuts and bruises. Accompanying Matilde as she did the day's shopping, I was almost overcome by a passing sense of guilt but was at once recalled from any possible commiseration by the Boy's incorrigible devotion to base mischief. As they entered the chemist's, I saw his good hand stealthily tug at the wool of his grandmother's home-made cardigan, unravelling the knitting stitch by stitch.

Dr. OCHOA

1

The mismatch among humans never ceased to amaze me. Even in the days, now long ago, when the body was in fine mettle and desire made the limbs tremble, it would have been utterly unthinkable for me to mate with a Chihuahua or mount a Pekingese. With humans instead one saw the oddest couplings, short stout balding men with tall willowy brides, prosperous matrons rounded in the middle and with other rotundities strolling contentedly with shrivelled males the size of their forearms, shrunken old men teetering on the edge of their graves tottering alongside young women fresh and radiant as the morning's new bloom. But no mismatch was as striking as the one between Donna Flora and her husband.

Her considerable girth notwithstanding, Donna Flora was an angel come to earth. Angel she would have been, even without the heavenly mansion whence she might have hailed, by virtue of the patience and forbearance with which she put up with Dr. Ochoa, not the devil incarnate perhaps but certainly with an address in the netherworld. Marriages, I heard it said, were made in heaven. The location of Donna Flora's's union with her husband was best left unspelt.

Dressed in a layered gypsy skirt and a long-sleeve white linen blouse trimmed with lace and embroidered with red roses, Donna Flora resembled a costume doll, the pink rounded cheeks in the neat oval face aglow with health, the light eyes framed by pencil-drawn eye-brows, small lips pursed in a perennial kiss. The fine dark hair drawn back into a roundel was held in place with a small red comb.

Always she sat back a pace from whatever the company, passive with the calm of serenity, her silent presence exuding an ineffable sweetness that filled the room, as if to make amends for the brusque and bristling presence of her husband.

Dr. Ochoa had instead been everywhere and seen everything and what little he had not seen was not worth seeing. In another age he would have spent most of his day drawing out his rapier and running people through or, else, passed endless misty mornings engaging in duels. For he took umbrage at almost anything one might say, his propensity for being offended not limited to his own person but covering the entire gamut of human interest, history, geography, art, architecture, through to philately and animal husbandry. On occasion even to wish him good day could provoke a mild ire, as he queried irritably: "And what, pray, is so good about this particular day?" Matilde had in fact stopped greeting him when he visited.

On the last visit but one, when Gretchen was still with us, at table Dr. Hammes had inadvertently thrown caution to the winds and casually remarked that "for long Spain has been a mere appendage of our continent." The conflagration was instantaneous, as though a tiny mindless spark had grazed the most volatile of substances. "Intolerable!" Dr. Ochoa barked bounding to his feet. "Intolerable and ingrate!" Haughtily then he reeled off an interminable list of his country's gifts to humanity. The discovery of the New World, the riddance of the vile savages in the Southern Hemisphere, the boon of the Inquisition – so ignobly wasted by the lily-livered Italians! Goya, Picasso, Dali, Miró, down to a sausage called Chorizo.

The company at table rushed to placate the inflamed spirit, Gretchen gently reminding him that an appendage could be a jewel, a precious stone, a diamond no less. "How very true!" the Professor added in swift accord, while a penitent Dr. Hammes nodded vigorous confirmation. The wind taken out of his sails, soothed by the precious idea, Dr. Ochoa sat down and poured himself more wine as Donna Flora looked on with fond patience as a mother would with a truculent child.

Nor was I spared his prickly barbs. The coal-black eyes behind the tortoise-shell glasses surveying my somewhat heavy rump one day, with unnerving joviality he said, "Growing at this rate, dear Alberto, you could end up providing a Korean household with dinner for a week!" I failed to catch the drift of his words but felt that it was not meant to be an altogether friendly compliment.

2

Severo Ignatio Ilario Ochoa y Esperanza was the twelfth of the twelve children of the Grandee of Esperanza, a noble so minor that neither he nor any his ancestors had ever been received at Court. The family's only brush with royalty had been accidental and circumstantial.

It was said that travelling towards the coast and crossing the parched highlands of the Meseta, a young lady who often privately entertained the King with a variety of games and gymnastics had felt faint in the high summer heat and sought a night's refuge in the small dusty town of Esperanza. Warmly welcomed as a rare guest with intimate access to the Sovereign's person no less, lodged by the Grandee in the most spacious bedroom in the sprawling brick and clay alcazar, which was the family home with one whole side around the courtyard taken up by a chicken run, the young lady was generously entertained with a lavish meal of eggs and haricot beans, which only worsened her malaise, causing her to expire the next morning. Repeated petitions to the court for the reimbursement of the funeral expenses went unanswered and the bones of the sporting lady remained interred in the dilapidated cemetery of the fly-blown town.

Severo's grandfather, who had buried the King's young lady and who in youth had promoted himself from mere Hidalgo to Grandee, albeit of the Third Class, suffered from several eccentricities. Occasionally he would release a number of chicken and, giving them a head start of an hour or two, would start off across the arid countryside to hunt down the emancipated poultry with an old musket, the fowls ending up on the evening table. Or else, out for a late walk after dinner, on his return indoors he would insist on entering the house through a darkened window. It gave him the thrill of an illicit amorous adventure.

Lean, emaciated almost, dark deep-set eyes in a long melancholy face elongated with a short, pointed beard, he had seen in young Severo a close image of himself. So that dethroning his own son and skipping the males among the first eleven grandchildren, he had decided that the mantle of succession should fall directly on Severo, who at the tender age of nine became the youngest Grandee in the land.

The eccentric endowment marked Severo Ignatio for life. At college the Jesuit teachers would smile wryly behind their hands at the pose and posturing of the "Pequeño Grandee," his school mates taunting him with a variety of irreverent names, Petit Grandee, Miniature Grandee, Pocket Grandee. Of slight build, frail in body and unable to repulse the jibes with physical force, young Severo spent his days in a vexation of permanent pique and indignation. It was to become a habit of life, so that ever after he suspected offence in every other remark, read affront in the most innocuous of words.

Not quite impoverished nor enjoying the splendour of true nobility, the Ochoa family lived in modest rustic comfort, the arid land offering a tolerable sufficiency; and there were always the chickens. On festive days the plain everyday fare was supplemented with rice and almond cake, oranges from the south. Then, of a sudden, the family fell on its feet on the right side of history.

One day the King was gone, Severo's grandfather seeing in the royal departure divine retribution for the failure to meet the lady gymnast's funeral expenses. In the civil strife and turmoil that followed and laid waste the nation, Severo's father's sympathies found him among the ranks of the victors and the foreign friends who had lent no mean hand in their victory. An anonymous provincial from a remote corner of the country, with narrow views and even narrower tastes, his reading of the days to come rapidly converted him to the cause of the race that was to rule the world for a thousand years and made of him an ardent Germanophile.

So enamoured did he become of the invincible race that he set his children to study the history and geography, the music and literature, the rites and rituals of the noble country. Of a summer evening, when the parched heat of day gave way to the cool of nightfall, around the courtyard of the family home could be heard the strident notes of warriors riding towards Valhalla, the music rising in surging waves above the cackle of the fowls settling down for the night; while the younger members applied themselves to the legends of the Goths and Ostrogoths, the tales of the Brothers Grim and the atrocious vengeance of the merry Piper of Hamelin.

Even after the vision of the thousand year hegemony had crumbled in rubble and ruin, Severo's father's conviction remained unshaken, so certain was he that the fallen race would one day raise its phoenix-head from the ashes and set out to conquer the world anew. So that years later, when Severo Ignatio came of age, it was thought fitting that the young scion of the family conduct his further learning in the promised land, at the University of Humbug – or perhaps it was Hamburg.

The choice could not have been a happier one. The years in the windy Hanseatic city saw the young man bloom into the touchy, argumentative and mercurial spirit he was to become. Both mastering the language and distinguishing himself in his studies, he also found time and occasion to release the long-suppressed rage from the years of boyhood, the jeering and jibes of his school fellows. Finding fellowship in the company of those, not a few, who still secretly nursed a yearning for the elusive thousand year dream, he vent his spleen against the Anglo-Saxon peoples who had undone the prophetic vision, robbed a race of its destiny.

Severo Ignatio might have gone far in life but for the suspect mind that read innuendo and offence in the most innocent of remarks, the coiled tongue springing to whiplash the offender. Positions of prestige and eminence had come his way, in academia, in government, but almost every occasion had been thrown to the winds by the intemperate tongue. Once at a reception he had even threatened to topple a Finnish Chargé d'Affaires from the balcony for suggesting that the Iberian peninsula had remained anchored in the 16th Century. Startled by the menacing words the diplomat had hurriedly stepped backwards, lost his balance and fallen off the balcony anyway.

For several years in the service of a famous publisher, now in late middle age Dr. Ochoa had made a modicum of peace with his fellow humans, occasionally letting pass the odd suspect comment, putting down his rapier after the shortest of duels. A late marriage, to Donna Flora, had also contributed to blunting the razor-sharp edge, her soft presence muting his bristling call-to-arms.

Over the years, too, the unquestioning reverence for the elect race had faded, giving way to a melancholy disillusionment, for the Teutonic warriors had abandoned their historic destiny and settled down to a humdrum bourgeois existence making automobiles and endlessly apologising for past misdeeds. Now afflicted with merely an indignant patriotism, he could brook no word against his country, its history, its much-medalled leader, its cuisine and wines; going so far as to stubbornly insist once that the Rio Tinto grape variety was the one from which Noah had extracted his wine before succumbing to unseemly conduct with his daughters.

The Professor was fond of him, looking on with good humour at his irascible outbursts. And in turn Dr. Ochoa had served him well over the years as an expert and able translator of his books. Unsaid and perhaps unadmitted, there was mutual esteem, Dr. Ochoa seeing in the Professor the figure of the man he might have become, composed, wise and distinguished; and the Professor perhaps secretly nursing an odd admiration for the Spaniard's quixotic foibles. What neither could have imagined nor ever wished was that one day soon the incorrigible quirkiness of the one would bring the other to grief without remedy.

3

Unaware of Fräulein Carin's prominence in our lives and the position she had assumed in our house, Dr. Ochoa mostly ignored her presence at table that evening. A librarian, she might have been for him a mere sales person in a book shop, a handler of bound pages with neither cognizance nor appreciation of the contents. The Captain, who was once again with us, as so often lately, he regarded as a sort of mute fixture in the dining room. Only once did he address the young man, fixing the blue uniform with a dubious expression to remark that a nation of unwilling warriors was a nation lost; to which Captain Ebi smiled vacantly before popping the umpteenth roast potato in his waiting mouth.

Fräulein Carin was not accustomed to being a wall-flower, a mere decorative presence by the Professor's side. But the exclusion was plain and visible. Her attempts to join the table talk were set aside by Dr. Ochoa, who responded to her remarks by addressing the Professor or Dr. Hammes, as though her disembodied voice issued from an empty chair.

Kindred souls, both silent and apparently submissive, Donna Flora and Ebi had taken to each other. Oblivious of the storm clouds gathering over the table, they looked at each other with quiet, almost tender smiles. She nodded in encouragement passing him the dish of potatoes, he nodded back in gratitude helping himself generously. The secret liaison however did not go unnoticed by Dr. Ochoa. Immersed though he was in a monologue on his travels in South America, the dark eyes had been following his wife's repeated efforts to satiate Ebi's famished spirit. Enough was enough and, suspecting some nefarious game underfoot, he shot Donna Flora a sinister look of such intensity that she refrained from passing Ebi the glacéed swedes.

In Gretchen's days ours had been a convivial table. Friends and visitors came and dined amidst amiable talk and quiet mirth, at ease in the cordial peace that reigned in the house. The frequent presence of Dr. Hammes lightened the air with a dry wit, the Baron brought grace and good humour, the occasional visit by Burgomaster Schultz livened the table with an earthy cheer. Even Matilde smiled at the odd sly remark on her culinary skills.

Altogether different this evening, the air in the dining room crackled with a frightening static. The Professor looked tense and anxious, Dr. Hammes forced a smile and lowered his eyes as though counting down to the moment when the lightening would strike. Matilde served and each time hastily retreated to the kitchen. Not desirous of being in harm's way, I sat fast by the door. Placid and pleased in their secret compact, only Donna Flora and Captain Ebi carried on as though picnicking under a serene sky, the one passing a dish, the other emptying it, exchanging courteous nods, brief satisfied smiles.

Coiled in her chair, venom in her eyes, Fräulein Carin looked on as Dr. Ochoa held forth unperturbed on the Aztecs, the Incas, the Olmecs and Tolmecs, musing on how the great Spanish Conquistador Pizzaro had failed to finish the job; so that the handful of savages who had survived the great civilizing mission of Christiandom had in time multiplied once again and now occupied the Andean heights in prolific numbers.

"Civilizing mission!" sneered Fräulein Carin unsolicited. "Nowadays they call it genocide."

Dr. Ochoa's protruding eyes swivelling around and locking her in the vice of a deadly gaze, in a voice that seemed to issue from a cavernous tomb he said, "Señorita, those with a proper upbringing are taught that one speaks when spoken to. As the Duke of Wellington …"

"Another famous Spanish Grandee, I presume!"

Startled by the hauteur and impertinence of the librarian, Dr. Ochoa could hardly believe his ears. He had spent an entire lifetime putting people in their place, but this!, from a small town librarian at that. At an earlier time he might have reached across the table and closed his long gaunt fingers around her swan neck, or as with a soiled plate simply asked a servant to remove her from the table. But with age had come the odd occasional restraint, so that now merely dismissing Fräulein Carin from his sight, contemptuously banishing her from the room, he turned to the Professor, whose uncertain smile of courtesy masked a mounting anxiety.

"Don't you think, Ernesto," he said, "that had our great General Franco been alive today …"

"Had it not been for our Luftwaffe," said Fräulein Carin with a short sneering laugh, "the great General Franco would still be sitting on the outskirts of Marrakesh munching dates!"

And then the heavens opened and the thunderbolt struck. But not before Matilde had scuttled back to the kitchen muttering "And where am I to get dates at this time of the night?"

Like a maddened jack-in-the-box Dr. Ochoa shot to his feet, thumped the table hard, so that his frightened desert spoon leapt off the table-linen.

"Intolerable!" he barked. "Intolerable and unacceptable! That the Caudillo should be spoken of in this manner. No, no! I cannot allow the memory of our great Generalissimo to be so profaned by this…this…woman. Whoever she might be!" Turning to the Professor he added, "Forgive me, Ernesto, but I'm obliged to abandon your table. Florita!" he commanded with a brusque gesture towards his wife. "We leave!"

The Professor's usual pallid colouring had taken on a light scarlet hue as, dismayed and distraught, he stammered helpless conciliatory sounds, saying "Come now, Severo! Please! Do please sit down."

Dr. Hammes had risen from his chair and chimed in to support the Professor. "It's all a misunderstanding. Certainly, Carin had no intention of offending your Generalissimo."

"My Generalissimo! My Generalissimo?" Dr. Ochoa drew himself up to his full height, as the orbs of his dark eyes protruding dangerously devoured the poor doctor. "Francisco Franco, Sir, belongs to humanity, which shall be forever indebted to him. For saving Western civilization from the Red Hordes."

"And the Yellow Hordes," Dr. Hammes added meekly.

"Please, Severo. Do sit down," the Professor pleaded. "I'm sure Fräulein Carin didn't mean to…"

Infuriated by the seemingly grovelling appeasement of the Spaniard, Fräulein Carin in turn sprang to her feet. "I meant every word!" she said looking down at the Professor with cold contempt. "No, don't bother to get up Ernst, I know the way out." With that she drew Ebi up by the arm, dislodging the last of the roast potatoes which he was about to insert in his waiting mouth, and steered him towards the door on the heels of the Ochoas.

Not a moment later Matilde bustled in with a small plate of dates. "They were in a jar at the back of the cupboard," she announced satisfied. "Oh!" Noticing suddenly the vacant places at table, perplexed she said, "I thought they wanted some dates! Where have they gone?"

"Powdering their noses, I expect," Dr. Hammes replied quietly, shifting through the remains on his plate.

There was an echoing silence in the room as soundlessly Matilde cleared the table. Pale and exhausted, eyes cast down, the Professor looked aged beyond his years, as though the weight of time had abruptly borne down on him, turning the silver of his head to a dull grey, the face lined and haggard. The two men sat on in silence, Dr. Hammes tracing invisible patterns on the linen of the tablecloth.

"Have a date, doctor," Matilde offered breaking the hush.

"Thank you. I think I need one."

"They say dates are good for the heart," Matilde said holding out the plate towards the Professor. He smiled wanly, took one and looked up at her expression of motherly concern. "If you say so, Matilde."

The two old friends sat there, going through the dates, mindlessly chewing the soft pulp in silence, as though applying themselves diligently to a sombre task; occasionally placing the stones on the plate gently so as not to disturb the perfect peace that had descended on the room.

The Professor sucked at the last morsel. "I just can't understand it, Thomas," he said pensively. "The way people are at times."

"Oh! Nothing much to understand," Dr. Hammes smiled wryly. "I've been convinced for sometime that Nature's been getting humans cheaply assembled in some dilapidated workshop on the outskirts of one of those grim industrial towns in China or India. Quite simply, an unreliable product!"

Matilde wordlessly beckoned me in to the kitchen for my dinner.

LOVE

1

Born into the kingdom of men, ever since puppy-hood I had heard the word, uttered ad infinitum and ad libitum, not to say ad nauseam, pronounced by the young and not so young, by the ageing and the old, the senile and the dying. It was said that cobbler Freitag on his death bed had croaked that he had never been loved, his very last words.

It came up in conversations sober and solemn, cropped up in exchanges facile and frivolous, punctually appeared in moments of heat and anger. As when Fräulein Carin one day told the Professor with some malice that he had never really loved. Ever spare with words, Matilde herself once said to gardener Bauer that one could well live an entire life without love; looking forlorn the old man could only stammer. Even school teacher Vogel, immersed as he was at all times in higher and recondite matters, occasionally mentioned love, but only to assert ominously that it was the one venom in man that would sooner or later see the human race off the face of the earth forever. Martha was more laconic. Love just happens, she said, clearing the dishes.

Dr. Hammes was philosophical about the matter. "Love comes and goes," he said as I lay on the surgical table with my legs up in the air. "Mostly it goes." Saddened by his words, Fräulein Ulrike remained silent the whole time I was in the surgery. Clearly it meant many things, different to different people. The Baron once hinted, half seriously, that his mother's love would one day empty the air of the oxygen around him. Butcher Udo, on the other hand, feigned total ignorance. "Love!" he exclaimed when teased that he might be in love with chambermaid Lulu. "Seen it only at the cinema," he added stuffing meat into the grinder.

True to the spirit of his calling, Pastor Shaffgott often declared that "Love is Charity!" Curious though that he firmly turned away the old gypsy woman begging alms on the steps of the church. Contrasting the clergyman's sententious sermon on the subject, Frau Gärten at the flower shop saw the matter in keeping with her gentle, dreamy soul: each day without fail she placed a single white rose by the grey pewter urn that held the ashes of her long-dead husband.

Perhaps it was not given to one of my kind to understand. Swirling around one's head, floating in the air like snow flakes on a winter's day, the word eluded my comprehension. I never did manage to understand it, never quite deciphered if it meant affection or affliction, or merely appetite. All I knew was that love had cast a lugubrious shadow over our lives, dimmed the light in our house, turned the Professor into a recluse. obtuse and melancholy. And I wished and prayed that the very same love, with its seemingly untold mystery and manifold power, could somehow lift the gloom from our days, restore our home to the ease and peace it had once known.

Oddly, I now prayed for Fräulein Carin to return in our midst, for her to sit in her floral silk robe beside the Professor at the breakfast table, artfully remind Matilde that the gravy the night before was a trifle too rich and bad for the heart, adding hastily "Everyone's!" before the housekeeper could ask "Whose heart?"

The wish brought with it contrition, for then I thought of Gretchen, the imperceptible fading of her spirit, her tenuous presence lingering only in the memory; her place in the home usurped by Fräulein Breitfuss. But in sorrow there was comfort that, banished from the hearth, yet she lived in our heart, her silent presence like a secret palimpsest whose faded words only we could decipher. Was this then also love? I could only wonder.

2

It was several weeks before Fräulein Carin came to the house again after the tempestuous evening with Dr. Ochoa. She was accompanied by the Captain. An imperceptible change seemed to have come over her. The burnished hair drawn back, severe in a metal-grey turtle-neck sweater and black skirt, her face was set with a firmness one had not seen before. Gone was the usual irony of the faintly mocking smile, the veiled provocation of the teasing words, the finely drawn eyebrows raised in query and dissent. It was as though something inside her had irremediably hardened, a tenacious resolve impervious to reason or argument.

Entering the house she looked down at me as I sat by the door. The hardness of her face was in her voice as well, as she said, "This creature doesn't look too well."

Matilde met her gaze squarely. "He's not the only one."

Losing interest in my well-being and ignoring Matilda's words with a brusque nod, she stepped into the house.

Gardener Bauer, sweeping up the dead leaves under the cherry tree, had overheard the brief exchange. "The Fräulein's upset," he said timidly.

"She's not the only one!" Matilde retorted with unaccustomed severity as she made for the kitchen.

"Ebi, please wait for me," Fräulein Carin called from the door, "I shan't be long."

Squatting down beside me on the lawn, "Silly bitch!" he murmured under his breath as Fräulein Carin shut the door behind her. I was still wondering why he should call her a canine female when he quietly added with a sneering guffaw "If only that fool of a Professor of yours knew what I know!"

The Professor described as such would at another time have called forth a growl from me, at the least. But age had blunted the spirit of quick indignation. The most I could now muster was a yawn of protest. Besides, I had never disliked Captain Ebi and this new persona of his was quite out of keeping with his usual self, easy-going and amiable.

Lately the Captain appeared to have lost interest in contributing towards the defence of the nation and had seemingly decided to take up permanent residence with Fräulein Carin at her cottage. He had shed his blue uniform in favour of a pair of green trousers, maroon jacket over an open-neck shirt. The braided military hat gone, tucked underarm he carried the slender briefcase.

Boyishly debonair, idle and carefree, waiting for Fräulein Carin to finish her day at the library, he loitered through the afternoon, feeding the swans in the park odd crumbs from his briefcase, making costly purchases, invariably leaving without payment. Oddly meek and uncomplaining, like an obedient seneschal Fräulein Carin would go in afterwards and settle the bill.

An aimless gadabout, wandering through the town, peering long at the shop windows, he would enter and ask for whatever caught his wastrel fancy. One day it was a whole leg of ham from Prague at Glockner's. Every other day he looked into Udo's and ordered the best cuts, the butcher enthusiastically introducing Ebi to the pricey Tuscan Chianina steak which he had discovered on a holiday in the south with Lulu the previous summer. Adolf was only too delighted to find in the good Eberhard a willing buyer for the blue porcelain ocarina that had been lying among his not excessively antique antiques for several decades. No less delighted, Ebi left Adolf's blowing heartily into the instrument while attempting to extract his little finger from one of the holes. And then there was the incident at the florist's.

The exorbitant price of the ocarina must have upset Fräulein Carin. Intending to soothe his sibling with a gallant gesture, Ebi ordered an outsize bouquet of exotic flowers from Frau Gärtner. The inebriating scent from the medley of blooms in the little shop must have gone to the young man's head. No sooner had the florist made note of the order when, without the least warning, Ebi's arms folded around Frau Gärtner in a close embrace while he sought to plant his lips on her slender neck.

Caught unawares and disconcerted, the comely florist attempting to disengage herself inadvertently introduced the orchid bloom she had been holding in her hand into Ebi's left ear. And was thoroughly astounded. Not long ago Adolf had recounted gleaning from his studies of the occult in the Orient that certain orchids coming in contact with delicate parts of the body had the power of momentarily paralysing the senses. Ebi's arms did indeed fall away and, with his ear stuffed with purple orchid petals, the ardent admirer sheepishly walked out of the shop. The gentlest of souls, Frau Gärtner afterwards felt a tinge of regret at not having been a trifle more generous with the young man's ardour.

Now sitting in the garden, sipping the beer Matilde had brought out for him, dipping into the bag of crisps he had taken from the briefcase, offering me the odd one, Ebi looked lost in thought. "Ah, Albert!" he said in a tone of resignation almost. "One can get tired of games and pretending. And pinching pennies." The melancholy of the pensive expression cast a shadow over his face that made him appear much older. No longer boyish with an easy contentment, it was an Eberhard one had never seen.

Wordlessly he opened the briefcase, peered inside and extracted a curious item, a sheaf of white cardboard sheets with rows of buttons sown on them. Oddly, each button was different, in colour, shape, size. There were buttons made of metal, cloth, leather, tiny round shirt buttons, colourful ones the size of the crisps Ebi occasionally popped into my mouth.

Pouring over the sheets as if trying to decipher some secret code, stroking my back with one hand, Ebi muttered to himself. "Just you try, friend, making a living selling this stuff," he said with an edge of bitterness, defeat almost. Fishing out a notepad from the briefcase he flicked through the pages. "That damn fool!" he muttered to himself making a note in the pad. "Mother of pearl. Size 6. Four dozen. May the devil take Farber and his haberdashery!" he added under his breath putting away the pad and the sheets of button.

The sudden loquacity was not a little surprising. In the space of a few minutes he had uttered more words than in all the time since he had come into our lives. Surprising, too, the unexpected weariness, the pent-up resentment, his inconstant spirit alternating between animosity and pity for self, as though Fräulein Carin, the Professor, shopkeeper Farber and the entire world had come together in league against him. "Look at that silly old fool!" he hissed with a peculiar acerbity watching Bauer as the gardener went about his labours. I could not understand the uncalled for jibe against the old man, an inoffensive soul if there was one.

I had never asked to understand humans. Nor in truth did I. It was not given to the likes of me to fathom impossible depths.

3

Under Burgomaster Schultz's interminable mayoral tenure it had become a tradition to hold open-air concerts in the park through the summer months, weather permitting. The musical programmes were mixed, eclectic by necessity. Limited municipal funds put full scale orchestras and ensembles of greater or lesser renown beyond reach. The town had to be content with local bands, duos, trios, solo singers accompanied on the piano by music teacher Forkel, with his odd creature Florenz invariably seated at his feet and raising a leg each time the teacher struck a note. It had to be admitted that despite her doltish canine expression, Florenz had developed an admirable musical sense, which occasionally was more than could be said of some of the performers.

Few of the soirées were memorable. Judging by the quality of the local bands, it would not be unfair to say that the inhabitants of the area were on the whole musically deficient. Not surprisingly, rather then the horn, the trumpet and other such demanding wind instruments, the playing of the triangle and the cymbal was much favoured. The drum, too, was a favourite. This often placed severe limits to the range of music offered to the public. The foundry men's band, ambitiously named FIRE & WIND, was an apt illustration. A dozen triangles, several drums and half a dozen cymbals entirely obscured the lone oboist and a good hour of incessant tinkling, the repeated crash of cymbals, and drums booming with the full force of the foundry men's mighty forearms made for a deafening but peculiarly dull musical evening.

There were exceptions. A quartet of mouth organists playing almost without pause had received a deservedly long, standing ovation for having successfully navigated various obtuse musical scores. And some years ago the entire town had extended its heartfelt admiration to a violinist who in the middle of a solo recital had broken down and helplessly dissolved in tears, so powerfully had he been touched by the music. It was later discovered that the loud sobs were caused by the young man's lady friend bidding him a firm and final farewell earlier in the day.

Every year, too, Burgomaster Schultz, who considered augmenting the sum of human happiness as the main task of his office, offered the townspeople a grand variety show at the end of the summer. A stage was erected in the park, seating provided for a couple of hundred and a motley group of performers assembled, folk dancers, retired opera singers, jugglers, contortionists, belly and ballet dancers, yodellers. These minor artistes touring the country through the summer months gladly accepted the modest sums the Municipal coffers could offer, so rounding off their earnings of the season.

In fairness to the Burgomaster, he did supplement the small monetary payments with free bed and board at Henschel's Gasthaus, as well as a tankard or two at Eichel's beer house. On occasion the thoughtful largesse was subject to abuse, with the odd artiste stretching the hospitality, eating inordinate quantities at Henschal's, ordering rare wines and costly liquors at Eichel's. Once an itinerant fiddler found the lodgings so comfortable and the fare so wholesome that he refused to budge from the Gasthaus and had to be evicted by force, but not before his fortnight's stay had caused a significant dent in the public treasury. "No more fiddlers in my place!" Henschel had sworn when afterwards it was found that the guest had removed an ashtray and decamped with a face towel.

The previous year the final summer show had been enriched with spectacles never seen before, made possible by a somewhat more generous purse at the disposal of the Burgomaster. Herr Schultz was infinitely delighted to present, among other rare performances, a whole hour with the White Heather Dancers from the Hebrides as they pranced, pirouetted and leapt through reels, polkas and Highland flings, and the public gazed mesmerized at the underwear beneath the flying kilts.

Herr Schultz had also somehow laid his hands on a pair of wandering dervishes and the endless twirling of the white-frocked figures, the red conical hats spinning away like tops, to the reedy music of the ney and the incessant drumbeats from a recorder thoroughly hypnotised the audience. Regrettably so intense was the trance into which the duo had fallen that rotating at almost lighting speed one of the dervish dancers spun right off the stage and crashed to the ground, smashing both legs. The contretemps cost the Municipality dear, for the injudicious dervish was hospitalized for a prolonged period before getting to his feet again and joining his partner in their whirlwind round of engagements elsewhere.

This year Fräulein Breitfuss's "Summer of Arts" had so thoroughly drained finances that Herr Schultz was hard put to it to book a reasonable number of artistes able to offer minimally acceptable entertainment. But ever a man of hidden resources, the Burgomaster would not admit defeat, managing in the end to put together a show featuring several rare and exotic numbers. The Peruvian Stompers and the Stick Dancers of Transylvania were outlandish enough, but small change compared to the Hermit of Hindustan, a real eye-opener if ever there was one.

4

The single sheet programme note, handed out by Municipal clerk Schicketanz as he leered at and lingered with the women in the audience, said that the Hermit of Hindustan had retreated inside a cavern in the eastern Hindu Kush mountains when little more than a boy and emerged as an octogenarian, having in the long intervening decades practised and perfected the unique discipline of the Dancing Iris. Indeed, it was claimed that he was the sole practitioner in the world of the ancient art that went back several millenniums to when the Aryans first arrived in the Orient and took to rolling their eyes continuously to avoid the blinding glare of the meridional sun. Emerging at long last and descending from the mountain heights, the recluse had rapidly found an agent and taken to the road, giving much acclaimed performances across the five continents.

Seated now on the stage on a square of white sheep skin, the holy hermit presented a singular figure. Untouched by a razor or a pair of scissors, the dense beard of an immaculate white had grown down to his loins and beyond, descending to the knobbly knees. Untrimmed and unchecked, the cloud of hair of the same pristine whiteness fell back from the head like a bridal veil, covering his back and shielding from prurient gaze the view of his posterior. Entirely dressed, front and back, solely in the hirsute growth held in place with a regimental tie knotted around the waist, the sage sat on his shrunken shanks in what the programme note described as the "immemorial lotus posture".

After Burgomaster Schulze's resounding introduction of the "Holy Hermit from the Hindubush," the figure sat perfectly still in the immemorial pose, while the subdued giggles and titters at the ascetic's choice of costume died down and a hush fell on the public. After several minutes of meditation the eyes in the round baby face covered with down opened wide and a gasp went up from the onlookers. The iris in each eye had begun to rotate clockwise, slow and deliberate at first, picking up speed then, ever faster, until they blurred into faint dark spots. Coming to a halt quite as suddenly, the rotation began in the other direction, again speeding up, fading to a blur once again.

The audience rubbed their own eyes in disbelief as the dance routine of the eyeballs began in earnest. Magically the irises now

310

spun in opposite directions and then, by force of some mysterious will, they began to move to and fro, darting from one extremity of the eye to the other, making policeman Bock's cross-eyes look like an amateur attempt at best. Unmindful that some of the weaker spirits among the public were beginning to experience a certain giddiness, the hermit introduced a further variation. Still rotating while racing from side to side, the dark circles of the iris started a rhythmic up and down movement. Soon they were ricocheting like mad little pin-balls, spinning, gliding, flitting. Simply to watch the frenzied dance brought on a spell of dizziness.

And then the unexpected happened, causing Frau Gärtner in the front row to faint and slump against Burgomaster Schultz. The irises had disappeared entirely, leaving only the white of the eyeballs. A murmur of shock and horror rose from the audience as at the same time the blind hermit's mouth opened wide and out came a pale pink tongue the likes of which one had never seen, so long that it slithered down snake-like past the chin and came to rest on the beard.

People held their breath as the old man sat there for several long minutes, perfectly immobile, not a muscle moving, nor a wisp of hair stirring. Just as Uli who was seated behind us said, "Ma, I think the gentleman's dead," it dawned on Dr. Hammes, who was with the Professor in the front row, that in fact the holy man might have breathed his last. "Get a doctor!" he called out getting to his feet and was about to make his way up to the stage when the hermit silently toppled over in a single piece like a statue in stone, the pose intact, the immemorial posture and all, one buttock exposed to view.

In the course of the years occasional accidents had occurred during this summer spectacle. Apart from the flying dervish fracturing both legs, once the entire stage had collapsed under the considerable weight of a large chorus of Tyrolean yodellers, the stout singing men in their leather hoses going down in a heap as their epiglottis emitted an impressively high falsetto; providentially the only damage suffered being nothing more than the large bump raised on the head of the leader of the yodellers by the sizeable cowbell that followed the group in their precipitous descent.

Another minor mishap involved the Magical Sword-Swallower of Dushanbe, who thrust down his throat the entire length of a broadsword that never reappeared again; albeit there was some ground for suspicion that the sword was in fact made of caramelized sugar. Perhaps the most poignant misadventure befell the Manchurian fire-eater with a rich head of hair, whose long flowing locks went up in a blaze as he skipped around blowing long tongues of flame; the singed head with the odd burnt-out black stubble of hair made for an atrocious appearance.

But a deceased performer the town had never seen. Atrophied in the lotus pose and lifted bodily, the Hermit of Hindustan was rushed to the hospital. To the immense relief of all, Dr. Süssmayr declared the anchorite to be alive, the diagnosis being that the man had hypnotised himself, which posed a disconcerting conundrum, for he alone could release himself from the state of immersion; though how he was to do this without first coming out of the catalepsy Dr. Süssmayr's medical expertise was at a loss to explain. But as there were almost no further secrets for modern neurological science, the eminent doctor assured Herr Schultz, the puzzle would be cleared up on dissecting the patient's brain. The Burgomaster walked out feeling faint.

For several days the hermit sat on the hospital bed, perfectly still in the immemorial posture, unseeing and with tongue out, without batting an eyelid or the twitch of a single muscle or nerve. Force-fed through a tube down the throat, on the third evening, as the attending nurse pressed liquidized custard through the apparatus, abruptly the patient came alive. With lizard-like alacrity the tongue withdrew into the mouth. Head cushioned comfortably on the nurse's prosperous bosom, the hermit smacked his lips sucking voraciously at the custard, while the irises, first one and then the other, rolled back in place and the eyes looked about with the beatific innocence of a new-born.

The hermit was released from hospital the following day and departed with his agent, without damages being claimed, much to the relief of the Burgomaster. And medical science was much enriched by the incident, it being thought that a decisive step forward had been achieved in the treatment of self-induced catalepsy. Some months later Dr. Süssmayr had a much-acclaimed paper published in a prestigious medical journal under the title "CUSTARD AND RELATED APPLICATIONS IN NON-TERMINAL PATHOLOGIES."

5

While Burgomaster Schultz waited anxiously at the hospital for news of the patient, his perplexity growing ever more acute at the passing mention of possible damages by the hermits agent, a lean Scotsman wound in a saffron robe and peculiarly called Swami Sri Sri Saradananda Hamilton, who moreover added that in the event of decease the hermit would need to be cremated on a pyre at the confluence of two major rivers, an imperative to assure the mystic a higher avatar on rebirth, and not on the banks of the sort of modest country stream that ran on the outskirts of the town, Municipal clerk Schicketanz had taken charge of the evening in the park and was acting as master of ceremonies. "The show must go on!" he announced drawing himself to his full height, which as it happened was below average, and adjusting his glasses repeatedly to focus better on Frau Adler's mildly daring décolleté.

And the show did go on. But the performances that followed were small change after the Hindu Kush hermit's life-threatening act. In any case the festive spirit of the evening had been dampened by the precarious condition of the holy man. The audience wearily watched the Peruvian Stompers, who stomped through their act, the short stout barrel-shaped figures with rugs draped over one shoulder tediously banging the boards with such vehemence that it was feared that the entire stage would come crashing down at any moment, with the incessant stompers meeting the fate of the Tyrolean yodellers.

Before the Professor and Dr. Hammes decided to desert the rest of the show, Schicketanz grandly announced the Somerset Somersault Duo. A depressing spectacle, if ever there was one. A brief act presented by a short lady, in tights and a sky-blue tutu, and her partner, a small mongrel with a patchy brown and black coat. For several minutes the duo somersaulted from one end of the stage to the other and back again, the animal following close on the heels of his mistress, turning head over heels as best as he could, more often than not banging his head on the boards. One could not but avert one's gaze from the sorry sight.

Humans might display scant regard for self, often parading themselves in a demeaning fashion, without décor or shame. But for one of my race, albeit of unknown parentage and of an uncertain but undoubtedly inferior breed, to lend himself to such an unutterably humiliating exhibition! It filled me with an unexpected sadness. My heart went out to the poor creature, such abject ignominy to earn the day's bread. There but for my Maker…, I thought with a grateful heart.

The Somerset somersaulters were more than enough for the Professor and Dr. Hammes, as well. I followed on their heels, as Schicketanz, eyes still burrowing into Frau Adler's décolleté, prepared to announce the première attraction of the evening, the Stick Dancers of Transylvania.

In the mild end of summer evening the closing twilight shadowed the park with an inky green, the trees dense, solid almost against the darkening sky still empty save for the first star of the night. Behind us the Transylvanian stick dancers had already begun their act, the dozen performers bent double and hopping about like wounded locusts on wooden rods tied to their legs. The loud clatter receded as we strolled out over the green.

Stalls set up for the evening here and there in the park were serving people drifting away from the show, Lulu handing out tankards at Eichel's wooden hut, Frau Daecher and widow Fruehauf devouring at Henschel's stand finger-thin frankfurters, a speciality invented by the hotelier's grandfather during the Great War that contained mostly husk, stale bread crumbs, and a minor quantity of fine-ground meat trimmings.

Conversing quietly the Professor and Dr. Hammes walked towards the lake, stopping by the bench at the water's edge where a sizeable, square tent had been pitched. The doctor laughed aloud reading out the words on the large board set out in the illuminated entrance:

MADAME SHAKIRA NOSTRADAME
FATE & FORTUNE FORECAST & FORETOLD
MINIMUM 100% ACCURACY
GROUP DISCOUNTS

"After you, Professor," he said with a broad sweep of his arm.

Taken aback, the Professor looked at Dr. Hammes with an uncertain smile. "You don't believe in this sort of nonsense?" he exclaimed.

"A hundred percent minimum accuracy. It doesn't come any better, you know!"

"You're not really going in there to have the young woman read your future?" the Professor asked unbelieving.

"Not mine. I have none. It's your future, Ernst, that's worrying."

"Oh!" Shying away from his friend's words, the Professor looked around awkwardly. "I must say, Thomas, some of us never quite grow up!"

"Why bother? Excessive growing up can be painful."

Boyishly cheerful, bantering and cajoling, step by step Dr. Hammes inched forward towards the fortune-teller's den. Taking the Professor lightly by the arm, he suddenly parted the curtain, to announce loudly: "Madame, here we are! May we come in?"

"Salaam and welcome!" came a raucous cry from the twilight gloom of the tent. "Please come! Entrez, entrez!"

6

A threadbare carpet underfoot, a dark blue canopy overhead printed with silver stars and an outsize milky quarter moon, Madame Shakira Nostradame sat at a red formica-covered round table with a large glass ball in the middle encasing a low-wattage bulb that cast a timid pink glow. Dressed in an ample blouse, printed with stars and of the same material as the canopy, the pleated folds seeming to choke the thin crinkled turkey neck, the frizzled head of hair was adorned with a circular cheesecloth trimmed with tiny blue glass beads, of the sort used in summer to cover carafes of water against midges.

The shadowed features of the elongated mule face gave the impression of indeterminate age. The length of the teeth, hardly ever seen on humans, was however impressive. Gold-wire rings the size of saucers hung from the curiously elongated ears and each finger wore a large lozenge stone of a different colour. The dark haggard eyes came alive as the visitors entered the gloom of the tent.

"Salaam and welcome," she greeted busily, half rising from her stool. "Come gentlemen! Come!"

"Madame Shakira?" Dr. Hammes asked in a faltering voice, peering into the penumbra.

"It is she, Monsieur!" the raucous voice assured with some enthusiasm. "At your service, Gentleman. Please take a seat. S'il vous plaît!"

The Professor looked around hesitantly, as if searching out a quick exit. The doctor holding him by the arm introduced himself. "I'm Dr. Hammes. This gentleman is a patient under my care. He's not well. We seek your guidance, Madame."

"Yes, yes, guidance you shall have, Monsieur. Please be seated," the fortune-teller urged indicating the only seating, a frayed imitation-leather office chair on three wheels. It was then that her eyes fell on me as I stood behind the doctor. "Can't tell *his* future," Madame Shakira said with the merest edge of contrariness in her tone. "Animals have no future."

Good to know. I settled down by the Professor's feet as he seated himself unsteadily on the mobile chair.

Dr. Hammes took the proffered sheet, narrowing his eyes to read in the dim light. "Ah, I see. Charges based on the number of years in the future. Plan A: 1 Year. Plan B: 5 Years. Plan C: 10 Years. Special Plan: 25 Years. Well! What do you think, Ernst? Shall we go for the special platter?"

"It might be overdoing it, at this age," the Professor remarked with equanimity, falling in with the doctor's play-acting.

"I agree. Madame, we'll take Plan A."

The Madame was not pleased. The long fleshy nose wrinkled as she muttered, "In this town only Plan A." She reached for the Professor's right hand, clutched it in her claw-like fingers, dusted it perfunctorily, passed her own hand over the palm several times as though meaning to soothe it; then peering closely traced the lines with infinite slowness.

"One question, Madame," said Dr. Hammes quietly rocking on his feet. "Do you also read misfortunes?"

"No money in misfortune," the fortune-teller rebutted dryly. Producing then with a sleight of hand a pack of cards, she spread them evenly on the table. Each card bore the garish illustration of a bizarre image: a harlequin with a lolling tongue, the entwined figure of a nude man and woman under a shower of rose petals, Beelzebub rising through tongues of flame, the Dark Reaper seated on a throne of skulls clutching a scythe in one skeletal hand, an old crone astride a curled-horn aurochs, a leering satyr leaping on its hind legs in pursuit of a pale maiden.

With thin, prehensile fingers Madame Shakira picked the card with the satyr and, pressing it to her forehead, shut her eyes. After a pause of several minutes, during which she appeared to have dozed off, abruptly she came alive with a flutter of the lids and, fixing the Professor with unseeing eyes, began to speak in a thin disembodied tremolo that sent a chill down the spine.

"I see a shadow behind you. I see a shadow in front of you. In the shadow behind I see a Halo. In the front shadow I see a Halo."

317

"No halo over the head, I trust?" Dr. Hammes interrupted quietly.

Sunk in a trance, Madame Shakira ignored the disturbance. "Back Halo good. Most beautiful Halo. Many years in your life. Much happiness. Front Halo different. Young, pretty. But coming and going. This Halo causing pain. Beaucoup d'agonie! Now…" Pausing in her divinations, she shut her eyes briefly. "Oh, what do I see? What *do* I see? Another shadow with the front shadow. Another Halo. Halo no. 3. Bad halo. Mal, mal!"

With shadows front and back and halos everywhere, the message was confusing. "Yes, alright!" Dr. Hammes interrupted impatiently. "But does the young one, Halo no. 2, love the gentleman?"

The query recalled Madame Shakira from her trance-like retreat, the voice returning to the former husky croak. Parting the fleshy painted lips in a brief grimace, she raised one bejewelled hand as if to dismiss the question. "Ah, no Monsieur! No. L'amour! Un grand mystére. Très difficile, très compliqué! "

"But…"

"Much work. Extra charge. Not included in Plan A," she added in a brisk, business-like manner.

"But that's what we're here to learn," the doctor insisted.

"Please ask this gentleman," she replied curtly, tapping her left breast. "His heart knows. Better than these," she added shuffling the tarot cards.

"The future, Madame?" the Professor queried meekly.

"Now you will see." Eyes shut once again, her hand groped over the spread-out pack. She rubbed the finger tips, held them under her nose, drew a sharp breath and picking up one of the cards placed it beside the satyr leaping after the maiden. Opening her eyes she looked down at the result of the draw. Lips pursed, her brow creased in a frown. The second card figured the Dark Reaper holding aloft the scythe.

Hastily dismissing the figure of death and removing the card, the nimble fingers picked out the nude couple and set it down beside the card with the satyr. Visibly heaving a sigh of relief, she looked up, but seemingly still at unease, just as the Professor asked, almost apologetically, "How will it end?"

"Ah! C'est ça l'enigme! Sometimes it ends. Sometimes not. L'amour. Très mystérieux!"

Madame Shakira inviting a return visit, for a Plan B reading, and Dr. Hammes's wallet modestly lightened, we left none the wiser.

THE PROFESSOR

1

The days shortening, the late afternoon light had begun to dim when we took leave of the Baron. Stretched out in the back as the Professor drove through the silent woods mellow with the summer green turning to pale ochre, I thought of the vague unease that had passed through me like the shadow of an obscure presence as the Baron stood on the steps of the mansion and waved us off down the gravel drive. Perhaps it was the ulterior sense my Maker had endowed me with in lieu of speech. But I did have a fleeting sensation, a vague foreboding, that we would never again see the Baron nor ever again set eyes on this secret Arcadia with its rolling meadow, its thousand roses and Hubert's august oak.

The shadow of the premonition was beyond my understanding. Yet it remained with me, like the blurred, unidentifiable vision of an image flitting through the dark. And later in the nocturnal hour, as the shades fell and I drowsed towards sleep, a dream of desolation rose from the fathomless depths and I found myself alone on that undulating pasture, now a vanished world with the venerable oak gone, the rose garden a patch of bare earth, the mansion crumbled to a heap of stones overgrown with furze and thicket, Hubert's castle devoured clean by an impenetrable forest that seemed to advance by the minute, minatory and malevolent. Devoid of life and the living, steeped in an echoing silence that made the heart race, the forlorn landscape was bare, save for Baroness Gertrude's upturned wrought-iron wheelchair, as though the brute hand of a spiteful giant had simply brushed it aside. Standing there in the wasteland among the rubble and ruins of memory, perhaps I wept in the dark of the slumbering night.

Perhaps imagination had conjured up the chimera of the phantom sight from the day spent at the Baron's. It was a visit different from all the others, so many over the years, with Gretchen and the Professor, and then with the Professor alone when she was gone. Nothing had visibly changed, the castle still brooding at one end, the rose garden at the other, the rambling ivy-clad mansion sitting stolid in its accustomed place, Hubert's oak as majestic as ever. Yet change had come, soundless and imperceptible, like an unseen spirit, permeating the land and its inhabitants with sudden age and decay. A matter of mere weeks, but it was as though the Professor and I had returned to the scene after long years.

Frail and gaunt, Baroness Gertrude's skeletal frame sat stooped in her wheelchair, faceless almost under a black lace shawl draped low over the head. Never a figure of elegance, Elfriede today was more blowzy than ever, the wrinkle-creased round face, under a dishevelled head of hair, set with the stoical forbearance of a silent decrepitude as she moved about in an almost aimless shuffle, as if her legs had forgotten the sense of direction. And Otfried leaner and more cadaverous than ever, the grey mask of his face frozen with a lifeless passivity.

The Baron too appeared to have suffered the abrupt onset of age. Less boyish in gait and movement, it was more the inexplicable absence of his usual light-hearted cheer and ease of manner that was surprising. Never less than cordial, yet a sombre weariness seemed to burden his spirit, as if weighed down by thoughts of transience and decay. "Yes indeed, Ernst," he said with a sighing tone of resignation when the Professor remarked that it seemed much longer than the mere month since our last visit. "Time passes our way and leaves us stranded in its wake."

Nor had Schwarzbauer been spared the hand of this mysterious change. Seated on the ground among the roses, welcoming me as he always did with arms opened wide to gather me to himself, enfolding me in his embrace and whispering my name, oddly something appeared to have dampened the exuberance of his spirit. As the Professor strolled over to greet the Baroness before going in for lunch, I sat a moment with the gardener, my head on his chest, the beat and throb of his stout heart in my ears. And as he often did, now too. slowly rocking me back and forth, he softly crooned a melody, wordless and hesitant, coloured as if by a dull resignation, the halting voice of one lost in a barren wilderness with neither direction nor destination. It was a Schwarzbauer I had not known before.

2

Lunch was a desultory affair, the fare spare as never before.

Shapeless in what must have been the Baroness's nightgown, the discoloured flannel threadbare from age and wear, a soiled apron loosely tied around where once there had been a waist, moving laboriously Elfried limped and shuffled between the kitchen and the dining hall.

Wandering about at a funereal pace that would have tried the patience of the dead, Otfried served from a tureen a thin, watery stew so bland that hardly a whiff of the meat reached my nostrils as I sat by the door to the terrace. He ladled out the meagre helpings with such deliberation that the Baron, normally indulgent with the butler's usual somnolent pace, remarked that the Baroness would shortly need to go for her afternoon rest. Unmindful of the pointed hint, Otfried continued with his lugubrious ballet.

Baroness Gertrude herself appeared to be not all there. Her usual crotchetiness had given way to a silent, remissive presence, as she sat humped with head bent forward, as if about to fall face down on the plate of stew. The accustomed liveliness of her eyes now dimmed, the vacant expression, still and mindless, gave the impression of a spirit spent and absent.

When at length, meandering aimlessly, Otfried had managed to serve the diners the potatoes and turnips, the Baron lowered his head and spoke into the small horn of the tubular hearing device that ran under the table and protruded with a similar horn where his mother sat at the far end. "Shall we start then, Maman?" he said mustering a forced liveliness, meaning to catch his mother's attention. But his voice carried through the tube came out as a muffled "Shall we part then, Maman?"

The Baroness looked up, the barest hint of life animating her gaze "Not yet, Armin," she said in an almost forlorn whisper, adding, "The time will come."

Odd, this unlikely resignation. One would never have expected the merest admission of mortality from the old lady. How the Baron's eulogy at Freude's funeral had raised her hackles, when carried away by the oratorical flight he had augured a reunion on the morrow with the little creature in the Elysian fields. Even in times recent Baroness Gertrude had made it amply clear that she quite expected to outlive Hubert's oak.

Despite the poor fare, lunch at the Baron's was usually a pleasantly light hour at table, the master of the house gently bantering with the Professor, extracting from memory little pearls of erudite minutiae; while the Baroness interjected pointed remarks of no relevance at all, whimsical recollections from her youth, antique proverbs that no one had ever heard. Today instead it was more the repast of a wake, spare, consumed in wordless company. Only once did Baroness Gertrude speak, addressing the Professor in a throaty whisper, to ask if Gretchen was well. The Professor nodded with silent complicity.

I wandered out onto the terrace as the meal proceeded in mournful aphonia. The air outside was tinted with a strange greenish-grey hue, as vast islands of cloud dragged themselves ponderously across the sky, the light hesitant and flickering, as if a spent sun was slowly extinguishing itself. A sudden gust of wind drove drifts of dead leaves across the parched grass of the meadow. At the end of its season of glory, the rose garden too looked like a mere patch of discoloured shrubs, unkempt and sterile.

Perhaps it was the strange light hovering uncertainly, or merely the dimming sight of my ageing eyes, that gave the scene a dismal air, arid and melancholy, as if like all things living, the trees, shrubs and blooms too had wearied of the incessant repetition of morning and noon, night and day, the tedious succession without end of the seasons. Or perhaps the scene was as pristine as ever, the onlooker's vision altered by the decay of his own mind and spirit.

3

Afterwards the Professor accompanied the Baron on his annual visit to his father.

We set off past the rose garden, up the meadow to the tree-line and along a forest path through the phalanx of evergreens massed densely on all sides. Strolling at a leisurely pace, the two men fell deep in talk. Composed and earnest, the Baron spoke of his father, of Baroness Gertrude, the mismatch of his parents, of his little sister Renate who had left them before he was born; and of the life he might have wished for himself but had not attained. "But," he added, "I think you'd agree, Ernst, most choices in life are limited to either/or. And then sometimes it's neither!"

Of different provenance, quite as diverse in character and the life each had led, yet there was a friendship between the two men that allowed for an intimacy of sorts, enabling each to divulge thoughts and sentiments not so much as private matters but as impersonal, almost academic subjects. So that the Baron spoke about himself with a non-confessional ease and, in turn, the Professor too shed his reticence, confiding in a detached manner, recalling the long years with Gretchen, the obstacle course with Fräulein Carin, the emotional cul-de-sac in which he found himself.

"I don't know about you, Ernst," said the Baron with a small laugh. "But I can tell you I wouldn't wait to be asked twice if I received a proposal from a young woman like Carin. And remember, a woman spurned…!"

"It's not quite that easy. And at this age…"

"Age! I expect only the dead are ageless. The rest of us carry our years as best we can. And I'd say you're not doing badly! The thirty odd years between you and Carin…"

"Besides, Gretchen…"

"Do you know, I used to envy you Gretchen. We all loved her and we'll carry her with us. The dead bring sorrow, but I think they wish us well. I think she would want you to start living again." The Baron turned to the Professor with a playful smile. "Besides, I've not been asked to a wedding in a long while!"

The trees fell away and the path led out of the forest to a wide open space, the green sloping field planted with graves weather-beaten and darkened with age. Below and beyond the rise of the cemetery lay the countryside, the rooftops of a small village in the distance visible on a clear day, the church steeple rising in the air needle-thin.

The Baron led the way through the thicket of headstones, dilapidated and leaning precariously here and there, the odd stone cross askew and threatening to topple over. Tall grass wreathed the tombs, the epigraphs, names and dates grown faint, erased by wind and rain and time, like the memory grown faint and gone of those who lay beneath the earth.

"Hermann Schenkel. The chap who donated the town library," the Baron said pointing out a large grey slab of clear Siena marble with a squat tombstone sculpted like an open book and inscribed with the words SCIRE EST VIVERE. "True!" the Baron remarked nodding his head. "Knowledge is life. But what then is death?"

A wide, weed-choked gravel path cut across the cemetery, separating even in death those of lesser lineage from the high-born. The lower portion was inhabited by the remains of Hubert's henchmen and their descendants, who had settled in the countryside around. The top of the rise, a gently sloping plot of ground, lodged the members of the House of Montfleury-Pischendorpf down the centuries, the tombs laid out at a discrete distance one from the other, row on row, neat and regular, the stone or marble headstones elaborately sculpted, the large lettering of the inscriptions clear to the eye.

Hubert's grave alone, a massive square of black stone covered over with moss and mould, bore the air of neglect and decay, the headstone nameless, as though time had worked its patient hand to erase from memory the traces of a life that had so little of the human. Beside him a more slender grave housed the remains of Ludmilla Beate Franziska, the girl-bride he had taken in old age, who had assured him posterity but not honoured remembrance.

Strolling along the wide spaces between the dead, the Baron came to his father. "His ninety-ninth year today," he said quietly, running his hand over the plain headstone bearing only the name and the span of his short life. There was no sorrow in his voice, merely thought and an undertone of vague regret. "Mother's never once been here since the day of the funeral. I don't think somehow they were made for each other. Whatever that might mean! But he was a kind and simple soul. Looking back now, I believe he never quite got over the loss of his little girl."

"Renate?"

"Yes. Gone before I was born. Odd to think, Ernst, that father spent a great deal of time with me when I was a boy, yet I never knew him. Not then, nor even later. I'm not sure … do we ever really get to know another human being?"

The Professor shook his head doubtfully. "Probably not." And then he uttered something surprising that made the Baron look up. "I thought I knew Gretchen."

The two friends stood in silence for a long moment, the grey calm of the repose of the dead broken only by the idle cawing of a crow in the trees. In the slow afternoon light the surrounding countryside receded in dull pastels towards the horizon swollen with sullen, colourless banks of cumulus. With not a breath of air, nor a blade of grass stirring, the still landscape seemed bereft of life, as if all living presence had deserted this corner of earth.

Gently patting the headstone of his father's grave and moving away, at length the Baron said, "Ah well, I expect one of these days it'll be my turn here."

"Oh! Early intimations of mortality, Armin? For all one knows," added the Professor, "I myself could be gone tomorrow!"

"No, you can't. There's Carin, things to look forward to. Unless, of course, in the meanwhile you decide to throw yourself on the railway tracks, à la Karenina!"

The Baron smiled in recollection. "As a boy I was unusually impressed by the cover of the book I once saw on father's table in his study. A young woman with arms up in the air, head thrown back, picked out on a railway track by the garish yellow head light of a locomotive rushing forward with a long plume of smoke. Can't imagine why it's stayed with me all these years. Mind you, it's a little less romantic nowadays. What with these super fast trains, one's run over even before you decide to do yourself in!"

4

Autumn at the door, the weather threatening to break, since morning the leaden sky had rumbled with echoes of intermittent rolls of distant thunder, as if a giant workshop above the dense layers of clouds was readying the machinery to release a second deluge.

In contrast to the grey world outside and the gusts of moist breeze blowing in from the north, life and warmth had returned to the house. Up earlier than usual, the Professor appeared unusually busy. Gone was the obtuse apathy, the resigned withdrawal of the past days and weeks. Hardly had he then stepped out of the house, received few callers, almost shunned friends and acquaintances. Seemingly suspended in time, emptied of substance and apparently incapacitated, incapable of the small quotidian gestures, he had moved about the house invisibly, sitting at the dining table with alarming frugality, wordless with Matilde, answering the phone with impatient brevity. Coming in to ask if he should change the broken panes of the small glass house in the back garden, even poor gardener Bauer was met with the same brusque dismissal.

Today, unexpectedly, the ashen look had given way to his usual composed, mild-humoured appearance. The curved back had straightened, restoring the trim figure to its height. It seemed the years had abruptly fallen away, the blood in his veins running anew, the spirit revived, renewed with a new will. The sullen hibernation over, his movements brisk and purposeful, he sat down to breakfast with the appetite of the new-born, Matilde quite taken aback with the cheerful greeting that met her. "Are you alright?" she could not help enquiring, to which the Professor responded with the expectancy of a famished guest, saying "And what do we have this morning?" With furrowed brow the housekeeper hurried back to the kitchen, with half a mind to call Dr. Süssmayr.

Watching the almost youthful stride as he moved about the house, put books away on the shelves, arranged the papers on his table, rearranged the furniture here and there though nothing was particularly out of order, one wondered at the curious, almost miraculous change that had come over him since the visit to the Baron's. It was as if he had been freed from the constraints of some secret struggle that had enchained his mind and spirit through this long summer's end. Unshackled now from whatever the doubt and debate that had raged within, he had found his way back to his old self, his presence once again felt and heard in the house, in the small details of daily life.

With patient good humour he sorted out with Matilde some of the summer clothes to be put away and asked for a heavier duvet now that the nights were turning chilly; asking too for orchids from the florist for the sideboard in the dining room. Matilde looked up quizzically.

"Fräulein Carin may be coming for dinner tomorrow," he informed her, his tone at once both hesitant and yet curiously assured.

"Will she? I'll need to do some shopping."

"I'll tell you in the morning." Leaving the room humming to himself, the Professor stopped at the door. "Oh yes, please tell Bauer to change the panes in the glass house."

"The young lady's coming back," said Bauer afterwards, sitting by the kitchen door.

"She is," the housekeeper agreed distantly, scraping the carrots with an odd gravity. "And for good."

The gardener nodded with sympathetic approval, adding "In old age one needs company."

"Depends on the company."

Bauer sighed. Putting down the mug, for the first time doubt crossed his mind that he would ever gain the companionship of this woman.

5

The sky turning ever more oppressive, the ponderous masses of cloud pressing down as if intending to obliterate the pale mid-afternoon light, Matilde hurried around the house shutting the windows against the keen breeze blowing steadily down from the woods, chilling the air with an almost late-autumn cold. She had had an unusually busy morning, changing the bed linen, putting out fresh towels in the bath, cleaning, dusting, polishing, even though nothing was particularly amiss and the house was as usual in good order. In between she had run down to Frau Gärtner's to fetch the orchids the Professor had asked for. The mass of pale white and violet flowers on long stems now crowned the tall cut-glass vase on the sideboard in the dining room. It was as if the house was being readied for the return of the prodigal.

The Professor's day, too, was unusually animated. Burgomaster Schultz dropped by late morning to ask the Professor if he could spare the occasional hour to stand in for Frau Botticelli, who read to the elderly at the old folks home twice a week but had left the day before on a fortnight's holiday in Venice.

"It would be a great honour," the Burgomaster added meekly.

"And what should I read? Tarzan's adventures?" the Professor asked teasing good-humouredly.

Herr Schultz looked abashed. "No, no!" he exclaimed with his eyes on the floor. "Your choice, Professor. But nothing too long." Because, he explained, the previous year Frau Botticelli had begun "Gone With The Wind," but even before she had got to the burning of Atlanta, several of the audience themselves were gone.

"Gone where?"

Herr Schultze clicked his tongue. "Departed," he said with a sorrowful expression. "And poor widow Pumpel, who had never missed a single reading, passed away with one chapter from the end!"

"Sorry to hear that."

"Yes," the Burgomaster nodded thoughtfully. "Life's just too short for some of these big books."

No sooner had Herr Schultz left, assured that the aged would not be allowed to depart without first satisfying their literary yearnings, when Dr. Ochoa called. It was to discuss details of the work at hand and the Professor retired to the study to talk over the speaker-phone while he consulted the papers on his table. Ears ever alert, despite the distance Dr. Ochoa must have sensed an unusual nuance in the Professors voice, for halfway through the conversation he suddenly said, "Ernesto, you are happy!" adding in a suspicious tone, "¿Por qué esta felicidad?"

Cactus-prickly, often outrageous in word and manner, yet the man was a friend of half a lifetime, partisan yet uncommonly loyal. Thinking then the better of it, the Professor told him.

"¡Caramba!" the Spaniard burst forth with a loud intake of breath. "¡Bueno! ¡Muy bueno! I'm happy for you, Ernesto. Happy! You know, my old friend the Marques de Estanyol used to say: love when young, marry when old! Wise words. And the lady...?"

Abruptly the words died in mid-sentence. There was a prolonged pause. "Still there, Severo?" the Professor asked.

After a long moment, Ochoa's voice finally came through, the spirit of joyous felicitation vanished, replaced by a grave, almost inquisitorial tone as he said, "The woman from the library. Yes, Ernesto?"

"Yes, Carin," the Professor confirmed.

"¡Madre de Dios!" Ochoa exclaimed in a sibilant whisper, as if pronouncing a malediction.

6

The world, it seemed, had decided that its last hour had come. The town emptied of human presence, the good people had shut themselves indoors when late in the evening the Professor and I left the house and set out for Fräulein Carin's.

Ever stronger, seemingly fed by its own rage, the wind rose in violent gusts, tearing through the trees, obliterating the bleary street lights with the wildly dancing shadows of the branches overhead. I cowed behind the Professor as long streaks of lightning raced across the black void of the sky, blinding sight, making day of night, and the deafening thunder came rolling in waves like the volcanic wrath of all the gods.

The Professor clutched the raincoat to his throat as the first drops turned to squalls of driven rain. It was not for me to understand the need to be about on this of all nights. But there was an urgency of purpose in his step as we hurried past the old stone houses and up the cobbled rise.

Widow Slusser's cottage was the last house at the end of the road. Beyond lay a large meadow sloping down towards the river and the old abandoned mill. The cottage, set in a small garden untended and overgrown with weeds and shrubs, was an old two-storied building in black stone with the front almost entirely obscured by an ancient wisteria which reached up to the slate-covered roof and whose gnarled and knotted branches seemed to hold the house in a mortal embrace.

Periodically rented only by outsiders, the house held the memory of a sanguine night long ago. People in the town were careful to keep their distance, especially after dark, crossing over to the opposite pavement if they happened to chance along that way The place was said to be spirited, the elderly claiming to have seen through the windows a large figure with a bloodied apron stalking through the rooms with a meat cleaver in the hand.

There might have been some truth to the claim. Widow Slusser's father, a butcher by trade, a giant of a man with an outsize bald head, coming home early one day had found the garçon from his shop in bed with his wife. The young man's fate was sealed on the instant, the body hacked in pieces, carried back to the shop in a canvas bag and ground with belly pork for stuffing, this latter act being deemed by the judge the most heinous aspect of the crime.

It all happened a long time ago but some of the older folk still recalled with a shiver that butcher Slusser's act of carnage had meticulously spared a tiny limb of the injudicious lover, the offending member being nailed to the headboard of the conjugal bed to remind the sinful spouse of her errant ways. Oddly Slusser was known in the town as a gentle soul, kind and soft-spoken, his one silent pastime the grinding and sharpening of the innumerable knives in his shop.

Thereafter the house had lain vacant for many years, the gate fallen loose from its hinges, the garden a wilderness of tall grass, the wisteria spreading out to gain an ever firmer stranglehold. People hurried past the benighted habitation with averted gaze. Decades later Slusser's daughter, now a widow, had cleaned up the place, repaired and renovated, and started letting out the cottage. Fräulein Carin's predecessor Dieckhoff had lived there for some two years without mishap; though the first tenant, an out of town nurse, had fled within days, running out into the night in her négligé screaming with terror.

7

Now as the wind raced and roared with the gathering force of a gale and the rain came slanting down in blinding sheets, the cottage rose before us, the squat black amorphous shape coming to frozen life under the sudden bursts of blinding illumination as streaks of lightening lit up the sky for long moments. The house was plunged in darkness save for a pale glow in one of the windows.

Sodden and chilled to the marrow, frightened out of my wits by the cloudbursts that rang inside the head like the clanging of hammer beats, limply I followed the Professor through the gate and up the short path. The wind had forced the front door open. Stepping into the gloom of the entrance, the Professor called her name, his voice drowned by the bellow of the thunder that seemed to hover above the house.

The pale light of a shaded lamp half-lit the large living room at the back. A small fire had burnt itself out in the narrow chimney, a few embers still aglow on the grate. On a white sheepskin rug spread in front of the fireplace lay two figures entwined as one, the unblemished pallor of their naked bodies almost ethereal in the penumbra. Headless under the spread of Fräulein Carin's mass of burnished hair, Captain Ebi's narrow, boyish back wound in the serpentine embrace of slender arms arched like clean sculpted marble.

Soundless as in a dream, the two bodies seemingly sunk in a trance, motionless save for the slow encircling caress of slender scarlet-tipped fingers on Ebi's hips, the stillness of the tableaux was broken only by the flickering blue of the lightning beyond the curtained window. And the thunder, less menacing, more ponderous now, seemed to be receding from the rooftop.

How long we stood in the twilight corridor I could not tell afterwards, perhaps a mere instant, or several long minutes. Finally the Professor turned away, his tall height suddenly stiff and cadaverous, as though the joints of his body had locked with sudden atrophy. We retreated towards the entrance, slipping silently out into the dark.

The rage in the heavens subsiding, with only brief flashes over the horizon, the skies now opened. Soaked to the skin, cold and comfortless, we made our way home under the torrential downpour. His face frozen in an expression which was hard to decipher in the dark, silent and bent forward the Professor hurried through the deluge, as though pursued by an unseen presence.

The downpour had spent its copious flood. We reached the house under a slow drizzle. Chilled to the bone, my coat soggy and dripping, I could not wait to make my way to my room at the back and stretch out on my little cot. But at the door, abruptly, the Professor stopped me. "No, Albert!" he said blocking me in the doorway, his voice curiously distant and disembodied. A firm hand on my neck, he pressed me down into a crouch with unaccustomed force.

The door shut behind him, opening again a minute later as he emerged with a towel in his hand. Half-kneeling he rubbed me down briskly till my coat was almost dry. An odd gesture then took me quite by surprise.

Ever since my puppy-hood the Professor had been for me the gentlest of men. Thoughtful and considerate at all times, tolerant of my youthful pranks, later good-humoured with the failings of my ageing limbs, a better father I could not have had, nor a kinder master. But unlike Gretchen he was not given to the small intimate gestures of a hug, a caress, an embrace. It was almost as if he shied away from the open affectations of affection.

So now it surprised me as he took my head in his hands and held my eyes in his gaze a long moment, his look sombre yet tender with a yearning regret. "Albert!" he said, with a sigh of weary resignation almost, pronouncing my name with a sort of finality, a salutation. And then, regaining his self, in a brisk, harder tone, "You stay here."

The purpose of his command escaped me. I had neither the ability nor the disposition to watch over house and home, safeguard humans and their chattels. It was not in the nature of my breed. And now in age, dim of sight and slow in limb, I would have been at best the tortoise to the intruder's hare.

The Professor turned in, shutting the door firmly behind him. Still puzzling over his intent in leaving me outdoors on a damp and chilly night such as this, I stretched out on the doormat. The rain had ceased, the odd drop trickling down from the eves. Patches of pale clearing had begun to appear in the still overcast sky.

I must have dozed off. It was a brief uneasy slumber in which the Professor and I were again caught in a thunderstorm, hurrying under a deluge as at a short distance behind us butcher Slusser came running with the meat cleaver raised in one hand. The road stretched out before us, familiar yet unending. The air turned to water, the silent rain beating down on our heads, we went forward and still he came, the giant figure bearing down on us, the cleaver glinting in the dark.

In the soundless vision the Professor walked at a brisk pace but strangely unafraid as the distance closed and suddenly Slusser was on us. The one-eyed hatchet was about to descend on us when, gasping for breath, I woke to the sound of a loud shot that reverberated through my head. Yet the sky was almost swept clean, the immense black canopy pricked here and there with the dim flicker of immeasurably distant stars.

The clean, crackling sound seemed to have come from within the house. Or perhaps I had merely imagined it in the stillness of that darkest hour before dawn. I lay myself down again, and slowly slid into a sleep without dreams, a black void where the world had ceased.

END-DAYS

1

Night falls as I crouch on the edge of the wood. In the evanescent twilight the trees grow silent as the chattering ceases and the birds nestle to sleep. Below me, mirroring the first stars in the darkening blue of the sky, small clusters of light come to life in the town. There's a nip in the clear autumn air.

On this solitary road skirting the wood there are few passers-by. The baker's boy idly wanders past whistling on his way home. But my gaze is fixed on the backyard of Martha's restaurant at the bottom of the slope. In a little while Uli will open the kitchen door and step outside to place a large bowl on the steps. He will stand guard for a minute or two, ensuring that there are no strays around, before going back in and shutting the door behind him.

Rain or shine, punctual as the hands of a clock, good-hearted Ulrich never forgets. No matter that the restaurant might be crowded with diners, a wedding party, a celebratory banquet. Rushing about taking orders, soliciting his mother in the kitchen, serving, removing dishes, yet he always remembers. Unfailingly, at the appointed hour, he steps out with the bowl of food for me.

The ancestral custom of hunting in the wilderness, racing in wolverine packs across frozen wastes in frenzied pursuit of a prey, tearing its limbs apart and getting down to a gory repast is at best a fragment of imagined memory lodged in some dim recess of the mind. Cushioned by the comfort offered by humans, fed, loved and pampered, I have never known the wilderness, nor hunted for sustenance and survival. Nor did one ever have the heart to corner and kill some poor creature to dine off its carcass. The savagery of bloody pursuits is beyond the nature of my breed.

So Uli heaps the bowl, generous as ever and ever careful to discard outsize knuckles, joints and bones, which would certainly dislodge my aged molars. And never is the bowl filled with leftovers, the odd bits and pieces left by diners on their plates. As if one of the family, I sup on what Uli and Martha set out on their own evening table.

Now as I wait to hurry down to the small stone-flagged yard for my day's repast, the recollection of other such evenings comes to mind, walking alongside the Professor as he made his way towards Martha's for dinner.

And I remember, too, on occasion catching the fleeting glimpse in the dark of a black and white mongrel rummaging for scraps in the bins at the back of the yard. Thinking, then, with pity and horror, of what it might be like to be an orphan, alone and homeless, cowering stealthily in the dark under rain and snow, wandering unblessed through the days of a life bereft of the warmth of care and kindness, the heart's fullness with love received and love given. At the sound of our steps the miserable stray would scramble to hide in the shadows, fearful, silently whining with the pangs of hunger. And each time I thought: *There but for my Maker go I!* For surely it was a mere trifling accident of birth that I instead should be trotting contentedly beside the Professor towards the comfort of light and the satisfaction of a full belly.

Uli goes back into the kitchen. But I feel his eyes on me, benign and watchful, as silently he peers through the cracks of the old wooden door while I devour his bounteous offering. Chewing through the last morsel of meat, licking the white enamel bowl clean, once again the thought assails me, that I could have had yet another home. Uli would have taken me in willingly, I could have lived at Martha's, in comfort and ease, nourished in this life's closing season with care and companionship. But it was late in the day. And as ever the stubborn doubt lingers in the mind, of the impossibility of rekindling in an ancient heart the fealty and love without reserve of once long ago.

2

Yes, I could have another home, other homes, I thought with leaden heart as Uli and I stood on the rise above the cemetery in the flickering autumn afternoon light. Below us the gently sloping ground dotted with tombstones ancient and recent milled with the black-garbed crowd of mourners. The Professor was well-liked, respected and esteemed, and half the town seemed to have come together to bid him farewell.

Dr. Hammes and the Baron were there, of course As were Burgomaster Schultze, Frau Gärtner whose wreathes and floral arrangements covered the long wooden coffin polished to a dark gold. Bank manager Adler had come with his wife, for once sans her permanent scowl, and brought with him clerk Schiefferdecker, looking more gaunt and with such a pallid hue that he could well have become the subject of the ceremony.

Many of the tradesmen who had supplied our house over the years stood together in a group, Udo with chambermaid Lulu on his arm, baker Gerstner who had exchanged his usual flour-dusted jacket with a severe black suit a size too small, Gerber the haberdasher whose perennially solemn expression was naturally apt for the occasion. Antiquarian Adolf stood aloof, squinting over the top of his pince-nez, a black mourner's handkerchief hanging loose from the breast pocket of his ancient suit.

Faces peered into the dark earth of the open grave at the head of which stood Pastor Schaffgott, his cadenced voice drifting up to where Uli and I stood. But the words were lost in the open air, as also school teacher Vogel's slow and halting eulogic diction.

Martha's arm around her, Matilde dabbed her eyes from time to time, Frau Botticelli by her side briefly whispering words of comfort in her ear. In the circle and throng of bowed heads nowhere was Fräulein Carin to be seen. She had not come, nor Ebi.

When finally it was over, the coffin lowered into the earth and the Professor laid to rest beside Gretchen, the assembly dispersed, lingering here and there for a moment in ones and twos, in small groups. Ilse Krause paused by old widow Ansel's grave, Montevideo perfectly quiescent in the wicker basket as though quelled by the solemnity of the occasion. Unrecognisable almost in a weathered felt hat and a rustic jacket, gardener Bauer was almost the last to leave after laying a small wreath of bay and carnation on the raised earth.

When the field of the dead had emptied and Uli, bidding me to follow him, hurried down to join his mother, the mild autumn afternoon filled with the stillness of a hush that seemed to emanate from the earth and rise upwards, filling the vast spaces of the sky. As I went down the slope to sit in the entombed silence by the fresh earth laid with the wreathes and blooms of mourning, already in the valley below narrow ribbons of mist floating above the waters of the river had begun to spread, dissolving the season's colourings of red and gold in a pale milky whiteness.

3

The days are now timeless, morning and noon merging into a single eventless continuum of wakefulness. Darkness falls early and the night envelopes me in sleep in the secret retreat of the bunker. Dawn and daylight, and the cycle starts anew, unmarked by occurrence or episode, like the pages of a book blank and unwritten. Only the clock in the body ticks soundlessly, registering cold, hunger and thirst, the fatigue of the ageing limbs. So the daylight hours pass, until it is once again time for me to sit in patient expectation, waiting for Uli to open the kitchen door and place the bowl on the steps.

I wade through the russet mantle of dead leaves in the wintering wood. The denuded trees are silent, the birdlife flown to more clement airs. Occasionally the odd raven flutters among the tall branches, renting the air with its ill-omened cry. The snow is yet to come, the hibernal sky perennially grey and brooding, marking time before whitening the earth.

Confused in spirit, uncertain of the days to come, dragging this ancient body I roam the woods, in search of what the mind itself seems not to know. Or perhaps simply searching for the past. Hard to tell. Time ceasing in days suspended and eventless, thoughts float up, with nowhere to go, without destination or finality.

I stretch out in the empty afternoon by this old trunk of a larch fallen long ago, where she would rest during our walk in the woods, often alone, at times with librarian Dieckhoff. And always I at her feet, Gretchen's hand reaching out to smooth my fur. Later, when she was gone, the Professor too would stroll up from the house, to sit here reading an entire hour when the weather was kind and the air mild; looking up occasionally from his book to cast a benign glance as I sat by his side. Halcyon days to which the mind returns with the irresistible pull of an anchor-tug.

Down below in the town the past lives on. Sometimes sitting on the edge of the wood my dimming eyes can still catch sight in the distance of familiar figures, known faces. Ilse Krause doing her morning rounds, still lugging Monty about in the wicker basket. Adolf lounging idly outside his shop, a theatrical bow for every female passer-by. Frau Gärtener ever graceful and brisk as she hurries down the street with a plant, a bouquet of flowers. And in the distance, on the steps of Schenkel's library Frau Botticelli still sits for a brief moment drawing on her cigarillo, but often now there is a little girl by her side, who at the close of day walks hand in hand by her side, a slight limp in her step.

Matilde one rarely sees, and then my heart fills with a strange yearning. I shut my eyes and see her move about in the kitchen, hear her sigh as she finally places the baking dish in the oven and straightens her back, wisps of aroma of the roasting meat once again reaching my nostrils; and hearing, too, her voice, low and laconic, as she tells Bauer seated by the kitchen door that overfeeding flowering plants with excess manure is quite as harmful as the lard and cream that Fräulein Carin has been discouraging lately. Old gardener Bauer himself, nursing his seeds and seedlings in the solitude of his country retreat, I have not seen since the funeral.

One other sight that fills the heart with longing is that of the Baron's little, black beetle-humped car when sometimes he drives into town and brings with him Schwarzbauer. A sudden urge takes hold, to rush down the slope and bound towards the gentle giant as he stands at the kerb, to leap up into the embrace of his powerful arms, his voice deep and tender as softly he calls my name, the guileless eyes luminous with the radiance of a joy pure and true-hearted. Save for mother Gretchen and the Professor, of all those encountered in my journey across the human landscape Schwarzbauer was the one in whose hands I could have consigned my life without thought or reserve.

The past lives on but there is novelty and renewal. One day late in the morning a small gathering congregates outside Pastor Schafgott's church, crowding the small green, lining the gravel path as, unheralded, Udo and Lulu emerge from the arched entrance. Barely recognizable without his butcher's striped bib apron, Udo is all elegance, flaunting an ample tail-coat over a white frill-fronted shirt. Nor, out of her vaguely coquettish chambermaid's clothes, is Lulu her usual self, now sheathed in an immaculate bridal gown sweeping down to her feet, the long fair tresses shaped into a bouffant atop which sits a vaporous bridal veil. Oddly enough though Lulu's middle seems to have a curious bulge under the wedding dress. Cheered by the gathering, man and wife stroll down the path, with Pastor Schaffgott at the door, one hand raised in a final cautious benediction.

But hardly a day goes by without my quotidian pilgrimage. Work on the Professors grave now completed, I sit for a long afternoon hour between Gretchen and the newly-laid grey slab of marble. And crouching on that hallowed ground, looking out across the valley at the autumn-tinted woods that fade away undulating towards the horizon streaked with the pallid brightness of a waning sun, I feel an unaccustomed lightness, as if abandoning the prison-cell of dull and inert flesh my spirit had flown loose to become one with the ethereal peace that seems to descend from beyond the skies.

Then again, some nights, the town fast abed, I slip down from my sylvan retreat to wander through the slumbering streets. Not a soul about, I pause here and there, a street lamp, a shop front, the flight of steps to the library, the lake in the park with the pair of swans dormant among the reeds, sites incised in the memory of a vanished world.

Up past the old cobbled road that turns down on itself, I stop by widow Slusser's cottage. Fräulein Carin and her Ebi are gone, taking with them the untold secrets of lives recondite and mysterious. Vacant and abandoned, with the low slate roof hooding the front, the knotted and gnarled reptile arms of the ancient wisteria clinging to the façade, the house offers an appearance of brooding dereliction. Probably, too, butcher Slusser has once again taken to stalking through the rooms with the raised meat cleaver.

Down the long avenue of trees until my somnambulist progression brings me to the front gate. The house is shut and shuttered, the grass grown tall in the garden. I sit out on the pavement, patient and expectant, waiting for the lights to come on, to see the Professor's tall figure in the doorway, catch a glimpse of Gretchen at the window. I shut my eyes, awaiting the miraculous chimera of rebirth and renewal, the magical return if only for a fleeting moment of days so blessed with grace and gladness, beloved faces, voices that soundlessly echo in the reaches of my dreams. But nothing moves, darkness prevails, and the myriad images of a lost world remain entombed in the interstices of the heart's endless grief.

And grieving, trudging through the shroud of silence back up to the woods dragging this senile body, I make my way to the sepulchral refuge. Weary in limb and spirit, in the black air I lay myself down on the damp bed of dead leaves. And as my sightless eyes begin to shut and darkness seeps into the mind, this night too, as every other night now, a wordless plea rises from the heart:

If there is a God in heaven,
And if there is a God for those of my kind
Then Lord hear this my one and only prayer.
Give me wings that I might rise and fly
To that abode of light, to be with those
Whom I have loved above all else
To dwell with them never again to part.
To sit between them on the Elysian fields,
Under the celestial canopy of eternity,
For ever and evermore, Time without end.

This is to acknowledge my immense debt to:

Dr. Paolo Ienne of the École Polytechnique Fédérale de Lausanne for his constant guidance in the Romance Language passages in the text

Prof.essa Lilliana Ravasio for her meticulous translations into Latin

Ing. Giorgio Sibella for his unfailing assistance in ordering and setting the digital text.

dimmed with her going are never to be rekindled anew, the warmth never to return to our lives again. Drowsy by the dying embers on the grate, the vision floats through my idle mind of the glow that once filled the house, festive days when the euphony of her voice rang through the rooms, the amiable talk and easy laughter of guests and friends, the ring of crystal and silver at the laden table, Matilde's brisk pace as the housekeeper emerged from the kitchen with tureens and dishes whose cornucopian aromas filled the air, woke the senses to the earth's goodness and abundance. All now gone, gifts given, gifts reclaimed.

I wake with a start to find the Professor bent over me, one hand gently brushing my head. "Hungry, Albert?" he says as I open my eyes and look up. "Shall we go?"

I raise my weight laboriously and get to my feet as he puts on his loden cape and we make our way across the back garden, scaling the steps up to the road that winds past under the woods. The still evening air greets us with an icy sharpness, frosting my nose, sending a frozen shiver through the body.

Under the limpid darkness of a sky set with tiny shards of glass, glazed and star-still, the wintering wood seemingly carved out of the blackness of the night sits massed and ponderous, the gnarled and knotted arms of the bare branches raised heavenwards as though in some secret supplication. Below us, a faint glow here and there through frosted windows, the town lies shrouded in the hibernal silence of life shut fast indoors, the elderly already abed.

The road turning down, we descend towards Martha's. As the slope levels off and we come within sight of the dimly-lit, stone-flagged yard at the back of the restaurant, a scurrying sound breaks the quiet. In the faint light we catch sight of a black and white mongrel rummaging in the bins filled with trimmings and garbage from the kitchen, leftovers from diners' plates. At our approach the cur raises its head, leaping down then with a limp to hide in the shadows, a thin whine like a spent plea for mercy escaping its lean frame.

The Professor walks on, but I pause for a moment, my eyes seeking out the cowering figure in the half-light. And for a moment

MARTHA

1

Mother and mistress, she looks down on me as I lie under her benign gaze, the pensive tenderness of the violet eyes resting on me like a silent benediction. Her unvoiced presence fills the room, the house, the air suffused with the fragrance of her breath. And somewhere in the far reaches of memory, echoing soundless and ethereal, her voice comes to me as she calls my name.

It has been like this ever since Gretchen left us. The days emptied of her presence, the long winter evenings are immersed in solitude and silence as the Professor sits at the table bent over his books and papers, faceless in the penumbra of the reading lamp. Stretched out by the fireplace under her portrait above the mantelpiece, inert and enervated I doze intermittently, waiting to hear her steps once again, the melody of the voice that has ceased, departed from our lives for ever.

It has been an endless winter, days of mortal cold, sleet and snow, the fleeting grey daylight enclosed by the frozen darkness of interminably long nights, a sullen sun rising laboriously over the etiolated dawn horizon. Adolf the antiquarian, a studious pupil of the esoteric tomes in his shop, quotes an ancient sage to say that winters now will be ever longer, stretching into summer and beyond. The antiquarian's oracular words half-froze widow Ansel's weary marrow, the old woman now in her ninety-ninth year and patiently awaiting the return of more clement seasons to warm her nonagenarian bones.

Our first winter without Gretchen and it seems that the lights